THE DANCE OF GODS

THE SEVEN ISLES
BOOK FIVE

A.R KNIGHT

CHAPTER I
HARROW'S EDGE

Every day, Eujo would wake up thinking she'd never been colder, then the next morning would prove her wrong. Their foursome, Eujo, Wax, his sister Bliss, and the thief Torny, crossed Whent's frozen isle by night and day, thanks to the skars wrapped around her wrist and hanging from a necklace 'round Wax's neck. The little gems were with her every morning too, whispering nonsense colored with emotion in her mind, chit chat that, by now, Eujo forced into a buzzy background.

Bliss slept next to her in the ramshackle bed, while Torny and Wax sprawled on straw scattered about the skin-flint room. Wood and rock bonded together to form the ill-fitting inn they'd been staying at for near a week now, preparing and recovering in equal measure. Selling their stolen sledge, the exhausted oxen, and extra Najahn gear they didn't need bought the quartet their stay, their meals, but time kept moving on, and soon they'd need to as well.

Rumors would spread, even if Harrow's Edge seemed a town where everyone had secrets to keep.

The inn's morning crew, slurping gruel and bonemeal

soups in torchlight, with dawn still some time off, greeted Eujo's descent with nothing more than flicked eyes and silent nods. Dressed in thick furs, warm leathers beneath, hard work's dirt brushed over her skin, Eujo looked nothing like the queen she was, nothing like the Renewal she had been. When she asked for her own bowl, the barkeep presented it to her without ceremony, complete with a small stone cup filled with fresh snowmelt.

Save the world, save your isle. A queen's burden, or so Eujo had been told after the Najahn put out the Renewal call. Gather the skars from each isle, ascend the Aegis's throne, and hold back the fiends until you become a withered husk. An honor, and, for those first few weeks, one Eujo bought into. The ultimate destiny for a street rat with enough luck to wind up at the top: immortality among the saviors.

Now she was as hunted as Eujo had ever been. The Najahn, for reasons Eujo didn't know, ended the Renewal. Demanded the skars and their power for themselves. Her own isle, Kance, and its other queen were doing the same, attempting to horde the stones as a bulwark against dangerous creatures. Against, possibly, more dangerous isles and their armies.

Which left Eujo adrift, which left her spooning gruel into her mouth, the warm fat and grain running as easy now as it had in her childhood. Comforting in a bland way. Like seeing her old shanty at the bottom of Kance's towering sky spires, knowing it still existed, the rags and ruins giving someone else a small reprieve from life's terrors.

"You like eating alone?" Wax asked, the Vis almost unrecognizable beneath his layers. He, too, had his own steaming bowl, sitting across from her on the small wood block table. A fire burned—always burned, with the cold so harsh outside—behind them, a blackened hearth guiding the heat.

"I thought you were asleep."

"You're not as sneaky as you think."

"Is everyone awake?"

Wax shrugged, left a slight smile. "Bliss and Torny weren't ready to get up yet."

No secret what that meant, not anymore. Enough hazards, enough time together, had sparked a fire between Wax's sister and the bandit. While they'd yet to out and proclaim it, since escaping the Najahn at the Golden Gash, Bliss and Torny had been even more inseparable than before. Eujo and Wax had guessed at what nudged the pair into intimacy, and Eujo's bet lay in the days after the flight, when she and Wax had been stuck in a delirious unconscious, the effort stolen by the skars to effect their escape draining them to near nothing.

Torny and Bliss had guided the sledge, had prepared their meals on the tundra, pitched camps and kept them moving. A shared stress that must've let their hearts open.

"Good for them," Eujo said, dipping back into her gruel. "At least our Guardians are having fun."

Wax drifted his spoon in a lazy line around the common room, getting more crowded as other guests and Harrow's Edge locals came and went, the day's start edging closer. "What, you're not? In this place?"

"It has a charm."

"Daily fiend attacks, treasure hunters, wild rumors, and everyone thinking about knifing you?" Wax laughed, low and quiet. "Definitely has something."

"At least nobody cares about us." Eujo took a deep breath, inhaled some soot from the hearth and coughed once, twice. Shook it off. "We should have received the reply by now, if Deux ever got our message. I say we go. We're ready."

"Ready to do something none of us have ever tried, you mean?"

"Isn't reckless bravado your thing, Wax?"

"Sure is. I'm game. Let's run the ice, see if we make it to the other side."

Eujo chuckled. Hard not to, faced with Wax's merry, glinting look. The Vis had a guileless charm, and Eujo wasn't stupid enough not to see, feel its gradual effects. They'd been adventuring together for nearly two months now, in almost constant company, and despite some near-deaths, some deep questions about their lives and their purpose, she and Wax had helped each other come out the other side. She didn't doubt those questions still lingered behind Wax's grin, but, if anything, getting tossed from celebrities to outcasts had only emboldened the Vis.

As if winning now, getting all those skars and . . .

"What're we going to do?" Eujo asked, not really Wax and not really herself. A question to the gods, but one Wax decided to answer anyway.

"After we get them all, you mean?"

Eujo nodded.

"Easy." As Wax said the word, though, his grin faded to a serious line. A hand reached up to his necklace. "Eujo, we know what these skars can do. The fiends come from the Dark Below. If we can't replace the Aegis, then I say we do what she can't: use the skars to stop this, forever."

Harrow's Edge lay on Whent's eastern coast, its farthest tip and amid an inhospitable blend of mountains, forest, and cragged cliffs. The town itself sat above the water, a place where little more than small fishing boats would dare risk sandbars, hidden rocks, and, in the winter, sudden jagged ice. Isolated, and not Eujo's intended destination after their frantic escape from the Golden Gash. A place Bliss and Torny chose after catching words on the way from small tundra towns, words suggesting the Najahn would pursue, that the obvious, larger ports to the southeast would be flush with bounty seekers.

A good place to watch the world turn.

Now Eujo looked away from the rumors, the small homes and hunters tending them to a fractured sea, one whose gray surface undulated like a thing alive. Balancing on its swooping waves were the floes, white patches catching sunlight here and there like beacons. Some held sway over massive sea patches, almost islands in their own right, while others scurried about on the slightest current, like insects searching for food. They'd need to use them all, make the precise jumps, plant their spikes and grapples just to keep from slipping off.

"At least here you'll get a few seconds before you die," Torny said, the bandit looking overstuffed with the large pack on her back. She and Wax would haul the emergency rations. Bliss played scout and assistant.

Eujo would pull the small sledge, the Kance skar whispering with her the whole way.

"Ready?" Wax asked, standing down the beach, where ice intermingled with dirty sand. "The day's not getting younger, and there's no way we're hopping these in the dark."

Three days on the floes. That's what the Harrow's Edge ice hunters said. A straight crossing to the northernmost tip of Tamas. How far they'd have to travel then, and through what, Eujo didn't know. The hunters here didn't care.

Tamas wasn't their kind of place, save for the ale that drifted north in the sweeter summer swells.

'When you are,' Bliss, Wax's sister, signed. She'd bartered for another weathered staff and slapped a pointed pick on its end, giving her a strong pole for the ice. She'd ensured similar sharp points laced all their boots, ready to grip.

Preparation Eujo appreciated, preparation she'd learned about as it happened. For a Queen, she'd spent enough time in the darkest, dirtiest places. But gutters didn't teach you about the wilds, about the gear necessary to survive a night on a frozen sea.

If, though, any fear threatened, Eujo found it easy enough to ignore: Wax took her attention, took all their eyes, and more than a few watchers from Harrow's Edge, wondering what these fools were doing. Wax leaned down, put his hand just over the lapping ocean's edge. The sea shivered, ripples breaking against the current, before the surface turned a lattice white, snowflake patterns spreading and vanishing in turn as solid ice shot forth from the beach towards the floes. A clear path to walk, wide enough for the sledge.

"Practice, practice," Wax said, standing. "Who says a skar can't be taught?"

Bliss took her brother's words as a signal, stepped onto the ice bridge like she had the others over the last few days. They'd come out here for hours, forging bridges until Wax would nearly collapse. Eujo did the same now as Bliss walked along, testing the ice with her pole. The Queen's Kance skar picked up her desire, Eujo's furs going almost weightless, the effect tracing along the straps flowing from her shoulders to the satchel-stuffed sledge. What'd taken the whole group to guide down to the beach now creaked as it rose a hair's height above the sand.

"Ready," Eujo said, the Kance skar humming in her ear.

With Torny taking up the last spot in the queue, the quartet marched onto the ice, a journey made possible with magic stones, the same ones that'd saved the Seven Isles for so long and that might again.

And yet, as Eujo walked over those waves, the ice crackling beneath her feet, the skar's energy flagged. Felt its first drinks, the power drawn not from some dead god's might, and instead from Eujo's own will. Like a ceaseless exercise, devouring her muscles, her mind, her everything to keep the sledge afloat, her pack light.

The Aegis died quick as the skars sapped her. As the crunching walk stretched before Eujo, she could only wonder how fast the stones would drain her too.

CHAPTER 2
THE JUNGLE ISLE

Her sweat marked her a foreigner, that and skin not so touched by the sun. Annalyse watched the day come into being from the inn's center, a fanned out bamboo floor sprawling several times her height off the muddy forest ground. She'd been in Kitaye for several days now, bartering time to think with her minor possessions. Fish, fruit, and sweet wine parlayed with her hours, suspicious glances nibbling away the minutes, and sudden ideas snapping at seconds only to be dashed with an odd despair.

Annalyse, just a few weeks ago, had everything. A lab and assistants better than any in the Seven Isles. Almost unlimited resources. Even fiends to test her ideas could be captured and hauled in with little notice, as if her whims served as guidance for untold dozens. At first, a heady thing, a momentous position, and one she'd carved into world-saving efficiency with Gladdring's help.

All that, now, gone. What she could save packed into a satchel, given a freezing swim and a secret escape aboard a vessel delivering Rana rice and equipment to Vis. A short, miserable journey laying low below deck, and now here she was, unseen and utterly useless.

What was it Quik had said to her? Flee to Vis, restart her work, and return better than ever?

Annalyse, a hot coffee, warmed over coals, in her hands, pictured the hunter without much effort. She'd been talking to his image, muttering asks late in the night about this or that Vis curiosity. A distraction, and one she needed to put aside.

Today was the day. She'd packed, procured extra food and footgear suitable for hiking through the wet winter jungle. Even a knife, big enough to ward off sniffing predators, lay on the table before her, sharp and ready. The trek wouldn't be a short one, but Annalyse had a destination, given to her, again, by Quik.

They'd swapped stories in the sand, with Quik kept in his prison on Ami's hard orders. Annalyse would talk about Whent, about the stone soldiers, the schools, the isolation imposed by hard winters and harder laws on doing, well, anything for the other isles without getting a profit back in return. Hardy folk, her own, and ones not caring much for the rest of the world.

Quik delivered his own version of the same: Vis, jungle tribes resplendent in their own perfect place, and as unwilling to leave it as the Whent were their tundra. Yet visitors weren't shunned, weren't turned out for what they had and then tossed back into the sea. No, Quik had said, a person could come to Vis if they wanted to escape, to start again, or simply to disappear.

Svarde had. The old Guardian. Quik spoke about the barbarian's cabin, somewhere to the southwest. Past a great fen. A solid building, and now Annalyse's hope. She could get there, bring her tools, her skars, and start again, without fear some Najahn spy would slip a drug into her drink, a dagger into her heart.

Because Gladdring had been a traitor, and Fassle did not suffer traitors.

Two satchels tied together on her back, a water skin at her waist with the big knife opposite, and the skars tucked away in a pouch along her thigh. Annalyse had traded off her Najahn clothes, too heavy here, for Vis weaves, the thinner plant threads resting lightly on her skin as she walked towards the city's southern edge. Loose and scratchy compared to real cloth, the jungle apparel nevertheless drew eyes away from Annalyse as she moved, casual glances confirming she likely wasn't a trader seeking a deal or a traveler ready to be sold something she desperately didn't need.

That perception held true until Annalyse reached Kitaye's southern border, where the main road split into several paths, each one offering advertisement on its destination by way of their upkeep. To the left and west lay the sturdiest road, the ground padded with constant steps, rutted here and there with cart wheels, and occupied by comers and goers. The middle, a straight south journey aimed, so Annalyse understood, at Vis's central lake and its surrounding luxuries, showed care and enough travel to walk unafraid.

The third, to the east and bending south, gave warning with muddy tracks and a hunter standing by, leaning on his spear and watching Annalyse with mild interest. He chewed on some spiced leaf. Others bent their way around the scientist, ignoring the odd jangles from her satchels as metal instruments bounced into one another. They picked their paths, none choosing the eastward road.

"Why?" Annalyse asked the hunter as the crowds eased. "No towns that way?"

"There were," the hunter replied, giving Annalyse a look that said her prospects that direction were, well, dim. "The fiends destroyed them, or scared the people enough to bring them back here. When the Renewal's done, we'll take them back."

"The Renewal's over."

That word had come fast. The Najahn declaring it was time to march on the fiends directly, a compelling idea curdled by their insistence that all the isles had to obey Fassle's commands, give up their skars and obey Najahn soldiers. Annalyse figured Whent would laugh the suggestion away, much like the Vis had.

Like this hunter was right now.

"Our Renewal is still out there," the hunter replied, grinning. "He'll gather up the skars and take the throne, no matter what those weak bones in their towers say."

"The Najahn hold the Wound, though?"

"If they won't let our Renewal through, then Kitaye will march, and the Najahn will see what the jungle can do."

Confident, this one. Then again, weren't they all? Annalyse had noticed the displaced villagers in the city, the ones living now in lean-tos and hasty thatched shelters on the ground while the city's residents kept their homes in the trees. That living location was the only difference she'd found, though: even the ones who'd lost family carried themselves with a defiant vitality, diving back into the jungle to gather fruits, hunt prey, or craft new tools. They fought life's hard turns and showed no signs of breaking.

Maybe the hunter was right, maybe the Najahn would regret pushing Vis.

Not that she would be here to see it.

She took a step past the hunter, away from the intersection and onto the softer ground. Was about to take another, break into mid morning and onto her journey, when the hunter's spear swept up from the dirt to bar her path.

"This isn't the road for you," the hunter said. "It's dangerous."

"So am I."

The man's eyes twinkled, the same look Annalyse had seen in Quik, a laughing appraisal.

"Then what are you looking for, dangerous one? Only fiends, the fen, and death wait that way."

"A fresh start, for one."

"Then take it at the lake shore. Or walk to the eastern mountains to Mottilan, those cursed fishers. You can lose your years like they do, throwing nets and whining about us."

Annalyse snorted, "A compelling choice."

The hunter let his smile fade. "But one you don't intend to take."

"I know where I'm going." Annalyse started forward again, and this time the hunter let her push past his spear. "I'll be fine."

He said nothing as she walked by, said nothing as she wobbled on her first muddy steps, her Vis shoes lighter than the Whent boots Annalyse had worn her entire life. Only when the road began a bend, one encroached upon by unnamed thorns and grassy stalks, did the hunter call out one more time:

"Stay off the ground at night, fair one, if you want to see the morning."

Annalyse heeded that warning at the first day's end, an altogether pleasant hike below the thick canopy. Bugs that might've been unbearable amid summer's heat poked and prodded with lackadaisical curiosity. Animals Annalyse didn't know and barely caught peeked at her from behind trees and ferns. No fiends, nor evidence of them, made an appearance. Still close enough to Kitaye for regular patrols, she assumed.

How long that would last, who knew.

Fear didn't bleed in as the sun dipped. Instead, adventure took its place, a confidence in herself and her abilities, in the tools Annalyse carried with her. The skars, silent in their pouch, but ready to be grabbed and deployed. Far from helpless, ready to handle the wilds. Annalyse, the first Whent in who knew how long to tackle Vis's mighty jungle.

She might've grinned the whole way up the big tree, a climb Annalyse made after far too many attempts, after hacking out handholds with the knife when branches didn't seem enough. She carried up one satchel and then another, rising far enough up to ensure a fall would break a few bones, but probably wouldn't kill her. She tied the satchels to the tree—Vis seemed to operate entirely on ropes—then set about balancing herself between two thick branches, unwrapped a smoked fish package and added some scavenged tubers, a found mushroom.

Back in Kitaye, once she'd decided on her course, Annalyse had spent her time learning what she could about the jungle. Pestering hunters, merchants, and anyone who came through the inn on how to survive among its verdant environs. As ever, she had her small notepad, taken from the Whent university and kept with her all this way, now filled with scribblings about what to eat, how to tie herself to the branches at night so she wouldn't fall.

How to survive alone.

In the dark, a dead dark with so little Sichi light flowing between the leaves, Annalyse took a skar from her pouch and listened to its whispers. A Rana one, this time, and it picked out the dew forming as the night cooled. With a little concentration, Annalyse let the skar suck some moisture from the air, pool it into her hand, and give the scientist a fresh, pure sip.

"You're my friends now," Annalyse whispered to the stone, feeling only a little strange as she did so.

She'd have to get used to this.

She would, too, have to get used to the noises. The rustles, the howls, of creatures making their way. Some trundled right beneath her, putting proof to the hunter's advice. Others whistled by overhead, either swinging or flying. A strange noise, but not too far from the urban music Annalyse knew, and one that served to sing her to sleep before long.

When morning came, when Annalyse twitched only to find herself unable to move because of her own ropes, the scientist set about to untie herself. She sat up, her back aching from its hard branch bed, turned to reach for her water skin, and stopped. Her satchels, so carefully tied to the tree, were gone.

Her branch bent, the air moved, and Annalyse looked back ahead. There, balanced on the branch's end, one foot before the other, holding a spear so feathered and lethal it belonged in a myth, stood a huntress.

"Welcome to my jungle, Najahn," the woman said. "Tell me your story, and if it's good, I might not leave you for the fiends to kill."

CHAPTER 3
HUNTERS OF THE DARK

The turn had come some time ago, though Ami couldn't tell precisely when. The days had disappeared, time tracked only in exhaustion, in their dwindling supplies, buttressed by what they could forage, could kill in the dark. They traveled by luminescent mushrooms and mosses, the dim light the skars in Ami's face could give off when their whispers turned up in the Guardian's mind. The cave floors started the same, but as their boot soles wore down, Ami could tell the difference between rocks, between slippery grains, between the grooves worn with running water and the ones etched by a fiend's claws.

Ami had come to favor the monsters and their distractions. The fiends came large and small, with the human pair avoiding the more dangerous ones and preying on the less. Sawi was a capable enough hunter, able to slink around a fiend and either pelt it with a stone or distract it for an Ami ambush. The pair would set traps, draw the creatures into fashioned spikes or a shadowed strike.

After, they'd start a flickering fire, hot enough to cook

whatever monster meat they'd found. In those moments, Ami would catch Sawi's face behind the meat, filthy yet vibrant, eyes always distant but not gone.

"Home," Sawi would say when Ami asked her thoughts. "Vis."

At first the response carried some hope they'd find the isle eventually, that their abilities would lead them unerringly south to the jungle isle. A foolish dream, one required to even undertake vanishing into the Dark Below. Else their odds would've been better darting around Noctia, waiting for the spring thaw and a secret ship. Instead that delusion faded into fragments, a lurch here and there whenever the tunnels seemed to veer in a southerly direction only to die with the next descent, the next dead end.

"We'll be down here forever, won't we?" Sawi asked later, as they hiked through a gnarled stretch with low ceilings and a dying stench. "We'll never see the sun again?"

"Start talking like that and you definitely won't."

"What, the truth?"

"You'll warp your mind."

Foti had enough stories like that. Miners lost in tunnels that went too deep, found days or weeks later muttering about the dark. Smarter groups strung lines behind them now, an easy rope to follow back to the surface. Cheaper ones, well, they relied on easy labor to replace the lost.

Not that anyone would replace Ami, not that anyone would want to.

"How're you holding together?" Sawi asked, her voice, like Ami's parched.

What water they found came courtesy of cave streams, stuff they'd drink after boiling it over their little fires. If they had the chance, anyway. Otherwise, what did sickness matter when you weren't going to make it out of here anyway?

"Vengeance is a powerful motivator," Ami answered.

"Is that all you have, vengeance? Ever since I met you, that's what you've gone on about."

Revenge upon the Circle for what they'd done to Catya, the Aegis. Revenge upon Gladdring for stuffing Ami away in his tower. Revenge upon Svarde for abandoning her and his Guardian's oath to go squat in a cabin for ten years . . . Ami could go on.

"It's easier than forgiving."

Sawi laughed.

"Is that what you really believe, Ami?" Sawi asked. "Because I don't think you stuck around Noctia this long because you're angry."

"No? Please tell me, Vis. You're half my age, haven't seen anything beyond your vines and these dark caves, but you want to tell me what keeps me going?"

"Anyone who's been in love can see it in someone else."

Ami stopped. Fast enough for Sawi to run into her satchel, jostle their gear. "What are you saying, Sawi? Speak carefully, or I might gut you here."

The Vis laughed again, the same chuckle that'd had real life back in Gladdring's tower. That held none of it in the dark.

"I'm saying everyone knows," Sawi spoke soft now, realizing, perhaps, that she'd tread far from random bluster. "I'm saying we, Annalyse and I anyway, respect you for it. For standing by her so long."

"I took an oath."

"Then maybe that's your reason, right?"

"Why do you care, Vis?"

"I . . . I don't know. I'm sorry I brought it up."

"Don't be sorry, and don't question me again. Not here, not anywhere."

Sawi didn't reply.

They kept on.

The sounds came after they'd settled in for the night, a whistling hoot bouncing through the tunnels, every burst followed by rapid scratching. Both Ami and Sawi sat up from their bedrolls, each one grabbing their weapons. Ami had her harpoon, Sawi a large fisherman's knife. Without speaking, they split to either side of their narrow chamber; every day's walk ended when they found a suitable resting spot, one with a single entry and exit. Easier to defend, easier to secure.

Easier to lure some unsuspecting creature into a trap.

Ami nodded towards the entry, the jagged arch. Sawi knew the signal, didn't protest, slipping into the tunnel beyond. Ami shifted to her right, turning to press her back against the cold stone. Purples and blues, shallow glows, clustered around their backpacks as the ripped off mushrooms and mosses fought for life. They'd fade, get tossed, and new ones picked within another day or two. Another cycle down here.

Her gloves, worn down, passed through the harpoon's chill. Its touch brought the Vis skars, all two, in Ami's golden plate to life. Their curious whispers filtered through, like a dream's fading touch. Ami couldn't understand the words, the god's old speech, but she knew their tones well enough: what stupid thing was she up to now?

The hoot came again, the scratching, and this time the noise carried a hungry edge. Sawi's footsteps, louder than they needed to be, pounded back Ami's way. The Vis scraped her boots on the rock, ran her knife along the stone to draw the creature further. Sawi was getting better at this, proving to be adept bait.

Ami slowed her breath, tensed her muscles. The scrabbling, the hooting, drew closer. Without warning, Sawi dashed through the entry, slipping a hair on the stone and scrabbling towards their packs. The Vis rolled, put her back to the satchels and drew the knife, eyes wide and mouth open, an extra terror sprinkle to draw the creature in full.

And the fiend bit.

One Ami hadn't seen before. A shallow body like an arch, bent and frothing with feathered claws, the bird-like thing hooted its triumph as it darted in at Sawi, those far-too-many points reaching towards what should've been dinner.

The attack stopped quick when Ami struck. She didn't aim to wound with the thrust, but kill, a blow right at the monster's waist, at the arch's bottom where the thing's claws shifted their stance and became talons. The harpoon bit right on through, the fiend's feathers a poor defense against a well-aimed blow. The monster straightened, its hooting breaking with surprise, with anger, with obvious pain. Its head, continuing the arch in an unbroken line, twisted Ami's way.

Just in time for Sawi to cut in with the grace note, right beneath the monster's noisy mouth.

It didn't utter another sound.

Hope dwindled, hope sprang, hope survived by the dimmest lights. Sawi and Ami found another as they cleaned the monster's odd skin, picking off the gnarled, dirty feathers. The creature seemed meant for bright skies, not the tunnels. An unlucky twist for it to find itself down here. But lucky for them.

"Is that a bolt?" Ami asked, more to herself than Sawi, as she pulled the feathers free from the creature's back.

Hidden amidst their gray fronds was just that, a narrow, short shaft with crow fletching. It'd burrowed into the fiend's back and stayed there, offering a curious question.

"Where'd it come from?" Sawi asked, leaning over the dead thing to get a closer look.

"No chance this fiend passed the Aegis's net," Ami said, referring to the protective shell the Aegis cast over the isles with her skars. A fiend could fight through it, and plenty did, but they'd earn burns, hard penance for their efforts. This one seemed far too unscathed. "Which means someone shot it down here." Ami picked at the fletching. "This is in good shape too. The wound must've been recent."

"Who'd be down here shooting random fiends?"

Ami sat back, shook her head. Blinked. Rumors had come south from Whent in the weeks before everything fell apart. A warlord and an army, an expedition into the depths. One led, in part, by a former Guardian with too much bravado and not enough brains.

"I have an idea," Ami said. "Go see if there's a trail."

Sawi didn't need more than that. The Vis slipped away while Ami continued the butchering. The scrawny fiend wouldn't make for many meals, but anything helped. Her work went faster now, her mind slipping away to the possibilities, the Vis skars lighting on Ami's renewed enthusiasm to whisper thrills.

"It's there," Sawi said, coming back as Ami finished the last of the feathers. "Thank Vis this thing has so many claws. We can follow the scratches."

Amazing what a little possibility could inspire. For the first time in too long, the pair had a plan, and with its fire they moved fast, finished carving and cooking up the fiend, ate, and would've started right out if Ami's sense hadn't taken hold. They'd already walked for hours, and the Dark Below remained deadly. Sawi, stating jungle rules were much the same, didn't argue. The scratches were both numerous and deep enough that they wouldn't vanish fast.

Ami expected sleep to be fitful, but it came on quick, as if pushing despair away made it easier to relax. Yet, even as she drifted away to dreams of civilization, a niggling worry remained: the bolt had been in good condition, yet the fiend lived.

What, then, had happened to the shooter?

CHAPTER 4
THE BANDIT LORD

Leaving the Najahn quarter always felt like blinding a thousand eyes. Gladdring kept the thick hood pulled up, the bulky winter furs matching the stature, if not the Najahn's purple and black, of someone who meant good business. Dodging an Adept's finery for less notable clothes was one thing, sacrificing respect for a disguise was another.

Neither guard, in their glossy black armor and skyward voulges gave him a glance. A success, albeit a minor one. Still, campaigns like Gladdring's depended on minor victories.

Noctia glowed in Winter's depths, its many stone windows greeting the midday with a lantern's flicker. Snow piled in the corners, shoveled off, sometimes with hands alone, by those who needed bread, soup, survival. Gladdring passed by several more now, hacking at ice with stone chisels. The boys would get their labor's due, enough to sate their stomachs for a night, enough oil or wood to keep their homes warm.

At least till tomorrow came and demanded it all over again.

The thought drew Gladdring's eyes skyward. Scattered clouds, a scant sun. No storms on the horizons. Bad fortune for the street cleaners, good for him. Perhaps the job could get done sooner. Perhaps . . .

No, hoping for this very night would be setting himself up for disappointment. Undo haste would mean risking—

Gladdring scowled at nothing and nobody, tromping along the manors scaling the westward cliffs, making his way south. Private guards and well-dressed groups shuffled to business or pleasure lunches, though the winter meals in Noctia lacked summer's cosmopolitan flavor. Vis and Kance fruits and fish, what Whent potatoes had been stored, would suffice until things thawed. His palate ached at the thought.

No, haste. Moving fast was what brought Gladdring here in the first place. Too much attention paid to overthrowing the Circle's irritating leader and not enough to shoring up his own position. The skars were weapons, Gladdring had proved that now, but the guards he'd entrusted to keep his secrets had decided their loyalty to the purple and black lay above loyalty to him. A problem Yarvick would fix, among several.

If only Masayo still lived. She understood, as Gladdring did, that true power lay in saving the isles, not keeping them in chains.

A statue to Demion, the first Aegis, dominated the plaza Gladdring now walked through, as if confirming his own statement. Cruelty and iron fists didn't create legends. Deeds worthy of remembering did. Demion had been the first to gather the skars, to put all the world behind their power. Gladdring would do one better than her, would marshal the skars and the Najahn together to obliterate the fiends at their very source.

Funny how that direct idea came from one particular Guardian, a Foti lost to his own ambition. Gladdring had been there that day when Svarde raged his proposal at the Circle, declaring a strike into the Dark Below the only sure option for saving their lives. In that moment, Gladdring found his direction, a larger purpose than simply deposing Fassle, a goal subtly shared among all the Tenets, as it had been as long as the Circle existed.

The argument, of course, was who would take over once Fassle's reign ended.

Icy stairs to a southern beach marked a poor man's path, one whose residents, carved into cliffside hovels, couldn't afford to keep clear. Instead, as Gladdring noted while passing several, the people living here jammed nails into their boots for traction. Damage the soles to save the skin. Gladdring himself fell on old traits, a perfect balance honed in a childhood on Tamas where one's ability to hold a pose made as much of a man's life as his skill with a sword.

Eyes found him now, but Gladdring didn't get the shivers he'd find back in the Najahn quarter. These were curious looks, tired ones. People who had too little incentive to move for something that didn't promise food or a fire. Of those, the flickering orange flames, Gladdring saw plenty, smelled them too: not the wood-burning luxuries back north, but loamy, smokey flames fed by mosses and trash.

Survival.

Gladdring could never forget what it took.

The caves beyond the hard, frozen sand offered little more than darkness for the first several strides. Only once he'd passed a few jagged black obelisks, again using a dancer's eyes to keep track as the daylight died beyond the rock overhangs, did Gladdring spy a home's glimmer. Here too he felt stares, had detected the shift once his feet hit the beach.

No, Gladdring himself hadn't. The stone in his pocket, set by Annalyse in a ring on a left hand finger. That's what let Gladdring know the impressions directed his way, and he'd best not forget it, not if he wanted to keep a level head.

Because here was a place where hands could be lost if one's head went the wrong way.

What looked to be a ragged sea cave broadened through unnatural efforts into a large chamber, one with straw-matted platforms scaling the sides. Rope bridges criss-crossed above the central floor, where several fires burned, some cooking, some cleaning, others serving as warmers for the human variety on display.

"Truly, all the isles can't compare to what you have here, Yarvick," Gladdring said as he approached, drawing no looks from the people inside, save one. They knew who he was, had probably known he approached since Gladdring left the Najahn quarter in his bumbled disguise. "A collection of skills no—"

"Quit your flattery," Yarvick, the only one who'd turned his way, said. The bandit lord held a wight's appearance, as if he'd risen from some rat-infested grave mere moments ago with ironic vengeance his sole cause. "It's been some time, Gladdring. When Fassle caught wind of your little plot, I expected your head on a voulge. Pity."

Yarvick grinned as he finished, showing off resplendent teeth long ago bereft of their natural white. Instead, gold, emerald, and other gems shone through, hewn down to fit and sharpened to glittering fangs. A casual look might assume it a power's play, a sop to strength. Gladdring knew better, knew what whispers echoed in the bandit's mind thanks to the unusual dental work.

"I convinced Fassle my death would be more annoying than otherwise." Gladdring stopped his advance on the cavern's edge. To move further without an invitation would be . . . unwise, said the whispers. "I hope my continued survival can prove profitable to you."

"It already has." Yarvick rose, a stone plate with picked over fish in a hand as he strode Gladdring's way. Lanky, with more meat seemingly on the fish than on the man's own bones, Yarvick moved with a slithery lurch, Gladdring unsure which direction a step would take the man until it arrived. One of Yarvick's many unnerving traits. "But I like your thinking. How can you help me, Gladdring? How will your new Adept raiments help the Nimble Fingers?"

"Fassle has no love for you."

A truth known to them both, but best to establish facts.

"Fassle has uses for me, and I him," Yarvick countered.

"But he would prefer you dead, and all your thieves."

The bandit only grinned further at that. Let him try, glimmered those teeth, and Gladdring had to agree any eradication would probably be a futile enterprise, with too many knives in too many backs to be worthwhile.

"He's announced a change," Gladdring continued, taking Yarvick's silence as an invitation to keep on going, "The Najahn are stealing all the skars, because I've shown him what they can do."

"We know."

"Then you ought to know too it won't be long before he's surrounded by the god's stones, and once he gets that power, we won't be able to stop him. Enough Vis skars, and the man might live for centuries."

"Enough Vis skars, and so might you. Or me."

"Better us, then, than him," Gladdring said, keeping his hands in his pockets. The whispers suggested Yarvick was amenable to Gladdring's argument, a fact Gladdring would prefer to remain with him and him alone. "You thrive on secrecy and backdoor power. I would give you both."

"You failed, Gladdring."

"I failed up, Yarvick. I'm closer to Fassle now than ever before."

"Easier for him to watch your steps."

Gladdring tilted his head, acknowledged the truth. "Even so, I'm here because there is an opportunity. I can't wield the knife, but I can get Fassle where you can do it."

Gladdring hesitated, Yarvick kept his gleaming grin going.

Not a no.

"Before I go any further, I need your word. Your binding word."

"How much is a bandit's word worth, Gladdring?" Yarvick's ash-grated voice echoed around the cavern, and Gladdring realized every other conversation had died. "A traitor comes to a thief to ask a favor, who can trust who?"

"Profit and power, Yarvick. The only currencies you and I care about. A promise on those."

"Well then, spill your secret, Gladdring, and we'll see if you have any power left to trade."

The Tamas skar on Gladdring's finger hummed. Words in a language beyond Gladdring's understanding, but flush with tones Gladdring knew well. He'd failed in his first attempt to overthrow Fassle, a rushed skar-driven rebellion put down with grim authority. That'd been too open, too kind.

In Yarvick, in the man's thieves and their many knives,

their crossbows, their poisons, Gladdring had a different tool, and a plan to go along with it. Yarvick, as Gladdring gave the details, kept up his grin, said nothing when Gladdring finished save an ask to leave.

A message, one way or another, would find its way to the Adept soon.

"Until then," Yarvick called after Gladdring's retreating steps along the ice sand, "stay alive, Adept. You're so much more fun than that Circle you serve."

Stay alive? For once, Gladdring's own grin matched Yarvick's.

He planned to, and far more besides.

CHAPTER 5

HOPPING THE FLOES

Hopping the floes became familiar fast, even with the skars aiding in the adventure. Eujo, growing up in Kance gutters, spent more days than she wanted to admit scurrying along narrow lines, leaping between buildings and floating sky islands, and that sure footwork made its benefits known as the hours, then the first two days, burned in a gray blitz along the ice. Clouds and cutting gales completed the scene, frothing waves tilting the smaller floes as the foursome ran across the snow-slicked surfaces. When energy flagged or light dimmed, they'd find the biggest ice block, chisel in spikes to tie down thick bed rolls, and all burrow in together.

They lost their tent on the first night, ripped away by a howling bluster. After, they stuffed themselves together, forgoing impossible fires for body heat and Foti skars.

The ale-slopping drunks back in Harrow's Edge esti-mated four or five days on the ice to reach Tamas's tip, and halfway through the third Bliss thought she saw a smudge on the far horizon, a line visible as twilight neared thanks to the clearing skies and mellowing bluster. A break, as if

Tamas itself wanted to extend a welcome. The alacrity made sense with the skars boosting their speed, and Eujo allowed herself a bit of optimism rather than the dead certainty their lives would be lost forever among the ice.

So, of course, things went wrong.

Chiseling out their nighttime shelter went as fast as ever, the quartet splitting hammering duties sped up with the hope that they were close to salvation. Eujo, the Foti skar leaping at the chance, sparked up some salted fish in the lone pot, long salt-encrusted itself. The god stones succored themselves on Eujo's own exhausted energy, but the fish soon sizzled, and, paired with potato scraps and some ragged bread, they shared a meal amid the setting sun.

Torny told another tale of her thievery gone both right and wrong, some chuckle-worthy pilfering of a Noctia mansion and its owners after a drunken revelry. She'd fled from an unlucky Najahn patrol, leading the cursing guards through one dock warehouse after another before eluding them by clinging to the underside of a pier, only to lose the stolen gains when a curious fish nipped the hanging pouch off her hips.

"Such is the life of a thief," Eujo said when Torny's story concluded, a dramatic sigh dropping off her lips. "Even when you think you've done it all right, it goes wrong."

"Ever try something like that?" Torny asked Eujo, the venom that'd started off their relationship dying out with their dastardly bond.

"I stole for food, not for a career." Eujo grinned to keep the words from cutting. "If I'd had the chance to get something better than moldy pears, I would've. On Kance, it's not so easy."

Torny seemed to measure the statement, as if deciding

whether to boast about her own prowess, only for Bliss's snapping hands to draw their attention.

'On Vis, we don't keep valuables for ourselves. No thieves.'

Wax coughed, "Well, no good ones anyway. Those who try get shoved into the worst jobs, so nobody bothers."

"Sounds great," Torny said, "but wait, I just remembered, you guys live in trees."

'Better than this.'

"What wouldn't be," Eujo added.

As the meal died down, the stars emerged, as clear a blanket as Eujo had ever seen covering the night sky. Normally a fire's light, at least, would disguise some of the beauty, but here, wrapped in their thick clothes, winter wind kissing their noses, nothing sat between Eujo and the glittering above. Beautiful, breath-taking, and more than a little bit frightening.

"Do you think the gods made all those too?" Wax asked.

He lay next to her, Bliss next to him, and Torny on the outside opposite Eujo. The subtle pairing was obvious to them all but went unspoken nevertheless, as though by acknowledging the way Torny and Bliss stayed close to one another, their soft glances, their signed jokes, would be to ruin some just-sparked delight.

As for Wax, well, Eujo wasn't sure what to think.

"If they did, then what went wrong with us?" Eujo's whispered reply rose above the wind, the waves brushing up against the ice.

She and Wax kept one Foti skar between them, the other passed over to Bliss and Torny. The small stone added to the blending, forcing both Renewals to keep their hands in its pouch to draw the skar's warmth. Fingertips touched, an ignored sensation with survival at stake, but now, with their success seemingly assured . . .

"Wrong?" Wax asked, returning Eujo to her own words.

"They killed each other here. Why? What was different about this place?"

"Us, probably."

Eujo blinked, flicked eyes towards Wax to see him still searching the stars. "Are we so bad to drive the gods against each other?"

"Or too perfect. Maybe they all wanted to keep us for themselves. They couldn't share, and now look."

"So every one of those lights is a broken world the gods left behind? An experiment gone wrong?"

Wax sniffed a soft laugh, "Better than the alternative, right?"

"Which is?"

"That we're the worst of them all, and that's why they died."

"Wax, knowing you, that's absolutely the case."

He laughed, she smiled, and they shivered beneath the thick blankets while the stars flickered overhead.

Until the damn floe lurched. Eujo's eyes snapped open as the berg tilted sideways, putting their chiseled stakes to the test. Wax, Bliss, and Torny rolled through their blankets, yelping and cursing in equal measure, to mash against Eujo as her view shifted from night sky to frothy sea, one no longer just waves but bearing an unmistakable otherness.

A fiend.

No, Eujo changed her assessment a second's fraction later, as the floe lurched back the other way, landing with a splashing crack on the waves. Not one fiend. Many. And they were boarding.

Like a jelly mass, the roiling shapes surged around the

berg's sides, crawling up on too many tiny legs. In the silver starlight—Sichi was nowhere to be seen despite the clear skies—the critters, looking like eyeless lumps, came at the foursome from all sides. The tiny legs scratched the ice, a raspy skittering sure to haunt Eujo's nightmares from then on.

If, of course, she lived.

"Skars!" Wax shouted, an obvious order Eujo decided not to call him on, reaching instead for her forearm and the Kance stone waiting there.

Its whispers, light and flighty, were the first she'd heard, escorted to Kance peaks by her soon-to-be traitorous Queensguard. They'd picked out the stone, with Najahn watching, and gave her a polite bow when Eujo slotted it into the bracelet, the first mishmash flowing into her mind. The skar's words remained gibberish now, but its actions were easy to understand as Eujo gave it a panicked order..

The closest fiends, their skittering dull purple forms, blasted away as Eujo stood. They rolled and flipped, splashing into a sea that'd no doubt return them soon. Nevertheless, time bought was time used, as Eujo reached for her staked pack and drew the rapier she'd carried with her ever since her royal ascension.

The thin blade made a poor weapon to execute small masses, but the Kance skar continued to play its starring role, changing its bluster from a blowing gust to a swirling one, whipping the fiends up and around Eujo so they bobbed, helpless, in the air. A simple skewering, one after another, the surprise fading with every stab.

"They bite!" Wax called again, and Eujo turned from her latest stab to see the Vis Renewal waving his thicker blade in an awkward dance, feet shuffling closer to the berg's edge, more mite-like fiends coming up behind him.

The Vis's main concern seemed to be the mite attacking his boot, wrapping its body around his front toes like some latching cloth. Wax smacked it with his sword, scraping off the shell but leaving the wriggling monster beneath. He cursed and Eujo darted in, forking the bug and wrenching it away. The thing bounced into several of its friends, bowling them back into the water.

Bliss, at least, had more success: she and Torny whirled in a weird concert, the Vis sweeping the fiends away with her thick staff while Torny stabbed any making it close. Holding their ground, for now.

"We need to move," Eujo said, relying on another Kance gust to give her time to slip on her pack. "Grab your gear and go!"

"What about the bedding?" Wax asked, flipping the blade to his off hand as he grabbed his own satchel. "We can't—"

"We can and we will. Now."

The Queen's guise fell on, a habit she'd cultivated quick once they placed the sky diamond tiara on her head. Giving orders, expecting them to be obeyed, a commander's calm fell on Eujo as she repeated the order, as she guided Wax towards their two Guardians. Bliss and Torny didn't question the idea, falling in fast as they leapt to another floe.

The fiends followed.

"Here," Wax said as they dashed along a narrow icy line, its edges a smudge against the dark water. "Let me go last."

Eujo, already huffing as the Kance skar sucked at her energy, was happy enough to swap places with Wax, brushing by him on the ice. Only to stop at Bliss's concerned look towards her brother. Torny, beyond, kept right on running, as she ought to.

"Go," Eujo said. "He'll be fine."

Bliss signed something Eujo didn't catch, let Eujo get by her. Loyalty to sibling and Renewal. Admirable, but unnecessary. Wax had an idea, best let him—

The flash tripped her, a sudden flare skipping Eujo ahead into a flat fall along the thin ice finger. She skidded, turned, saw Wax doing what the Renewal always seemed to: blowing fire back at the ice behind them, the trailing fiends igniting like so many poppers in the dark, their forms rolling off the floe into the sea. Bliss tugged at her brother, their forms only shadows against the Foti skar's light.

Too much, and not enough. Eujo planted her hands, started to rise, felt Torny's helping grasp on her shoulder, but that wasn't the concern: Wax, his big moment done, almost collapsed into Bliss's arms, his sister twisting to help the Renewal along the ice.

They hadn't slept long, the skars hadn't recharged from a day leveraged to run along the ice. Worse, the fiends weren't done either. The roiling mass, their many legs seeming to work in concert as they bobbed as one in the dark waves, moved around the flame, circling the floe, cutting the quartet off from their next jump.

"Surrounded," Torny spat, drawing her daggers again. "Guess we go down fighting?"

"We're not going down anywhere," Eujo snarled, flipping the bracelet around, engaging a different, slippery whisper. "Hold on."

"To what, this is an ice berg?"

"Hold on to me, then."

If Torny made another crack at that, Eujo didn't hear it. Instead, she told the silver skar what to do, and the stone responded, leapt at the idea, at the far horizon holding Eujo's eyes.

And the floe, surrounded by fiends, began to move.

CHAPTER 6

THE WARRIOR'S DEMAND

Amazing how a spear to the throat brings out the truth. The Whent academy wasn't much for torture, for interrogations—such things, on the rocky northern isle, were best left to the Pits and their hungry, angry rabble. Instead Annalyse and her friends asked questions, ran experiments, sought the truth through trial and error. Knowledge earned over years and years, bought by Vis now in moments on a tree branch.

"So that's why they want the skars," Deshiva said, the two of them sitting in a soft clearing after a night swamped by conversation, by slight threats and easy turnabouts.

Annalyse gave the hunters what they wanted and more besides.

What did she owe her old home, that'd cast her out?

"There's power," Annalyse agreed, "but that's not the only reason. Control too. The Circle's always afraid of what the isles might do. Gladdring told me as much."

She'd given up the Tenet's game, explained his whole plan: overthrow Fassle, unite the isles with the skars and work together to destroy the fiends. Annalyse didn't have an answer for Deshiva's skepticism at the idea: Gladdring's motives had always rung true to the scientist.

"That, at least, you have right," Deshiva replied. Fresh coffee, boiled up over the campfire, cooled in small wood cups in their hands. Shadows moved around them, Deshiva's hunters keeping a perimeter. "The Najahn are only interested in control."

Deshiva looked every bit the wild Vis rumors told of the isle, sporting a dress Annalyse hadn't seen much of during her brief stay in Kitaye. Tight woven clothes streamed around inked skin, sigils Annalyse would've loved to learn about, interrupted by holsters and straps for a bow, arrows, and more tricks than Annalyse dared imagine. Deshiva's hair split into twin taut braids, tied with a slim, corded headband matching the summer ocean's clean blue.

That Annalyse felt more than a little out with her fresh weaves, her scant satchel—returned after the hunters cleansed it of tools and treasures—and utter lack of deadly weapons would be an understatement.

That Deshiva didn't care one bit was equally clear.

"Vis skars belong to us," Deshiva said next, unprompted, jerking Annalyse up from her coffee. "We've let the Najahn keep them for the Renewal long enough. They cannot have them for their own wants."

Annalyse blinked. "What does that have to do with me?"

"You're going to help us."

"Help?" Annalyse looked left and right, hoping some hunter would be there, ready to disabuse Deshiva of the notion this Whent woman far from home would be any help at all. "I'm not a fighter."

"Now you're the one who's lying." Deshiva smiled. "You've spent the last hours telling me, in detail, how Gladdring had you working with the skars to develop weapons, to turn armor into more than just a metal wall. You'll do the same for us."

Another blink. A dull lack of surprise found its hold. Gladdring sounded much the same, albeit without the threats, when he first came to Whent, found her amid the few skars in the Academy's stores and asked whether she believed the stones only belonged to the Aegis. That conversation, her showing off what the skars could do, had brought her here, an inflection point she saw again rising up over the campfire's dwindling embers.

Dive into the fray again? Get used by someone again?

Quik flashed. Their conversation on the dock, in the Najahn port while they dried off. Escape, survive, and maybe save the world. Optimism in a hopeless situation? Maybe, but wasn't that why she'd left her warm, cliffside workshop on Whent?

THE MARCH DIDN'T GO RIGHT BACK to Kitaye, the hunters veering east off the main path, finding a way through thick trees and plants that Annalyse didn't know existed until the flat, leaf-coated forest floor appeared before her next footstep. Two days blurred by, Deshiva monopolizing the mornings and nights between the long walks to scrape the scientist's mind for more.

Annalyse, eventually, did the same in turn. Had Deshiva and the hunters show their methods, how they tracked and fought, turned a fiend or a hanoko's assault into an ambush. How they held their weapons, and where a skar might find its best place. Habits died hard, and Annalyse scribbled page after page on her charcoal pad, diagramming ideas, pitching them to Deshiva, and when they arrived at the southern lake, all thoughts of Svarde's cliff-side exile had died a simple death: buried by possibility.

Treehouses circled the lake, many beginning low on a thick trunk before spreading up through branches to neighboring trees. Spidering rope bridges kept the Vis off the ground, making Annalyse almost feel like she was back on Noctia, where people were always above and below. Fronds and ferns replaced the stones and slate, tropical birdsong matched the cawing gulls, though the air lacked Noctia's endless soot, an industrial tang Annalyse didn't miss in the slightest.

"This is you," Deshiva said, escorting Annalyse personally to a squat, wide tree near the lake's eastern end. The water lapped a verdant border, a sole beach kept clear by Vis attendants, and fish frolicked, jumping, splashing, and getting carried away by happy raptors. A natural miracle put on pause when Deshiva opened the thin bamboo door. "We built it to what you said."

"What I said? You mean when I told you what Gladdring had for me?"

Annalyse asked the question, but the answer was obvious. Much like in Noctia, a central slab, this one a hefty stump chopped and cleaned, dominated the space. Smaller tables ringed it, each holding a small chest. A rope ladder led to a lofted bed. Netted windows spaced the wood floors and walls, letting in far more light than Annalyse ever had in Gladdring's grim tower.

"This is what you had, it's what you need, right?" Deshiva asked, her tone at once risking frustration for a missed detail and hoping otherwise. "There's little time. The Najahn are already fortifying."

Annalyse didn't take a step inside. Not yet. If the walk, if the discussions had filled her notebook, that'd all been a theory. Everything for Gladdring had been science, tests for practical application, but not yet a manufacture for war, for death. And that, too, had been for use against fiends.

"I . . ." Annalyse started, faltered.

Deshiva grabbed Annalyse's shoulder, twisted her so the scientist saw the Vis leader. The sun descended at her back, giving Deshiva's inks a fired glow, her eyes an intensity stealing what remained of Annalyse's thought.

"This is not a choice, Annalyse." Deshiva said, mauling each syllable. A promise and a threat. "You will do this. Without it, the Najahn will overpower us. They will take this isle and subjugate everyone on it towards their ends."

"Which might be noble. They might—"

"If the Circle wanted our cooperation, they would ask for it. They have not asked. They will not. You know this. Pick a side."

Deshiva said the words like Annalyse had a choice, but grim looks, both from Deshiva and two waiting hunters said otherwise.

"Do you even have any skars?" Annalyse asked, and Deshiva at last gave a slight smile, nodded past the scientist into the treehouse.

"We have yours." The smile dwindled to a frown. "Your skars and the first pieces for them are inside. You'll work tonight. We'll leave tomorrow."

"Leave? We only just arrived?"

"A short trip," Deshiva said. "A Najahn ship has docked at Kitaye. They're going to take the skars. We won't let them."

"I'm not a fighter, I don't—"

A smirk now, "That's not true. Fiends, the Najahn. If you aren't yet a fighter, you are now. Get to work, Annalyse. This is it. What you were meant for."

Those words stuck with Annalyse as she went into the treehouse workshop, looked over the space. The chests held her pouches, the skars Annalyse herself had carried making a start. Hardly enough to equip an army, though, or enough to fight the Najahn. Annalyse went from one stone to the next, picked them up, heard their whispers. What'd once been so marvelous now sounded different, almost sinister. Not a new universe to explore, but one to exploit.

Her colleagues would be ashamed, in shock, or disappointed. As they'd been when Annalyse first announced she was leaving with Gladdring. Her first step away from science towards something practical. This was just the next.

What she was meant for.

The Vis were raiders, stealthy and swift. Nothing like the Najahn, like the massive Whent armies back home. A few skars, put right, could change everything. The scientist looked over at the spears, the weaves stacked inside the treehouse door. The first things she was to work with, to transform into something special.

They wouldn't do.

The hunters did as she asked, running into the twilight. If they found what she asked for, then maybe, maybe, the isle long written off by the rest of the world would have a chance.

Or Deshiva, Annalyse, and all the hunters would find themselves speared on a voulge's end.

CHAPTER 7

THE KING BENEATH

It wasn't long into their first stretch following the bolt's blood trail before Sawi admitted she wasn't a hunter. Not in the formal Vis sense, anyway. Not one of the dangerous trackers who'd helped lead Ami, Svarde, and Catya through the jungle paths to the Great Sana ten years ago.

Instead, she was barely an adult, one tossed into gathering fruits and watching the days pass without a threat.

"You could've mentioned this earlier," Ami said as they slipped down a narrow crevasse, a break off from their tunnel but one still sticky with the fiend's drying, bluish blood.

Not that the blood itself glowed that color, but the mosses coating both traveler's satchels painted it as such. The blood's reflection helped, but Ami found the strong iron smell a better guide as they stepped slow and careful among the Dark Below's too many twists and turns.

"You would've known it already if you'd even once asked about me."

"Stopped doing that when my friends kept dying."

Sawi, a couple handholds below Ami in the descending gap, paused and glared up, her eyes putting up a good flare as Ami hesitated.

"Quit acting like some sort of martyr. I'm over your act, Ami. Sorry about Catya, but she knew what she was doing when she became the Aegis. Friends that died? Who? You certainly didn't seem depressed when we were working with Annalyse. Every morning, barking orders, demanding this and—"

"Keep moving. Keep talking if you want, but keep on moving."

Sawi took Ami's points, both of them. She rattled on, a raging flood obviously building for some time. What prompted the outburst now? Ami's tossed off remark, a line tinged with truth that simply sounded good in the moment?

Or was the Vis beset by more problems than her traveling companion?

Lured away from home by Gladdring, stuffed into an experiment and then an attempted overthrow. Told to ignore a close friend. Left to rot in a cell with certain death the only outcome till Ami happened on by?

That might bend someone's mental state into a broken place.

"I've been there," Ami said when Sawi's rattle dwindled, when the two reached the crevasse's bottom.

A last drop, high enough to for Ami to catch herself on all fours, the harpoon jagging against her back. Scrapes and cuts tweaked, itched, and were ignored. The Vis skar embedded in Ami's faceplate whispered. She'd pop it soon, give it to Sawi at the walk's end to prop the Vis back up, and endure a painful few hours. A penance, of sorts.

For what?

"Yeah, you've been everywhere," Sawi muttered, crouching before Ami until the Vis located the blood trail. "Experienced all there is to see. We're all just repeats to you."

"I'm trying to say there's no use in self-pity."

"Who's pitying themselves? I'm telling you we're going to have to work together to track this thing, and you're talking about self-pity?"

Ami laughed, once. Sawi had it right. The Guardian had gone down another mental rabbit hole for no real reason.

"The dark does strange things," Ami finally said as they started off again.

"I swear, Ami, if you lose your mind down here, don't expect me to carry you home."

"As if you could find it, gatherer."

Sawi shrugged, a silver-blue shadow amid the encroaching, mossy dark. They kept going. More hours burned. Conversation picked up and maintained, dropping to whispers if either heard another noise, but the fiends had grown quiet. Either listening to the pair bumbling through their territory or, like the one Sawi and Ami had killed, leaving. Where to and why, who knew.

Hopefully the bolt's owner was the reason, and hopefully they were friendly, because Ami had long since decided she and Sawi had no path, no plan, and no chance of getting out on their own.

"It ends here," Sawi said, slowing to a hunched stop in a small chamber. Several tunnels interconnected, leading off in different directions. "There's a mark where the bolt hit. Then nothing."

The pair gave the chamber a good once-over, found no other markers. Ami was about to declare the spot good enough for a night's rest—the multiple entries weren't great, but small tunnels spread noise. They'd have warning and close quarters to defend, better against higher numbers. Yet, just as Ami sloughed her pack off into the dirt, Sawi whistled.

Soft, low, and curious.

"Look at the splatter," Sawi said when Ami asked. "The bolt struck, there's a spray back this way, most of it. Whoever shot the thing would've been standing in this tunnel."

"Then that's the way we go." Ami re-shouldered her satchel. "Nice work, Vis."

Sawi threw Ami a skeptical side-eye, "Thanks, but that was kind of obvious."

"Not to a Foti miner."

Sawi snorted, but Ami swore she saw a little grin play about that face. Sawi did, too, lead off the walk with more spring than before. Ami started to rationalize it, throw a secondary reasoning into why she'd given Sawi the compliment, then stopped herself. Shook her own head in the purple-blue gloom.

Sometimes, a kind word could just be that. Just because Gladdring tried to turn everything into manipulative layers didn't mean Ami had to.

As if rewarding Sawi's efforts, the chosen tunnel didn't branch for a long time, instead snarling in a curling dance without choice. It descended—of course it descended—but the pair could at least believe they were following the right trail, going until their legs felt leaden, their eyes were have shut, and Sawi began bouncing off the walls as her steps veered.

An easy state for an ambush, and one commenced as the tunnel widened, split into a fork. To the left, darkness and further depths. To the right, as Sawi's sucked in breath announced, a crossbow and a curious stare behind it. No lanterns, but as the pair's moss cast its light, Ami recognized the outfit: a fur and leather collection, albeit thinned out as the Dark Below settled into a warmth cozier than the frigid winter above.

"Whent," Ami said, striding up next to Sawi and keeping her hands free. No drawn weapon, no decisive kill, or so Ami hoped. "You're a long way from home."

"So are you, Foti," the scout replied, a grizzled woman's tone emerging from the thick cloak. "I don't recognize the other, which means she must be a Vis. An odd pair."

"With a stranger story." Ami let her left hand drift towards Sawi's, putting it in a spot to grab the Vis before Sawi could do something stupid. "Yet I bet yours would match ours."

"It might."

A long silence. Both sides gauging the other. Ami tried to place what a Whent expedition might be doing this far down. Too deep for mining, but maybe not for scouting. Some small party whose delusions of hidden treasure had taken them far off course? Or—

"We're lost and desperate, dammit," Sawi said, breaking the standoff. "We were trying to get to Vis through these forsaken caves and need help."

"To Vis? Through the caves?"

With Sawi breaking them open, Ami didn't try to stop the Vis. She spilled it all, except their branding as traitors by the Najahn. At least clever enough for that. Without the gear or willingness to pay the high price for winter travel south, Sawi said they'd tried to be enterprising and found themselves doomed instead, and when the scout pointed out their weapons, the fact that they were still alive, Ami seized the opening.

"We're good fighters, hunters," Ami said. "And we'd be glad to put off our trip if you need our skills."

That drew a different look from Sawi, more curious than angry. A swerve to their intended plans, but if Ami was judging the scout right, from the well-filled water skin, satchel, lantern, and gear in top-notch repair, then she belonged to a Whent party with good supplies. Supplies Ami and Sawi could use.

And, though she'd never say it aloud, Ami was ready to be done, at least for a time, with blind walking through the dark.

"Then pledge an oath," the scout said. "Right now. Promise you won't injure, steal, or hinder our efforts in any way. Do so, and keep your hands clear of your weapons, and you can come with me."

"Hinder your efforts?" Sawi asked.

"You've found Jochi's expedition. My name is Olgata and, down here, we are going to save the Seven Isles."

A declaration like that deserved some back-up, and Olgata delivered, albeit over two days travel. The scout, after a slow trust thaw gained through shared dinners and stories, though Ami and Sawi continued reserving their Najahn status, gave Jochi's whole plan away. The warlord had built a network over the last month, grinding outposts into the Dark Below all the way from Whent's surface. Scouts co-opted from across the isle patrolled neighboring tunnels, warding away wandering fiends and mapping chambers for useful ores, pools, and plants. Meanwhile, Jochi himself had set up camp near the Wound's base, in a place they now called Dreamhold—a basic name, Olgata admitted, but clear enough in purpose to attract adventurers—where he sought a way to close the gates.

"The gates?" Ami asked.

"Where the fiends arrive," Olgata replied. "There are seven, matching our isles, and through them come all the monsters. Our problem, now, is how to destroy them."

The tunnels they walked through grew brighter as they approached Dreamhold, with lanterns hanging and signs, already, of engineers shaving off rougher edges. The air no longer smelled mossy, instead crackling with ash and industry. Words, indistinct but still actual words, drifted along between hammers, drills, and saws. Ami found it hard to keep a smile off her half-plated face. Somehow, they were going to survive. Somehow, they were going to—

The tunnel broke into a larger one, a massive tube overlaid with production, with rolling carts. People, from Whent soldiers to miners, to the merchants supporting them all churned, and most in one direction. Ami stopped, stunned at the sheer number.

"How?" she asked Olgata. "How are there this many so far down?"

"Winter in Whent normally means hiding, waiting out the cold with ale and boredom. Now, our isle has possibility instead. A chance to do something new, something incredible." Olgata glanced at the pair, giving them another once-over, a search for something she didn't find. "A chance, too, at glory, at resources beyond what Noctia and the Najahn could hope to match."

"I thought this was about the fiends?" Sawi asked.

"The fiends, and throwing off the Circle's oppression. This is more than a chance to save the isles, Vis. It is the way to break the chains binding them."

Whatever Ami's feelings about those chains—the Najahn seemed impossibly distant down here in this underground world—she forgot about them soon after, as Olgata led them through another massive chamber, this one sealed along one side with glittering, pointed iron fortifications, and into a strange city. The houses and buildings seemed oppressive, flat walls and empty windows just starting to get dressed up with repairs.

Sawi noticed it first, the Vis's experience keeping any scream away from her lips: many doing the work bore blotchy skin, faded eyes, or missing limbs. They didn't speak, didn't have satchels with food or water nearby, and lurched about in doubtless purpose. Yet, Whent people didn't spare them a second glance, or worked alongside the shambling strangers.

"What are they?" Ami asked, following Sawi's discovery.

"That answer," Olgata said, "waits where we're going."

As for who gave it, the most impossible turn yet. He sat on an odd stone chair in the center of the town's largest, only temple, up stairs and behind smooth walls. A gigantic, jagged blade sat in one hand, its point driven into the clean slabs at his feet. Nearby, as if waiting on him, stood two others, watching Ami and Sawi approach. One, a wild-looking woman with wide eyes and a fierce grin, almost menacing, and the other, so laden in furs and with a beard so big as to be Jochi and nobody else.

Yet Ami found her focus on the man in that chair, the one who had no right to be alive, whose body looked more gray and scar-coated than ever, yet in whose bright eyes and set smile lingered real hope.

"Ami," Svarde said as the pair entered the chamber. "Are you ready?"

CHAPTER 8

WHAT QUEENS DESIRE

A visit to the Circle's private chambers never came easy. Even now, wearing an Adept's gold-gilded garments, Gladdring took the carpeted steps slow and with a scowl. The broad hallway narrowed in its descent beyond the main room, where the vast round table served as meeting place for anyone seeking help from the isles's greatest power. Lanterns burned, portraits spaced the walls, holding the grim visages of Circle leaders past. Their eyes didn't seem to follow Gladdring, but instead stare off into a hard distance, as if their struggles against the fiends, against hostile isles continued long after life left them behind.

A rosy prospect for his own future, but then, nobody who sought real power was blind to its consequences.

Or, at least, he was not.

Neither, it seemed, was Fassle.

The man waited alone in a circular room with a central table and three chairs, all plush and immaculate in their Noctia purple framing. Fassle himself wore a plain black robe, a silver necklace vanishing beneath its high collar. No gold, no medals, no ceremony. A hot tea pot smoked in the table's center, two cups already poured. No guards stood nearby. The only observers a single portrait pair, Demion and her long lost Guardian, drawn from hearsay, the oils giving them a determined, brave stand against their unseen foes.

Would that Gladdring could find the same courage. At least, with Yarvick's knives at his back, Gladdring wouldn't worry about weapons.

"Three times," Fassle said by way of greeting, nodding to the chair opposite him. "Three times I've summoned you to these chambers, and yet this will be the first in which, I hope, we can work together."

Gladdring didn't need reminding on the first two. One, a simple series of threats laying out Gladdring's coming doom, followed by stripping his Tenet rank and throwing him into the Circle's secretive, most desolate prison. The second, when Fassle decided the skars could be more than just propaganda, could prompt a revolution, had been to drag Gladdring from the offal and offer him an Adept's cloak instead. Loyalty's bargain.

An easy one to take. Far easier to overthrow Fassle from his side than in a dungeon's deep cell.

"I was surprised to get the summons," Gladdring said, sitting. "I thought we were well on our way?"

"Any grand plan runs into problems." Fassle lifted the tea, drank. Gladdring had to copy, tasted the anis from Tamas, a little cinnamon tossed in for flavor. Hot and perfect for winter. "Your reputation as the Trade Tenet— and not as a traitor—brings you here."

"How may I serve?"

A frown. "Don't be dumb with me, Gladdring. I know every word out of your mouth that isn't cursing me causes you some pain, so let me appeal to something that, I hope, makes some measure with you: the Najahn's cause."

"What cause would that be?"

"The skars, Gladdring. The damn skars. The key to keeping our power."

"And stopping the fiends."

"Yes, of course," Fassle dashed off the words, shook his head. "Not every Isle sees our approach as welcome." The frown carved harder lines. "No surprise. The fiends remain. They grasp at what weapons they can find."

"As they should."

"No. If your little show proves anything, it's that the skars can't be wielded by those who don't know what they're doing. Already, the Whent outpost has sent word of Renewals using the stones to destroy their buildings, ruin the path to the isle's skars. A single fool. Can you imagine the same everywhere?"

"I can. Disaster."

A sharp nod. "Then you know we can't let that happen. We must control the skars, and we must bring them here. Foti, Rana, and Tamas are already ours."

Gladdring sat forward, "Foti? I thought—"

"They have no leaders. Only merchants and miners. We slapped down their petty attempt and they turned back to their forges quick enough." Another swirl and sip of the tea, its burn seeming to settle Fassle back into the moment. "Whent is under repair, but the Golden Gash remains ours while the rockbiters send all their warriors into the Dark Below."

"A doomed effort, no doubt."

"A lucky one for us. By the time any, if any, return, we'll control every city. Their remaining powers want security, and I've delivered it to them. But that's not why you're here."

"Oh? You didn't call me just to complain?" Gladdring let a raised eyebrow linger.

"I called you here to give you a task. One worthy of your skills."

"Then tell me."

Fassle sniffed. Gladdring shifted his right hand, sent it into his robe's pocket to the Tamas skar nestled there. The stone's whispers brushed Gladdring's thoughts, caught Fassle, and suggested truth. What the Circle was about to ask would be genuine, not some trap.

"Vis and Kance are the only two isles with any doubt remaining," Fassle said. "I'm sending more forces to the south. The shipping lanes remain free of ice, so we will crush those jungle dwellers should they protest. Kance . . . is a different matter."

Ah. Invading the sky isle would be a disaster. Other than Noctia, Kance was the only isle with real leaders, with martial abilities beyond random raiders and haphazard warlords. The two Queens commanded loyalty and lethal troops, enough to make a Najahn incursion both bloody and long, if not impossible.

"They've removed our soldiers from the outpost," Fassle continued, "stripped them of their weapons and sent them home. We have no presence there any longer. None."

"Kance won't trade their skars?"

"Trade? Gladdring, I thought you understood. This isn't about trade. We take, because if we do not, then there will only be turmoil. You must convince the Queen of this. You must break her resistance. Offer anything, save the stones. Turn her mind, and be rewarded, not just by me but from all these isles you claim to serve."

"If she won't make a deal?"

Fassle refilled his cup, made to do the same to Gladdring's. "They have two Queens, yes? If the one coming here will not play her part, perhaps the other will."

As to what might happen to the refusing Queen, Gladdring held no illusions.

THE ADEPT IGNORED the snow as he waited by the private Najahn docks. Quiet in winter, with ice blocking most isles, he stood now amid a crowd of purple and black. Some with voulges and the sharp chakram discs, others ready with nothing more than ropes and a willingness to get a ship into port. And what a ship it was, too.

The Kance Queen came in on a vessel that seemed to float on the gray waters, gliding along the wave-tops, never descending into any roiling valleys, instead flagging its sails with such precision as to rest alongside the black rock pier without ever once touching it. Anchors, silver-stained, dropped from either side to lock the three-story craft and its sloping cabins into place. Workers scurried, ramps descended, and the retinue disembarked at speed: a full ten soldier squad of Kance Queensguard, their glimmering armor the perfect version of armed cold, double that many in servants carrying chests, gear, and shrouded heads. Several advisors came next, all approaching Gladdring with welcomes and receiving them in turn.

And last, of course, the Queen herself. Somewhere north of Gladdring's age and frosted with Kance's classic demeanor. She swept down the ramp wearing thick boots beneath an equally burly cloak, one frilled with silver feathers at its edges, as if she might suddenly decide to take flight.

Then again, with a Kance skar, such a move wasn't a total impossibility.

Some nameless Najahn assistant whispered pointers into Gladdring's ear, ranging from Kance's harvests and notable trading partners over the summer to the Queen's preferred foods, daily habits, and apparent love of the lelune flowers filling the Wound's crater. Gladdring only kept that last, shuttling it away as a potential evening destination.

The best diplomacy happened out of doors and away from listening ears.

The Queen had her own sources, as she marched down the pier without an eye or a look at anyone else save Gladdring. If she was impressed at his regalia, nothing showed on her face, shrouded like her various underlings in a silk, silver-blue hood. Beneath, as she squared up to Gladdring —those boots put their heights close enough to match stares—Gladdring saw not the killer Fassle made the Kance ruler out to be, but rather someone curious, compelling, and ready with a question.

"Are you Fassle's lapdog, or do you have a mind of your own?" the Queen asked, loud enough for the mousey assistant at Gladdring's side to hear. Her voice had a crystal's clarity, each syllable announced like a dart's strike into the thick boards dotting so many Noctia taverns.

"I do what the Circle desires," Gladdring replied, his traditional honey tongue a poor match.

"And that is everything Kance owns?"

"If you would give it." Gladdring grinned. The Queen didn't match his lips. No joking to be found here then. His fingers rubbed the ring, the skar, but he pushed away its offered advice. Too much reliance on the skar would dull his own instincts, and the stones could be stolen at any time. "If not, then I hope we can find a way to keep both our Isles, and all the others, safe."

If the words touched the Queen, she didn't show it. Instead, she seemed to trace a line around and through Gladdring, measuring him in every way. Gladdring had done the same many times before, to a partner on the Tamas stage before a rehearsal, a performance, an audition. He let her, hid nothing.

"Fassle invited me here," the Queen began, "with a letter. It said the Najahn needed help, that I had to let them take all of our skars. He stuffed his lines with pointless words about unity, fiends, and nonsense."

"But you came anyway."

At last, a grin's fraction. "I came because true power doesn't hide in her castle or behind a closed door. I came to tell Fassle to his face that the days of Najahn supremacy are over. The isles are not yours to claim. You can have your trade, but you will get nothing else from us. Ever again."

For the first time in far too long, Gladdring felt his heart tremor. A smile rose as he gave the Queen the slightest bow. The world might be under assault, the Najahn might be destroying centuries-old tradition, and the consequences could mean the end of everything, but this, this would be fun.

CHAPTER 9

THORNS

Gloved hands gripped ropes, each other, anything on the ice to keep themselves from rolling off. Splashing into the dark ocean wouldn't just mean a soaking, but would guarantee a fiend swarm, a quick numbing, and a slow death below the waves.

That dire fact hummed along Eujo's periphery as she let the Kance skar run with its own wind, shoving the lanky ice floe holding their distraught foursome across the churning sea. Sometime after its lurching start, Torny collapsed on top of Eujo, pinning the Queen to the ice with her own body and a desperate chisel hold. Curses streamed from the bandit, only growing as the skittering bug-like fiends continued to clamber over the floe's edges.

But not so many: the fiend-filled waves broke as the floe shot forward, those grubby monsters not already climbing up left behind as Eujo's skar-fueled desire shattered their creature created raft. Behind, according to Torny's more lucid moments, clung Wax and Bliss, the sibling pair riding the floe's trailing edge after Wax's Foti bomb failed to do more than light up the sky.

The skars, like the gods that made them, were fickle friends.

Eujo's silver stone sang, a melody rising like a new dawn, though the night around them held only stars. Strong and joyous, Eujo found herself wincing at the volume, the skar's song picking up speed along with the floe. The ice tilted, threatening to throw its front end beneath the surface only to surge free, a shift narrated by Torny's frantic shouts to Wax and Bliss to stay at the floe's back.

"Not a boat I'd choose, but I'll take it," Torny snarled near Eujo's ear, swapping the chisel hold to her left hand and drawing a knife. Ahead, two clawed, shelled fiends picked their way across the ice. "Don't suppose you can slow this ride a second, Eujo? Give me time to pick off these bugs?"

The Queen parsed the words, wanted to find a reply, but the skar took it, a mad rush siphoning Eujo's air. Her lips sagged, her eyes drifted near shut, and Eujo found her hands and feet numb. Movement seemed impossible, improbable, a folly against the skars continuing song.

"Guessing that's a no," Torny muttered. "Don't blame me if you get a bite then."

The fiends spread, each sliding, picking their way towards Eujo from either shoulder. The Queen couldn't find the energy to move: trying felt like attempting to shove a whole ship on shore by herself.

Panic.

A skittering fear washed her, blotted out the skar's song as the fiends closed. She couldn't do a damn thing, not a thing to save herself. For all her life, since she could remember, Eujo could always, had always depended on her skills to steal food, to escape pursuit, and, if necessary, to turn that pursuit into partners when they caught her. Now her fate depended on a bandit, a fickle thief who—

Torny moved, climbing up and pressing down on Eujo's shoulders. Her dagger, a flash to Eujo's right, lanced and speared the first fiend. Yellow goo flew free, splattering down the floe, onto Eujo's hands, her face, and she couldn't do a damn thing about it. With a flick, Torny sent the fiend flying, shifting to go for its partner.

Too late.

Eujo wanted to scream, the skar's tune jolting, sending the ice slashing leftward. Stinging pain radiated from her left wrist, Eujo rolling her eyes that way to see Torny stabbing the second fiend, pushing it off and away with yet another, somehow different, curse.

"Sorry," Torny hissed, moving again to clamp down on the red leaking out from Eujo's coat sleeve, staining her glove, the ice beneath into a lurid pink. "Bugs move fast. How bad is it?"

Eujo didn't even try to answer. With the fiend's dispatch, her last lingering focus dissipated, her eyes lolling back towards the horizon and Tamas's shrouded line. The skar sang, and its song, like the wind slicing through the palace among the sky islands, swept her away.

"You try, then," Torny's voice again swam into Eujo's muted world, quiet, dark, and wet. "It's not like I'm some sort of strongman."

"Then get out of the way."

Wax? He sounded alive, at least. Better than Eujo, who seemed unable to open her eyes, to do much more than breathe. Her every muscle twinged in exhausted depletion, unable to muster even the slightest twitch.

The Vis skar, now, led the whispers, all the others barely a murmur. The jungle stone's fierce muttering told Eujo all she needed to know: wherever they were, however they had survived, the drain to get them there had nearly killed the Queen.

Something pulled at her shoulders. Eujo felt herself slide, dirt or sand beneath her shifting away as someone—Wax, likely—dragged the Queen up some slope. Questions dashed, Eujo too tired to hold on any single one, gave into frustration instead. Easier to be angry at what she couldn't do than be rational about it, especially now.

When she couldn't even see.

The Vis skar reacted, spiking up into a curious burble. Eujo's eyes itched, a sudden bloom, as if a crusty coat were being cleared.

"Look at you. A sword's length. So strong."

Torny again.

"At least she's off the ice now." Wax, the reply.

Silence, then a Torny laugh, "Your sister's right, Wax. Want to be the Aegis, better bulk up. That way there's more of you to waste away, because right now I'm guessing you'll be all bones in a week or two."

"Maybe I'll hand you all the skars once we get them, see how you like it."

"Sure, then I'll sell' 'em right back to Fassle for his stupid war."

Torny's cut didn't land, the group fading to a more awkward silence than the first time around. Eujo, so close to opening her eyes, could guess why: always hard to laugh at a real disaster.

Tamas emerged in a blink, a blank black to beauty. Oranges, purples that would've taken Eujo's breath away if she had any to spare. Her sight's bottom chunk was only the beach, its black grains a sharp cry from the white and brown sand elsewhere. Further up, where the small dunes ran into Tamas proper lay vivid life: swooping leaves dangling from gnarled bushes, squat trees dotted with spiked indigo flowers, and all tinged with winter's frosty kiss. Roots ran over the ground, reaching high enough to, Eujo figured, smack her knee with a wayward step. A thick loam meshed with the ocean's salt, odd enough to prompt a cough, which Eujo turned into a sputtering groan.

"Hey, she's waking up," Torny said, bending over and staring Eujo right in the eye. The bandit, for her part, looked both worn and well, an arduous trek survived. "Guess she didn't kill herself after all." The bandit glanced away from Eujo's face, over the Queen's back, and frowned. "I know she was breathing, but just because the body's kicking, doesn't mean there's anything left upstairs."

"I'm here," Eujo said, the words a bare whisper.

Torny sighed, clicked her tongue. "Too bad. Coulda fetched a great price for those skars. Guess we'll have to do things the hard way."

The hard way, such as it was, would have to wait. As Eujo crawled back to life, a step-by-step emergence aided by devouring what little remained from their reserves—Wax and Bliss had both lost their satchels in the fiend flight—they learned reaching Tamas wasn't the same as, well, reaching Tamas. Their landing point, marked by the floe's crunching beaching on the black sand, seemed remote, with nothing so much as a chimney's smoke marking the morning's chilly blue sky. No trails made themselves known to Bliss and Wax as the Vis pair took up an initial scout, returning to report the thick roots lay in every direction save one: a walk down the coast.

That gave them a chance in the early afternoon, when,

with Wax's helpful shoulder, Eujo forced herself to put one foot in front of the other in a halting walk. The ice floe hadn't even left their sight, though, before their beach walk began to disappear.

"Tide's going to cut us off," Wax said.

The Vis had been throwing Eujo one concerned look after another all morning, but he'd kept his focus where it ought to be: keeping Eujo upright. Now they stopped, Bliss hiking up the sand to the snarling root-and-plant combo with a shaking head.

'It's going to be worse than snow in there,' Bliss signed. 'Every step's a trap.'

"Why don't our magical friends here burn it?" Torny asked. "Clear a path, send up a signal, and give us some warmth. Three things I'd be happy with right now."

"Don't know if either of us have the energy for that," Wax replied, the waves now kissing their boots with every splash. "Wait this out, and go at low tide?"

'We'll starve before long.'

"Or go cannibal," Torny added, coming to help Wax walk Eujo up the beach. "Bet you're pretty gamey, Wax, but I'd give you a try."

"Thanks."

"Torny's right," Eujo said as they joined Bliss, looking at the roots. Thick, brown, and constant. "We're low on food and water. Any town might be days away. We can't wait, and we can't struggle through this." As she finished the words, her voice dropped to a near whisper. "We shouldn't need much."

Wax sighed, felt beneath his coat for the Najahn necklace. Its slots, now more filled than not, shined in the dull sunlight.

"A little," Wax said. "That's all. No explosions."

"No explosions," Torny agreed, as if she had any say.

The bandit and Bliss helped Eujo away, leaving Wax staring at the plants, one hand wrapped around the necklace, the other reaching out as if he was going to give the plants a nice pet. At first, nothing happened, no sound save the wave and some far off bird calls Eujo couldn't identify. Then the air shimmered, a blur between Wax and the closest roots. Wax began breathing hard and the roots blackened, smoke rising before the first faint orange flicker burst up. Several more joined quick, a small fire lighting before Wax stumbled back, falling to a knee on the dark shore.

"Well, look at that," Torny said, only for the fire to sputter and die. "Oh."

'They're alive and wet,' Bliss signed, going to her brother's side. 'Burning them won't work.'

Eujo looked to her right, hoping for a chance and finding one, though not quite how she expected. When the ocean filled her view, the Rana skar on her wrist piped up a new note. A possibility, if only Eujo wanted to swim. The skar would push the water around her, propel Eujo all the way to anywhere she wanted to, a shapeless urge defeated by Eujo's own exhaustion and the fact that they had two skar-less people with them.

"But," Eujo muttered, drawing a curious eye from Torny, "maybe we don't need to swim."

"You're right, we don't need to swim," Torny said. "Not getting back in that drink, Aegis or no."

"If I'm right, we won't have to."

Eujo took a step towards the approaching tide, Torny getting the gist and helping her along. The Rana skar caught the Queen's idea and leapt at it like a dog to its dinner. Beyond, as if someone took a spoon to the incoming wave, the water split, the wave washing up around Eujo and Torny but not touching them. A bubble of sorts, and temporary.

"We take turns," Eujo said, catching up to Wax and Bliss. "Keep the waves away, keep walking, as long as we can."

CHAPTER 10

LIFE STRIKE

Through properties unknown, a wielder could feel a skar's power through a handle, a jewelry band, or just by holding the stone. Annalyse hadn't found a metal, wood, or other material that would block the skar's whispers, while at the same time hadn't found any way to conduct the skars save by touch. In other words, no matter how close she hovered her hand over the Vis skars piled before her in the treehouse, they remained silent.

As did the small collection set in boxes around the room, once taken and now returned to her by Deshiva, arms for the hunters going into battle against the Najahn the next day. She'd been tasked with slotting all these stones into spears, daggers, and whatever else Annalyse could devise.

How the Vis would handle the skars suddenly in their minds, their whispers urging the warriors to this and that, Annalyse wasn't sure, so she planned to play things as safe as possible.

Vis skars only, for now. Wrapped into weaves, slotted

into bracers. A boost to keep Deshiva's warriors alive without causing wild catastrophe. An edge that might let the Vis win the battle without charring the jungle to ash, causing a river to flood a village, or simply stealing everyone's souls.

The opals, all three, lay separate from the other skars. Annalyse regarded them as the night ticked on, the Vis skar in a simple necklace helping keep the scientist awake. Among all the tests she'd done with Ami, Sawi, and Quik, she'd kept the Noctia skars away. Saved those for later, a later Annalyse never really wanted to arrive, a plan Ami had agreed to.

The power over death was too fraught, too frightening, too strange to gamble with until the other stones had been mastered.

"And I'm definitely not giving you to them," Annalyse muttered to the black stones.

She kept her voice low, given the two hunters guarding the treehouse door. The bamboo building up the shelter wasn't exactly sound-proof—the noise from the lake's multitude still went strong, music, whooping calls, laughter and song ringing out in hard opposition to the methodical war-making going on in here. Annalyse would expect those guards to report everything they heard and saw to Deshiva, who'd probably jump at the chance to throw whatever death those black skars could deal at the Najahn.

Najahn who, Annalyse had to remind herself, were mostly made up of the Isle's poor and desperate. Recruited and shoved into roles, hardened both with pledges and the security that came from hot meals and soft beds. Weapons and the training to wield them. Not evil, just opposed interests.

Which was why Annalyse had been tucking skars into wrist and shoulder wraps too. She'd pitch the plan to Deshiva: anyone who took a bad wound could have one of these around till help arrived. Keep the Najahn alive, and maybe Vis wouldn't find itself crushed in a brutal war. Maybe Annalyse wouldn't have nightmares waiting every time she settled in to sleep.

Her eyes drifted to the bed, a leafy mat sprawled off to the right. A slight concession to reality: Annalyse would have to sleep sometime, and, despite the Vis skar's best efforts, the day's march and her subsequent hours burned here had taken their toll. A collapse seemed in order. She'd already prepped a dozen weaves, half again that many bands. More than double that many Vis skars still lay waiting, but Deshiva's own people could copy Annalyse's efforts quick.

The scientist deserved a rest.

THE STING WOKE HER. Sharp, in her shoulder. Annalyse blinked into the dark, the Vis skar still on her chest rising in a spitting fury, gibberish flush with effort. She rolled her head left, blinked again. She'd doused the lanterns before laying down—it seemed foolish to leave a fire lit, unattended, in a treehouse—so the only light coming through came from Sichi's pink glow and distant torches, small rays dancing through tiny gaps in the bamboo slats. Enough, just enough, for Annalyse to see the dart sticking up from her shoulder, black and purple fletching visible.

A Noctia weapon.

The realization, along with the spreading burn had Annalyse sit up, throw the mossy blanket off her. Her eyes ran along the space, saw nothing in the shadows. Until a shape landed, cloaked and quiet, in a crouch before her. A hand reached inside robes, the person's face unknowable beneath the hood.

Annalyse opened her mouth, tried a scream, and only sputtered instead. Her throat spasmed, croaked as the dart's poison seeped further. The assassin—who else could it be, Masayo's Third Hand following Fassle's orders—drew a thin knife, angled it towards the scientist. A single jab would be enough. The killer stabbed the blade, and Annalyse threw her arm across, intercepting the strike, catching the knife in her hand.

The pain seared, Annalyse's right palm blazing as the first blood dripped, but the knife drove past her neck and stuck into the wood behind her head. The assassin dropped the hilt, reached back into the robe with a soft curse.

Annalyse didn't. The Vis skar roared, the poison simmered, and she pulled the knife free even as it cut deeper. Her backhanded swipe had little skill, had desperation, and it cut across the assassin's shadowed face. A hot spray told Annalyse she'd struck, and the assassin stumbled back, abandoning the second weapon draw to catch themselves on the treehouse's center table, the one holding all those skars.

No sound save the lightest creaks as the assassin's soft shoes pattered on the wood. Nothing to draw those guards.

If Ami had taught Annalyse one thing during all those training sessions, it was to never let up. To press until you found success or failed hard enough you either died or had no option save to change. Annalyse held to the Guardian's fire now as she rose from the bed, let her grip on the knife slide to the hilt, wet with her own blood. She noticed, with no small satisfaction, the blade's tip held red not her own.

Again Annalyse tried to find her voice, again she mustered only a croak, a soft rasp.

"You should be dead already," the assassin snarled back, pushing off the center table into a swift charge.

Annalyse swung the knife to meet it, found her hand blocked by the assassin's left arm in a simple parry. A new, bruising ache erupted from Annalyse's stomach as the assassin's other hand struck, pushing her down to the floor, back shoved against her own bed. The assassin followed the punch, pinning Annalyse's knife arm to the floor and bringing up their right hand to grip her throat. Taut Najahn leather pressed in, stealing the scientist's breath away.

No way Annalyse could fight back against that strength, no way she could out-skill a Third-Hand killer.

Not alone.

Annalyse twitched her right hand, a flick—all she could manage with the killer pinning her down—that sent the stolen knife skittering across the treehouse floor, the metal clunking where it struck the boards. The assassin jerked their look after it, kept their grip on Annalyse's throat.

And Deshiva's guards proved their worth.

The wood door swung in, ropes creaking and a question flying from the first guard's mouth, one dying into a wordless, angry whoop as the guard found the scene, met Annalyse's eyes.

The assassin cursed again, the killer's grip went steel, as if deciding a quiet choke was no longer fast enough. Annalyse, her every nerve afire, the Vis skar keeping up its frustrated hissing, bucked. Kicked up her knees, flailed her left arm in a push against the assassin's face, and nudged the hold off just for a second.

Long enough for the spear to arrive.

The assassin leaped back as the Vis hunter stabbed

between them and Annalyse, the feathered spear cutting like a pink line between the pair. From their robes—Annalyse still couldn't catch a good look at who lurked beneath that cowl—the assassin pulled a short sword, used it to deflect the second guard's lunge. The killer hopped onto the central table, scattering skars across the floor.

For a moment the foursome seemed caught in time, Annalyse on the ground, trying to catch her breath, the two guards aiming their next strikes at the assassin just above them. A frozen dance that snapped back into motion as the assassin broke at the second guard, flicking a snared skar at the guard's head. The hunter moved their shoulder, deflected the stone, and missed stabbing the assassin as the killer vaulted past, breaking for the door.

With another whoop, one answered now by coming reinforcements, the first guard broke after the killer. The second turned to Annalyse, concern pairing with frustration on the huntress's face.

"You're alive?" the huntress asked.

Annalyse nodded, the poison starting to subside, a cooling following the acid spread. The Vis skar doing its work.

"Noctia," Annalyse said, the words a struggle.

Exhaustion followed in their wake, sudden and confusing. How could Annalyse be ready to collapse this quickly after a fight for her life, with her hand still bleeding onto the wood at her side?

The only answer seemed to be the words streaming in her mind, the Vis skar filling Annalyse almost to bursting with its unintelligible ramble. Working to keep her alive, and at the same time . . . draining her?

The huntress was talking again, Annalyse realized, a slow blink taking her focus back to the guard as the Vis wrapped the cut on her hand. Already another hunter pair had entered the treehouse, were lighting the lanterns and scouring the place for more hidden killers. They found the entry fast enough, a thin cut in the thatching overhead. More whoops echoed outside, the chase continuing.

"They'll catch him," the huntress said, "or her. It won't matter. These are our jungles, not theirs."

Annalyse would've like to believe that, would've like to put her faith in the Vis, but the Third Hand didn't send scrubs on missions like this. Gladdring mentioned them often enough as another weapon in his Trade Tenet arsenal, willing and able to put a fatal, or the threat of a fatal, end to anyone standing in Noctia's way. The man hadn't been afraid of Masayo's group, but he'd respected them, a fact that had Annalyse even more nervous.

That the Najahn cared this much to send one of their assassins after her?

"You're alive," Deshiva's voice, somehow not sounding tired in the least, broke Annalyse's soporific slurry. The guard had lifted the scientist back into her bed at some point, pulled up the blanket. "I don't need to ask why, or how that poison didn't kill you."

Deshiva loomed over her, tapped at the necklace Annalyse still wore and the skar within it.

"You'll keep it on at all times. And we'll make our own for my hunters." Deshiva looked back over the treehouse, a strait-laced stare, as if judging the attack on facts and facts alone. "Noctia doesn't want to let you go, which means you're even more valuable than we thought. Your guard will be doubled. One will stay in here with you at all times." Deshiva turned back to Annalyse, reached down and pulled up her blanket. "We haven't found the assassin yet, but we'll keep looking." Now she knelt, her words falling to a whisper. "We cleaned up the skars, but there are some missing. The black stones. What can they do?"

Annalyse said nothing, sleep snatching her away, but not before fear's cold spike promised death's own nightmares.

CHAPTER II

WRANGLING THE DEAD

"What are they?" Ami asked as she and Svarde, crouching, peered through a narrow hole into a brilliant abyss.

Seven circles spun in the deep pool below, a pit as wide as a small city and bordered by sloping rock. Water rippled, frothed on its surface, a sign no peace waited beneath. Every circle held its own color, the shade matching a particular skar. It was, as Svarde had said on the walk over, not hard to link those spinning discs to the isles and the gods that made them. Harder, though, was why they existed here, deep down beneath Noctia's craggy shores.

"We only have ideas, not answers," Svarde said and Ami suppressed the flinch this time. Her old friend's voice had lost its timber, sounding raw and shallow now, as though its life had been ripped away. Which, Ami supposed, it had. "The Dead King and Demion with him never found out what they were, only that the fiends come from them. Doorways, portals, pick your word, but they open to places beyond our world."

"Or on the other side of it."

Their tunnel, a small branch leading off the battlefield chamber, where Jochi and Svarde's dead minions continued building, enhancing fortifications, had been expanded by the Whent engineers. Small globed lanterns flickered every few strides, buttressed by planted purple-blue moss patches. The end goal, one achieved just a day before Ami and Sawi arrived, had been to get an eye on the fiends, on what the enemy planned.

And what they planned was invasion.

The burning obsidian monsters launched their constructs from the pool seemingly every minute, small and large muttering machines climbing onto the stone, sometimes pushed, other times gnawing up the ground to find a cliff or a new, built platform to rest upon. Metal works latticed the space above the black waters now, worked on continuously by the flashing fiends. Buildings unknown and strange, some mere skeletal frames marking activities while others became enclosed bulbs, dotted the massive chamber's gray rock sides.

Jochi had the grate Ami looked from now occupied at all hours, spies watching, learning, wondering what the fiends might do. What they'd learned had been passed from Svarde to Ami in the walk here, a day-defining list of fiend activities, everything from their sleep patterns—the fiends seemed to cool, their hot skin swindling to a soft orange as they stood stock still for hours—to what the monsters did for joy: throwing burning stones towards one another only for their target to hit the scalding rock with a metal bat, the fiery missile launching over the dark pool to land with sizzling smoke. Then the next would step up, a contest to see how far their blasts could go.

"Even if these doorways opened across the ocean, that

wouldn't answer why now, why at all," Svarde said. The great, jagged blade that never left his side jiggled against the stone floor as Svarde shifted, planting a curious look at Ami, one she forced herself to take, the man's gray visage as unnerving as his voice. "The fiends attack more frequently now, in greater numbers and with more desperation. Even these burning creatures are bringing in more than they can handle, faster. Look."

The fiends had families, though the only dynamic Ami could pick out lay in size: smaller, sparking versions dashed around the pool's edges in clusters. Parenting seemed to be shared among the working, larger monsters, with rotating supervision, a necessary fact given that the other portals hadn't quit.

Even as Ami watched the five children—hardly that small, all matched Ami in size, their four arms, two legs, and glittering dark stone heads as alien as ever—the pool frothed near their cleared rock field. Play, kicking around some ore fashioned into a crude ball, stopped at the first splashes. A full-grown fiend stomped down from their watching perch, unlimbering their flail while the smaller set scrambled up metal stairs, sparks following their every step.

Two more familiar fiends, flesh-colored, tooth-and-clawed creatures limbered onto the rock and snarled at the large firewalker opposite. There was no negotiation, no discussion of shared purpose in invading the isles. The obsidian fiend swung its flail, the chain and iron whistling through the air to strike the first dog and send it flying back over the pool, splashing into its deep center.

"It'll drown before it gets back to shore," Svarde muttered. "Let's see if the other can do any better."

As he spoke, the two scouts Jochi had posted at the

grate whispered side bets to one another. Ami frowned, she didn't object to the gambling, but one of these small fiends against a full-size firewalker?

The dog thing didn't hear Ami's doubts, instead barking up a wheezing, spittle-infused storm and charging the firewalker. The big fiend yanked back the flail, sweeping the return along the floor to catch the charging fiend's feet.

Too slow.

A leap, all four claws extended, teeth wide, seemed destined to strike the firewalker as the flail slid harmless beneath. Destined, but denied.

A rock, burning, struck the leaping fiend from above, barreling into the creature's front left shoulder and spinning it aside. The attacker hit the firewalker with its naked right, driving a wild bounce to the floor, the fiend steaming from the firewalker's skin. The shock only lasted a moment before the firewalker slammed home with its other three arms, a triple strike driving its enemy into the ground, one of several that—

Ami looked away, back down the tunnel. She'd seen enough death.

"Can we go back?" she asked Svarde, who waited till the hits ended, watching every one.

"I try," Svarde said as they walked the narrow tunnel home, "I try every time to find a connection. The Dead King never could, but I think it's possible. I've tried with the firewalkers who've died, but their bodies turn to ash. They burn all the others."

Another tale folded in with all the rest in the short time since Ami had arrived. The Grave Blade, or so Svarde had come to call the sword. How the Noctia skars blended with the dagger Vis forged so long ago to tie its wielder to those lost bodies around them. At first, the connection came with instinct, a spastic sensation like a lingering dream, a feeling of being somewhere *other* than yourself.

"Like understanding the skars," Ami replied. "They all have their own language, and once you learn it, or at least enough, they'll give themselves to you."

"And take."

Ami nodded. If Svarde had stories to tell, so had she and Sawi. The god stones and their powers seemed behind most everything warping their lives, and accepting that the skars inset to her face weren't tools but dangerous, fickle friends, made more sense. Just as the gods themselves had obviously been flawed, so were their creations.

"But if I can break through, then we'll have a chance," Svarde said. "We can drive the firewalkers away and do what the Dead King never could: fortify and contain the pools, all the fiends."

"Forever?"

"Until we find a way to close Noctia's gates."

"So we sit tight while you play with your sword, is that what I'm hearing?" Ami asked.

"Even Jochi doesn't have a better idea. The firewalkers have too many constructs. Any drive up the tunnel would end in slaughter. They're not stupid either. They've poked what we've built, lost their fiends in the process. They won't try it again till they're ready to break us."

"So it's a race, then. You against them, with us caught in the middle."

Svarde grinned. "Once again, you need me."

"Nah," Ami countered. "Catya and I could always find another way."

"She's not here this time."

"But Sawi is."

Svarde didn't follow Ami to the plain house provided to

the pair as a sort of living quarters. Set across from Svarde's hollow, gloomy cathedral and its throne, the severe block of a building stood several stories high, kissing the dangling cave ceiling with its roof. The rough construction, with slabs seemingly sheared off with endless whacking by bodies who knew no end to their endurance, made the building seem like a child's puzzle squeezed together: touch it hard enough at the right point and the whole thing might come down, hit it at the wrong spot and it might withstand a giant hammer blow.

Gray and black shades dominated, broken up here and there by Whent lanterns and the ever-present moss. Smoke and ash filtered on through, overpowering the underground's natural loam flavors with cooking mushrooms, fiend meats, and whatever else the Whent scouts managed to dredge up from the dark.

Sawi had some soup now, shoveled into an earthen bowl and scooped with a concave rock into her mouth. The Vis, as Ami walked through the doorless entry, seemed to stare at nothing as she ate. Not in silence—the Whent crafters, their dead assistants, worked too hard and too constant for the caves to ever be free from ringing, cracking, slamming sounds—but in relative peace.

Not contentment, no. Ami picked the stress out from Sawi's tight jaw, the way she sat rigid on the stone bench, the slab table low before her. Sawi's hair and skin collected dirt just like Ami's, but the Vis hadn't taken a trip to one of the watery spots nearby, where streams and small pools offered a chance to clean off. Neither had Sawi ventured to any Whent cookfire to talk about, well, anything with the warriors and workers sharing their space.

Ami had found Jochi's hardy force a refreshing change from Noctia's political populace. Everyone here seemed more concerned with smashing the fiends and finding their next mug of ale than who might stab Fassle in the back. Better still, the Vis skars meant getting drunk came without hard consequences the next morning.

"I have a job for you," Ami said, announcing her entry and drawing a slow look.

"I don't want a job," Sawi said, a little soup dribbling from her lips end. "I want to go home."

A short laugh, "Vis, if you think that's an option, then you've already forgotten our wandering."

"You don't need to come with."

"If you want to die, Sawi, then go ahead. But don't do it uselessly."

Sawi flinched. The snap action found her focus, and when Ami sat across from the jungle hunter, gatherer, whatever Sawi wanted to call herself, the young woman didn't seem quite so lost anymore.

Anger was ever the cure for despair.

"What do you want, Ami?"

"I want your mind and your ambition," Ami replied, leaning forward, clasping her hands above the table. Just the way Gladdring did when he wanted to manipulate somebody. "Svarde has a slow burning plan. I want to speed it up."

"How?"

"I need you to find us some fiends."

CHAPTER 12

A NOTE AT THE END

The request came two days later, after the Kance Queen had her welcome feast and her first meeting with Fassle. Gladdring listened for word and found it through the usual channels: loose-lipped guards with too much ale, ones who in turn heard the results from the Queen or Fassle's angry muttering. A refusal, no alliance, no easy access to the Kance skars and their wind-warping powers. Plans made for crossbows able to launch bolts buttressed by a gale's force were neutered before they could even begin.

A tragedy.

Gladdring mulled over the reports delivered to his room every morning, an Adept's due. They described a Najahn force on the move across the isles, solidifying holds on Foti, Rana, Tamas, and Whent while struggling with Kance and Vis. All fitting with reputation: Rana cared more about raiding and drinking than their own governance, Foti wanted to forge and gamble, Tamas obsessed more about the stage than strategy, and Whent . . . well, most of Whent seemed to be missing, disappeared into the Dark Below for weeks upon weeks now with no sign of return. Fassle was already salivating at the thought of migrating Noctia's more miserable citizens to the north, turfing them to the deserted villages and farms and calling it a gift. Loyal expansion.

And, for once, Gladdring couldn't find much fault in the man's argument: valuable land ought to be used, and if Whent sent its people to the fiends' slaughter, then why not raise the petty from poverty?

A better opening in their political power game arrived that same morning, however: an invitation from the Kance Queen to take her to the Wound, a last viewing before she embarked for home tomorrow.

Why Gladdring and not Fassle? The letter suggested the Queen wanted someone with a more interesting tongue and less blatant objectives. She'd already refused the Circle's leader, better to talk about flowers, fiends, and the isles's future with someone less greedy.

If only she knew Gladdring.

Nevertheless, he put on his gilded purple-black robes, this time atop a cozy wool undershirt to keep Gladdring warm amid Winter's continuing clutches. Noctia's snow blanket had by now reached the deluge stage, where wide streets became single lanes as drifts overwhelmed the isle's ability to cast off the thick flakes. Ice floes clogged the port, a checkered white and gray visible through Gladdring's tower window. Ramming boats, their prows bolstered with Foti-forged breakers, cleared lanes for essential trade, scuttling back and forth like frantic insects. Smoke spiraled into the gray sky from a thousand chimneys, their acrid scents showing Noctia shifting to mosses, coal mined from the cliffs, and whatever else would suffice for heat.

The Najahn quarter wasn't immune to the change, and

Gladdring joined the coughing crowds as he walked through the squares en route to the cliffside trail. Scholars and soldiers alike hustled, clanking armor and boots mingling with glib conversation, an excited energy ever-present since Fassle's announcement. A world at last going to war with its monstrous opposition demanded enthusiasm, and if that war called for some subjugation of lesser isles, well, that was only a small price to pay.

The heroes had to go on.

The Queen waited for him, standing so alone that Gladdring didn't recognize her at first. The silver-blue robe and regal bearing should've given it away, but against the snowy stones and without her guards' usual glittering armor, Gladdring walked right on by, stopping only when she spoke.

"Not as sharp this morning as usual, Gladdring?" the Queen started, the arch tone as ever accompanying her words.

Had she ever uttered a sentence with love?

Gladdring wouldn't bet on it.

"Distraction is a constant these days," Gladdring said, spinning as well as his frame allowed and dipping into a bow. "My mind is always afar."

"Then bring it back. I didn't request your company to be bored by it."

"I shall do my best, your majesty."

The Queen, head shrouded by an indigo frill along her silver robe, gave Gladdring an icy nod, then glanced up the trail. "I came here once. When the Aegis was installed. My mother was still Queen."

"And you were . . . ?"

"Horrified." The Queen began the walk, leading with strong strides, confident despite the hard ground and frosted pebbles. "I'd never seen a man so withered. He nearly died the moment he left that awful throne."

"Less than a year for most, when their time is done," Gladdring acknowledged. "A terrible honor."

"An easy one to leave for someone else."

A bold thing to say aloud, no matter how real or common the sentiment, or that Gladdring agreed with her. The Queen didn't let those words linger, instead launching into a retelling of the last two days, of how Fassle had hounded her, pitching one offer after the next for a Kance capitulation.

"Surely not his word," Gladdring said.

"Surely his meaning," the Queen replied.

Getting feted and giving the same was, of course, a familiar refrain for the Kance Queen, and she rebuffed the Circle's advances with the cold logic she'd displayed throughout her reign: The Najahn couldn't do without Kance's trade, and if they wanted the Sky Isle's skars, they could buy them at an appropriate price. There would be no surrender, no more Najahn outpost.

"So then came the other offers," the Queen said as they neared the guard station outside the Wound's tunnel. "Ships and swords, food and medicine from across the isles, all delivered to our shores by the purple and black."

"You were unpersuaded?"

"Fassle seems to think I cannot strike my own deals. He, you, and this isle are not the center of everything."

Gladdring's skar, the topaz lingering in the ring on his hand, trembled at that. A whisper dangled in his mind, suggesting the Queen's certainty faltered there. Noctia did lie at the literal center of the Seven Isles, but Gladdring figured the skar had something deeper in mind. The Queen worrying, perhaps, that Fassle could starve her people.

He chased the connection as the Queen continued running along her many partnerships with other Isle leaders. She'd come here to tell Fassle no to his face, something that could've been done by letter, or even via the ambassador every isle sent to this one. No, she'd come in person because the refusal wasn't meant to be so blunt. A massaged decline, one meant to open as many doors as it closed.

"He's not listening to you?" Gladdring asked, stalling off what'd become an almost embarrassing rant, the Queen's hot words spilling steam into the chilly morning.

"Fassle only listens to himself. You know that."

Gladdring let a slight smile touch his face, a slighter nod. Solidarity, beginning to smooth the way for what would be coming, for what Yarvick had passed along the night before. His thieves, listening around every corner, reading every missive, had discovered Fassle's real plan, and now Gladdring had that same revelation in the pocket opposite his skar, waiting for the right moment.

Fassle would die by a knife to the back like many other men, but ascending to his position, and securing the isles's safety, would mean allies. Few would have more measure than Kance's Queen. With her backing, the other Tenets would fall in line, and Gladdring's position would be secure.

"I said, stay here," the Queen snapped as they reached the outpost. "You're daydreaming again."

"You can't expect me to listen to all this without considering what it means."

"What it means? I've told you. Fassle won't shut up. I can't wait to leave this miserable isle and its stupid games."

"Stay but a little longer and you might find its games not all that stupid."

The guards on station gave the pair nods as Gladdring and the Queen went beneath the stone arch, entered a tunnel lined on both sides with busts of Circle leaders and Aegises from years past. Torchlight—no lanterns, here, by tradition's writ—replaced daylight, the shadowed ceiling closing in around them, both dropping their voices to near whispers under the lifeless stone eyes.

"Don't tell me you're planning another party, Gladdring. It's gauche, with so many suffering," the Queen dished off the words with a sigh.

"A party, no. But your attendance will be required nonetheless."

"Do tell me more."

Gladdring slowed his walk, keeping them in the tunnel, alone. The Queen matched his dragging stride, her face as placid as ever. A read impossible without the skar in his pocket finding the curiosity.

So he sated it. Asked for a partner in a fatal scheme. A bold request Gladdring might never have made save for the night when Fassle broke his earlier moves, left Gladdring a breath away from death. Once you'd all but kissed that final goodbye, inviting doom for another dance came, if not easily, than without the sweats, the trembles, the doubts of another life that'd visited him the first go around.

The game unfolded fine at first, the Tamas skar encouraging Gladdring to continue. The Queen was rapt, it said, and her eyes did indeed stay locked on his, taking in every word. He found his confidence, declared that once Fassle had been removed, his allies would put Gladdring on top, with her help, and together they could—

A keen pain stopped Gladdring mid-sentence. Not a dart, a stab, but the skar, warning Gladdring the scenario had changed. The Queen's expression stayed the same, flitting now to a frown as Gladdring fell quiet, but she was no longer a willing partner. Instead, the skar spoke of sadness, disappointment, and fear.

"Did I say something wrong?" Gladdring asked, putting on his best funeral smile, ingratiating and yet sad.

"Wrong?" the Queen's frown deepened, quizzical furrows forming on an otherwise perfect brow. A sniff, then, as she answered her own question. "Of course. A skar. Nobody else could read me, and neither could you, without those damned gems." She tilted her head. "Which one is it? What isle's god gives you another's mind to read?"

"My question first."

The Queen held up a single hand, a single finger. The white glove wrapping it gave a golden glint against the torches, a signal, and Gladdring wasn't surprised when the tunnel's openings on either side found new shadows.

"Don't take it personally, Gladdring," the Queen said as the shadows, purple and black Najahn, advanced. "Fassle promised he would leave my isle alone if I could prove your loyalty, one way or another."

A hollow gesture, one proven by the note in his pocket. The Queen grasping at hope when there wasn't any to grab.

"Fassle won't keep his word." Gladdring sighed. "He never does unless it's best for him."

"For my isle and its people, I have to try."

The guards neared. Another moment only. The Tamas skar continued to whisper its warnings, and possibilities. The Queen hadn't yet closed herself off to him: the skar rasped her sadness, and Gladdring used it. Fell forward, as if slipping on the rubble, into the Queen. She gasped, tried to separate, and succeeded when the rushing guards dragged Gladdring off her. The rough and ready warriors gave Gladdring the traitor's sentence then and there, the

Queen backing up their accusations, declaring she had ready testimony.

But as the soldiers started Gladdring away towards what would be a cold, lonely cell, he caught the Queen reaching into her own pockets to find the letter, and Gladdring's hope.

CHAPTER 13

THE FIRST ACT

S he'd really walked only one time in her life: when Eujo first went to Vis, embarked off the *Storm's Edge* and set foot onto Mottilan's shores, under those towering cliffs and suspicious eyes. After their trade-less arrival prompted little more than derision—Wax would clarify, later, that the whole city was still sour at his Renewal ascension—then Eujo, her guards, and several hired hands bearing their packs walked up and through the mountain passes to the Great Sana.

That had been the only time her feet had earned blisters, her legs weighed down with fatigue, and every breath came in a lurching gasp after the one preceding. And yet, even then, the feelings were fleeting, knowing rest was close at hand, that she had supplies aplenty and there was nothing to fear.

Walking along the Tamas coast held none of those comforts to assuage the deadening load born by Eujo, and more lightly by the others. The soft sand was at once mesmerizing and a struggle, the grains shifting under her weight and dragging her feet, a trick harder to handle with

88

the Rana skar sapping her strength. When Eujo swapped with Wax, a change triggered when one or the other inevitably stumbled, her shoulders lightened, her feet sprang from one step to the next, and those heavy breaths became pleasant, sea-breeze gulps.

At first.

By the day's end, her tired legs found little reprieve even when the skars were quiet. By the time Bliss and Torny flicked up a small fire with what frosted roots and branches they could cut, that Wax could power up with a skar, Eujo wanted nothing more than to sleep. Or to eat. Or to take a bath.

A thousand small luxuries the Tamas coast forbade them.

Bliss and Torny agreed to split the watch, giving their Renewals a night unbroken, and Eujo took it, walking as far up the beach as they could before laying down, winter's hollow dawn bringing with it aches forgotten in blissful dreams.

What had those dreams been about?

Eujo couldn't remember, but if they looked anything like what they saw in the afternoon of their second day, she wouldn't have been surprised.

Torny acknowledged the shimmers ahead to the south, their arcs bounding over the brilliant bushes and their crimson-hued leaves. Spires too, albeit ones with odd-angled points and stranger colors, yellows and blues to go with crimson dashes, pierced the clouded sky. Doubts, questions, hopes traveled with them after that, flagged energy restored at salvation's sight.

The beach gave them some good fortune by running right up to the spires' edge, an unceremonious ending to the wilds coming with a carved clearing, voices, song, music, and smells so rich as to make Eujo's stomach snarl. They held hands, the four of them, each one helping the other along up the dark sand to the first of the bodies, the watchers, the odd figures in outfits too foreign for Eujo to recognize.

"Haven't you been to Tamas?" Torny muttered as they closed on the half-dozen forms clustered around an ocean-going pier, one dotted with fishing spears, nets, and poles. "Does it always look like this?"

"Only the southern coast," Eujo replied. "There it's not so different from Noctia. Better ale, more water, friendlier people. That's it."

Friendly or not, the daylight cast the eclectic figures in a mystical glow. Despite the chill, as Eujo and the others approached, the squad turned their way and revealed fluttering outfits, bands of cloth strung about one another in dashing silk, in waved linen, sheer meeting with opaque, and all leading to sprawling or svelte shoes, all of which seemed to float on the sand.

"New friends?" came the first welcome, from the largest figure in the group's center, one whose yellow and cherry-red costume billowed up around him like a jellyfish's shroud. "From the North? It has been some time!"

The man concluded his welcome with a deep bow, complete with an arm sweep, and the others mimicked the motion, all the while skittering along the sand in sideways steps. A distracting motion when mingled with their colors, and fast enough that Eujo didn't notice what they'd done until Bliss flashed her fingers.

'We're surrounded.'

Torny responded first, hands dropping into her coat folds to find what Eujo suspected were dagger hilts. Eujo herself could've snagged her rapier, the sword hanging along her thigh, but instead put her left hand along the bracelet on her right. Unnecessary to summon the skars—they were always there, always whispering—but covering the stones might keep their secret a moment more, preserve surprise. Wax, with his necklace, matched his sister in hands-free appraisal.

The Vis would talk in a moment, make some hackneyed introduction. Better not let that happen.

"We crossed the ice floes between Tamas and Whent," Eujo started, taking a half-step before Torny, Wax, and Bliss. Establishing leadership. "Along the way, fiends attacked, so we are low on supplies, tired, and in need of food."

"A trying tale, I'm sure," the man replied, rising to pull a short silver horn from some hidden place on his person. He put it to his lips, puffed several clear notes loud and far, before dropping the instrument to reveal a showman's grin, the kind Eujo had seen far too often in the Sky Palace's court. "But we are a home for the needy, and often an absolution for the same. Be glad you've found our little corner of the isles, for here you might find all you will ever need."

"You give that speech to everyone who comes here?" Torny piped up before Eujo could find a more diplomatic reply. "We're asking for some soup, not for you to save our souls."

"Sometimes both can come together, if you find the right place." The man's smile didn't falter. A shine in eyes ringed with black makeup caught the trailing sun and sparkled. "And you have most definitely found the right place, my friends."

He turned at his own words and beckoned up the beach, where those spires and swirling shimmers waited.

"Come, follow, and you'll find what you need and so much more besides."

"Wait," Eujo said as the man took his first step. Too much suspicion, too many wrong turns made a blind walk, even here, even with her every bone wanting to lie down and devour dinner, an impossible choice. "What is this place, and what were you doing?"

"Rehearsing, of course," the man replied, and jingles bounced as the rest of the group nodded, clapped, or jumped a simple hop, various jewelry snatching sound and light. "What else would you do here at the day's end? The ocean, after all, is a most respectful audience."

"Guy's lost it," Torny muttered.

"As for the Animas, it is the place where Tamas finds its purpose. The ritual of all rituals, the stage where the artist meets her maker, and her meaning."

"I vote we keep walking," Torny continued, the man either not hearing or not caring what she said. He continued up the beach, beckoning with both arms, while his friends remained where they stood, a shallow circle around the quartet.

"Guess we have a choice," Wax said, looking at the gleaming, all too quiet and all too happy faces around them. "Either we follow that guy, or we find a way past these people."

"Find a way to where?" said one, a slim woman who nearly stood in the ocean's waves.

"There's nowhere else to go, not unless you travel the main road," continued a second, and Eujo closed her eyes, took a deep breath as the obvious continued its way around.

In alternating phrases, like, indeed, the few Tamas performances Eujo had seen on Kance, the actors relayed the quartet's predicament: the beach would turn to crags in another few hours march, while the only way through the snarling plants and bushes was right here. And, of course, should they choose to come into the Animas, then they would find warmth, possibility, happiness.

"Our throats cut and skars stolen, more likely," Torny said as they followed the first man's footprints up the beach. "Noctia has its share of spiders setting traps, but I'd prefer any of them to these nuts."

"A choice we don't have," Eujo said, and appreciated Wax's nod in agreement. "We're starved, lost, and without friends. We take their offered meal, a bed, and try to go on our way in the morning."

To that plan, the bandit, at last, had nothing to add.

The Animas folded out much like its actors's outfits: if Eujo saw the spires first, their spindly tops rising high, then every step up the beach revealed both more and less. Sense stated how homes should be built, but the Animas eschewed that guidance, instead sending its buildings, framed by those same roots found everywhere else and separated by stiffened canvas, into manic shapes. The skeletal structures rose high, jutted out at angles, their root scaffolding painted in all colors, often a blend of several, but always with white connecting them. The skin between the bones. Ladders clung to various sides, steps big and small occupied by actors coming and going, sometimes other workers, their smiles just as large, carrying sets, props, and people from one place to the next.

Tents and carts, carriages and cook fires spaced the grounds between the Animas's canvas buildings, showcasing a more understandable life: one of food, trade, survival amid the Isles. Conversation traveled like it did in any other town, though its tones here differed, often carrying on in the flavor of memorized lines, speeches delivered, or witty comebacks proffered to applause.

On the whole, like Torny, Eujo found herself increasingly on edge and had to tamp worry down with cold logic: just because a place was different, didn't mean it was deadly.

Daklin, their guide and the same man who'd given them the welcome on the beach, led the Renewals and their Guardians to a broad tent filled with bench-bordered tables. As they passed through the wide, whipping flaps, Eujo found the source of those shimmers: carved glass tubes, wending their way up from small pits in the ground to soar into the tent and out beyond it, into the Animas proper.

"What're those?" Torny asked, again saving the Queen from opening her mouth. "Some kind of decoration?"

The tent's populace, more than thrice their number sharing in the same early dinner Eujo wanted right that moment, all stopped their words and turned, listening in as Daklin gave a swift, proud explanation: Tamas, a sandy isle, offered glass aplenty, and in digging a little beneath its trembling surface, gasses could be found and lit, sending heat around the Animas to keep them warm when fires alone wouldn't suffice.

"Do you see great trees here for burning?" Daklin asked, spinning around to take in the tent as he did so, heads shaking at his sight. "Any Noctia coal, so we could warm ourselves in its filth?" Again shaking heads, and Eujo found herself among them, much to her own annoyance. Still, the man had a way of speaking, of catching you in his turn that pushed you into his realm, to play his game. "Neither do we have furs like Whent, lava like Foti. Our god gave us the gas and the glass, and that is enough for us."

Tamas apparently gave the Animas enough food too, with fish and tubers aplenty, cooked into a steaming broth and delivered to their table in ceramic bowls, each one painted with a figure series. When Wax asked, Daklin said the bowls played out scenes from one of their plays.

"Because that is what we do here at the Animas," Daklin continued, that grin ever widening even as his foppish cap sank over his bent head, "we entertain, we enlighten, and we bring people the happiness they deserve."

"Great," Torny said, the soup vanishing quick with her rapid spoonfuls, "good luck with all that. Sorry we won't be staying, though. Things to do, isles to save and all that."

The man nodded, seeming almost sad. "Your quest can wait until the morning. Tonight, at least, take in a show. See what you have found." Again that twinkle, that sparkle. "You may even decide you'd like to stay."

CHAPTER 14

FIRST FIRES

Alone, walking through Vis's jungle had been a relaxing, almost transcendent experience. The music, even in the winter, of birds, bugs, and the breeze took away the journey's effort and replaced it with a nourishing wonder. Annalyse could've walked beneath those boughs for months, years, a lifetime in happiness.

Running with Deshiva's hunters at dawn, after scant sleep, shared little with that trek even though the trees remained the same. Even with a Vis skar settled against her chest, the same one that'd kept her alive through the assassin's poison, keeping Annalyse energized, the sprint flagged her spirit, stole the enchantment. In part because of the spears, the feathers, the set faces flitting between branches around her.

In part because they were running to war.

The isles existed in a fragile balance with one another, each so reflective of the god that'd made it that they relied on each other. Open warfare blocked trade, sentenced too many people to misery, so aside from Rana raiders and occasional skirmishes from feisty bandits or broken souls, Annalyse didn't hear of war. Now she was in one.

The run lasted most of the morning, leading them east from the lake towards the Najahn outpost. Even from afar, the Great Sana rose above the horizon, caught in glimpses between leaves as Annalyse ran through the trees, always aware Deshiva and her spear sprinted at her footsteps.

The lead hunter didn't speak much, save when she showed up at Annalyse's treehouse in the morning, demanding the inset armors and Annalyse's participation. It hadn't been a question. Just an order, and one the scientist followed without protest.

Gladdring had taught her that much: no sense making enemies when there were no options.

She almost struck the hunter ahead, stumbling to a stop through a thick fern just before his inked back. Orange and purple lines, forming fruits, animals, and sigils Annalyse knew not provided the last barrier before the cleared Najahn fields. His outstretched hand, palm towards her, served as a catch, one Annalyse didn't need.

"You did well," Deshiva said, coming up behind Annalyse, as silent as the rest of her band. "Most Vis would struggle on such a run." Deshiva, her own face marked, hair pulled tight to her head, nodded towards the stone. "Then again, most Vis run alone."

"That's their problem, not mine."

A slight smile, "Good. You'll need that spirit today." Deshiva nodded ahead. "Are you ready?"

"For what? I'm not a fighter."

"Today, you watch. Learn. Use what you see to make us better tomorrow."

"What am I watching for?"

Deshiva glanced to her right and left, bending to see

around Annalyse. The hunter to the scientist's right moved, stringing a narrow bow. The weapon's size said it wasn't built to fire long range, but then, shooting far in a dense jungle likely wasn't needed. The slim quiver suggested, too, that the Vis rarely—

"Study us later," Deshiva interrupted. "I need your eyes on the Najahn. Tell me if you see anything strange. Otherwise, learn."

Deshiva brought her fingers to her lips and blew. Not an outright human whistle, but a high-pitched, short noise, like a bird saying hello to the sun. Too quiet to carry far, but it didn't need to: Deshiva's signal found repeaters around, the whole jungle seeming to awaken with the peeps.

Beyond, in the fields, animals, pigs and cows imported from other isles, perked up. Tamas chickens, their brown feathers fluttering, circled in their thin pens. Wood piles, neat in stacked rows, stood waiting for mealtime immolations. Four or five Najahn milled about the scene, doing the day's work with little look to the outskirts.

Abundant order.

Easy targets.

Arrows flew, the bowstring thrums heralding the burning lines as they arced through the air and landed on those wood piles, on thatched sheds. Not many—Annalyse would've dismissed the assault if the desire was Najahn casualties. Only a couple arrows seemed to catch on wood dampened by winter rain.

But the shots drew attention, and by Deshiva's grim nod, that was the goal.

The Najahn swarmed like slovenly bees, the sort Annalyse used to see ambling about the Whent tundra flowers in fall. Awkward shouts, astonishment, and stumbling from the outpost's central buildings. Armor clanked as Najahn soldiers rushed to put it on. Someone found a horn and sounded a three bleat blast. Deshiva signaled a second volley, and now three wood piles burned, and with those sparks, the hunter began the next play.

At a second whistle, seven Vis hunters, clad in dark weaves, dashed from the jungle's edge towards the animal pens. All drew long knives, their curling ends showing original intent to butcher meat. This time, as the Najahn formed their lines, the first few drawing voulges, finding crossbows and the necessary quarrels, the Vis used those knives to sever ties holding fence gates closed. The hunters shouted, squawked, and slashed, scaring the animals from their pens in frenzied flight. As each one emptied, the hunters pursued their emancipated quarries, shuttling them towards the jungle, the road, away from the Najahn.

"Amused?" Deshiva asked as the armored warriors finally gave some pursuit, firing fruitless shots at the hunters, sending lumbering soldiers in far-too-late defense.

"I've never seen a fight like this."

When the Whent warlords decided to struggle over territory, their battles were pitched, drunken clashes. Masses met on the plains and battered each other till one side gave up, new kegs were tapped, and the losers accepted into their new fold without malice. One warlord would eventually gobble up most of the isle, as Jochi had done, until, old and frail, their small empire would splinter.

"With Vis on our side, nobody will die today," Deshiva said. "We can persuade the Najahn they have no hold here, and they'll leave in peace."

"If you believe that —"

Deshiva's sudden glare cut the words. "Don't let your cynicism murder hope."

"I would call it reality."

"Then you need to change your reality."

Annalyse shook her head, watched the Najahn slow and stop their fumbling pursuit. Nearly thirty armed and armored soldiers were in the field now, a narrow-faced captain barking them into formations. Deshiva gave another low whistle, repeated again through the trees, and the Vis forces sank deeper into the jungle, several strides. Annalyse only tripped twice, an achievement.

"We're running?" Annalyse said, catching up to Deshiva and squatting next to the hunter. Bugs made friends with her hair, ferns tickled her arms. A thorn caught her shoe. The jungle wasn't much for space. "Already?"

"It will be hard to prove this was more than thieves," Deshiva said, "if they don't catch the rest of us. Yet, if they push after, we will surprise them."

"Straightforward."

Again the frowning look, "Are you so unversed in combat?"

Before Annalyse could reply with the obvious, Deshiva squinted at the Najahn, then cursed. The soldiers, harder to see this deep, but still unmistakable, had turned around. Were marching back behind their palisades. Forfeiting their fields and their creatures. Annalyse would've cheered: a victory without a loss, without a single wound?

Deshiva, though, looked like she'd swallowed a lemon.

"The worst response," Deshiva said as afternoon dwindled the day away, Annalyse and several other leaders joining her around a clearing's cook fire.

The Vis had withdrawn to a makeshift camp thirty minutes away from the Najahn outpost. Hunter groups continued to gather up the freed livestock, meaning to get the animals back to the lake where their former destiny could be restored. Those that they couldn't lead would be left to fend for themselves, likely hanoko food.

"Why?" Annalyse waved her wooden soup spoon at the convivial camp. "Nobody hurt? Objective achieved?"

"The easiest victory, with the fewest benefits. We didn't test your skars to know if they'll work. We didn't really punish the Najahn. And now they'll hide behind their walls until reinforcements arrive, too many for us to fight at once."

"You don't know that."

"Says the scientist," but Deshiva nodded as she spoke. "You're right, however. I don't know what the Najahn might do, what might happen. I can't control their actions, just like you cannot know when a hanoko might pounce. Instead, we must focus on what we can control."

"Which is?"

"Your skars."

Annalyse reached for the necklace on instinct. She had four on there now, a Vis, Foti, Rana, and Tamas stone. Their murmurs bubbled. The Tamas one gave some clue to Deshiva's moods, but her pensive ambition was obvious even without the whispered emotions.

"What about them? We'll need someone to get in a fight to see how they do." Annalyse kicked up a smirk, noticing a circle forming where hunters seemed to be wrestling with one another. "Who knows, maybe we'll get lucky over there."

"Not the Vis skars. The others." Deshiva reached, pulled a stick off the ground and stuck it into the cook fire, empty now with dinner depleted. "The Najahn are hiding behind their wooden walls. Your Foti skars can break them."

"Or destroy the one who tries."

Another sharp look, and this time Annalyse listened to the Tamas skar, found in Deshiva's severity a taut weariness, someone who'd been pressed for a long time and who wasn't bound, anymore, by temerity. Deshiva would press and press until she delivered victory for her isle.

"Your people could die. Will die. And even if they succeed, what will you do then? Run back to the trees like we did today? The Najahn will prepare the hole."

"But they will be scared. They will know we can do things they cannot."

"We? You mean your hunters? Right now, the skars are still mostly a secret, Deshiva. For hundreds of years only a few have tried to use them for anything other than the Aegis. You open that door here, the Najahn will respond. They have more skars than you, and deadlier ones."

"The scientist again seeks to counsel me in ways of war," Deshiva replied. Her stick caught fire and she withdrew it, a torch in the dark. "The Najahn control us through order, but haven't you noticed? The fiends have stopped coming in high numbers. It's like the Aegis has been restored, but no new Renewals won the Wound. There's no reason to fear anymore, no reason to give the Najahn their hold. If they want to take our most valuable resources, they will have to fight for it."

"Even if it means letting the isles run wild?"

Deshiva grinned, "Unless those stones are more powerful than you've let on, Annalyse, a simple spear will kill someone with a skar just as well as it will you and me. Justice will come about as it always has, through the strength of those delivering it." She cast the stick back into the fire. "I've already sent runners to gather the rest of your skars. I'll have volunteers by morning. Tomorrow night, we put the fear of Vis into their black hearts."

CHAPTER 15

MYSTERY

Living in Noctia, among the Najahn, Ami could choose when to care about the fiends. Seeing Catya at the Wound would bring the monsters and their lethal danger into fresh light, but that tension would dwindle as she returned to the food, fires, and culture amid a city comfortably defended. Going down through the Dark Below with Sawi had flipped that switch, put Ami on a constant guard, and finding Svarde's dead-ridden city and Jochi's warband hadn't flipped it back. Goals weren't murky experiments, oblique loyalty to an Aegis already surrounded by protectors.

Here, the objective was clear: find a way to destroy the firewalkers, then close the gates. Stop the fiends, save the isles.

She repeated that mantra to Sawi as they walked the tunnels to the south, following Olgata to the controlled outskirts. Jochi's engineers and soldiers, a grumbly, ale-swilling bunch, nonetheless claimed territory with enthusiasm, burrowing in checkpoints and slaying any monsters wandering by. Those fiends, so far, wouldn't help Svarde link to their bodies, given that they'd been chopped up and added to the army's next meal.

"A couple weeks ago, I'd have called that gross," Sawi said as they past the last one, taking their first steps without Olgata beside them. "But, consider my eyes opened."

"Some of them are even tasty." Ami licked her lips, a gesture lost given Sawi's straight ahead stare and dim light from their gathered mosses.

Her tongue also picked up the tang, the golden face-plate and the burn beneath, healed to a rough patch by her Vis skar. She fought off a threatened wince. No sense getting wrapped up in something she couldn't control, couldn't change. Without the skars and Annalyse's quick thinking, she'd have died. A career fighting fiends and thieves ensured Ami already had enough damage to turn any beauty into a grim picture of lost possibility.

Sawi stopped, and Ami jerked herself free from her own head.

"What?" Ami whispered, lowering her voice as Sawi had a hunter's knife in her hand. She had a spear slung over her back too, but this tunnel pressed in close enough to make a long weapon a fool's choice.

"You didn't hear that? Listen."

A scratch. A scrabble. Not large and heading their way. Ami tapped Sawi's shoulder, nodded down at the knife. The Vis returned the gesture and Ami sank back several strides, kicking up some cave dirt and holding the torch low. Sawi peeled off her mosses and tossed them to the tunnel's far side, shading herself. A risk: the fiend could be able to see in utter blackness, but even then, Ami could charge in with her new Whent blade and offer a surprise strike.

Besides, after this long, both of them were comfortable killing in the gloom.

The skittering came on, picking up speed. Ami smiled. A predator smelling food. What did it take to get through those gates, to swim from the pool and climb into these tunnels?

Not light work, surely, and wanting for some reward. The kind that would get this fiend killed.

Sawi struck without a sound. Ami only knew she swung at all because the creature announced its injury with a burbling yelp, like a bird getting punched mid-squawk. Ami darted forward, torch in her left and Whent blade in her right, to find her efforts unnecessary. Sawi had the fiend spitted on her knife, a dart more than enough, given the monster barely outran her blade in length. Nevertheless, the fiend captured its otherwordly origins, with a swirling skin seemingly made up of writhing pink worms. The mass shivered on Sawi's knife, held at arms length by the frowning hunter.

"A lovely specimen," Ami said, wrinkling her nose up in a nasty smile. "The gods truly do have awful imaginations."

"The gods?"

"Of course, the gods. Who else would've created these things?"

"I . . . " Sawi shivered. "I guess I hadn't thought about it. The fiends, the gods."

"You thought these monsters just appeared from the ether, ready to devour us?" Ami knelt, gave the fiend a closer look as its skin settled into cold death. The creature's blood, a pale blue, leaked down into a puddle at her feet. At least it had blood at all. Some fiends . . . "Though I suppose, if you're feeling fanciful, you could say the fiends came from other gods looking to mess with ours."

"Does it matter?" Sawi set the knife and its prize down, put her tossed moss back on her satchel. "Either way, we still have to stop them. Doesn't make a difference how they were made."

"That way's less fun."

"You're a weird one, Ami."

"What clued you in? The faceplate?" Ami straightened, stared on down the tunnel. "But you might have a good idea in there."

"Wow, a compliment? From you?"

"I'm already regretting it." Ami started off down the tunnel, not back towards Jochi's camp.

"Isn't that the wrong way?"

"Depends on what you want."

Sawi hissed, a noise telling Ami she'd done something right, and the Guardian kept right on walking. When the Vis caught up, knife and its attendant fiend held behind her very much like the torch Ami still carried, the Guardian gave up their new destination: the big chamber and the gates inside it.

The Vis pitched questions, as she liked to do, but this time Ami didn't shut her down with grim certainty. Instead, like Ami often had with Svarde and Catya on their Renewal journey, the Guardian played Sawi's questions into her own plans, fleshing out the details and building confidence. Sawi herself just grew more bewildered, but that didn't matter: Ami would see the gates up close, do what neither Svarde, the Dead King now in Svarde's thrall, or Jochi's scouts had. And when she saw those swirling lights clear and clean, Ami would figure out how to shut them down.

"Blind hope's not your usual speed," Sawi muttered

when Ami batted away her latest question. "You're risking us getting ambushed, cut off, or lost."

"You'd rather place your faith in Svarde somehow raising an army of dead monsters to fight off other fiends, forever and ever?"

"I mean, it's a start?"

The tunnel twisted and turned a while longer, with forks and small chambers splitting off here and there, though the right passage was always obvious: fiend feet, claws, and who knew what else had ground down the way leading to the chamber, and Ami swerved that direction without stopping.

Even if she performed a miracle and shut down the gates right now, the walk back would be long, and their legs were already heavy. Best to make it fast, get back to Svarde's camp for some awful Whent ale and more bone-meal and mushroom soup.

Another wince. After she made it back to the surface, Ami would never have soup again.

The chamber appeared without ceremony. The tunnel, dark and constant, stopped without preamble, throwing Ami and Sawi onto a broad gray rock cliff. Stones, same as the ones on Jochi's side, lay about in sizes ranging from pebble to boulder. Many bore scratches, stains of blood and worse things. Bones. A natural graveyard but without dirt for the burying.

Black water lapped at the edges below them, a decent hike down but nearer than the overlook they'd used to spy on the firewalkers yesterday. The reminder pushed Ami's eyes up, across the great chamber: a glow rose from what would've been the horizon on the surface, stretching its meager lines across the walls and ceiling in their direction.

Too far to see anyone distinctly, too far to fire a shot, to patrol.

"At least we're alone," Sawi said, drawing her spear and holding it without much confidence.

Ami had taught the Vis better than that. Maybe another lesson when they returned. No lapses now, not here.

Again, though, Sawi made a point: without a fiend on the cliffs, it was time to inspect the gates.

The swirling lights looked much the same from this side, as if their size and shape held no matter how Ami looked at them. As she walked down, Ami noted off their colors, their sparkling dots spinning, dashing, driving through the water. Jochi's watchers said they never changed, not even when fiends emerged.

Beautiful constants, and one for each god.

Foti's orange-red burned on the chamber's left side, seemingly equidistant to the chamber's two shallower ends, the ones fiends tended to go for. Why, then, did the firewalkers always head towards the Dead King's city? Why did most fiends choose that side?

Ami glanced back the way they'd come, saw no hints near their small tunnel's entry. The narrow path might deter the larger monsters, though the Dead King insisted the biggest passages lay beneath the waters. Even so, something must draw them—

"The Wound," Sawi said, following Ami's eyes across the chamber. "The Wound's back where we are. Maybe that's why there's fewer fiends this way."

"How would that matter?"

"You said this is all about the gods, right? All our stories say the monsters came when Vis and Noctia fought, when he stabbed her. If that's true, then that might be what created these gates and caused all this."

"Maybe, Sawi, you should write these ideas down. You're quite observant, for someone destined to pick fruit all day."

Sawi glowered, Ami laughed and made her way to the water's edge. She reached down, ran her fingers through the ripples. Cold, but otherwise the same as every other pond, lake, or river Ami had set foot in. Not salty, though. Not like the ocean. At least Ami wouldn't die if she drank a sip, at least Jochi's scouts could come here, gather more water to boil for the army.

Her fingers, too, didn't burn. Didn't come away coated with some monster slime or turn splotchy with some parasite.

Ami stuck her whole arm in, soaking her linen shirt. Withdrew it, watched with the torch held near.

"Anything?" Sawi asked.

"Like a clean bath, albeit a chilly one."

When the water treated her arm like it had Ami's hand, she began taking off the rest of her clothes, save the barest beneath. Ami handed the torch to Sawi, who asked what Ami thought she was doing, and only sighed at Ami's response.

But the Vis didn't stop the Guardian as Ami, blade in her right hand, dove into the waters and kicked down, down towards those swirling lights and the only answers that mattered.

CHAPTER 16

RECKONING AND REWARD

Fassle couldn't have asked for a better killing night. Clouds blocked Sichi's pink glow, driving snow slicked stones and keeping people inside. Howling wind mingled with surf to cover any unfortunate screams.

If the gods were alive, Gladdring might take the weather as a sign they'd turned against him.

Indeed, he wore little more than a ragged shift, a bruised and battered body numbing fast as his assassins dragged him through narrow gaps between towers, down neglected stairs, and, slipping, bleeding, stumbling, towards a particular cliff. One Gladdring himself knew well, had used for this very purpose more than once.

Among the Tenets, certain advice circled, such as where and when it was easiest to dispose of an annoying scholar, a pesky soldier, or a merchant whose self-worth had grown too large. In better circumstances, Gladdring might've laughed, pointed out the coincidence to the mute murderers walking him down. Instead he kept his mouth shut and his mind open.

Fassle came to him quick after his guards tossed Gladdring in the tower cell, stripping the Adept—though had he already lost that title?— of his robes, regal ornaments, and the several skars secreted about his pockets. The shift had replaced them, and in its sallow plainness, Gladdring couldn't muster up the glare Fassle deserved.

"Spying on me already?" Gladdring asked first, denying Fassle the opening motion.

The Najahn leader stood beyond the bars and converted whatever he'd been about to say to a wordless sigh. Unlike Gladdring, the man kept on his raiments, looking as if he was about to pronounce some grand vision to an assembled mass instead of skulking about a disheveled prison tower. And not the nice one either, reserved for those lucky souls the Najahn would ransom for one deal or another from their home isles.

"I never stopped," Fassle said, the voice settling its weasel bones amid the lanterns, the laughter and cries of guards and prisoners. "Would you let a dangerous animal roam free in your home?"

"If it only bit my enemies, I would."

Fassle laughed, "Gladdring, you are my only true enemy."

"There are more knives at your neck than mine, some deadlier still."

"Those will all be rooted out in turn." Fassle reached into his robes, drew out a ring, a familiar one. "I'm learning more every day. Useful in ferreting out true intentions, both for me and a few I really do trust."

Gladdring couldn't tear himself away from the skar. He knew the stone's ridges, how the pointed end would cut his finger if Gladdring grabbed it wrong. Years upon years, since the last Renewal, they'd shared every minute. An easy lift from the Tamas outpost where he'd been stationed, those ale-addled people, his very own, easy to deceive because they didn't care to, well, care.

They might if Fassle's purple and black forces stamped their order on every Tamas theater.

"The skars don't tell you everything," Gladdring said, seeing as Fassle was waiting for him to speak. Leaving a door open for Gladdring to spare his own life, or just fishing for more information? Did it matter? "They won't tell you why we want you gone."

"Then it's a good thing I'm here. I'd much prefer if you told me." A glittering grin. Gladdring picked out dinner remnants, fishy bits, in the man's teeth. "Is it just power that pushes you into these awful moves? Or something more grand? Delusions about saving the isles?"

"It's your insufferable smell."

Fassle, taking a breath to launch into more rambling offal Gladdring didn't care to hear stopped with a mix of gulp and growl. Then came the glare, one Gladdring met with settled exhaustion, retreating to rest on the thin bench at the cell's back. They hadn't bothered to cover it with a sheet. Meant Gladdring wouldn't be staying here long.

Now, if Gladdring could guess, he'd just chosen how he'd leave this place.

"That's it?" Fassle asked through tight lips. "After all this, after I've given you one last chance at absolution, you offer a joke?"

"Not a joke. You're rotten, Fassle. Can't breathe when I'm around you."

Red rose in those sallow cheeks. A man withered by his own vanity, corrupted by endless sycophants and lack of challenge. Fassle couldn't cope. Had been lucky to make it this far. Gladdring would've loved to drive the dagger into the man's heart himself and clear the way to a better world.

Now somebody else would have to do it.

"You won't be breathing at all in a few hours," Fassle hissed, sending some spit with it for good measure. "You could've been so much better, Gladdring. Instead, you'll die knowing I'll be reaping the rewards for all your work. The Najahn will finally control all the isles, and you'll see none of it."

Fassle threw up one final sneer as the man turned, but for all his bluster, the clenched hands along his robes gave Gladdring the true grin. Fassle might have thousands ready to wage his war, man his fortresses, and batter his enemies, but Gladdring had pierced the man's defenses nonetheless.

THAT GOOD FEELING didn't do much against the cold. As they reached the cliff, Gladdring realized he'd lost all feeling along his arms and legs. His teeth clattered like some mad machine, spasms running along every muscle. His eyes hurt, seared by the snow, the wind. The fall and the swift end that'd come with it almost seemed worth it.

"Walk to the end and jump," said the toneless voice, one of the killers. Gladdring looked, a slow turn, to see they'd both drawn Foti blades. "One chance to keep your dignity, or we gut you and shove you off."

One chance to make this look like his own choice. The man didn't say as much, but Gladdring knew what'd happen if, when his body washed up near the port. Fassle would put out a notice in the morning, declare Gladdring missing, and when his drowned corpse drifted in, there'd be all tragedy and no turmoil.

Less pain, too, for him. At the end, why would Gladdring want to feel a sword through his skin?

He took a step out onto the jutting rock, barely wider

than Gladdring himself. Ice ran through, along the stone. Snow built up along those same lines, shifting as Gladdring planted his feet, the wind running the flakes along.

"Faster."

Had he been delaying? Gladdring couldn't be sure. Ahead he saw only swirling snow and darkness. Cold pierced his world. A thundering heart took over, and again Gladdring wished for his skar's whispers. His friend, with him at the last.

Two more shuddering steps and Gladdring reached the edge. Looked over, saw the dimmest whorls where the waves bashed Noctia's stones. Reached, took one more frozen breath.

"Stop right there," the executioner said. "Turn around. Slow, so you don't slip on your frozen toes."

The odd request pierced Gladdring's numbing soul and he managed a slow, shuffling twist, scraping his soles across the rock. At the end, both killers stood facing Gladdring, but not with crossbows or blades drawn. The lights behind gave their silhouettes a patient appearance, waiting, not driving the action.

"Out with it," the same speaker said. "Yarvick wants to know how you'll be paying back your debts."

Gladdring would've laughed, would've cried save the thought of tears, of breathing in more frozen air pitched too much horror to countenance. Instead he only gaped, found a question and asked it.

"What debts?"

"The ones you're incurring right this minute by still standing, all through his good graces."

"Then Yarvick knows what I'd do. What I intend to—"

"Intentions are all well and good, but they don't keep the fires lit. Don't get us any more skars neither." The killer took one step towards Gladdring, hands dropping to folds within his cloak. "Yarvick's asking for more than a promise, Gladdring. One bought with your life."

"Name it, then." Gladdring hated his teeth for chattering, his legs for twitching. "I'll pay it. I have no choice."

"Not enough." The man matched Gladdring now, up to his chest, and the killer's breath stank of old fish and older ale. "After tonight, you're his. What he asks, you do. What he wants, you get. And when the time comes to give what you can't now imagine, you'll do it, because of tonight. Do you agree?"

"What choice do I have?"

"Say it. Promise it on your damn skar."

"A skar I don't have."

The words were barely a whisper. The wind snapped. Warmth, though, came from Gladdring's left hand, where his killer's gloved palm withdrew, leaving two tender stones. A topaz, glinting, familiar, and shorn of its ring. Next to it, a twinkling silver rock.

"Promise."

Gladdring couldn't tear his eyes from the skar pair, but he said the word. Gave the killer what he wanted. The word had barely left his lips before the killer gave Gladdring a hard shove, his numb feet slipping on hard stone. Gladdring fell back, the wind snatching at his shift, the cliff suddenly rushing by.

Still, Gladdring felt no terror. His old friend had returned, and with company.

CHAPTER 17

THEATER CAMP

The theater beat the performance. Benches grown over with soft black and blue mosses, globe lanterns lit with long poles hanging from rafters, musicians embracing the evening chill to play well enough to bring Eujo back to the Kance court and its many, far too many, luxuries. All this for a small crowd, barely one section of three with any populace, and most of those offering little more than polite claps.

Torny joined Eujo in caring less about what went on stage than what was around them, taking to their predicament like a prisoner eyeing an escape. Because that's what they were, prisoners, and none of them counted anything different.

Their swift dinner had ended when Daklin returned, somehow more made up than before, skin glistening with powders to go with an outfit more frills than not. He'd offered up a bow and a gesture, declaring the Animas's last show of the night to be starting in mere moments. This apparently amazing experience attracted no attention from the others in the meal tent, all of whom had spent time casting curious looks at the newcomers and offering nothing else. No introductions, only inquisitive stares turned away whenever Eujo met them.

Daklin took Torny's excuse of exhaustion and tossed it aside, saying all they'd have to do was sit. And if they fell asleep, well, that was judgment enough on the entertainment. All declared with a grin covering iron beneath, hard enough for Eujo to overrule Torny's follow-up and get them moving. Neither Wax nor Bliss cared to protest, their international innocence giving them a blissful shot at enjoying the evening.

'We'll have a window after the last act,' Torny flashed, sitting to Eujo's right. The Kance Queen had the aisle, matted wood stairs descending towards the stage. Wax and Bliss sat on Torny's other side, by turns mesmerized and confused by the mishmash going on before them. 'They'll be too busy congratulating each other to notice us.'

'And go where?' Eujo replied, fingers snapping in the adopted Vis sign language. 'Run away into the night?'

'We don't want to be here. It's not good.'

The way Torny bit at her lip suggested the bandit wasn't a total novice to Tamas traps. The isle had its reputation as a floppy plaything, producing ale and good conversation, but nothing dangerous. What too few bothered asking, what Eujo had learned not long after ascending to royalty, was why nobody, not Whent, Rana, Kance, or even the Najahn, had tried taking the isle for their own ends.

The murky truth was that people who went to Tamas with ill intent, or who earned the ire of its people, didn't tend to come back. Not as themselves, anyway.

'They won't hurt Renewals,' Eujo said, flicking her

attention back to the stage to gauge the time as scattered applause burst out to a few bows.

Moving into the third act, then, if Eujo had it right. The play was a mistaken identity farce, but the actors weren't on their game, forcing lines and missing spots on the stage. The costumes carried the production, all feathered, fili-greed versions of Najahn armor. Someone must've spent innumerable hours plucking, dying, and stringing together the feathers, and the effect as the shimmering, bird-like forms danced and debated around the stage should've been entrancing.

But Daklin's constant presence put a damper on things.

Their chaperone rarely left the bench two rows behind them. His grinning stare kept Eujo and Torny to the finger flashing, and even that done with their bodies in the way, blocking any downward spying.

'You say that like we're Renewals anymore. That's all over, remember? We're just bums looking for stones now.' Torny winced as the third act opened and an actor tripped over their absurd feather leggings. 'We're nothing, and we have nothing.'

'We have the skars.'

'Oh yeah? Going to have Wax burn this place down too?'

Eujo turned her head away to buy herself time. Torny liked to spiral, wrap herself up in a dire cloak to justify some dumb, reckless act. At least, that's what Eujo saw, and what she'd have to prevent right now.

She stood, twisted up from the bench and walked the steps to Daklin's row. Her friends's eyes followed Eujo, but she ignored them as she nodded next to Daklin. Their guide flickered a frown but scooted himself over, letting Eujo sit down with prim polish. A Queen's ways weren't easily forgotten, despite their journey often preferring a peasant's posture.

"Why are you keeping us here?" Eujo asked, slipping the whisper between lines in what appeared to be a hopelessly dramatic speech about the Wound, the fiends, and destiny on the stage. "What're we to you?"

Daklin didn't turn to look at her, said nothing as the speech died down to an anguished end. Some love lost, some hope died. Eujo couldn't pretend to pay attention.

"You're an opportunity," Daklin whispered back. "Not just for us, but for yourselves."

"Opportunity for what?"

"You seek our skars, yes?"

"It's what Renewals do, Daklin."

"Then this is your test. Work with me, and I'll grant you your souls."

The word, like lightning, like the feel of a stiff breeze, triggered a memory. What the Tamas diplomats kept offering in trade for sky diamonds, for herbs and minerals needed for their wines, their endless play productions. An elite currency, proof you understood Tamas values. Get a soul, and you could get the best of the best. Doors would open, stages would be lit, and, perhaps, a skar could be obtained.

The slant to Daklin's smile, the eyes and too-smooth skin spoke of a dangerous deal. A man used to getting his way while making others think they were getting theirs. Eujo, back on Kance, would've tossed the man out, had him watched. Here, with her purpose destroyed by the Najahn, their possessions meager, and their knowledge even more so, Eujo only saw one way.

"What do you need?"

.   .   .

THE LINES CAME FAST, thrown at Eujo for her to repeat back with the same tempo and tone. She and her partner, a squat woman calling herself Bayan, stood amid the gnarled roots and scragged trees beyond the Animus. They were rehearsing, as Bayan called it. The other three did the same: bantering their lines, learning their places, and trying to do something they'd never done before.

At least Eujo and Torny could fall back a bit on their bandit pasts: subterfuge was only a different sort of stage.

For now, Eujo wore the same robes she'd carried with her from Whent, though Bayan promised a costume would be coming. In two days time, they'd start full rehearsals. In four, a practice show. At six, the first live performance to advertised audiences.

Daklin had broken down the schedule that morning in a near-dawn wake-up, tea and bread practically thrown at the foursome in their shallow tent. After a night spent on clotted hay with her clothes for blankets, Eujo took the walk with Bayan to their rooted rehearsal spot to shake out her sore muscles, clear her head for what became one cringe-inducing line after the next.

"I'm not much for a farce," Eujo said after Bayan finished a slashing critique. "It's not my thing."

"Oh, I'm sorry, we'll have them write another play just for you, that's you're thing." Bayan spoke in quipped snaps, a bird squawking a few notes before clapping her beak shut. "Do it again. Lean into the character."

A musician who'd broken her last lute string and on the hunt for more, prompting a bizarre quest where she joins up with three other misbegotten music-lovers, all solo artists who come to realize that, together, they can form a band and be greater than any of them alone. Bayan had read the synopsis to Eujo on their walk out, and even in the carly-morning fog, Eujo had felt something die at the description.

The best Tamas plays were a marvel, a departure from the isles and their oft-miserable existence. This? This *was* that miserable existence, just put on a stage. Still, if it earned Eujo and Wax the souls to get the skar, she'd push through.

The Kance Queen read the lines again. Then again. Finally, on the fourth time through, Bayan, with a sigh and a shrug, declared them good enough.

"How many more?" Eujo asked, reaching for the water skin and trying not to shiver. A cold and clear day.

"That was only the first scene," Bayan replied, riffling through the stiff parchment, another Tamas production. That paper, so rare and useful, was wasted on this . . . Eujo fought off the grimace. "Another five in the first act. Be ready."

Steps came next. Motions across their gnarled grove, Bayan barking at Eujo to stand here, move there, add some flounce to the motion. A disgruntled artist didn't move like a queen, a thief. The audience had to believe.

"I can't believe this myself," Eujo said, the skars on her bracelet catching her frustration and muttering in her ear, suggesting something dangerous. "This isn't me."

Bayan softened, letting the script dangle at her side and reaching a hand towards Eujo's shoulder, one the Queen evaded with a back step and a glare. If the wind didn't get colder, it certainly felt that way.

"You're here, by chance or by fate," Bayan started, her clipped tone sticking around. "You can walk away at any time. Daklin won't put someone on the stage who won't try. We don't care if you can act. We care that you're willing to make the effort."

"All while people die across the isles? While fiends rampage? You want us, Wax and I, to dance?"

Last night, in the Animas, Eujo had accepted the grit, agreed with Daklin's absurd offer. Cut the distance between those words and the actions they demanded, though, and Eujo found her patience lacking, pushed along by slim food and exhaustion.

She hadn't left Kance for games.

"If you can't find joy in this, then why bother fighting the fiends at all?"

"I find joy in good wine and a warm fire."

"Then think of that when you're on the stage, and you might find your soul. Don't, and I'll tell Daklin to send you packing. Maybe another troupe will give you a better chance."

Unmoved by the plight of thousands. Typical for a Tamas. Eujo summoned up some spit—the Rana skar only too happy to pull water from the air—and shot it to the side. Followed it with a Kance curse.

"Show me the steps again," Eujo snapped. "And do it slow this time."

CHAPTER 18
POWER UNLEASHED

Waking nightmares. A thing Annalyse had never experienced until she spent the hours after Deshiva's raid lying down in a makeshift camp. Ropes tied the scientist to a thick branch well above ground, ropes that did nothing to ease her comfort nestled between leaves and insects. Other Vis, those who'd spent the night running along as Annalyse had, seemed to find sleep fast amid the ferns and bark, the sun's light splintered into dancing shadows.

Those shadows spawned the horrors keeping Annalyse tight, eyes flitting between closed and open as foreign sounds added their own surprises. A hoot might prompt a look at a rustling branch, a gloom behind those leaves where someone might lurk. Annalyse kept one hand grasping the Vis skar worn on her necklace, its soothing whispers tending to the bug bite litany covering her.

Too late, Deshiva had offered oils to ward off the bites, claiming after that she'd not realized Annalyse didn't know how to protect herself on the isle.

A fugitive didn't have time to study.

The runner swung in on vines early in the afternoon, satchel looped over his shoulder holding the skars left behind on the expedition. A few from every isle, save the already-incorporated Vis and missing Noctia stones. Annalyse took the satchel and rebuffed another request from Deshiva to give her own warriors a lesson in the whispering rocks.

"I'm not going to be responsible for killing them," Annalyse dished off in a reply.

Instead, she sipped more Vis coffee, the bitterness keeping her awake around a forest floor fire. Her hands drifted from one Foti skar to the next, catching its tones and comparing them. The skars weren't all the same, their personalities coming through in eager gushes or quiet sighs. Riven from the same god, Annalyse wasn't sure how the skars had those differences, relegating it to future research.

Assuming she lived that long.

When Deshiva brought over an evening meal, fresh mango and fresher meat from some jungle beast Annalyse didn't know, the hunter confirmed the Najahn hadn't left their self-imposed palisade prison.

"They're waiting behind those spears for us," Deshiva said. "Time to give them a reason to leave."

"It's been a single day, Deshiva. Can't we wait a little longer?"

If Annalyse had asked a question Deshiva didn't anticipate, the scientist hadn't seen it yet. Instead, the hunter, wearing a darker weave, her spear bereft of feathers, kept her patient look, her solid stance. A negotiation where one side wouldn't give.

"The Najahn aren't trying to decide," Deshiva said. "They're waiting for reinforcements. Once they arrive from the Ringed City, with their armor, their voulges and chakrams, we'll lose any chance. I'm not asking a question, Annalyse. I'm making a request."

Gladdring had done the same after he'd pulled Annalyse to Noctia. Polite inquiries turned into suggestions turned into directives, many given in the same tone Deshiva had just used: presented as a choice, in reality an order.

"I'll do it, but I've never done something like this before."

Deshiva nodded at herself. "That's why I'm going with you."

THE EXPLOSIVE RISK with Foti skars put Annalyse and Deshiva on the nighttime mission alone. Again Annalyse found herself at the jungle's edge, looking across empty pens and half-burned sheds towards the Najahn outpost. Sichi shone clear, the soft pink coating everything. Other hunters climbed the trees around them, settling with bows, darts, and eager spears in case the Najahn decided to do something rash.

Whether any counter would be able to save her, Annalyse didn't wonder. She focused on little else save the Foti skar in her left hand, the most reasonable of the bunch and still urging the scientist onward. Destruction, fire, and fury thudded along with her thoughts.

Deshiva tapped Annalyse's elbow. The signal. The hunter started first, crouched and creeping with her spear in her left hand, her right clearing ferns as she moved. Annalyse followed, the fresh, dark weave clinging tight, all to minimize shapes and shadows. Special shoes, ones Deshiva claimed belonged to Vis's Lira—whomever they were—melded to Annalyse's feet, letting her bounce off the leafy floor with little more than a rustle.

Sneaking narrowed things. Thoughts of Noctia, Whent, the skars and her research disappeared as the scientist focused on planting her feet in Deshiva's trail. The hunter moved like an animal, every stride leading into the next, slanting to one side or the other to stay among the tallest grasses, to weave behind fence posts or into a shed's shadow. When Sichi struck them full on, Deshiva sped up, forcing Annalyse to do the same.

Her toes struck a tangle, some weed forcing Annalyse into a stumble. Her right hand flung out, ready to catch her, only for Deshiva's spear to slide in her path instead. Annalyse caught her chest on the haft, looked up to see Deshiva already pulling her along, into the next pen's shadow. The hunter's look carried not judgment, but a calm acceptance.

There would be mistakes. They would not be fatal.

The last dash up to the palisade was a clear run, a dirt path offering a few scant stones and nothing else. Lantern glows rose over the wood wall this close. Annalyse couldn't make out a watch from where they sat, tucked in behind a storage shack stuffed with feed for winter. The thatched roof had been singed the day before, its charred scent mingling with the bright air. Conversation, too muffled to parse, drifted along the breeze.

"They haven't seen us," Deshiva said, the words barely a whisper. "It's time."

The Foti skar heard as well as Annalyse and responded with a roar, demanding the scientist let the fire god's power flow. Annalyse closed her eyes, pushed back, in much the same way she might resist a stomach ache, a bad cramp.

After a long moment, the skar subsided, dwindled to a merely boiling anger.

"All right?" Deshiva asked, and Annalyse nodded. "Ready?"

Another nod. Annalyse's heart picked up this time, its beating outpacing the skar in speed, thunder.

When Deshiva broke cover, the scientist came right behind. They padded along the dirt, the two dark dots on the move. Annalyse expected a shout but none came. Blind hubris, not to set a watch the day after an attack?

Were the Najahn so confident in themselves?

The Foti skar threw an edge at that, one Annalyse agreed with. The Ringed City would pay for its arrogance. Hopefully, though, not in lives lost. Never that. Never death.

Deshiva reached the gate first, turning her back to the wall and settling her spear's base into the ground. Annalyse came up beside her, stayed facing those sturdy logs bound by rope and metal. A gate that must've stood for years upon years. Hers, now, to destroy.

The skar begged her for the chance.

"It will be quick," Annalyse muttered. "Back away."

Deshiva gave her one step, twisted and angled the spear, ready to skewer any sudden charge. Annalyse put her right hand out, pressed her palm flat against the wood. The skar snarled, almost barked its nonsense. The scientist breathed in deep. It'd all happened so fast. So quiet. No resistance.

Now the world would know what a skar could do in war.

Annalyse guided the skar, spoke to the stone in impressions, imagined visions, and straight up desires, just the way she, Ami, and Sawi had all those days beneath Gladdring's tower. The Foti skar didn't ask for clarification, didn't reply, save to unleash itself.

Like a bad flush, Annalyse went warm from head to toe, the feeling swimming to her fingertips and out into the wood. In the pink, the dark log sizzled, an orange spreading as the first outer bits caught the skar's energy. Annalyse wanted it to burn a hole, set the gate afire, and in the first seconds, with the first lick, the skar seemed to be doing just that.

But a taste does not make a meal, and the skar lunged.

The first lick blew outward, one flaring ring after another pulsing from Annalyse's hand and flying over the gate. Blazing ripples, ones earning shouts from inside as they crested the gate's top and kept right on going, leaving flames in their wake. Annalyse wanted to move her hand back, but the skar pressed her to the wood, demanded she keep the connection, that the skar would do what she wanted, if only Annalyse could give it everything in return.

What choice did she have?

"Annalyse?" Deshiva's voice, loud, over the shouts.

The scientist felt a hand on her shoulder. Felt the skar run over her last resistance.

The gate burst. Exploded inward, those ripples tightening until they became a solid rush, boiling and burning away the barrier into a scalding rush. Annalyse pressed her eyes shut against that nova, opened them to see shadows lit aflame. Four Najahn soldiers, those sad curious souls, ran, stumbled, fell as the metal cloaking their bodies blazed, melted, green and blue pyres. Others, not so close, merely caught searing shards to faces, arms, legs. Dry winter grasses and the tents near them lit, completing the chaos.

Deshiva's hand pulled Annalyse away, twisting the scientist from the fire. Deshiva's grip only tightened as

Annalyse tried to keep her balance, tried to find a thought, words beyond the Foti's skar's pulse for power.

The stone wanted more. The skar, as if Annalyse was sprinting, was lifting something far too heavy, sapped her and sent energy running through the stone, through her fingers and feet, the fire now without direction, burning gouts flaring up into the night. Deshiva, a halo behind Annalyse's flame-shrouded eyes, let go, wringing burning bits off her own hand.

Annalyse wanted to scream, tried, but found her throat and voice as missing as the rest of her. Without Deshiva's hand, the scientist fell to the ground, the impact launching sparks in all directions. The smell of burning hair, dying screams, and Deshiva's shadow, all overcome by the skar's fury.

She reached, tipped what little of that skar power she could into her right hand and held it towards Deshiva. The hunter's dancing shadow darted, leaping and ducking flames, a black line twisting in Deshiva's hands.

Help me.

The words, if Annalyse said them at all, vanished in the skar's crackle. What didn't, what held steady to the last, was Deshiva's black line, snapping towards her.

CHAPTER 19

THE OTHER SIDE

Swimming was better with Rana skars. Ami knew that before she stepped into the cool water—not cold, the whole Dark Below seemed to gain some constant warmth this far down—and Ami knew it after she'd submerged her head, her golden face, and her battered body beneath the calm, vast pool.

On Foti, only sailors bothered to treat the water as a place to be. Everywhere else, you were more likely to dive into lava or a stream so sizzling as to sear yourself a tasty medium-rare. Ami hadn't learned otherwise till they reached Rana, when Catya, who'd grown up in Smythe and splashed among the rocks, declared she wouldn't lose a Guardian to a river's current. They'd spent the long raft ride north dipping into the summer waters every night, learning the strokes, kicks, and held breath that brought Ami, now, towards the swirling motes.

Beneath the water, the seven clusters spread. Their sizes all seemed similar, the motes swinging in and out on crazy orbits around central objects Ami couldn't see. They sprawled across the chamber, keeping space between them, as if placed in their precise points by some caretaker.

Noctia, the goddess?

The dead goddess, Ami reminded herself as she kept up the kicks, diving deeper for the dazzle closest to her. Teal motes danced, their color like Rana raider gear, sticking out amid the gloomy water. No mushrooms, no glowing moss beneath.

Her lungs issued their first pang. A warning, nothing more.

The first mote neared as Ami kept her feet kicking. The Guardian struck out with her Whent blade, angling to stab the light, and the mote dodged the stab, flitting beneath it like a small insect might evade a haphazard swat. Intelligent, then, or instinctual?

Either meant alive, or more so than a torch's glow, a fire's spark; the closest things Ami could put next to these swirling lights.

She kept on.

The motes surrounded Ami fast. They slid around the Guardian, across her eyes, above and below her body, stopping not the slightest as they kept along their speedy circles. Ami stabbed again at one, then another, trying to see if she could catch them, but her experience was no match for their smooth ease.

Until she went for the deepest one, closest to the center the lights rotated around. Ami missed the mote—her lungs ached again, a harder stress this time—but the blade bit into something else. The teal lights gave Ami vision, the pool's water clean enough to let the Guardian keep her eyes open, and she saw the sword's point disappear into a fold.

No, not a fold: skin.

Ami pulled. Found the sword stuck, her yank only

bringing the Guardian deeper still. This close, Ami expected to see a body, see, perhaps, some strange fiend-belching creature waiting beneath the waters ready to summon forth more horrors. Instead, nothing save murk found her eyes. The weapon's target held to its invisibility.

But it couldn't hide from her touch.

Shifting the blade to her left hand, Ami reached out towards the pierced point. Felt a ribbed, threaded surface. Not a ferrite's rock skin, but not far from a less molten lizard's. Felt, too, her fingers press in, like on an old fruit. Almost without trying, her hand disappeared into the scales, sinking through with little pressure.

Her lungs ached now. She'd have to kick up soon if—

The skin parted, peeling away around Ami's wrist like a blossoming flower. The sword swung free from her grip, wheeling away as the dark waters vanished before her. What'd been black and blurred morphed in a single instant to a foggy gray, shapes resolving as best they could through a watery sheen into things Ami recognized: hills, dotted with odd-looking trees. A clouded sky. A muddy plain stretching before her.

And it was under attack.

The sky wasn't just cloudy, it split and shattered with lightning strikes. The bolts rained across the ground and darted between the clouds. Those odd trees looked so different because they were bent almost in half with some driving wind. What rocks Ami could see, smoothed and large, shook and split, the earth shaking. Some smoke in the distance suggested a fire, even as clear blue water stormed over the mud. A world in ruin, a world at war with itself.

Spots blotted her vision. Ami's breath running out. She tried to pull her hand back, found it tight. Ami crossed her left hand over, grabbed her right, pulled. This time her hand budged, this time, as pain split her skull, as her lungs demanded air right this minute, her hand came free, threads of that blasted world coming with. The lines spilled into the black water, dissipating around the motes.

Ami kicked once, found the move hard, found her eyes still drawn to the madness beyond the liquid curtain. Saw a new shadow find its way, smearing across the view. Yellow eyes, embedded in some deep skull, matched Ami's.

In a rush, like a friend diving in, Ami felt the water buffet her aside. She was drowning, her kicks weak, her heart thudding, her lungs screaming, and she was no longer alone.

THE PEBBLED pool's edge cut Ami's skin. Glorious scrapes and grit, none of it associated with the coughing, gasping pain bracketing her lungs. She fluttered her eyes open, blinking away the black to see not her expected savior—Sawi—but a slithering, snapping, thing. Webbed claws, wide, spotted in faded and white, scurried up the pebbles. Ami felt herself move with the creature, realized then the fiend had her left leg scooped into a crescent-like mouth.

A leg, Ami realized, that wasn't bleeding, wasn't broken.

"Ami!"

The call, both relieved and far too late, came from Sawi, just coming to her feet further up the stones.

"What is that?"

Ami tried to answer, a spitting curse that would've shown Sawi just how much the Guardian appreciated being left to drown—that this was all a consequence of Ami's own actions was all too easy to shove aside—and wound up spitting up more water. Her head knocked a larger pebble on its journey up the chamber's slope, a splitting flash interrupted by familiar whispers.

The Vis skars, unwilling to quit.

Neither would she.

Ami tugged on her pinched leg. Felt it shift inside the monster's mouth. The fiend stopped its rush, the six webbed claws freezing, jutting out longer, sharper talons to secure the fiend's place. Those yellow eyes tilted Ami's way, revealing a full scaled face, albeit one with ochre hair tufting out at the joints. The Guardian didn't see malice in that stare, only curiosity mingling with fear, panic's left-overs fading slow.

Beyond the fiend's visage, Ami caught Sawi shifting, picking up a sharp stone and lofting it for a strike. A welcome move, except the damn fiend didn't seem to be killing Ami right then, and a rock whack might change its mood.

"Stop!" Ami gurgled, the pool's quiet helping the watered words to carry. Sawi hesitated, her frown little more than a fuzzed line as Ami's eyes continued coming back from near-death. "It's not hurting me."

She did, though, tug on that leg again. Hard enough to yank the fiend's head a little more back towards her.

"Let go," Ami said, trying to put what force her sput-tering self could muster, while also trying, trying so hard, not to seem threatening. "Please."

The fiend shivered, a running shrug sending water spraying off its scaled form. The leering eyes blinked, and as they did, Ami saw they split through the middle, separating into eight pupils, each angling a different direction. Now they all focused on the Guardian, her battered form naked on the stones, bleeding, matted.

Perhaps it found pity, perhaps it decided Ami wasn't

the food it needed, perhaps it only wanted to leave and dragging a human with it wasn't a good idea, but the fiend found its reason and opened its massive, bulbous mouth.

Ami had her leg back in a jerk, had herself kicked by a web claw in the next moment, the fiend scrambling up past her, past Sawi, and, banging its broad body into the tunnel's side, gone.

EXPLAINING what she saw was the easy part. Answering what it meant came harder, but Ami and Sawi had time during the long, slow tunnel walk towards Svarde's dead city. They had enough bandages, enough food to bring Ami back to some comfort while the Vis skars did the rest. Those little miracle stones stole Ami's energy, forcing Sawi to again let the Guardian lean on her shoulders as they traveled.

"Is this becoming a habit?" Sawi asked when Ami fell against her the first time, a question breaking the silence that'd fallen after Ami's tale.

"Just enjoy being useful."

"I will." Sawi wrapped her arm around Ami's waist, the two falling into a matched stride. "I'd enjoy it more if you weren't an ass all the time."

"You want me to be happy, find an answer for what I just saw."

"Sounds like a dream to me. You were close to drowning, started imagining—"

Ami cursed, cut Sawi off. "No. That fiend didn't come from a dream. I've never seen a place like that before either, and I've been to every isle. It was somewhere else, and it was in trouble."

"Vis gets bad storms sometimes. Like what you described."

"No. Not like this. Not earthquakes, floods, lightning all rolled into one. Sawi, this was annihilation. Apocalypse."

Sawi laughed, a hopeless, confused chuckle that Ami found herself matching.

"Ami, I don't know," Sawi said as the laughter died, its echos bouncing away before and behind them. "I don't know what's going on anymore. All I can do, all I am doing, is trying to survive, and maybe keep my friends alive too."

For now, that might be enough. Ami, though, replayed what she'd seen, again and again as the deep hours passed. The fiend coming through had been scared, had grabbed Ami in what might've been pure panic, and, given what Ami had seen, the monster had every right to feel that way.

Destroy somebody's home, and they would run any way they could.

CHAPTER 20
TYING THE STRINGS

Shadows fished Gladdring out, sopping, soaked, and surely dead save for the Rana skar. His old Tamas topaz was there too, crushed into his palm, a numbed grip and the only thing Gladdring was sure of. The only thing he focused on as oars slapped the sea, keeping the slim boat near enough to the rocks to evade onlookers.

Not that there'd be any on such a cold, scoured night like this one.

Gladdring didn't try to talk and the shadows, he counted three, didn't change his mind. They didn't speak between themselves either, silent couriers for the damned. Their route brought Gladdring north around the Najahn quarter and away from the Ringed City, away from any watching eyes.

The shadows did, though, offer Gladdring a small flask, the stiff liquid inside bringing a welcome fire to his trembling lips. Another debt Yarvick would add to the list, would call upon.

Though what Gladdring could offer now seemed an open question.

Yarvick, though, would know that. The thought brought Gladdring no comfort.

At length, at shivering, frigid length, the boat glided into a narrow gap between cliffs. Jagged enough to have natural origins, the gap nonetheless bore signs of Yarvick's touch: outcroppings where spies could keep watch, cages and boxes floating just beyond sight from outside, waiting to be picked up and carried off. Jobs done, prizes won, and deals fulfilled.

All in all, not that different from Gladdring's own, and with much the same risks.

Still, both professions had another thing in common: being bold was key to success.

Gladdring spent the last minutes in the boat wringing out his robes, smoothing out his gnarled hair, and gathering what confidence he could, a normally sturdy spire shaken when the shadows helped him—in little more than candlelight—onto a thin pier. Rocks curled up and around them, the grotto washed out by waves striking stone.

"Walk," said a shadow. Gladdring tried to pick out some details, some features in the gloom, but the trio always seemed to evade the light, tilt their heads in such a way as to leave only their eyes bright.

Where to walk, at least, was clear: the pier gave way to a narrow line running along the rocky wall. Wet and treacherous, Gladdring took every step slow, balancing with one hand on the stone. The darkness deepened. Hearing the oars slap behind him, Gladdring risked a glance and saw the boat shoving off, all three shadows aboard.

Alone with only one place to go.

Yarvick certainly had a flair for these things.

Musing on the bandit lord and his Nimble Fingers kept Gladdring company during the freezing walk. Yarvick had simply always been there, a presence looming across the Ringed City since Gladdring arrived on some balmy day in a smeared youth. They'd met by accident, Gladdring tagging along as a promising scholar with his predecessor at the Trade Tenet. His former master had planned to engage the Nimble Fingers to make off with some rare Tamas wine from the latest shipment. The move would weaken a Tamas merchant enough to force complying with the Tenet's demands.

Gladdring watched his mentor negotiate a price with an ale-swilling shamble in a tavern corner, every moment more surreal than the last, until the Tenet tried too hard to demand a cheaper trade. A point jabbed against Gladdring's gut when the Tenet finished, Gladdring's own gasp signaling the change in status. When Yarvick sauntered over from the bar a moment later, his bandits had both Gladdring and the Tenet under lethal control.

The Tenet accepted Yarvick's price then, hoping, no doubt, Gladdring would forget the sweat, the fear, the stutter in that moment. Gladdring never did, yet he'd wound up, now, in the same place as his former master.

How merciful would Yarvick be?

Slipping, cursing, and altogether making clear to any observer that Gladdring belonged in warm, comfortable halls, the former Tenet reached the line's end to find a scalloped rock wall. The water ran beneath it, gurgling forth from some deep wellspring to meet the ocean's waves. Gladdring looked, but the muted pink glow gave no clues.

Was this the trick, then? A cruel joke meant to leave Gladdring here, abandoned, only to rot away? The idea spawned a thousand others, paths where Yarvick's cunning could prop up an escaped Gladdring, manipulate Fassle to think his adversary lived, was still plotting against him, and in some mercurial future cause Fassle to go insane . . .

"You look about as dead as anyone I've ever seen," Yarvick's harsh voice, all rotgut and whiskey, came from behind.

Gladdring turned slow, keeping his footing and getting his back against the rock. There, standing on the line he'd just walked, was Yarvick. The bandit leader had a better get-up for a freezing night than Gladdring, and appeared dry, almost buried in the great Whent furred coat and leather boots. Yarvick held a merry torch in on hand, the other stuffed inside the coat's pocket. Where Gladdring had to keep an eye on his feet, Yarvick stood like he might on solid, dry cobblestones.

If he lived, Gladdring promised, he'd try to reacquaint himself with some physical prowess. This whole thing was too great a weakness to let stand.

"All part of the plan," Gladdring blustered, drawing up to his straightest stand.

"What plan?"

"The one I'm making up as I go along."

Yarvick scoffed a single laugh. "That much is obvious. You've fallen too far for it to be intentional. Especially for a luxury lover like yourself."

"I prefer to think I have good taste."

"How'd that sea taste, then? You're free to drink some more."

The Tamas skar sparked a whisper. Gladdring agreed. They were in the game now, he and Yarvick. The delicate dance of words.

"You saved me. Why?"

Best to set the stage. Settle on facts, so those same truths could be bartered back and forth.

"I'm trying to figure that out." Yarvick took a step closer, the torch bobbed with the move. The water shadows writhed around them. "Here I thought I'd made a bargain with someone useful. A bargain I don't believe you can fulfill anymore."

"For the moment."

Up close, Yarvick's splotchy, scattered gray and black beard sprang forth like a spider's legs from his withered chin. The skin around his eyes and face lacked slack, taut and discolored. Gladdring would've thought the man nearly dead. The reason why he wasn't, so some, including Gladdring, believed, lay in Yarvick's left eye: a black stone, a Noctia skar.

The Goddess of Death could be generous.

"Then tell me how you see this moment ending," Yarvick said, "and I will tell you whether I agree."

Talent. Gladdring and Yarvick both survived by having it, and knowing whether others had it as well. The bandit lord wouldn't go through all this for nothing, and now Yarvick was playing a particular game. He could simply order Gladdring to do his bidding, strike some life-debt promise here on the fractured edge, but Yarvick wanted more.

The Tamas skar fluttered, warm. Agreement, and with it a leap to the only thing Yarvick might want but not, not yet, have.

"A puppet," Gladdring said, not hating the words as much as he expected. "You want a puppet running the Najahn. And you want that puppet to be me."

Yarvick answered with a slight grin, a short nod. Silent still. Gladdring had started off down the right track, could he continue?

"Fassle's refused your offers and he keeps catching your

thieves," Gladdring spoke with measure, balancing every assertion with the Tamas skar's clues, with Yarvick's narrow hints. The former Tenet ran along Yarvick's hopes, his foul schemes and darker dreams, all possible with an ally controlling the Circle. "And when it's done, when every Tenet, the Adepts, the advisors are yours, what then?"

Yarvick kept his sallow smile. "Yours to wonder, mine to know, puppet. You know the terms. You spoke them yourself. Do you accept?"

"Is there any alternative?"

Yarvick flicked a hand towards the water. "You swam in those waves once. You can do it again."

No rescue boat this time.

"Then you'll have your puppet." Gladdring bowed, low. "What comes first?"

"Your rebellion, of course. Time to get you cleaned up and ready to spark some chaos." Yarvick laughed, dry. "The isles need some new blood running things. Today, we cut out the old."

With that, at least, the puppet agreed.

CHAPTER 21

THIEVES TOGETHER

It was a truth accepted by three of the four: acting was a torture to be inflicted on their worse enemies. Only Wax disagreed, lounging at the table as the evening after their third day rehearsing wore on. They'd watched another trial performance, this one open to the public, and grimaced through another group similar to themselves botching lines, flopping about the stage, and turning a tragedy into a farce. That inspired Wax to declare he and his friends could do better.

Eujo wasn't so sure.

Three days burned beating herself with the script, muttering and screaming lines in turn, being told to whisper that, smooth over this, to wave her hands not at all or like she was trying to flag down a passing ship. Whatever experience she'd learned hiding her emotions in the Kance court fell away amid the roots and her teacher's hard stares.

Some people lived for the stage. Eujo preferred the cheap seats.

"Oh, it's not that bad," Wax said. "You've just got to

relax, that's all. Get into the role. Be who the script says you are. Don't take it so seriously."

'Says the man who's never been serious in his life.' Bliss, already two mugs deep in the admittedly fine Tamas ale, signed. 'You know what they have me doing? Comedy. I'm supposed to fall over or point at people and pretend to laugh.'

"What, you'd rather give a speech?"

Bliss delivered the well-earned glare.

"At least you don't have to try the stupid accents," Torny said. She spun a knife in the table, the blade's point making a small hole as it whirled. "I've never talked like a Rana and I'm not going to start now."

The thief's defiant claim seemed challenge by the vocal medley around them, the various troupes taking their dinner amid the table swath. Most recited lines or critiqued the same. Ribbons had been thrown up around the place, bringing in a festive air for the guests witnessing the shows. There'd be a new one every day, culminating with Eujo, Wax, and their Guardian's performance.

Spread fliers advertised a rare dual Renewal event. That Eujo and Wax's pictures on the parched tan paper looked little like them seemed of no concern to Daklin, who cared only that, at last, art would have a big audience.

"Get through the one show, we get our passes, then we never have to do it again," Eujo said. She'd barely touched her own ale, the chill mug taunting her with a fun evening and a miserable tomorrow. Reading lines with a hangover ranked up among the worst realities. "If I can do it, so can you."

"You're the Renewal. It's your job. I fail to see where it says Guardians have to join in the nonsense."

Wax smirked, "A good Guardian supports their Renewal in all things."

Torny waggled her own mug, as if she was about to douse Wax with its contents. "This Guardian might reconsider her oath."

"Too late for that." Wax let his smile die. "Considering the Najahn and Eujo's Kance killers want our guts, I don't think it'd be good to split up anyway."

"Think they'll kill us on stage?"

Eujo and Wax had both protested the flyers, the publicity, which Daklin shot down without a second's debate. The audience would be checked for crossbows and, besides, interrupting a performance was a serious crime on Tamas. Any murders and assaults would wait until after the show, when the foursome, souls received, was no longer part of the Animas's group. Hardly a comfort, but Daklin again refused to budge.

Threats on their lives weren't his problem, so long as the show went on.

"Daklin assured us no," Eujo said.

"Ah, yeah, let's believe the actor." Torny spun the knife again. "What good is it getting those souls if we're kidnapped and killed right after?"

"Not getting those souls means we're stuck,' Wax replied. "It's a bad deal, I know, but we got away before. We can do it again."

"But they'll know where we're going this time. They'll follow us right to the Tamas skar. Then to Kance. We can't outrun them forever."

Wax reached into his frilly tunic—the outfits they wore were all flamboyant, absurd things covering up warming wool underclothes—and shifted his skar necklace. The wild yellows, oranges, and reds on the lace, the oversized sleeves marked them as Animas actors and were, so Daklin said, a requirement while the public shows ran.

"We might, with these," the Vis said.

"The skars only give for so long," Eujo said, mulling as she spoke. "Torny has a point. If we wait, we're stuck. If, though, we leave now, we might get a head start."

Torny nodded, "They'll come in a few days, expecting a performance, but we could be long gone by then."

'But we wouldn't have the souls?'

Eujo caught Torny's flashing eyes, the thief's slight grin.

"What can be given, can be stolen."

Wax and Bliss didn't protest much at the idea, especially when Torny smoothed it over, said she and Eujo would only take a look. If the souls, whatever they were, couldn't be snagged, then they'd find another way.

Slipping from the dining tent brought the thieving pair into the chilly Tamas night. Far from a soundless or lightless one, with glimmering lanterns hanging from poles giving light to practicing musicians, rehearsing actors, or the audiences taking all of it in with ale and stiffer stuff in hands or pipes. A hazy glow spread off encroaching roots and stumpy trees. Late falling leaves searched for homes on the breeze.

"Any idea where Daklin's at?" Torny said as they meandered towards the largest theater, an easy target sitting at the Animas's center. "Or should we just start asking?"

"Doesn't matter where he is." Eujo nodded at the big theater. "It's where they'll keep the most important things they own."

"In the theater?"

"As good a place to start as any."

The guess wasn't as random as Eujo made it sound. For one, the big theaters had rooms, hallways, levels unseen from the stage and the seats. Plenty of places to store things. Two, if the living quarters where Eujo and the others had been stashed were any indication, turnover was frequency and security lax.

Neither she nor Wax had taken off the skars since arriving, and Eujo damn sure wouldn't be leaving the bracelet anywhere off her wrist till they left this odd place far behind.

The Animas's main theater rose up from the dirt like some fabulous dream, its several entry arches spaced by carved stone sent over from Whent and patched with thick mortar. Active murals covered the blocks, some painted over in a blended way to combine new scenes with old ones, bright dancers darting through a stilted shadows, animal costumes cavorting with faded kings and queens. During the day, with all the action, the art disappeared. Now, with the lantern light and little else nearby, Eujo slowed, took it in.

"Not bad," Torny said, next to her.

"It's beautiful."

"You like this stuff?" the bandit sniffed. "Never had time for it."

"A luxury I learned to appreciate." Eujo found herself drawn to a forlorn woman sitting off to the side, staring at some unseen floor, coated in an off-white raiment. She reached out, ran a finger along the solemn face. "When you're locked into a role all day, you start searching for the truth where you can find it."

"And the truth is this sad lady?"

"I think she's trying to figure out what to do."

Another sniff. "Trying to tell me you're confused, Eujo? Because I thought we had a pretty clear plan here."

Eujo drew back. Nodded towards the closest arch, a big,

faux-gold three plastered over the middle. "We do. Get this skar, get Wax his Kance stone, and then march right to Noctia and get arrested. Executed. Whatever."

"Well, you put it that way, maybe we should re-evaluate." Torny fished her knife free, tossed and caught it. "Bet Yarvick would take us all in, since I have the diary. Could all be thieves then."

"I'm never going back to that."

They walked beneath the arch, a short tunnel splitting at the sides to wrap around the building. Going left, the lanterns more sporadic beneath a theater not expecting wanderers, the two glanced at hung playbills. Names they'd never heard of dominated in splashy flavor. Like the art outside, the credits had an air of useless immortality.

"Ah, so you'll go back to the Queen that wants to kill you then?" Torny quipped after a few seconds silence, the bandit perhaps waiting for Eujo to deliver a better answer that she simply didn't have. "Or are you stuck on your original idea, rotting in a Najahn cell till someone decides to hang you?"

"We'll find another way."

"Hope's a bad plan, Eujo."

"Better than planning to fail."

Torny flinched, again fell quiet. Had Eujo delivered a personal stab with that last line?

Either way, it didn't matter. They'd reached the tunnel's end, a door marked with the Animas's smiling sigil noting backstage lay beyond. Torny tested the simple handle, found the door stuck. Barred, likely.

"Another way?" the thief asked.

The longer they slinked around the theater, the more likely someone would catch them. Eujo stepped up to the door, delivered several sharp knocks, and almost fell over:

with every touch, the Whent skar leapt up in her mind, a shout demanding Eujo let it loose.

"You okay?" Torny offered. "Don't think anyone's answering."

"Then it's safe to go in."

"Not sure I—"

Torny stopped as Eujo put her palm flat against the door. The skars were dangerous, but, if she could massage this one just the right way . . .

The door shook, at first a ratting tremor that shrank to a tight, cracking buzz right near the handle. Torny felt the skar's warmth rush through her fingers into the door's wood, trace a line to the bolt keeping the portal locked, and with a sharp snap, one that echoed more than Eujo liked down the stone hall behind them, the bolt severed. With a whine, the door creaked towards them.

"Now that's a good trick," Torny said, easing the door open further and peeking inside. "Would've been real crap if you'd brought the place down on us."

Eujo, breathing hard, like she'd been sprinting, found her voice, "It listened to me. Just enough."

"Must feel good, having someone listen to you." Torny pushed the door open. "Lucky us, I think you're right."

At first, Eujo didn't see what Torny meant. The backstage area sprawled before them, crowded with sets and hanging costumes. Trinkets and fakery lay piled here and there, some mysterious system, or none at all, used to guide their placement. Eujo followed the bandit into the room, Torny striding with purpose, and after three careful steps, Eujo saw where the bandit headed: another door, this one tucked away, a glaring, dusty purple and gold sign declaring it off limits. A true keyhole lock, moldering from black to green, topped the knob.

Eujo didn't even have time to suggest the skar again before Torny had her tools out, plying at the keyhole with a thin metal file and a thicker partner.

"Just keep watch," Torny muttered as Eujo looked over her shoulder. "This isn't anything to get worked up about."

"What?"

"The lock. It's cheap. Same kind's used all over Noctia too. And I can guess why."

Before Eujo could get Torny to elaborate, the door clicked. Beyond wasn't so much a room as a closet, only with a single chest, left open, on the floor. In it sat stacked black tablets, each one with a smiling theater mask chiseled on, then filled in with golden dye.

The souls. What else could they be?

For the first time since drinking to a stupor on the Whent sledge, both the bandit and the Queen shared an honest smile, a dishonest victory.

CHAPTER 22
WROUGHT BY FIRE

Dirt seared her mouth. Grains burned her teeth. The first and only sensation Annalyse felt as she snapped awake, the pain gradually letting in the rest of her. Arms and legs both there, flat on the ground along with her chest and head. Face down. A hard fall, going by the tangy wet smearing across her forehead, joining the sand on her lips.

The whispers in her mind.

The skars were frantic. Vis, as ever, scrabbling about spouting nonsense, her wounds itching as the God of Life sent its essence after them. Foti, still in Annalyse's left hand, raged, hunting for targets and frustrated with the black earth before them. The ruby murmured satisfaction between the thrashing too, at a task more than completed. What that was, Annalyse didn't have to remember.

The sounds, the ones not whispered in her mind, told that sotry well enough

Crackles, snaps, and screams told a story about a burning fort. Whistles, the flash-fresh kind as fletching and wood shot past her ear, said a fight was still underway.

Clashing metal confirmed it, as did Najahn barking as they ordered their troops about a battlefield. Living in Noctia had given Annalyse enough exposure to those exercises that she recognized the short, clipped commands.

The armored rulers of the Seven Isles weren't doing so well.

With a press, Annalyse brought her head up, torn and matted hair falling across her eyes as she took her first real look up the soft hill. There'd been a gate once, now only a charred ruin, one door hanging by splintered thread, the other no more than snowy ash upon the ground. Through the opening and above it, arrows flew in scattered flashes, their tiny forms catching Sichi's pink in instants. Their targets lay beyond, hidden in smoke. Annalyse watched for a long second, but heard no crossbow clips, no return fire.

Either the Najahn were already dead, or they didn't see the Vis arrows as a threat.

Annalyse pushed away the strategies, the theories. She wasn't a player in the fight, not anymore. Deshiva's orders had been to blow the gate and run, had been—

The scientist twisted, the reason for her dirt kiss flaring through an exhausted haze. There, not more than a stride or two down the hill, lay the Vis leader. The cause wasn't hard to identify, as a burning ring marked the sight, a blasted black line leading right from Annalyse to the hunter. Deshiva's long spear, the haft of which must've cracked Annalyse to the ground, lay in pieces, all but the stone point simmering.

"No," Annalyse coughed, scrambling to Deshiva's side. She planted palms in hot grass, kicked away smoldering sticks. The Vis skar protested.

And Deshiva lived. The hunter's eyes were shut, but her chest rose and fell. Her open mouth breathed when

Annalyse held her hand against it. A minor miracle, one Annalyse could credit to the Vis skar on Deshiva's bracelet.

They were both alive, then, for the moment. Annalyse slowed her own breathing, let the panic fade. The arrows weren't for her. The Najahn orders, coming faster now, louder, weren't for her. Battlefield tactics, a required subject for anyone climbing Whent's academic ladder—Rana raiders and factious warlords demanded such things—said she and Deshiva, already casualties, would be ignored till the fight's aftermath.

Which, if the Najahn triumphed, would mean dark things for them both.

Annalyse looked over Deshiva, down the long hill and its haphazard pens, burnt sheds, all the way to the jungle line. Shadows flitted. Vis hunters stopping to stretch bows and launch arrows over the burning palisade. They couldn't possibly see any Najahn target, the arrows more likely to land in the dirt, so why . . .

The second part of the plan. Cover the retreat, if necessary. Deshiva hadn't told Annalyse that, but the move made sense. Don't go for kills, but keep the Najahn back. Scare them, slow them down until Deshiva and Annalyse could get back home.

Battlefield tactics.

Deshiva hissed. Her eyes still closed. Her body too heavy for Annalyse to haul. Not without help.

Annalyse raised her head, waved an arm. Against the fire's light, she'd appear a black smear, but the Vis hunters were sharp. Hopefully they'd understand.

"Getting us help," Annalyse said to Deshiva. Who knew whether the words would penetrate, but maybe. Even if they didn't, just speaking, her rasped voice gashing the words, helped keep the scientist in her place. Focused on the plan. "The Najahn aren't coming out. We'll be fine, Deshiva."

The hunter didn't move.

Najahn voices rose again. A single word repeated. Its meaning was no mystery.

Annalyse bent down, slid her arms against Deshiva's side. Tried to ignore the heat radiating from the hunter's skin, the charred armor, and pushed. Deshiva, equipment and honed muscle, didn't budge. A second try gave no different result, save Annalyse cursing a life largely led among academic confines. A few years out in the Vis jungles, and she might've been able to—

There!

Annalyse shot her hand up again as a shadow, a hunter dashed closer. Well within bowshot and moving fast towards them. Between the two, Annalyse figured they could at least drag . . . wait. The shadow slowed, started pulling a bow over their back. Annalyse frowned, waved her arm.

"No time for that!" the scientist tried to yell, a croaking noise that might've carried to Deshiva's ears and no farther.

Well, if they weren't going to help, then Annalyse would have to do it herself. Reaching up to her necklace, Annalyse popped the Vis skar free, dropping it from trembling hands. Aches, stings, and a very, very dry throat raced to her nerves, catching her breath. They abated for a moment, the Vis skar's whispers lighting up, when Annalyse picked the teal stone off the dirt, only to return when Annalyse pressed the gem into Deshiva's scalded left hand.

Their research on Noctia had been abundantly clear on this point: skars would amplify one another, and two Vis stones together could do far more than one alone.

An arrow whistled over Annalyse's shoulder, close

enough to move her burned hair. The sound made her twitch, the one that followed made her move.

A sharp metal clank, so close as to be right on top of them. Annalyse tried to dive and more fell to her side, another breeze lighting on her skin as a voulge's curling spear stuck the space where she'd been. Wielding it, black and purple armor carrying a fire's white ash flakes, face hidden behind a metal visor, stood a Najahn soldier. Behind them, more fanned out, breaking into three-man units in rambling runs into the grass.

If the Najahn was interested in surrender, the soldier said not a word. Only drew the voulge back, this time for a free skewer. Annalyse had no shield, no weapon.

At least, not one the Najahn could see.

The Foti skar bellowed and Annalyse let it loose, the right hand she'd stuck out as a useless ward serving as a conduit. The air between the scientist and the soldier shimmered before breaking free in a sparking dazzle. Heat struck her, slammed into the soldier, throwing the skewer aside and sending the Najahn stumbling back.

But no frying flame followed, no devastating inferno, even though Annalyse willed it. The skar seemed to gasp, as if for breath, and in its struggle Annalyse felt her own exhaustion. She'd been burned, wounded, ran out, and spent her energy letting the Foti skar torch a whole outpost. Any more would mean a long rest, food, and time.

She had none of those.

The Najahn recovered their balance. They brought the voulge up, but didn't close.

"Take another step and you'll die in that armor," Annalyse said, the rasp again losing itself on the wind. "You know what happens to metal when it gets hot?"

"Know what happens to a body when a voulge strikes

home?" the soldier replied, the helmet warping the words, telling Annalyse that inside the armor waited a woman, a tired and scared one at that. "I've seen it. Your friends are seeing it right now. The curved point makes a hook. And when I pull, you come with." She settled the voulge into a two-handed grip. "Surrender, or you die like the others."

Annalyse hadn't noticed, hadn't been able to focus beyond the right then, right there, but the Najahn's threat, like a curtain pulling aside, brought in the rest of the battle, the battle that wasn't supposed to be fought. Screams still sounded, but their tone changed. Less the agony of the burned, more the sharp, short shouts of ended lives. At the Najahn's nod, Annalyse looked back, saw the shadows meeting the soldiers.

The Vis had spears and arrows, weapons able to fell most enemies, most fiends. The Najahn marching against them had bulk, had metal, and had trained for war. Chakrams, those bladed discs, slipped off backs and launched into the night, slicing into the path of fleeing or charging hunters. Even missed throws caught edges and flipped, rolled into the wrong paths. Any Vis making it passed the discs found themselves facing voulges as long as their spears, and Najahn trios working in unison to divide, trap, and destroy.

Annalyse didn't need more than a few seconds to see the direction Deshiva's band would take if the fight continued. Didn't need more than a few seconds to know the swift end she'd be facing if she did anything other than surrender.

"Put down the skar," the Najahn ordered when Annalyse turned back, shoulders slumping. "I assume there's more in that pouch?"

Annalyse nodded. Behind her, Deshiva murmured again, a pained groan.

"Then they'll buy your life. Hers too." The Najahn tapped the ground at her feet with the voulge. "Throw the skars here."

"You'll kill me when I do."

Gladdring had taught Annalyse that much: never give up your only edge.

"This isn't a negotiation." The Najahn took one step closer, shifted the voulge across her chest. The screams beyond continued. Whistles, at last, called for a retreat. "Do it, or you die and I take them anyway."

Annalyse glanced at Deshiva, the hunter's eyes closed tight, mouth in a fierce grimace. No help coming. She reached for the pouch. In death, she and Deshiva saved nobody.

In life, in life there was always a chance.

CHAPTER 23
SPEAK ACROSS WORLDS

The fiend's corpse didn't move. Hadn't in the whole time Ami had been standing there, nursing a bland mushroom tea—all the teas down here were bland. She watched as Svarde paced around his stone chair amid the temple's great room. Light filtered in from above, so far distant, leaking through the Wound all the way to this spot. Sometimes Ami would look up to the tiny gap and wonder how long it'd take, if she set one hand after another, to climb the whole way back to Catya. A day, two, three?

And how close would Ami make it before a chakram or crossbow bolt knocked her off?

"Still no connection," Svarde grumbled. "It's not all invisible. Like my foot, my finger's asleep. It's there but won't respond."

"Try harder," Ami suggested.

Svarde grunted. "This isn't something you 'try harder'. Either it works or it doesn't. I tell those bones out there to move and they do."

"Maybe you're not speaking its language."

"Oh? Care to tell me how to talk to a dead rat like this, then?"

"Have to learn that one on your own."

Ami swirled her tea. Blew away the steam. Better, at least, to have the brew hot. Kept it smooth so the tea would wash the constant dirt and dust down here off her throat. The rest of her wasn't too filthy, at least: cave streams and springs made convenient bathing and refreshing options. Jochi's army didn't even bother with latrines, a blessing keeping the army's stench to a bearable level.

On the whole, Ami had to admit the Whent did a campaign right. Jochi's supply lines ran steady, with fresh ale, food, and equipment shuttling down from the surface every day. Outposts expanded, fortified, and plotted further growth into underground cities with every passing hour. To hear Jochi tell it, messengers had already been sent to every isle advertising cheap living and protection for work. Winter's ice would slow any migration, but Ami figured more than a few gutter grubbers would take Jochi's offer.

A few generations from now, the Dark Below might just be another land to travel like all the rest, towns, inns, and industry toiling away. If, that is, the fiends didn't destroy it all.

"Look at us, Ami," Svarde said, returning to his throne and sitting on it. By Ami's eye, the chair lacked any comfort with its hard seat, stiff back, and sharp edges. Svarde, though, hadn't asked for a change. "By rights, we should both be dead. I'm a faded thing dependent on this damn sword, and you've half a face, exiled from everywhere. Not the way I expected us to go."

"If you'd called this, Svarde, I'd have drank a lot more ale."

"We had enough as it was."

Truth. That first year with Catya on the throne had been a drunken blur. Sure, the isles celebrated a new Aegis as they ought, but Ami and Svarde took it to another level, indulging their celebrity and utter lack of responsibility with one revel after another. At the time, Ami rode the accolades, woke up in a hundred different beds and remembered few of them. Svarde did the same, both often stumbling into the same Najahn cafe a mess, not meeting the other's eye as they groaned through a breakfast, a day avoiding what Catya really meant to either of them.

"She had it the worst," Ami said.

"From the start," Svarde agreed. "She always pretended to be so stoic, but you could see it. Every time we visited, you could tell she hated being stuck on that chair."

"It was worse after you left."

Svarde didn't answer that, didn't make Ami describe how Catya withdrew further and further over the years. Began enduring the entertainments instead of enjoying them. More than once, Najahn guards would have to pull Catya back from the Wound, from a step over the edge. Ami would get a message telling her to come quick, and by the time she arrived, Catya would be placid again, plied to sanity by Noctia's best drugs: ale and various plants that'd send the Aegis into a numbing happiness.

"When I saw her last, she seemed herself," Svarde said. "In her mind, at least."

"Because she gave up two years ago," Ami replied. "She told me any chance at a normal life, at a normal death, was gone. That she wanted to feel everything now until the end."

"She's strong."

"No. She's weak, just like you and me, like everyone." Ami downed her tea, made to throw the cup until she remembered there weren't an infinite number of the damn things down here. "Catya couldn't make the effort to change her life and so she's going to die on that chair. We haven't been able to save her either, and the rest of the isles aren't even trying."

Svarde eyed Ami. "Your more dire than usual today."

"Have a reason I shouldn't be? Don't know if you've looked around, Svarde, but we're stuck underground, surrounded by a bunch of fiends and corpses—"

"You're forgetting Jochi."

"The warlord? Even if he finds a way to close those gates, he'll just take over. Pave the way for his empire."

"My empire?"

The Whent warlord, flanked by the man's ever-present bodyguards in their hulking leathers and seemingly endless beards, stood in the temple's entry. The warlord had his hands clasped, a patient smile. Neither guard matched his expression, giving a better hint to the man's real mood.

"A worry for another time," Svarde said, knowing enough not to give Ami a warning look.

She could be nice. For a minute or two.

"Good, because I have a worry for now." Jochi stepped into the room, gave Ami a nod. "Our friends continue to fortify themselves, but they've had a setback. A large fiend emerged. A thing I'm glad we did not need to face, and that caused enough damage that I believe we have an opening." The clasped hands released, opened with their palms to Svarde. "With your bodies and my soldiers, a strong offense now might be enough to drive the burning fiends back. Maybe destroy them."

"Back to where?" Ami asked. "The water?"

"Their home. Those gates."

The whirling storm, the quaking earth, swimming seas. A collapsing world.

"Do we know if they can go back?" Ami didn't expect an answer and received none, only a furrowed brow from Jochi and a slight grin from Svarde. The barbarian had found a new patience in his weird death-life, one Ami might investigate later. "Do we know why they're coming here at all?"

At Jochi's continued confusion, Ami relayed what she'd seen. The obvious conclusion, that the fiends were fleeing a shattered home, was met with a shrug by the Whent warlord.

"What matters is that they're here, and they're fighting us," Jochi said. "We need to destroy them."

"Or," Svarde suggested.

"Or what, negotiate?" Jochi laughed. "Try to talk them into peace?"

"The Dead King says they've been down here for centuries, fighting all the while. These fiends aren't animals. They might be as exhausted as we are. If we can find a way past this, if we can—"

"Welcome them into our home? Burning monsters?" Jochi set his face into a mask, looked at both Ami and Svarde as he spoke. "Even if, even if they find some way to an agreement, how could they live among us? Where would they go? Which isle would give up land to them?"

Ami sniffed, "Foti would welcome them. Bet that heat could go a long way towards keeping the forges hot."

"It wouldn't be without challenges, but we would save lives," Svarde added.

"A barbarian and a Guardian, suggesting peace?" Jochi spoke, then stopped. "I'm waiting for you to say this is a joke, but you're not." A deep breath. "We can't afford to fight down here. If you want to try to talk to these damned creatures, then do so. I won't stop you. But when they decide to roast you on a spit, I won't save you either."

Ami spent the tunnel walk heading towards the fiends, with Svarde and the Dead King walking by her side, wondering why she'd done the dumb thing and traded her blade for her mouth. Aside from Svarde's sword, they didn't even have any weapons. Didn't have a plan either except to try.

When she'd told Sawi, the Vis had laughed just like Jochi, wished Ami good luck. Sawi said she was spending more time with the scouts, trying to find the best path back towards her jungle isle through the tunnels. Ami wanted to call Sawi a coward when the Vis spoke, but instead she'd told Sawi to do it, to get out while she still could.

The tunnel's ending, its wide opening loomed like a dawning sun. Blasted metal of a make-up Ami didn't know hung around the edges, drilled into the rock to form a grate, supports for the ceiling and plates for the ground. Easier, maybe, to move those constructs. No lanterns, no torches save for the one the Dead King carried. Unnecessary for the burning fiends. The heat rose, sweat already drenching Ami, though she noticed neither Svarde nor the Dead King dripped.

Death's perk.

"Let me lead," Svarde said when only a few strides remained. "They know me. They'll respect me."

"Or they'll kill you on sight." Ami put a hand on Svarde's left arm. "I'm the one who should go first. They've never seen me before. I'm neutral."

"You're the only one of us who can die."

"That means I have stakes."

Svarde's frown said he didn't buy that argument, but

Ami didn't wait. Moving faster, keeping her hands from touching the scalding metal on all sides, Ami went to the tunnel's edge. Looked out, and shaded her eyes.

As the sheer brightness faded, Jochi's news of devastation proved an undersell. The odd iron homes the fiends had built along the chamber's banks lay in ruins, bars bent or outright shattered. The monstrous constructs had abandoned the tunnel, aiming their ballistae and fire-gouting turrets towards the pool, towards the bigger threat. Cold, ash white bodies lay in clumps while other fiends hacked at the gravel sides, trying to dig holes in ground too hard for it. Still more huddled around makeshift forges, heating and shaping new metal to replace the damaged old.

A frantic pulse underlined the heat-blurred motion.

Yet one stood as Ami approached, a larger fiend stood on the jutting cliff, holding a flail in one of its four arms. A damaged coat of chains cloaked its chest and legs. Nothing crowned its obsidian skull, the triangle shape seeming to float on an endless flame. The monster raised the flail as if to strike, then must've noticed Ami's outstretched and empty arms, her lack of a following army.

Instead, the creature faced Ami square, though it stood near double her height. The black stone began to spark, and Ami realized she had no idea what to say.

CHAPTER 24

ALES AND ALLIANCES

The Najahn prisons held several key advantages over Yarvick's bandit hideout: warmth and a reasonable bed being the first two, sanitation being a key third. While Gladdring figured the Nimble Fingers used the ocean as their personal toilet, like everyone on every isle, showers and laundry options seemed nonexistent. The smell permeating the cave network on the city's southern end dominated Gladdring's exhausted perception as he arrived, guided at first by Yarvick and then, after the bandit lord disappeared, several underlings through side alleys, further caves, and warehouses with trap doors to wind up here.

"Sleep," said the thin thief who dropped Gladdring off at some damp straw well away from the cave's simmering fires. "You won't get much."

Dreams came faster than Gladdring would've expected, owed, he supposed later, to the night's long and dire adventures and the bandit cave's odd quiet. The latter mystery resolved itself with a shaking wake-up, sometime near mid-morning. Gladdring and his ragged robes rolled off the straw with a bleary shake to find all the empty alcoves housing sleeping thieves.

Of course, an industry best done in the dark would have early morning as its most active hours.

Not Gladdring, though. While Yarvick himself didn't present a mission or drip any clues as to his ultimate objective, lackeys took the lord's place and tasked Gladdring with a simple start to his new puppet life: sit, drink, and call in debts.

The Tenet found himself guided to an old favorite restaurant well within the Ringed City's upper-crust quarters. High on the cliffs and flaunting winter's cold with well-shoveled streets, bright flags with house emblems, and the constant clatter of deliveries making rounds, the whirlwind shift from Yarvick's squalid camp, and only some few hours distant from a dip in the icy seas, put Gladdring in a blended, surreal miasma.

If someone were to tell him, now, that this was the true dream, Gladdring would not have argued.

Instead, the restaurant honored his appearance and request, helpfully submitted on his behalf by Yarvick's assigned bandit bodyguard, a weathered woman with a Rana's sharp tongue, to take over a back room normally reserved for special, small parties. Most Noctia restaurants in this wealthy level had similar spaces where secrets could be shared, privacy protected.

Never before had Gladdring used one to undermine the very force ruling the city.

Yet, with fresh coffee and an omelette steaming before him, Gladdring found himself recounting who owed him what and how much to the bodyguard, who asked here and there for a repeat, but otherwise wrote nothing down. When he finished, the bandit let slip a slight grin.

"Think that ought to be enough for one day," she said. "I'll get you another coffee."

He'd only taken a sip, and was about to ask what she meant by 'one day', when the bandit left the room. The door out didn't have a lock, but Gladdring didn't try to rise. The chair had a nice cushion, and Yarvick had ordered new robes, a fresh shave for the former Tenet that had Gladdring feeling some measure of his prior self. The Tamas skar—the Rana one had been gone when Gladdring awoke—added its own warmth, its ready whispers.

The game, so the bandit said upon her return some minutes later, well after Gladdring had cleared the omelette and started in on his second coffee mug, was simple: Gladdring would call in those debts, and when each person bent to his command, Gladdring would offer up a simple plan: when Fassle fell, their towers, their businesses, their families would pledge loyalty to him.

"That's too brazen to work," Gladdring said when the bandit finished. "Nobody talks that openly about treason."

"You do, now."

Gladdring squinted at the bandit, trying to decide if she was too inexperienced in the ways of power politics, or had some other reason to believe Gladdring could get away with declaring the Circle's end. The Tamas skar whispered only confidence on her part, suggesting the latter.

"Yarvick believes it'll be that easy?" Gladdring asked.

"Not belief. Fact. Fassle's time is coming to a swift end. You will ensure you're ready to take his place."

"If Yarvick could topple Fassle so easily, why wait till now?"

Again the bandit's grin, "Not my place to say. Yours to learn, I'd expect, if you don't muck this up."

Mucking up would've been hard. The bandit's prior

absence must've been to send runners throughout the city, gathering up Gladdring's debtors like the Najahn found would-be soldiers. Each one, from industry captains to Najahn scholars, ambassadors, and admirals found themselves across from Gladdring. Most looked at Gladdring like he was a ghost returned to life, a mystery clarified when one mentioned Fassle himself had proclaimed Gladdring's unfortunate demise.

Gladdring treated the surprise as anyone ought to: a tool.

Shock and subtle manipulation, courtesy of the Tamas skar, turned skeptics into subdued subordinates, each one accepting Gladdring's commandment with a mixture of doubt and relief. If Gladdring wondered about Fassle's support throughout the Najahn, the day's meetings confirmed the Circle's leader was overstepping his bounds. Most Najahn came from isles beyond Noctia, and hearing their supposed leader declare an effective occupation of their homes damaged once pristine loyalties.

Fassle might think rounding up all the skars, ending the Renewals, would help stem the fiend tide, but the move seemed to be eroding Najahn support instead. More than one volunteered they would've left already were it not winter, were the isles without any other means of defeating large fiend attacks.

Through each and every meeting, too, Gladdring noticed the bandit watching him. She never moved, didn't smile, cough, or offer any commentary. Only opened the door to let one cowed form out and escort the next one in.

Yarvick didn't trust his puppet. Not all the way.

Gladdring wouldn't either.

By day's end, reached with more coffee than Gladdring cared to contemplate, the former Tenet's head pulsed with a sharp ache, his throat ran dry from all the talking, and he'd started pacing around the table to nudge some life into stiff muscles. When the bandit announced the end to the parade, Gladdring could only nod, mutter an ask about what came next.

"That's up to you," the bandit said. "You did well today, based on what Yarvick told me to look for. Because you did, you get a treat."

Gladdring sent a skeptical eye her way, "A treat?"

"Pick a place. This one works, but I bet you've seen enough of the food here to last a day. A tavern. We'll go. Drinks on me till you get sloppy, then we go back to the caves. Do it again tomorrow till your list's done."

"That's my fate?"

The bandit folded her arms. "Hardly a fate to be complaining about. Sitting here, eating, drinking, blabbing all day long. You've a life of luxury."

"With a knife at my throat."

"How're we any different? I make one wrong step and it's a Najahn cell or a fiend's claw. Make your choice. If I've got to babysit you, I'd rather do it with a pint in my hand."

Any Ringed City resident assembled their own list of establishments according to their moral code. You could visit only the cleanest spots, the ones that hid the filth in the back and offered up a bright, fancy bliss to soak yourself in. The middle pack, restaurants and pubs that paid attention to their food, were dominated by those just getting up the ladder and wanting to prove it to themselves, their partners, their parents.

Gladdring preferred the bottom, the places that hid nothing and charged only a little more. His bandit escort slapped down some loose jewelry on the counter and they had ale, dark and fresh, before them in a moment. *Anchor's*

Rest, despite the name, wasn't close to the port. Instead it catered to the seafarers who'd given up the trade for the desk but didn't want to lose the spirit. Literal anchors hung about the place, used as stands for tables, lanterns, and seats. Everything on offer came via import, and all the drinks from Tamas.

The bandit didn't use the booze as an excuse to talk. She brushed off Gladdring's attempts to chat, leaving him to listen to a lonely strummer peel off mournful sailing tunes over muttered conversations. More subdued than usual.

Fassle's proclamation, or just seasonal slowness?

Either way, Gladdring let the bandit ply them both with rounds. She drained every mug, wanting to match Gladdring, who must've been three times her size. A bold play, and one that wound up with Gladdring, not the bandit, leading the pair outside.

Nearing midnight, a clear sky letting Sichi drown the city in pink. Gladdring let the cold shake off the drink's fuzz, the bandit leaning on his shoulder, muttering something about how Yarvick would be so peeved they'd both stayed out so late.

"Don't worry, he won't mind," Gladdring said, then steered the bandit onto a nearby barrel. He turned the thief so her head could rest on another, the stacked empties waiting for a ship to bring them home. "I'll be right back. Need to take care of myself before we walk."

The bandit might've replied, but any words vanished as her head buried itself against her arm. The Tamas skar whispered its greasy confirmation that the thief wasn't faking. Good thing, as when Gladdring turned down the alley alongside the *Anchor's Rest,* two people were waiting.

"You received my message," Gladdring stated flat to the clear-eyed Queen of Kance. Beside her, looking no less confused, was a burly Vis hunter, a man Gladdring had never met till right that moment. "As I'm still alive, I assume you agree?"

The Queen glanced at the Vis. "He tells me you held him captive in a cage. That you ran experiments on him."

"I would have killed the Queen tonight," the Vis said, discarding the Queen's comments, "for what she tried to do to my brother and our friends. Would have, except your warning promised something more important. So talk, and save her life."

The Vis's scowl matched his hard eyes. Gladdring doused them both with a smile.

"Those experiments will save the isles. More important than your useless revenge. Annalyse spoke highly of you, and I hope she was right." Gladdring gave the Vis a nod, then turned to the Queen. "Your royal squabbles are equally pointless in the face of what we can do together. Call off your hounds, if they still hunt." He clasped his hands before him. "Fassle is going to fall. We need to make sure I take his place. The alternative, I assure you, is far, far worse."

When neither one made a move to flee, to call for the guards, or gut Gladdring like a fish, the revolution truly began.

CHAPTER 25
EXIT STAGE LEFT

Victory spawned momentum. Slipping away from the Animas with souls in hand, out into a later yet more buzzy encampment, Torny and Eujo kept success off their faces with spoken lines. The two dished nonsense back and forth, delivering memorized quips whenever someone wandered close. An unnecessary precaution? Perhaps, but neither the current thief nor the former one wanted to risk anything.

Not now, not with escape so close.

Sichi's high location meant time ticked closer to midnight, the tenor changing from one of frivolity to drunken antics, as attendees from far away and relieved actors took to ales, to herbs, to each other to indulge a day well done. Impromptu songs trailed their walk, cheers and happy chatter bouncing between groups dressed from costumes to florid, thick coats. The whole scene had such a delighted air that Eujo almost doubted their reasons for running.

If Eujo stayed, she could have a few flagons and maybe catch some of this same fun.

If Eujo stayed, she'd find a dagger between her ribs or a poisoned drop in her drink.

Easy enough to ignore the blissful idiots, then.

Returning to their barracked tent, Eujo and Torny pushed through the flap to find the place nearly empty. Dinner tables cleaned off and abandoned, none of the slim cots occupied. A night to one's self was not an option, apparently, save for Wax and Bliss. The siblings didn't even notice the arrivals at first, Wax deep in a rambling scene, his character boasting about some amazing achievement. Eujo recognized it: she'd be entering in another minute, ready to cut Wax's character down to proper size.

Might as well play the part.

"I see you're ready to go," Eujo said, both direct and without the force she'd normally add. Keeping plans quiet had to be the game, here.

'Did you get the souls?' Bliss flashed back fast as Wax broke off his speech. From the hope in the Vis girl's eyes, she didn't share her brother's passion for the stage. 'Please say yes. His accent is terrible.'

"Hey," Wax protested, swapping to a whistle when Torny opened her own coat, revealed the four tablets stuffed inside. "Nice work."

"Told you, I'm good at this," Torny said, heading towards her cot and the pack leaning against it. "Let's move. There's a big enough party out there they won't even notice us leaving."

Reminded purpose shoved the foursome into quick action. Wax and Bliss hadn't been useless while Eujo and Torny were off pilfering the passes: they'd filled water skins, sneaked away snacks into the packs. Spare clothes, courtesy of their costumes, stuffed into the remaining space. Seeing the frilly absurdities panged a wish in the

Kance Queen for her better adventuring outfits, most waiting for her on the Storm's Edge, wherever Deux had the ship these days.

Would he return to Kance, give up the game if Eujo couldn't get word to him soon?

Another worry to cast aside. She couldn't do anything about it now.

They left after a few minutes, Wax leading the way from the tent. With the packs looped over their shoulders, the party didn't look ready for the revel, and looks found them fast. Curious stares put doubt right into the plan, dismantling the idea they'd slink away unnoticed within a few seconds. A passing trading cart, pulled by two shaggy Tamas ponies, even slowed as its driver gave the crew a long look.

"Well this was stupid," Torny said, as Wax started for the huge camp's southern edge. "Daklin's going to be on us before we get past this tent."

An exaggeration, but not by much. Time for something different, an idea inspired by those clopping ponies.

"Drop the packs," Eujo said. "Now."

"But—" Wax started only for Eujo to hiss the repeated command. "Fine."

Four packs hit the floor, Torny forcing a laugh into the air. "Told you these'd be too heavy to wear onstage, Wax. You moron."

Throwing her arms up, shaking her head, Torny turned towards Eujo, fingers flashing. 'Tell me you have a better idea.'

"Think it's time to celebrate that bad idea with a better drink," Eujo said, while her hands spoke something different. 'We distract. You and Bliss get a cart.'

Torny's head slanted while Wax dashed off for flagons.

Ale barrels and piled cups lay everywhere, ensuring no matter where you might step, inebriation was at hand. While he went, Torny, Eujo, and Bliss dashed off a plan in finger snaps, one Eujo hated, even though it was her own idea.

These people wanted a show, might as well give them one.

Wax returned with four filled mugs to find only Eujo standing around the packs. Despite the strange start, no real action bored the makeshift audience, who'd returned to their groups, their rehearsing, singing, and all the things one might do when they weren't trying for a desperate getaway.

"So what's the plan now?" Wax said. "Drink these? Act like idiots?"

"That'd be too easy for you."

"Ouch."

Eujo just smiled at him, "No, here's the real plan. We start our scene. Just like rehearsal, only better. Act like you mean it."

"Like I mean it? I'm never faking, Eujo. Never." Wax took the first flagon, gulped down the contents. Offered the second to Eujo, who did the same. "You know the scene. Ready?"

The ale took on a different taste, spiced with anticipation, with urgency, with dread of doing something she'd never imagined and the belief, the sheer damn certainty, she'd do it well. Eujo was a Kance Queen. She'd risen from the gutters to the throne room and would go farther still. She'd save the isles, she'd—

"Give me the other one," Eujo said, grabbing the third and downing it. Wax laughed, emptied the fourth and wiped some splatter down his chin. "Okay, now I'm ready."

Despite her declaration, few wandering eyes found the pair and their satchels. Instruments continued to spar with conversation, song, and happy shouts over the chill night. Enough to make Eujo wonder if she and Wax even needed to draw attention. Maybe they could slink away with a cart without needing to . . .

"Ah hah!" Wax announced, stepping back from Eujo, wide eyes, open mouth, and waving arms doing everything to destroy Eujo's stealthy dreams. "I've found you alone at last." Wax pantomimed a look around, holding a hand up over his eyes. "No servants about, no listening ears waiting to catch us?"

Eujo fumbled for the line. Remember the place, the plot, the point. A few curious folks turned their way, and their stares drove her right into the words.

"Not this time," Eujo said. "They've been misled. They think I'm preparing for the wedding."

"Ah, clever as ever."

"If only you were as well."

Wax tilted his head, put a hand to his chin. The Vis really did commit, throwing his every verve into the motions. Eujo fought off a blush, found an iron frown instead.

"Whatever do you mean? Isn't this what you wanted?" Wax asked. "This is it, where we decide the plot to put us in power!"

"Us? Oh, my dear, I think you've let hope go to your head again." Eujo began a slow walk around Wax, shaking her head towards the growing audience all the while. The looks heading back her way were mostly confused, not surprising given they'd started in the play's middle. "I'll have the power, and you get the pleasure of waiting on me."

Wax flashed a grump scowl for a moment, then

shrugged, smiled. "There are worse fates! So how should we do it? Poison? A bump on the head? A knife between the ribs?"

"All too obvious."

Eujo again looked towards their audience. Rolled her eyes. Earned a few chuckles. She tried to see beyond, find where Torny and Bliss would be coming with the cart to save her from this nonsense and saw a shape drifting by in the back. Someone shouted, but their audience didn't pay much attention.

"Instead," Eujo said, putting a hand on Wax's shoulder and spinning him to face her, "I think we ought to go with an accident. A little shove out a little window."

"What window? And when?"

Summoning up a power-hungry grin didn't take much. That, at least, Eujo had done aplenty in the Kance throne room, one of the first lessons delivered after her ascension. Always make traders, visitors from other isles think you would do anything to get, to keep your position and its benefits. Nevertheless, their lines would be drawing to a close soon.

"Have you ever worn a dress?" Eujo asked, to more chuckles.

"A dress? I—"

"Because I have just the one, and I think you'll look great in white."

Wax dropped his jaw. The crowd chuckled. Eujo let her manic smile slip at the soft patter of approaching hooves on the dirt. Rolling cart wheels. She risked a glance, saw exactly what she hoped for. Time to close this one off with some improvising.

"Now, time to get back. We both have some dressing to do," Eujo said.

Another few seconds. The cart, two ponies, and the two Guardians driving it, coming in fast. Eujo needed to hold the crowd, keep them from getting in the cart's way, from wondering.

"It'll all work out," Eujo said, then leaned in, gave a bewildered Wax a sudden smooch.

The move came as instinct, and it earned more laughs, covered the approaching cart as Torny and Bliss rambled near. Some cursed as the cart pushed them aside, a few more wondered questions as Torny and Bliss jumped off, grabbed the packs and threw them in the cart's back, but those pieces blurred against the kiss. Against Wax's return, the Vis not shying away, him holding the moment. Just as his character ought to, just as the scene demanded.

"Let's go!" Torny snapped, pushing Eujo and Wax apart. "If they see you, you're both dead!"

A line. Her line. The play. Eujo, the blush harder to fight off this time, spun on her worn boot heel and dove into the cart. Wax pulled himself up afterward, and Bliss cracked the reins. The crowd clapped, a few dozen hands, and ones quickly overwhelmed by angrier calls. As the cart rumbled forward, some ragtag merchant more in night clothes than not, came barging through, knocking costumed, drunken revelers to the side. The man pointed, shouted for help. The cart rolled on.

Eujo waved. Wax laughed.

"Amazing," Wax said as Bliss picked up their pace, breaking for the camp's edge. "Never knew you had it in you, Eujo."

"I'm the best actress you'll ever see, Wax. Just need a couple ales in me first."

This time they both laughed, Sichi's pink light washing down from above as the cart rolled along. Up front, Torny pointed out hazards, Bliss steered, and the chill seemed plenty distant. They had the Tamas souls, they'd dodged the play and the assassins that'd come with it. Now all they needed was the skar, and then . . . Eujo's elation died a quick death. Wax had settled into the satchels, still grinning. He even put a finger to his lips, glanced Eujo's way, lifted an eyebrow.

The Vis didn't have a Kance skar. But he didn't need it. She had one. Eujo could be the next Aegis.

She couldn't go home. Not now, not again.

CHAPTER 26
WHAT BLOOD BRINGS

The Whent Pits had a smell all their own: blood, sweat, and beer all coming together to create a stench best conquered by the same ale that made it. Annalyse had endured that particular blend once before, on what her father intended to make an annual trip. A vacation of sorts. That plan ended when Annalyse found the weapons, the fighting, the fiends a little too fascinating.

The bodies before her, the Najahn around her, smelled much the same, but Annalyse was only disgusted, defeated, drained. Fascination had no place in a suddenly brutal world.

They'd set her, hands tied, on a log to watch. The entertainment, the grim business, happened in chunks, as Najahn pairs and trios, most no longer wearing the bulky armor, dragged one body after the next into the roaring bonfire. A countdown, a toss, and another Vis vanished into the flames.

Annalyse hadn't bothered to start counting.

As she understood it, in the dim hours since the battle wound down and the clean-up began, the Vis hunters had lost their cohesion when Deshiva fell. Some tried to attack the Najahn, others broke to run, and still more did neither, waiting for a signal that never came. Crossbows and chakrams took their brutal toll on any hunter that left the trees for a better look, a clearer shot.

The Najahn didn't bother with prisoners, not that Annalyse saw.

Save her and Deshiva, the ones that could be useful. The ones that begged for their lives with a little bit of knowledge. Well, Annalyse had, anyway. Deshiva had mostly glared, cursed, and spat while the Najahn shoved her in a makeshift room and locked the door.

The scientist, though, could use the skars. That made her valuable.

Veritrus, the Najahn commander and bearing the absurd formal names Noctia's upper crust liked to lay upon their children like regal cloaks, sat on the log next to Annalyse. Barely room for two, the man bumped her, jangling the metal cuffs holding her hands together before her. He handed over a simple stone cup.

"Water, nothing else," Veritrus said. Narrow-faced and severe, the voice had all of logic's strength and no compassion. "Drink it."

She did. Deshiva had chosen defiance and look what it'd earned her?

"Will they come back?" Veritrus asked.

"I already told you what I know."

To a degree, anyway. That she could use the skars, yes. That Deshiva and the Vis had essentially forced her to help them. That Annalyse, a Whent, held no loyalty to Vis and would be happy to work with the Najahn instead. It'd earned her the log, the water, and zero beatings.

She wasn't on the pyre either.

"So you say," Veritrus replied, "but subterfuge is not your game, Annalyse. Your eyes flinch away when you approach a lie. Your hands tremble. You put more effort into your voice when you talk, as if by trying you can perhaps force the truth. Relax, and speak. You're safe here."

"What a thing to say." Annalyse nodded at the pyre. "I thought the Najahn were above brutality."

"And I thought the isles were too, yet here we are. Attacked by fiends every day, and now by Vis hunters at night. We protect these people and they raise their hands against us. Why?"

"Ask the Circle."

Veritrus nodded. They both stared at the flames. Two Najahn tossed another body on top. Nobody cheered. Nobody sang. Nothing like a Whent victory.

"Fassle's decision pits us against the fiends in a direct war," Veritrus said. "Not Vis. Not these jungle hunters. They could have listened, and lived."

Annalyse could've countered that, but stopped herself. When Quik had helped her get on the boat to Vis, he'd advised lying low. Keeping herself unnoticed while continuing her research. Puzzle out the skars and their mysteries at Svarde's abandoned cabin. She could still do that, now. Get out of this messy war and use her talents as she wanted to.

Problem was, she'd need to get her skars back for that.

"Deshiva's the one you want to talk to," Annalyse said. "You want to change their minds, you'll need her help."

"The one who spat on my face?" Veritrus smiled, thin and small. Unused to it. "Doesn't seem likely."

"That's not my problem."

A sharp glance. That smile died fast. "It is absolutely your problem, rockbiter. She came with you, and even if you were a hostage as you claim, you destroyed my gate and burned half my outpost. You owe a debt."

"You took my skars. Give them back, I'll show you how to use your own as payment."

"What satisfies the debt is mine to decide." Veritrus reached over, plucked the water cup from her hands. "You can start tonight. We have wounded, and you will teach them how to heal with the Vis skars. Do that, and we can see how else you can repay us for your actions."

Veritrus didn't give Annalyse a choice. As he finished speaking, the man raised a hand and two heavy grips landed on Annalyse's shoulders. Orders came after, stern, direct, and without question.

At least, where they took her, Annalyse couldn't see, couldn't smell the pyre anymore.

Breakfast came late, came slim, and Annalyse ate it outside. A cool and cloudy morning, misting with what would've been snow back home. Nevertheless, the fruit and fresh meat from some jungle game helped banish the bad memories of the night before. She'd spent several hours going from one wounded Najahn to the next, helping them clasp the skars, to accept the Vis whispers. Not a one had died.

Not a single Vis received the same mercy.

At least the chains were gone. Apparently Veritrus didn't think Annalyse likely to run off or take a knife to one of his soldiers, an assessment Annalyse agreed with. Eating, drinking without the cuffs weighing her down was a magical experience. A short torture it'd been, but long enough.

"We've had a visitor," Veritrus announced. He'd ditched his armor for clean robes, the man's face no longer holding a day's grime, a battle's grit. He stood while Annalyse sat, studying her with hands by his sides. "One that would have killed you already if I hadn't forbidden it."

Annalyse's enemy list ran short. Nobody on Whent cared enough to see her dead, despite some possible jealousies at her inventive prowess. Nobody on Vis knew her, save Deshiva, still locked away. Which left Noctia, and in particular, a skar-stealing assassin.

"Where are they?" Annalyse asked. "They have some skars of mine I would like back."

Veritrus laughed, genuine, so Annalyse believed, "You want to speak with them? Really? Either you're braver than I took you for, or just as oblivious."

"I'm determined."

"Foolish, more like." Veritrus tapped his left hand against his thigh, the robes shifting. "Do you know why my soldiers fought instead of running, after you destroyed our gate?"

"Because running's hard in all that armor?"

A sigh. "Because we believe, Annalyse. We believe in the Najahn cause. In our duty to defend the isles. Even if the Vis throw every man, woman, and child in their jungle cities at us, we will stay, and we will defend, because we are right." His hand rose, pointed at her. "The person who asked to take your life says that you don't believe that."

"You can lose a war in more than one way, Veritrus."

The captain nodded, understood. "Then help me again. Convince Deshiva to assist us, to make peace."

"What can you offer?"

"Lives."

THE ASSASSIN WRIGGLED. Spat both a curse and a wet line across Veritrus's boots. Shorn of his cowl, his Third Hand robes, the thin man seemed less threatening than a street pickpocket. Annalyse didn't look as two soldiers held him fast, Deshiva herself wielding her old spear. With a single thrust, the deed was done. Blood for blood, and Veritrus quick to give up the killer in his own midst.

"Here," Veritrus said, turning to Annalyse, not a feeling on his face. "These are yours, I take it?"

Three black stones. The Noctia skars. Warm and whispering their odd, nonsense poems when they landed in Annalyse's hands. Death takers, or so Ami had called them. Imperfect ones, from what Annalyse had seen: the animals they'd tested, inflicted a mortal wound with the skars attached seemed divorced from their instincts, wandering around a world they no longer inhabited.

"You're not taking them?" Annalyse asked.

"There are some stones I plan to use. Vis, foremost among them. The Goddess of Death does not need a place among my soldiers."

"But they have power—"

Veritrus closed Annalyse's hand over the stones. "As you said, there is more than one way to lose a war." He looked at Deshiva. "Satisfied?"

"Hardly." The hunter strode up to Veritrus, planted her bloody spear in the ground. "But I don't need more bodies. Not dead ones. Get going."

"Not much for patience, are you?"

"When I'm hunting something, I take all the time I need. When I'm kicking Najahn off my isle, I want it done fast."

"As you will." Veritrus eyed Annalyse. "I hope you understand the terms must be held. Otherwise Fassle will not be content, and everyone on your isle will die, one by one, until you surrender."

Annalyse expected Deshiva to offer up a counter, some brave threat, but the hunt master only scowled. An admission of truth, and perhaps, of Deshiva's willingness to honor the pact they'd made that same morning.

Equally truthful, obvious first to Veritrus and later to both Annalyse and Deshiva, was that the Najahn had nowhere to stay. The Foti skar's blaze had decimated grain stores, barracks, and the outpost walls, rendering the settlement an easy target for fiends and Vis assaults alike. Belief in the Najahn mission or no, the soldiers had to leave or find themselves joining the bodies in the pits.

Veritrus had known all that and still pressed for concessions, ones he earned at a voulge's edge.

The Vis skars would flow to the Najahn, and Annalyse would ensure it. In turn, Veritrus would guarantee her research, her safety from the Third Hand. Peace, independence, and a chance at saving the isles, all rolled into one.

So perfect, but as Annalyse watched the Najahn column march north, with Deshiva's whistled calls for her hunters to clean out the leftover loot, peace was far from her mind. The Noctia skars and their hungry whispers, growing louder with every passing hour, pushed that hope far away.

CHAPTER 27

HOPE'S BARGAIN

What do you say to a scorching demon?

Technically, Ami kept her mouth shut. Technically, she let the fiends talk for themselves, by pointing past the monster and its flail to the disaster behind it, the flimsy ruins scattered about the rocky chamber. Damaged, destroyed, dampened spirits seemed obvious, so obvious Ami wasn't sure how she'd missed it earlier when spying from Jochi's cave.

These burning beasts might be dangerous, sure, but they didn't look like marauders from here.

Her counterpart, a long several strides away and still just about burning Ami's breath with its proximity, didn't follow Ami's gesture. Or, at least, it didn't turn. Did they need to, to see? To hear? Did these things even operate on the concepts Ami was considering, the ideas of running, making war, invading a new home?

"Give it a chance," came a call behind her, a woman Ami hadn't met much, who struck the Guardian as a bit lost. Maena, the Rana captain. "They'll understand you. Watch the flashes."

As if Maena's advice proved a lost key, the obsidian triangle capping the fiend's burning body sparked up. A popping blue line rippled along the edges, snapping towards the center at random, until one jolt caught. The indigo flame formed a circle as big around as Ami's hand. On the triangle's opposite side, an orange burn lit, jumped, made a similar circle. The two shapes sat near another for one smoldering second before the orange one flickered, the circle fracturing upon itself. Sparks shot free. Just as the shape seemed to disappear into a single fiery gout, another line lashed out, snaking into the dark obsidian several times before finding the blue circle.

Ami had learned bar games tougher to parse than that. She nodded. Touched her head. And then what? Her heart? Would the fiends even know what that meant?

Ferrites. Think back to those. When Svarde had first found Kivi, the rock lizard had been as young and untamed as any wild creature. The barbarian, with Ami helping along as they, with Catya, ventured from isle to isle, taught with patience, with hands and encouraging tones until Kivi understood.

So Ami knelt, touched the dirty stone at her feet. Grabbed some of the dirt and held it towards the fiend. Sure, if the monster tried to touch her, Ami would roast, but if it understood . . .

For a moment, only the indigo circle remained on the obsidian as the fiend regarded her.

"We can share," Ami said. "Together."

The fiend watched for another long moment. The indigo fire faded. It bent to a single massive knee, scraped its right mid-arm against the rock cliff, throwing up sparks. Held the charred dust out towards Ami.

The obsidian flashed once, gold, bright.

. . .

"As introductions go, that was magnificent," Jochi said back in the dead city's temple.

The warlord paced while Svarde sat in the massive throne. The Dead King stood off the side in his armor, showing no sign of offense at Svarde's usurpation. Ami, arms and face salved with cooling lotions made by Whent physicians, leaned against the wall near the entry. While Jochi and Svarde plumbed Ami's fiend conversation for clues, the gold-plated Guardian marveled at the moment. Maena sat on the floor, sharpening a crude knife taken from some old corpse.

She'd had a real conversation with a fiend. A short one, sure, one broken off after the flash by Ami's realization her clothes were starting to sizzle. She'd begged off, the band retreating. No weapons drawn, no strikes fired. A door cracked open.

"Ami, I know we've said this already, but you did well," Svarde said, his formal tone making Ami twitch.

She preferred him more as a reckless warrior than a king, but fate loved to play jokes.

"Don't need the compliments. I'd prefer a plan."

"Oh, that's obvious," Jochi replied, the man's bearded grin doing everything it could to make Ami doubt the words that'd follow. "We send a delegation to Noctia. Explain what's happening. Meanwhile, we keep these fiends here. Help them set up camp right where they are."

"Around the pool?" Svarde asked.

"Where they'll do the killing," Maena added, ending with a sharp ting as she rang the knife along a whetstone. "Right, Jochi?"

"The Rana has it, loath as I am to give credit to a

river rotter," Jochi said. "The fiends are our new Aegis. They'll hold the wall against any new monsters because they'll have to. We'll provide any provisions they need, of course. Weapons, what have you, but otherwise, we get the best result: enemies killing enemies."

"They're not our enemies," Ami said.

Maena laughed, "You didn't see what they did to that Whent city. Burnt half of it to the ground. Nearly killed Svarde and I. They didn't come in peace, Foti. They came to take."

"Because their own world is dying!"

Maena jumped to her feet, pointed the knife at Ami. "Ours is too, if you haven't noticed? Monsters everywhere. The isles at each other's throats, all because the fiends won't stop coming. Jochi's right. This is the answer. Make'em fight each other till their homes collapse. Problem solved."

"Cruel."

Jochi shook his head once. "Ami, I'm disappointed. I would've thought you would know real cruelty. We could drive these fiends back to the water. We're giving them a chance."

Ami narrowed her eyes at the man, visions of swift decapitations running through her mind, then looked to Svarde. "What do you think, Svarde? You think forcing these fiends to fight for us is the right move?"

Svarde turned to both Jochi and Maena, one after the other, and nodded out of the temple. "Give us a minute. There's words need sharing you don't need to hear."

That the warlord and Rana captain didn't fight Svarde's order said more about the barbarian's power than anything Ami had seen so far. Apparently staving off death and having battle-broken corpses at your beck and call could get you far in life.

Far enough to forget where you started.

"You want to go back and offer them what, Ami?" Svarde asked. "Ale? A patch of land on Whent?"

"There's plenty of caves down here that aren't—"

"They'll start with what we give them, then take the rest. You've seen their machines. Better than anything we have. They're almost twice our size, can burn us to death without a touch. We unleash them into our world and we'll deserve what happens."

"So you'll condemn them instead?"

Svarde brought his hands together, the glittering black blade interrupting the clasped fingers. "What changed, Ami? Not two days ago you wanted to get me a dead fiend to control so we could drive these monsters away. Now?"

"Because I saw what they're running from, Svarde. This isn't a choice for them. It's desperation, it's fleeing something more terrible than anything we've ever seen."

"And?"

Damn Svarde for knowing her too well.

"We already did this to Catya!" Ami strode right up to Svarde. "We gave her up for the good of these rotten isles. Did that feel right to you? Was it worth it, to put her on that throne and watch her wither?"

Svarde, withered enough now himself, met Ami's stare and gave her nothing. The man's eyes, so rich with battle, lust, and bravado in the years she'd known him flashed no clues, no life. Infinity's trap.

"I ask you again, Ami. What do you think happens?"

"I don't give a damn what happens, Svarde. I give a damn that we tried, that we tried to make up for all the bad choices, for all the death, with something better."

"And what'll you do if Jochi refuses?"

"I'll kill the bastard, and the next, and the next until we get a Whent that understands."

Svarde, at least, laughed at that. "You would, wouldn't you?"

Ami found a smirk, folded her arms and backed off a step. "Violence has always been our answer, Svarde. For once, I'm trying peace."

Another long stare. What Svarde was searching for in that look, Ami wasn't sure. If he wanted the old Ami, the fiery, cocky swordsman ready for adventure, Svarde wouldn't find her. That one's time had passed. As for who'd replaced it, Ami wasn't so sure of that herself.

"All right." Svarde said the words as if convincing himself. "Get the fiends to pick an ambassador. Only one. In the meantime, we'll get those Whent engineers working on something for the monster to wear."

"To wear?"

"If we're going to bring a fiend to the people, Ami, they can't look like a fiend." Svarde chuckled. "I can't imagine Fassle taking it kindly if those floppy robes of his catch fire after he says hello."

"What if Jochi says no?" Ami threw Svarde's own question back at him. "Or Maena?"

"As you said, we can just keep killing the rockbiters till we find one that says yes." Svarde's quick smile faded. "As for Maena, she's too busy dealing with her own problems. Today she's against it, tomorrow she might be your biggest advocate. Don't worry about her."

Two wins in a day. Ami would have to temper her ego. The best way she knew to do that was by finding ale, in large amounts, and indulging till the next morning's hangover torqued her back to sanity. She descended the temple's stone steps, angling towards the dead city's one resuscitated tavern only to stop at the bottom, a familiar face waiting for her.

"Heard about your chat," Sawi said, the Vis looking refreshed. "Good move, making friends with the firewalkers."

"Firewalkers?"

"Gotta call them something other than fiends, right? If they're going to be hanging around?"

"That's no sure thing." Ami started towards the tavern and Sawi fell in beside her. "A lot of people need convincing."

"I'm sure you can handle it. That gold face of your's is pretty intimidating."

Ami sniffed, threw a side glance at Sawi. "Why're you so chipper? Sleep all day?"

"Almost. Does wonders."

"I'll take your word for it." Yet Ami didn't quite. A longer look confirmed Sawi's strong shape. New clothes, boots. A belt with places for a blade, knife, and several pouches. One made for a journey. "I like your new outfit."

"Thanks. Hope you don't mind, I traded off your harpoon for most of it."

"I'd be angry if the thing wasn't a crap fiend-killer." The tavern loomed before them, noisy jeers rippling out. Mugs clanking. Ale's soft malt in the air. "Why, though?"

"Because I'm leaving tomorrow, Ami. Going home."

Sawi explained the rest over several rounds. Whent scouts had gone far enough to gauge a good route underground all the way to Vis. Jochi had given leave for several to make the journey, and Sawi would be joining them.

She'd been away too long, needed the sun, the vines, the peach wine.

"Whent ale's not good enough for you?" Ami joked.

"It suits the dark, I suppose," Sawi replied, their two-person table socked away in a back corner, beneath a burning lantern. Slate walls, smoothed by dead labor, cast the whole place in a grim cheer. "I've had enough of that, though."

"Me too, Sawi. Me too."

CHAPTER 28

NIGHTMARE FOOD

Carrying a drunk was much easier with satisfaction's strength. It'd been a rough and raw couple days for Gladdring, but the curve seemed to be swinging around. So many idioms and axioms about waiting for luck to turn, and here it was, his moment.

Too bad he had to share it with vomit on his robes. A lurching step down as Gladdring left Noctia's more luxurious quarters for its better ones had the woman in his arms eject a fair bit of her ale, an event that only had him laugh. All the better to keep the Najahn guards patrolling the streets off his scent: what Tenet would allow such an awful coating?

Not that the Najahn patrols were thick, the night now nudging into early morning. As Gladdring walked down swept cobblestones, the descending side slotted with ridges to break up the slope, the city hung in that precarious interval between sober social hours and belligerent bar fights. Merry flakes spiraled down. A constant sea breeze threatened to whisk away the remaining warmth from Gladdring's ales. Burning wood and Foti-mined coal singed his nose. Gladdring's adopted city telling its tale across his senses.

One he could listen to forever, one that faded as Gladdring reached the switchback stairs down to the deserted southern beach.

The lanterns sputtering here spread farther apart, a few flickering as their oil dwindled. Noctia not so concerned with lighting the way for the huddled poorest, stuffing themselves in crannies carved along the slick steps. The conversations, what few there were, held a different glint, desperation's edge. Stress, hunger, fear.

And, speckled in the replies echoing out to Gladdring between the crashing waves below, hope's hint.

The Tamas skar picked it up, distracting Gladdring. He'd put the woman down some blocks earlier, now pushing her along as she muttered nonsense. The skar's whispers muted the blathering, instead passing along, like a leaf tickling his ear, those bright bits. Gladdring glanced once or twice as he scuffed by the caves, each time meeting cautious eyes, ratty blankets swept over sleeping forms.

A watch, he realized. They kept watches here, in the isles's greatest city.

The troubling idea stuck with him as Gladdring and his cargo reached the sand. So preoccupied, they all were, with the fiends, the skars, with their grand ambitions that Gladdring had missed all those so far below. Not as charity cases, no—that way would lead to weakness, to betrayals, to distraction—but as tools. Levers to deploy for his own position that would, in turn, elevate their own.

A revolution from the top might force change, a revolution from the bottom would guarantee it.

. . .

"Not the arrival I was expecting."

Yarvick and his attendant rasp met Gladdring as he and his intoxicated charge reached the Nimble Fingers's entry. Gladdring didn't for a second think Yarvick had been waiting there. More likely, some lookout had glommed their approach some ways back, allowed the bandit leader to ready a trap.

If Yarvick had seen Gladdring's meeting with the Kance Queen and Vis Hunter, that trap would likely be a fatal one.

The Tamas skar whispered no panic, so Gladdring refused to show any.

"We all have nights that get away from us," Gladdring replied, continuing to hold the bandit up against his shoulder. "No harm done."

"No?" Yarvick asked. "Perhaps not to you, but to me, a great grievance." Yarvick stepped full into the falling flakes, the snow building as the night slipped towards dawn. A narrow gray hat spilled into Yarvick's tangled, greasy locks before catching a broad cloak. No furs, only innumerable pockets, from which Yarvick pulled a small blade. Not longer than Gladdring's finger. "The Nimble Fingers are built, as strange as it may seem, on trust. A thief must know he can depend on his partners in all things."

Yarvick, with his free hand, grabbed the drunk bandit and threw her into the sand. She landed with a grunt, a groan, and little else. While lantern light and Sichi's clouded pink gave only a gloomy view, Gladdring picked up Yarvick's tight eyes, crisp frown. The Tamas skar didn't find sadness, just disappointment.

The blade glittered as Yarvick stared. What would come next wasn't hard to discern.

"Mistakes are only that, Yarvick. Errors to be learned from." Gladdring kept his arms folded. No aggression.

Advice offered, but Yarvick's to act upon. Manipulation was stronger the more invisible the strings.

"If that's your attitude, the answer to why the Najahn are so pathetic is now clear." Yarvick turned his glare on Gladdring, tossed the blade and caught the end by its point. "A mistake is a slip on a slick stair, a lock pick breaking in a tumbler. Unless you tell me that you forced her, held her down and poured the drink in her mouth, her state was her own doing."

That the Tamas skar might've nudged the bandit towards indulging herself, Gladdring kept quiet.

"Still, you're suggesting death," Gladdring began. "I'm here. Unharmed. She can learn from this, and your Fingers can see you're reasonable."

"That's your line? Bad choices cost nothing?" Yarvick spat to the side. "It's good you're going to be under my direction. These isles couldn't afford someone so weak." He thrust the blade handle towards Gladdring. "Take it. A single cut across the throat should suffice. With all that ale, she might not even feel it. As merciful a death as exists on these damned rocks."

Gladdring let the knife hang. Kept his hands in his robes.

"I will not."

Yarvick let the blade linger for another breath, then withdrew it. Slotted it back into his coat. The bandit lord squatted down near the drunk thief's head, patted it once, then slipped his fingers to her exposed ear. Pinched, pulled up. With a yelp, the bandit's eyes fluttered open.

"Understand this," Yarvick said, dead logic his tone, "this man has spared your life, but not your place here. You will find a way off of Noctia today. By tomorrow, all the Nimble Fingers will know to slip a point between your ribs, some poison in your drink, or a wire across your throat. Noctia is your home no longer."

You could not push people beyond a certain point, and Gladdring figured he'd reached the end of this road, so held his tongue. The bandit seemed to sober up enough to grasp something of the situation, slobbered out begs and apologies. The words died when Yarvick turned his look back towards the cave, waved a single cross-cut with a single hand. Two shadows materialized, swept towards the sobbing thief, and picked her up. The trio headed towards the stairs up, where Gladdring had little doubt she'd be dumped with nothing more than the clothes on her back and a desperate life before her.

"Is that better, you think?" Yarvick asked after the group disappeared, a watch done otherwise in wave-crashed silence. "Exile? She'll have to be worse, do worse to survive now. The knife would've been a kinder end." Yarvick inspected Gladdring. "You seem awake enough. Care to come with me, puppet? There's something you should see."

"What's worth seeing at this hour?"

Yarvick didn't answer. He walked, and Gladdring accepted the quiet hike back up the stairs. Halfway along, the two shadows, their faces wrapped in matted scarves, passed going back the other way. Of the drunken thief, there was no sign. When they reached the street level, Yarvick kept going to the east, along the Ringed City's southern quarter. Modest houses scaled the terraces here, some claiming small farmland in addition to their steep slopes and rain-catching gutters.

Gladdring expected deserted streets, but more haunted the icy avenues. They walked alone or in pairs, few words and fewer stumbles among them. Not drunks or revelers, then, but people moving with purpose. Yarvick gave them no notice, and Gladdring followed his lead. They took the leftward forks when the roads split, always angling higher.

Their destination emerged from tumbling, thick snow. Built into the cliffside like a Najahn tower, the wide building had a purposeful cast to it, little regard paid to finery, to impression. It sprawled, swallowing the road's end and stretching beyond, stone supports and retaining walls serving to keep its several stories and all their weight locked in place.

No sign declared its name, its reason.

"Don't say a thing," Yarvick noted, skipping the main entrance, a wide, barred wooden door, for a smaller single offering on the building's far end.

Gladdring kept quiet, though, when they stepped inside, he wanted to retch.

A short room, cluttered with desks themselves cluttered with thick paper volumes, lost any cozy charm with the monstrous stink suffusing its air. Yarvick didn't react, walking right on through and drawing no attention from the sole man etching numbers onto one yellowed paper book. Scrawny, smoking a pipe, the man's pallor put him as daylight's enemy. Gladdring had known more than a few of these night men, and all had their reasons for dodging the sun.

This one's were easy to grasp, as easy as the smell.

Through the room, Yarvick led Gladdring out to an overlook, a lip spreading away from their exit and over, on flat, rough stones, towards the large entrance. Wide stairs swept down from both, leading towards a massive pit. There, Gladdring saw the source of the smell, the curdling in his gut.

Hacking, chopping, skinning and stripping were hundreds, possibly thousands of people. They sat, stood, and moved between massive stone tables. Bodies occupied those slabs, but not human ones. Strange beasts, with scales, feathers, tentacles, and parts Gladdring couldn't name. All dead, though not about to be buried or burned. Instead, as pieces were cleaned, other workers clad in filthy aprons brought black buckets around, pushed the meat inside. Others wheeled wooden carts, shoveling in the viscera and departing with it far back beyond Gladdring's sight. Those same carts, sometimes several tied together in a line, would emerge minutes later with a new body ready to be carved.

"How your city feeds," Yarvick said.

"What? I know where our food comes from, I know what we trade—"

"Your food. Your Najahn luxuries." Yarvick scrunched up his face, as if he'd bitten a lemon. "Noctia is a blasted isle, Gladdring. There's not enough fish and crops to feed most of its people. So we use what we can, what the other isles give up on the cheap."

"Our people eat fiends?"

"The ones we can cook." A slight smile found Yarvick's pallid lips. "We test them all, first, on the petty criminals your Najahn don't catch. A suitable punishment, don't you think, to risk illness, death, to keep so many from starvation?"

Again Gladdring gulped down the remnants of the ale, threatening to make its way free.

"Why did you bring me here, Yarvick?"

"So you understand, Gladdring. Fassle's war to eliminate the fiends will starve his own city. Thousands upon thousands will perish." Yarvick trailed off as someone cursed below, some acid or other spouting free to coat a now-ruined arm. "Yet, this offal can't stay. Fassle's blind war, these terrible pits, the isles need to be remade. When we destroy the Najahn, Gladdring, we'll use the skars to stop all this. To bring about a new idyll."

"With you at its helm."

"Yes."

Yarvick ended his speech there, but Gladdring heard it continue as he watched the working poor below. Lives calling for change, needing it.

They would get it, and soon. As would Yarvick.

CHAPTER 29

AMID SNOW AND SUN

Their laughter flew into the night, blending with gnarled roots, Sichi's pink lights, and the rollicking cart wheels rumbling on the hard dirt path. Four people on a quest to save their home and winning, dammit, winning despite so many obstacles thrown into their way. Eujo listed them off one by one, calling the Golden Gash's avalanche, her traitorous Queensguards, and the ever-present fiends into the air for Wax and Torny to denounce in turn. Bliss, hands tight on the reins steering the confused, exhausted ponies added her own fierce grin.

"And we're still here!" Eujo concluded. "Take that, Noctia! Take that, fiends!"

Across from her, nestled into their satchels, ale's warm glow present in his moonlit face, Wax echoed her boast, before falling into a classic Vis whoop.

No pursuit rattled behind them, no danger loomed in front. For the moment, for this moment, they could bask in success.

Moments, though, pass, and so too did this one, rolling

to an end as the roots thinned out, faltering to a snow-dusted plain. Hills, jutting hard up and down with no friendly rolls to them, warped the road ahead, suggesting a curving line through clean country. In the far distance, to a horizon with no straight line, a gentle yellow suggested a town within reach.

Yet Bliss wheeled the cart off the path, let the sweat-sheened ponies, their every breath sending steam into the air, rest. The halt nudged Eujo from her slumber, something she didn't recall happening but that'd clearly given her enough awkward sleep to restore her vigor and render her back sore. Wax still snored.

"Awake?" Torny asked, her head appearing over the cart's bed. "Good, cause we'll be walking the rest of the way."

"Walking?" Eujo said, the words scratchy and prompting a lunge for her water skin.

Worn at her waist, body heat enough to keep the contents from freezing, the water nonetheless verged on numbing the Queen's throat when she drank it. Torny expounded, saying the Animas would be sending pursuit and they'd be hunting for a cart like this one. The ponies wouldn't travel much farther that night anyway, better to send them on a meander, throw off pursuit as long as they could.

"Won't anyone after us just head on to the closest town?" Eujo said, nevertheless easing herself from the cart. Bliss whacked her brother on the shoulder, startling him awake with a curse. "If they care that much, they'll find us."

"That's why we're walking. Any fast pursuit will beat us to that town, won't find us there, and then we'll be clear."

The pack didn't seem so heavy when Eujo scooped it onto her shoulders, a reminder they lacked provisions, gear for any overland travel. This wouldn't be like the hike on Whent. They'd find themselves frozen, starved, or both. Eujo reminded Torny as much, only to watch Bliss give the ponies a good slap on the rump, the empty cart vanishing with them into the dark.

"We'll take our chances," Torny said, though at least she didn't look thrilled with it. "I'd rather go a little hungry, shiver a little more, than wind up back on that stage with a collar around my neck."

A compelling argument, that. Eujo, though, didn't make any boasts as the group took their first steps westward, frigid grasses crunching underfoot.

That their overland route would leave a clear trail didn't escape any of them, a reality Torny addressed by having them cut back north in the pre-dawn light. The root forest's remnants kept the ground clean enough to disguise, so the bandit figured, a bunch of Tamas actors wouldn't be able to follow it.

"A bit dismissive, aren't you?" Eujo asked, walking with the bandit at the foursome's head. Torny had her daggers out, used them to hack away any nasty thorns, a dangerous business in the dark: they'd all earned a few scratches already. "Tamas isn't an isle filled with morons."

"Didn't say it was, but if I'm reading them right, Daklin and those fools aren't big on wilderness survival."

"And you are, bandit of the city?"

"As of this quest, you better believe I am." Torny waggled a dagger in Eujo's direction. "I've crossed four isles now with Wax and Bliss, more than most manage in a lifetime. Nature's my playground, Eujo."

As she finished the words, Torny, her look more focused on her dagger, smacked right into a leaning root.

Eujo laughed, "I see that."

Dawn found them back amongst the hills, heavy lidded eyes on both Torny and Bliss, while Wax and Eujo welcomed daylight with brighter looks. The heavy coated hiking kept the group warm, so the first rays struck not with heat but grandeur, splashing across a glittering rainbow land. Eujo shaded her eyes, Wax uttered a delighted whistle. Sparkles flashed in every direction, climbing up and falling away as the hills, each a challenge to climb, proved exquisite sunlit canvases. Tamas's native creatures emerged too, clear skies filling with hunting hawks while curious critters emerged beneath the roots to seek fortune among the frozen prairie.

And carriage wheels carried their clatter along the wind.

"Can you walk all day?" Eujo asked Torny and Bliss when they hunkered down on a hill's far side, the lump blocking view from the path and showing, far to the west, another root forest rising. "Or will you need to rest?"

"What I need and what we'll do are two different things, I figure," Torny replied, throwing a frowning look at Bliss. "She's worse off than me. I dozed, she had to drive."

Bliss heard them, or felt Torny's look, and gave them a weak smile. 'I'm fine.'

"She's lying," Torny said to Eujo, dropping her voice. "Where we're going, that town, we won't stay hidden long. If we can manage a few hours sleep here, I say we do it. The grass is comfortable enough once you mash it down."

Eujo took up Torny's request, pitched it to Wax and Bliss, and the Vis Guardian had her eyes closed lying on her pack within minutes, sunlight be damned. Torny joined her, the two nestling into a makeshift collected gear bed.

"I'll take first watch," Wax said, biting off a frosted

carrot leftover all the way from Harrow's Edge. "Sleep if you want it."

"I don't, actually." Eujo let her hand slide to her bracelet, the whispering skars. "Think I'll take a look around, see if that town's our only option."

The hilltop offered a grander view than below, though Eujo nearly shut her eyes to keep the glare low. She saw glimmering beauty, felt cold wind sneak beneath her coats, and watched Tamas play its morning away. Just watched. Pushed away the skars and their whispers, destiny and its demands to soak in the moment, the now, the peace.

No fiends, no knives, no traitors, no tormentors.

If Eujo made it, collected the Tamas skar, then the Noctia one—whether Wax would insist on going to Kance was a problem they'd address later—would it feel like this? Not so beautiful, stuck amid the Wound's crater, but with guards, with all her needs addressed at Eujo's whims. No responsibility except to sit there and decay.

That is, if the Najahn would even let her.

The thought struck a different note. She and Wax hadn't talked much about the Circle's declaration, an unspoken assumption that the Najahn would simply allow a completed Renewal to take the throne ending that conversation before it could really begin. And yet, would they? Even if Eujo collected all the other skars and presented herself at the Ringed City, would the Najahn just take the stones away?

If so, what then?

Eujo, saving her eyes, looked back down the hill, at the three forms lying against its silver. Wax waved, a lazy arc. Between them, they had nine skars. Nine little stones with a god's power instilled within. They could move mountains, burn whole cities, or froth up a flood from the calmest river.

The Najahn wanted to use those powers against the fiends directly. An idea that could work, but . . . Eujo snuffed a snort. The isles wouldn't give themselves up to the Najahn so completely.

The skars, used for anything other than the Aegis, would tear the isles apart.

So what, then?

Her friends didn't offer up any answers. Neither did the hawks in the sky or the snow at her feet. Perhaps, though, the solution lay in what she couldn't do, rather than what Eujo could. Returning to Kance would mean death or exile. Wax seemed willing to go back to Vis, and with Torny and Bliss growing closer every day, the bandit, after repaying her debt to Noctia's thief king, would likely follow the Vis girl to the jungle isle.

Could Eujo go there too? Give up the sky diamonds, the mountains, her home for a new one?

Maybe.

"FIND ANYTHING UP THERE?" Wax asked when Eujo returned to their makeshift camp.

"Answers, of a sort, and more questions."

"Like what the animals are eating out here?" Wax nodded across the small valley between hills at a scampering rabbit, tall ears and white fur doing well to blend it against the snow. "It keeps digging here and there, but I don't know what for."

Eujo chuckled, once, and shook her head, "Wax, I wish I could be as unperturbed as you about how things are going."

A small smile, "Eujo, I didn't come from much, I didn't

plan for greatness, so I'm going to find what happiness I can until I get home or wind up dead."

Eujo flinched, "Dead? That's—"

Wax shrugged, the grin falling away. "Realistic. My friend died after we found a single skar. We've seen so many more die too. Now we're being hunted by Kance assassins and the isles's strongest soldiers? Eujo, if we don't wind up skewered, hung, or eaten by some hungry fiend, it'll be a Vis miracle."

"Yet, you're still wondering about some rabbit's food?"

"A lot nicer than the other things I could be thinking about."

"Suppose so." Eujo stared at the furry creature as it flung up some more snow. "I bet it's the roots."

"What?"

"The rabbit. It's trying to get at the roots."

"Oh."

Eujo felt Wax's gloved hand land on her shoulder, squeeze.

"Don't worry, sky queen. Our quest might be danger-ous, our chances of success slim, but I won't let a single day go by without making you laugh."

Which he did, right then and there, and for all the worries wandering about Eujo's world, she let them fall away.

Just for a moment.

CHAPTER 30

DINNER DANGERS

Deshiva's hand pulled Annalyse back from the petal's edge. The Great Sana's brilliant purple and white sprawled, yet Annalyse kept finding herself tottering near a long, fatal fall.

"Again, Whent?" Deshiva asked. "How many times do you owe me your life?"

"I don't get it." Annalyse shook her head like a rat scattering water. "It's as though i'm drawn to the edge, even though—"

"A sickness common to those not used to heights. You've been too sheltered in the wrong places. A few days swinging from the canopies will cure you."

Deshiva patted Annalyse on the shoulder, turned back to the operation around the Sana's center. Annalyse tore her eyes away from the sprawling view, caught Deshiva whispering to another hunter and nodding the scientist's way. Passing off responsibilities. Annalyse felt a blush rising and killed it.

She couldn't do anything about the urges, so why be embarrassed by them?

Najahn and Vis hunters scoured the Great Sana's pistil, pulling Vis skars one by one and tossing them into satchels. The Vis seemed surprised as each new stone came free, muttering about the death of another lie, one Annalyse herself had believed until Gladdring showed her the gathered stores in the Ringed City.

For so long the isles had been told skars regrew in time with the Renewals, and only as many as were needed to secure the next Aegis. For so long that lie had been accepted without question, letting the Najahn mine and mine and mine the gods's fragments without the slightest suspicion.

So much trust misplaced.

Now these stones would be sent down, slotted into armor, woven into bracers, or placed in necklaces. The Vis and those Najahn who'd turned traitor—Veritrus sent those who refused on a swift journey north, where Kitaye would toss them back home by sea—would hear the Vis whispers, would find their wounds healing faster than ever before. A force able to keep on fighting well after their enemy succumbed to disease, gashes, infection.

To hear both Deshiva and Veritrus tell it, that force would never leave Vis. Would serve only to keep the jungle defended.

Annalyse had heard such noble announcements before, had seen what happened when those making them were threatened.

This time, she'd be staying out of it. The trip to the Great Sana's apex was a parting gift, a chance to see the best view on Vis before Annalyse could return to her satchels, her research, and her retreat to Svarde's cabin on the western coast. At least the trip up had been worth it, the Great Sana a fascinating ecosystem from bottom to top.

Those flashing butterflies and the wriggling caterpillars

alone confirmed Annalyse's choice as the right one, even if, again, the scientist found herself edging closer to the far fall.

A little attention, a couple focused footsteps, and Annalyse put herself back near the center. The view was plenty beautiful from right here, and she could ignore the plucking around her, its implications, if she tried.

THE RETURN BROUGHT Annalyse to an expected feast with unexpected guests. Veritrus laid out a good winter's spread, supplied with Vis's verdant fruits, fish, and what vegetables were salvaged from the torched outpost's stores. The mess hall's burnt bones loomed around them, makeshift thatching and initial repairs already underway. Tables were mashed together into a long line, enough to seat twenty, including Annalyse, Deshiva, and various hand-picked hunters and Najahn.

Joining them were the newcomers, the ones who'd arrived at a swift run from the East, from Mottilan.

Korrus claimed leadership over the half-dozen strong entourage, a bulky man with a hard edge, a familiar frustration emanating from his oft-clenched fists and narrowed eyes. Annalyse had felt, looked the same after many a failed experiment, but, for Korrus, the glower seemed his default mode. Nevertheless, the man parlayed his people's places at the table with a promise, so Deshiva muttered to Annalyse, of peace.

Ale flowed, the first bites proved as delicious as they looked, and Annalyse let the peach wine soothe away the day.

At least until Korrus started talking.

Veritrus wasn't a fool, and he'd positioned himself, Deshiva, Korrus, and Annalyse at one end of the table. Gladdring would've approved keeping the power players close together, better to keep sensitive discussions secret, though Annalyse found herself, as Korrus began his opening salvo, eyeing the blissful drinking at the table's far end. There, the conversation seemed focused on entertaining hunts and how accurate one could shoot with a bow after drinking several bottles of Kitaye's finest fruit wine.

"Mottilan deserves its share," Korrus started. "We're the closer city."

"And the smaller," Deshiva said. The hunter popped fish bites into her mouth with her fingers as she spoke, seeming to swallow them whole between words. "You're welcome, as are all Vis, to share in what's ours. Equally."

"Equally? Since when has Kitaye talked of equality?" Korrus leaned forward, elbows on the table. "Every Renewal, you take the mantel and share none of it with us. When Najahn or Kance plan for trade, your attempts to take every ship are ruthless."

"Friendly competition, no more."

Veritrus, like Annalyse, held his focus on the food. Some fights were best avoided.

"Your friendly competition costs Mottilan trade, costs us a chance at a better life. Kitaye shares no spoils with us, ever. And now you seek to claim equality when Mottilan is clearly the better choice."

"The better choice?" Deshiva asked, cutting the words. "The better choice for what, Korrus?"

The man swept his hands wide, almost knocking Annalyse's wine over.

"All of this. The outpost. The skars. We should control

the Great Sana." He narrowed his focus to Deshiva. "Of course, we would give Kitaye its share."

This time, Deshiva leaned forward, though she put her palms flat on the table. "I won't negotiate this here. Not now. Our elders should be the ones to decide. Not us."

"That will take time, time we don't have, unless you think Noctia will sit by and allow us to decide for ourselves." Korrus pointed at Deshiva. "Besides, I see what's going on here. Your hunters are already making their beds, building new tree houses on the outskirts. Time means Kitaye control."

"Time means just that, time."

"Fine. Then take your time elsewhere." Korrus glanced at Veritrus. "Your Najahn Tenet, Gladdring, promised Mottilan a greater part to play on this isle. It's time you fulfilled that oath."

Veritrus glanced up from his fish, carved up to eat in slow, measured strokes with metal utensils, unlike Korrus and Deshiva. "Gladdring? A traitor. His word is less than nothing now."

Korrus sat back, eyes going unfocused. A new plan finding itself.

"A traitor like you?" the man said.

"I'm not dead, nor powerless," Veritrus replied. "Glad-dring was hung on Noctia some days ago. That said, your quarrel is with Deshiva, not me."

"Then you won't take a side?"

Veritrus shook his head, and Annalyse almost choked when Korrus turned her way.

"And how about you, Noctia scientist?"

"How about me, what?" Annalyse looked at Deshiva, a glance yanked back when Korrus slammed his left hand on the table. Conversations dipped, eyes turned, Annalyse tried to find logic and failed. "I don't—"

"You do. You all do. I'm not a suspicious man—"

Deshiva coughed. Korrus reddened, but bowled on.

"As I said, you all have your agendas, just as I do, and mine is to see Mottilan respected. So I ask you, scientist, do you not care who controls the Great Sana? Will you sit out this struggle?"

That, at least, Annalyse could answer.

"I just want to be left alone."

"There." Korrus nodded, rose the same hand that'd slapped the table and placed it, heavy, on Annalyse's shoulder. "That wasn't so hard? Now you, Deshiva. Be honest. If I send my runner and call in my Mottilan hunters just up the road, will you give up this place?"

"Conquerors are not welcome on Vis," Deshiva said, her hands dropping beneath the table. "Power here is shared."

"But not with Mottilan." Korrus swiped a palm-sized fish filet off the wood plate, jammed it into his mouth as he stood. "You've made your choice, Kitaye. You will reckon with it shortly."

The man raised a single finger and the Mottilan hunters seated at the table all bounced up from their chairs, followed Korrus out the door and away into the night. Deshiva wasted no time, bounding after them, whistling orders, and in seconds the outpost's revelry shattered into new sounds, the clash, bang, and songs of war.

Veritrus, throughout the whole exchange, kept eating his fish and seemed not in the least perturbed. Annalyse, now the only other one still seated at the table, downed her wine. Without saying a word, Veritrus reached, lofted the wine skin, and refilled the empty cup.

"What just happened?" Annalyse said after finishing that one too.

"The reason the Najahn held these outposts for so long," Veritrus said, sparing a mournful look at his now-empty plate, "is because we kept the peace. Freedom is no easy thing."

"What are you going to do?"

"Tell my soldiers to stay out of it. I recommend you do the same."

Annalyse nodded. Gauged the empty plate before her. The food asked a different question. If she took her satchels tonight and set off, she'd have to scrounge on her own. Learn to catch fish, set snares, and harvest fruit on an unfamiliar isle. A dilemma she'd ignored in her first journey, had been about to ignore here.

Astounding how settling on one's path made it easy to miss the dangers.

"Unless Korrus has a thousand hunters," Annalyse said, "he'll never be able to overcome the skars. He'll be massacred."

"Or he'll do exactly what he means to," Veritrus replied. "Don't discount Mottilan scrappiness. The underdog knows what it takes to win."

Annalyse watched Veritrus help himself to more wine. So cool, so unperturbed. Why?

What would Gladdring assume?

"You're playing them both." Annalyse spoke flat, certain. "You want them to fight."

Veritrus stopped his sip before the cup reached his lips. Dark eyes glittered. Annalyse became very aware, in that moment, how empty the mess hall had become. War demanded everyone's attention, it seemed, save the two of them.

"The assassin had it right. You are trouble." Veritrus set the cup down, pushed back his chair and stood. "I think you and I should take a long walk, Annalyse, and talk about what this conflict means for Noctia, for the Najahn, and you."

CHAPTER 31
A SUIT FIT FOR FIENDS

Disaster proved a great hangover cure. Despite one ale after another the night before, perhaps aided by the Vis skars, Ami perked up quick, rolling off the straw slab that made for her bed at the first horn's blow. She replaced the ratty shift—Ami really ought to ask Jochi's traders for new clothes—with battle leathers, scuffed boots, and a strong two-handed sword delivered to her as a gift from Jochi last evening.

A reward, and thanks, so the warlord said, for sparing his forces from one endless battle after another with the fiery fiends. A strange admission given Jochi's position—warlord—and the Whent fascination with gladiatorial combat, but there it was. Perhaps being so far removed from their normal lives made the Whent rethink their opinions.

Whatever the reason, Ami slotted the sword into the sheathe behind her back and spared a silent look at the empty slab nearby. The straw had already been cleared, repurposed somewhere else. Sawi was gone, then. The little

Vis who'd braved the trek with Ami made good on her claim and disappeared.

She might be dead already.

Ami grinned. Not likely. The Guardian had taught Sawi more than a little during their days in Gladdring's tower and the Dark Below. The Vis had the skills to make it home. Whether she had the luck was a question Ami couldn't answer.

The horn blow's question, though, came with a clear explanation once Ami left the Dead City, joined curious and coerced soldiers, and Svarde-directed corpses, wandering to the front: no attack on the Whent soldiers, not yet, or the city. But fiends aplenty, arising from the chamber pool and assaulting the firewalkers.

Sawi's name stuck, prompted Ami to ask a soldier going the other way, their overnight duty ended, how they felt. The gruff reply came back that Jochi had deemed the burning fiends worthy of their own name, now that they had more than hostility to offer.

The Whent warlord waited near the tunnel barricades, surrounded by his stoic bodyguards and enduring one report after another from scouts scurrying to the battlefield and back. Ami caught the latest, a wild description of looming, watery bugs flying up from the pool and swarming the firewalkers. Both sides seemed to be dying in high numbers, the bodies piling up amid the gray stone slopes.

Jochi, hearing this, issued new orders to the assembled troops, living and not, pulling on their gear around him. The barricades behind, sealing the tunnel entry, remained shut save for the small door used by the scampering scouts. From what Ami could see, no Whent rescue would be charging forth.

And that was a damn waste.

"What're you doing?" Ami said by way of greeting, shoving her way past an older man tugging on metal boot covers.

"Letting our enemies take care of each other," Jochi said, holding up a hand to forestall those hulking bodyguards from making any move. Before him sat a simple table, various colored rocks seeming to show the battlefield makeup. "Any leader knows to stay out of the way when two problems collide."

"Except we just made friends with one of those problems."

"Did we?" Jochi tapped a reddish stone. "As I understand it, we barely have a dialogue. They could change their minds at any moment. If the firewalkers survive, they'll be weak. More likely to bend to our demands."

Ami caught herself, let the indignation die away as Catya taught her so long ago. A lesson she remembered at her own convenience, but that kept Ami's curses silent. Jochi had a point, but not the whole picture.

"What if the firewalkers lose?" Ami asked. "What happens if the bulwark we have now turns into endless unpredictable fiends again?"

"Yes, I've considered that. We'll wait till the right moment, Ami, then step in. A few crossbow bolts, so my scouts tell me, will ensure the firewalkers survive. Then we'll have their loyalty, their—"

"They're not stupid, Jochi. They'll know we see what's happening, that we could be acting, right now, and we're not." Ami reached down, shoved several gray stones near the red. "It's past time."

Jochi gave Ami the guarded glare she deserved. "Careful, Guardian. You aren't the commander here." He moved his eyes past her, to the assembling soldiers. "But I'll grant you what you want. Take those who're ready, move to the tunnel's edge, and assist." Those eyes found hers, none of Jochi's cocky mirth in them. "If you get a single one of my people killed helping those monsters, Ami, I'll never let you near a command again."

The plateau loomed over disaster. Ami and the twenty-odd Whent soldiers and scouts traveling with her—with Svarde busy elsewhere, Ami left the stone-tossing corpses behind—ventured beyond the tunnel's opening onto the jutting point without resistance. No firewalker stood watch, because battle engulfed their encampment.

Those great constructs had their nozzles and ballista launchers pointed back towards the vast pool, unleashing torrents and dark iron bolts in a steady stream. Smoke rose when lava struck water, the billowing gray turning the cave ceiling into storm clouds. Darting up and down within the boiling miasma were the firewalker's apparent foes, wild creatures half an ox's size and made up of wings, legs, and sucking, shimmering mouths.

"Down, commander!" called a scout at Ami's back and she dove, one of the creatures making a long glide their way.

Ami kept an eye on the thing, watched its whole body convulse as it flew, bunching up behind the snout before bursting out in a bile shower. The splatter struck the stones at the plateau's front, splashing and sizzling around every-thing it touched.

Acid, then.

The gliding creature leveled out its approach as Ami stood, grabbing a rock, but before the Guardian could make an ill-advised throw, a dozen crossbows clicked behind her. Quarrels struck the fiend like bee stings, rippling, tearing wherever they hit, like ripples through a crashing wave. The monster spiraled, those ripples cascading, and when it struck the rocks, the whole fiend popped like a bad bubble, scattering its few real bits across the slope.

"Ugly and awful," Ami muttered, resuming her approach to the plateau's edge.

Below, the firewalkers seemed at a loss. The water bugs rebounded to and from the pool, sucking up more water with every trip and using it to douse the burning monsters in fatal showers. The firewalkers tried to use their constructs for shelter, ducking behind the larger frames until acid melted the metal to slag. A lucky flail strike, a well-timed fiery gout scored hits, but the battle's outcome was obvious.

"Pick your targets, aim, and fire at will," Ami said to the Whents, and appreciated Jochi's discipline when the rock-biters did just as she asked.

Crossbow quarrels filled the chamber sky, most missing the fast water bugs, but enough catching to throw the liquid fiends off their quick flits. The firewalkers capitalized on every falter with a launched stone, a massive ballista bolt, to bring the water bug swarm down. Ami resorted to playing field general, calling out shots to her soldiers.

A new experience for one better used to getting her hands bloody, but not a bad one. Catya must've felt a similar satisfaction every time Ami and Svarde downed a fiend, solved a puzzle at her direction.

When the last bug splattered amid the firewalkers, its watery demise breaking white ash patches on the nearby burning fiends, Ami gave the Whent archers much-deserved congratulations.

Then sent the force back to Jochi, save a single runner, waiting near the tunnel's edge.

A gambit, and one that paid off when a firewalker

approached, a different one than before. Ami couldn't tell a lick about what lay beneath the flame-wreathed body, but the obsidian head held unique ridges, and those glittering sparks seemed a bit sharper with this one.

Brighter too, as the firewalker showered Ami with blues, silvers, and browns. The Guardian took a step back, breathing some air without searing her lungs. Another reminder that Jochi, with all his concerns about how these blazing things would integrate into the isles, wasn't wrong.

Yet four hands clasped with one another, a flail dropped to the dust, and a gathering of sparks combining into a single golden shine were gestures Ami understood, were ones she returned with a bowed head, a word of thanks, and a slow retreat.

"They owe us now," Jochi said, with Svarde joining them, near the barricade after Ami made her report. "Nice work, Ami. For the first time in the isles's history, you've brought fiends into our debt."

"Debt?" Ami asked, aware their trio stood amid watching eyes and listening ears as her Whent force tossed off their arms and armor. "And how do you think they'll repay us?"

"By not attacking, for starters," Jochi said, a grin climb up his cheeks. "And by wearing these."

The warlord raised a single hand. Several soldiers parted, either by moving back or getting shoved aside as at least ten engineers hiked in with a laden cart. Several black lumps lay in the center, each as large as Ami or bigger. They reeked of ash and soot, held no reflection, and looked to Ami like something dead had been roasted and laid out to dry.

One of the engineers, a squat woman with more muscles than Ami had ever earned showing through her tool-speckled vests, stepped forward, greeted them all with a solid spit off to the side.

"Dampers, ready as requested," the engineer said, clipping the words in the way more rural Whent tended to. "Stayed fine in the hottest forges we've got down here. If the damned fiends are hotter than that, then I'd say send'em back because the isles is no place for'em."

"Dampers," Jochi repeated, then nodded. "Good work, and right on time."

"As always," the engineer replied, not letting a smile or frown touch her set face. "They're not light either, understand, so don't be dumb and try to carry one of these yourselves. Firewalkers look big enough to take the weight, though."

"What're these, then?" Svarde asked, leaning on that great blade like it was some sort of cane.

Leave it to an ax man to mistreat a sword.

At Jochi's second nod, the engineer answered, "Heat blockers. Firewalker slips their arms through the holes, wears it like a vest. It'll block the worst of it from singeing ya." She eyed Jochi. "Material to make these isn't cheap or easy to find, so don't go losing them."

"Have any with sleeves?" Ami asked.

The engineer spat again. "You want sleeves, you prove these work. Not wasting any more time and leathers till we know this is worth doing."

"Well," Jochi said, "I think, if there's anyone here who can convince our fiery friends to try one of these on, it's you, Ami."

The Guardian folded her arms, thought about echoing

the engineer's spitting ways, but shook her head instead. "What for? We don't need—"

"Up, Ami," Svarde interrupted. "It's time we show the isles what's really going on down here. Stop the Renewal. Get the Najahn to support us."

"And you want me to do that?" Ami laughed. "A traitor?"

Now it was Jochi's turn to chuckle. "No, Ami. You get a firewalker or two to side with us, and even Noctia might change their minds."

CHAPTER 32
DOCKSIDE RUMBLE

Fassle couldn't have picked a nicer day to start a war. The Najahn leader, captain of the Circle, and overall moron stood atop the makeshift platform built overnight on the dock, beckoning several borrowed Whent galleons stuffed with armored Najahn soldiers. On most of those uniforms, slotted in during the weeks between Gladdring's ouster and his presence, now, as a cowled observer amid the morning masses viewing the send-off, were Vis skars. Pilfered over years, stored, and now set to use against their home isle.

Next to the Circle's leader stood a gritty woman decked out in Najahn medals. Noctia's Renewal, returned from Whent, where she'd been when Fassle's declaration ending the whole charade had gone out. She'd been hailed as a hero nonetheless, surviving fiends, bandits, and dangerous seas on her trek around all but two isles. Her efforts showed evidence around her neck, the classic jewelry laying over the woman's cuirass and on display.

Not a Renewal anymore, but a general, a leader, for the Najahn. By her stern smile, she wasn't disappointed in her change in fortune. Then again, who wouldn't be? A change in destiny from rotting on a stone chair to leading the isles's most powerful force?

At least, while Fassle still held power.

Gladdring wanted to take some pride in the plan he'd developed being put into motion: it'd been his idea to bring in Annalyse, to finally put the skars to the test after so long wasting their power out of fear, confusion, routine. He wanted to join Fassle on that platform and wave, confident they were turning the isles to a better future.

But to stand on that platform would be to die.

Yarvick would be ensuring that.

The former Tenet, his Tamas skar pestering with intuitions from the crowd around him, didn't try to pick out the bandit lord's insurgents. Fassle hadn't made the send-off a secret, giving notice aplenty for Yarvick to set his assassins. Gladdring, too, had his role rendered: take the stage after Fassle fell, proclaim himself the new Najahn leader, and send the troops on their way. The war on Vis wouldn't be stopped here, shouldn't be stopped, because if Gladdring, Yarvick, and Fassle agreed on anything, it was the skars's necessity as a military matter.

The question wasn't whether the Najahn needed to rule the isles, but who ought to rule the Najahn.

As Fassle launched into his conclusion, Gladdring pushed his way through the crowd. The seaside street, sporting wharfs and a rope fence barring the buzzing people from a swift drowning, had snow shoved up against its sides. Coffee and food vendors took bartered buys of all kinds, from pawned jewelry, homespun clothes, to chits for returned favors in the future. Those smells, warm and spiced, competed with frosted fresh catch and seaman's stink. A nervous energy pulsed, one Gladdring didn't need his Tamas to catch.

It'd been before all their lifetimes, the last time the Najahn marched to war. Then, it'd been against Kance, subduing the very isle whose Queen now lurked behind Fassle. Her face rested impassive beneath her silver-blue coat, far larger than the one she'd worn on arrival, as if puffed up on the inside. Near her stood the Vis hunter, Quik, playing into his position as escort and muscle. The Kance Queen had her own guards, of course. All wore voluminous coats, as if the whole cohort planned to travel in the coldest Whent tundra for a week.

Gladdring shivered. That, at least, would not happen.

Fassle reached up towards the blue, sunny, cold sky with a single clenched hand. As his words wound down, wishing good luck and the Noctia's own strength to his troops, the air around his hand shimmered before a blue-white flame shot upward, blossoming into a burning ball then fading away.

A skar. Fassle had a Foti skar and knew how to use it.

This wasn't—

Bolts flew. Small black darts lanced from nearby inns, warehouses, and probably from the street. At least three, maybe more, perforated Fassle's cloak. The man, his arm not yet down, jerked as they struck, moved back a step. The crowd picked up the strike, the screams began. Najahn soldiers not on the ships, the ones already casting off and moving south, drew weapons or dithered, confused. The two Adepts, standing in their glorious robes behind Fassle's platform, disappeared behind the grips of their own guards.

If Yarvick's bribes worked, those same guards would be cutting the Adept's throats in seconds.

Fassle's own protection swarmed the stage, four armored Najahn with their useless voulges swirling around in the air looking for someone to stab. They formed up around Fassle, with a fifth eschewing arms to bend down, pick up the body.

Gladdring edged nearer, easier now with the crowd flowing away. Too many people and too few exits for a swift getaway, though. Once Fassle left the stage, Gladdring would still have an audience, would still . . .

The black and purple robes fluttered. Fassle pushed away the helping guard and rose to a shaky stand, a furious, defiant glare on the man's face. Holes torn by the fired bolts only made Fassle look stronger, only made Gladdring smile wider.

Yarvick would have to commit now, and Gladdring had his opening.

More clicks. More bolts streamed in, this time bouncing off the armored guards surrounding Fassle. One took a hit in narrow band between helm and breastplate, collapsing. Another found Fassle again, lodging in the man's shoulder, only for Fassle to yank it out and throw it aside. He howled out a command, and at last the soldiers amid the crowd found their directions, running towards the buildings where Yarvick's assassins hid.

And clearing the way for Gladdring.

The former Tenet shifted away from the platform. Any chance of supplanting Fassle then and there was over. Even if Yarvick had more death to deal, the crowd would be too thin for any victorious overthrow. Instead, another plan whirled into motion, one Gladdring caught up with behind Fassle's platform, along the seaside street heading north.

"That went poorly," hissed the Kance Queen as Gladdring joined her, several Kance Queensguards, and Quik. "I thought Yarvick was supposed to be good at this."

"He is," Gladdring replied, letting Quik and a Queensguard, glimmering in their outlandish silver armor, take the lead. The Vis hunter spoke fast to the man, no doubt explaining the route. "Whether he's good enough to destroy Fassle, we'll see, but we can't depend on either."

"I'm depending on you, which I do not like."

"I never asked you to like it, only to believe it."

Around them, onlookers broke in different ways. Some found perches to stare back at the departing ships, the continued attacks on Fassle. New sounds rang, metal clashes mingling with shouted orders, Fassle's own voice haranguing his would-be killers. Others dashed through doors locked and not, battering through to disappear into shadows and wait out the chaos. Someone called for ale and a blade, in no particular order.

Gladdring's party turned inward and upward, scaling steps as horn blasts made their first calls through the city. An alarm heard more often of late, whenever a fiend made a near incursion, but still a startling sound. Najahn guards passed by, flowing out from the barracks, some adjusting their arms and armor on the fly. One slipped, fell down the cobbled steps near them. A Queensguard stopped to help them up, only to be ordered onward by the Queen.

The several days burned in Noctia taverns, turning loyalties and taking knowledge, re-ran through as Gladdring hustled. Their entire plan relied on a single fact, and if Fassle decided to change it, if that fact proved false, then . . .

Then Gladdring would have to hope Yarvick succeeded, and still saw a place for him. An eventuality to consider when, if, that dark time came around.

The gates to the Najahn quarter arrived faster than

Gladdring expected, though the sweat flowing through his heavy coat and cowl suggested he'd earned the passage. More guards than usual stood outside, voulges drawn, and two crossbowmen loomed with bolts ready across the gate's battlements. More black and purple soldiers continued rushing out.

Hard stares greeted them, hard stares turned by the Kance Queen's icy demand that Najahn keep its royal guests safe. No second looks came their way, no inspections. Quik, the hunter wearing Najahn robes, claimed himself as their escort, that they were en route to protected quarters.

Chaos proved a valuable ally, as the gate's commander gave no thought to why the Queen, part of Fassle's celebratory entourage, would be returning alone. Instead, they were hustled through, told to seek shelter.

They would, and did, just not where any Najahn soldier would expect.

Gladdring's familiar tower looked the same as it had when he ruled it. Fassle may have already appointed another Trade Tenet, but the new master had yet to stamp their mark. The same token banners, one for each isle, hung outside the door, now without a single guard standing watch. Another thought borne out: with the Circle under attack, who cared about a tower filled with scholars and trade agreements?

Quik and the Queensguard commander breached the door, a task made easy when panicked scholars lurched it open at the first knock. The Vis hunter bowled the robed pair aside, telling them to get back to their chambers, to not open their own doors until Najahn horns said otherwise. The hallway to the central stair lay empty and ripe for running.

The Queen gave Gladdring a nod, one he didn't return. No chancing success until it was guaranteed, until what they sought was waiting.

Two levels down and an obstacle. Three guards, armed and armored, standing before a door Gladdring knew too well. They stared at the entourage, confused, until Gladdring himself stepped forward and threw back his hood. With his hand, Gladdring pushed Quik back a step. He knew these guards, their presence here a surprise, and a suspicious one.

"Traitor," said the center one, their leader. "You're supposed to be dead."

"But I'm not." Gladdring threw a nod behind him to the waiting Queensguard, all with hands on their rapiers. "Lucky for you, a chance to balance your souls has arrived. Acquit your betrayal and let us by."

The guard laughed, "Betrayal? Acquit? We serve the Circle, have always—"

"I serve the isles," Gladdring announced. "I serve the people who live here. Your families, friends, sons and daughters. Fassle's wild whims will get them killed. I'll see them saved. You know this."

"Do I?"

Voulges weren't much use inside a tower's tight confines, so these three carried Foti blades, their bluish metals shimmering as the leader, and his two friends, drew them. The leader leveled his point at Gladdring, and the Tamas skar shouted a warning.

There would be no negotiating.

The Vis hunter saw reality just as fast, breaking hands now cloaked in gauntlets from beneath his robe. Shoving Gladdring aside with his shoulder, the hunter gashed the lead guard's blade, swatting it to the ground with his first swipe, putting the clawed points to the guard's neck in the second. Two Queensguard stepped up alongside Quik, their rapiers matching the enemy's blades point to point.

"Your lives, then," Gladdring said, cutting in before Quik could utter some useless Vis nonsense. "If the isles themselves count for nothing, then maybe your own survival does."

Mortality, as ever, broke old molds. The lead guard snarled a curse, let his hands go limp. The other two followed suit, dropped their blades. The Kance Queen said something, then, that sounded like gibberish, but both Queensguard surged forward, delivered temple-knocking strikes with their swords, and dropped the two Najahn to the ground. The leader protested for one short second before the same happened to him, leaving three bodies motionless on the stone.

"We're wasting time," the Queen said. "Go."

Through the corridor, past another door, and down one more spiral stair to the moment of reckoning, a hope that Fassle hadn't yet found a way to mobilize his new weapons. A hope delivered in the piles waiting. More skars than Gladdring had ever managed to collect sat in Annalyse's old chests. Yarvick's informants, the tavern insinuations from pliable Najahn bore out their accuracy: Fassle had claimed the old skar testing grounds for himself, for new initiatives not yet ready.

Many Najahn skars had been moved here, few deployed. Gladdring could well understand why: a Vis stone, with its innate healing, was simple to slot into a soldier's bracer, sword, or armor. A Foti or Kance skar, capable of leveling the soldier's own force with poor use, demanded training. More research. More time than Fassle had since his purge had thrown out the only experts in Najahn employ.

And now Fassle's own mistakes would be Gladdring's salvation.

"Gather them, as many as we can store. Hurry," Gladdring snapped, making his own way to the Tamas collection. His hands reached beneath his heavy coats, began stuffing the stones into pockets. "These moments buy our future."

The Queensguard, and the Queen herself, shuffled satchels from beneath their huge coats, sweeping skars with one swipe after another into the bags. Untold power packed into every one of those stones, and here dozens upon dozens were theirs.

"It's time," the Vis said, standing near the stairs descending further. "Let's go."

Gladdring swept another look around as the Queensguard tied off their satchels, began the retreat with their Queen in tow. Most of the skars were gone, the laboratory made a mess in the haste. What miracles might they have found here, if Fassle had been smarter, or too stupid to notice?

Regret, though, had little hold on Gladdring. It vanished, in fact, when his feet found the frozen sand and his eyes, looking to the narrow sea cave and its small pier, beheld the Kance clipper waiting at the dock.

Above, the Najahn horns sounded again. The battle still raged.

CHAPTER 33

NEW TOWN, OLD ENEMIES

Eujo embraced those frosted rolling hills for two days. The wildlife tantalized, with Wax and Bliss falling on old hunter habits. They marched westward first, finding more gnarled roots at the foothill's edge and, with them, possibilities. Using Torny's knives, Bliss and Wax whittled out darts and the hollow tubes to launch them. While the bandit and the Queen kept the fire lit, the Vis pair stalked the evenings and early mornings, pinning scurrying vermin and the occasional bird flying too close. They taught Torny and Eujo to dig through frozen grasses and discover thicker roots suitable for boiling, burrows where buried nuts offered snacks.

Skinning came next, a night time job to shed furs off the bodies and hang them off the stacked satchels to dry. When Torny remarked that the pelts were too small to wear, Wax pointed out they were big enough for mittens, hats, and boots.

"Unless you're thinking we'll get charity when we come into town, we'll need something to trade," Wax said, sliding the bandit's dagger beneath a light gray coat whose former owner sat on a spit over crackling flames. "Unless I'm missing my guess, without the Renewal's protection, we're just travelers like anyone else."

"He's right," Eujo added, though she kept her eyes off the grisly business.

Not that carving meat and fur made her uncomfortable—Eujo had seen enough humans put to gruesome ends to forbid that affliction—but the Tamas night was otherwise too beautiful to waste looking at blood and guts. They'd been blessed with a clear streak, starry skies and mild winds. As they tracked southward, though Eujo couldn't imagine they'd gone all that far, things seemed warmer too.

Sure, the small animals and scattered vegetables weren't enough to fill her stomach, but starvation wasn't imminent, violent death seemed distant. Hard to be too disappointed.

"Okay, but where're we traveling to?" Torny asked. "Sleeping on icy ground's just great, but I'd love a bed. Some straw. A mug of something other than melted snow." She held up a gnarled, boiled root and frowned. "I'd even take a carrot over this."

"There'll be other towns, with less likely pursuit," Eujo said. "Every day we stay away from the main roads, the chances we'll be caught go down."

"Says you. If they want us, betting they'll find us."

"Haven't yet," Wax muttered between knife strokes.

"Ever think there might be a reason?" Torny gestured with the root off to the north, where they'd come from. "Not easy to hide tracks in the snow. We'd have been caught by now. I'm thinking they've given up, gone back to their show."

"You're betting a lot on that," Eujo said.

"Yeah, my own sanity. 'Cause if I have to spend another

few days watching this Vis butcher meat, I'm going to lose it."

The Kance Queen cast around for Bliss, but the hunter was off doing just that. Bliss could usually talk Torny down from the bandit's caustic rants, fingers flashing something funny or suggesting a walk. Like a young child, Torny would get distracted, drop her crusade, and wander off with Bliss, muttered curses following their footsteps.

"Then let's compromise," Wax suggested. "I'm with you, Torny. I don't like the cold, the meat here is gamey, and there's no fruit in the trees. I'd trade a thousand pots of snowmelt for a single ale."

"At last, someone speaks sense."

Wax took the dead rabbit's paw, angled it south and wiggled it. Eujo crinkled her nose, Torny just laughed.

"The next town's not too far that way. Bet we could get there tomorrow if you're willing to walk."

"Willing?" Torny scoffed. "I'd run there right now if it wouldn't mean dooming you all to dying out here."

"You're the one keeping us alive?" Eujo asked. "You?"

"Of course. It's my knives you've been using to clean all these kills. Without'em, you'd be the food for these things."

Wax glanced up from his dirty business, "Rabbits don't eat meat."

"Tamas rabbits do. I've seen'em devour a whole ox. Swarmed it, gone in seconds." Torny flicked snow off her gloves as she spoke. "Terrors everywhere out here, kept away by yours truly."

Eujo sighed. Maybe it wouldn't be a bad idea to get somewhere warm, with other people to talk to.

A BAD IDEA. The town was a damn bad idea.

Sure, it'd started fine, when the bedraggled quartet made the tavern in a place about the size of the Najahn outpost back on Whent. The sun slid towards the horizon after a hard day, a storm finally seemed to be moving in, picking up snow with it, and the thought of a fireplace held enough allure for Eujo, Wax, Bliss, and Torny to make great time over the hills. They even passed by a slow-moving cart making its way from the eastern mountains, on one of several roads leading into the village.

Tamas-style huts abounded, mushroom buildings with centered chimneys and thatched roofs. Mud and stone walls. Few flags, less bluster than the Animas and its carnival vibe. Torny said something about meeting the real Tamas and Eujo couldn't disagree, could almost find common ground with the people shuffling around, tending to daily tasks in a manner she hadn't in so, so long.

But the tavern, that'd been the mistake, though Eujo wasn't sure how they could've dodged it. Marking both the town's inn and watering hole, the tavern stood off a sedate square, a sprawling single story whose roof rose up and down like all those hills they'd been walking over. Smoke and the roasting, spiced meat rolled out to greet their pelt-covered satchels as the foursome closed, as they stomped into the place and laid their first glimpse on civilized society in several days.

That look gave Eujo everything she needed to know, to see, to run from.

Livier, the Kance assassin, Vientas member, and man loyal to the wrong Queen raised a mug as they walked through the door. Two more, marking the same threesome that'd attempted a brunch battering of Wax and Eujo way too long ago on Noctia, sat with him, grins glittering. Bliss and Torny, who'd dodged that bloody breakfast, didn't notice, kept right on walking in until Wax snatched at his sister.

"What's up?" Torny asked as Wax and Eujo stood in the doorway.

Someone shouted to shut the sturdy barrier, stop letting the cold in, and Eujo performed a quick and dirty calculation: the day was late, they'd marched long with tired, half-starved legs. Their coats and satchels weighed heavy with pelts and bones for bartering. Even with the Vis skars whispering their readiness, there'd be no outrunning rested killers.

No escaping across a snowbound land with tracks as easy to follow as walking them.

"I'm done, Wax," Eujo said, finding a familiar bearing in the words. Setting a course and following it. "Get a room. Stay, rest. They won't care about you."

Livier and the other two stood, now. Started their way.

"I can let the Foti skar go," Wax muttered as Bliss and Torny picked up the mood, saw the approaching trio. Hands dropped to weapons. "Burn them and this whole place to the ground."

The rest of the inn hadn't yet noticed how near disaster lay.

"They'll probably kill you first, or the next ones will," Eujo said, pushing past Wax to plant herself before the oncoming killers. "The Vientas don't stop because one falls. They'll chase us till the very end."

"Eujo . . . " Wax started, that build-up Eujo herself had heard so many times from follow thieves, from Queens-guards, from the other Kance Queen. About to tell her what was right, what she should do, how she should act. "I'm not—"

"That's right, you're not," Eujo said, giving an icy glare as good as any at her friends. "Go. This isn't your fight."

"As your Guardian," Torny said, "I believe it is."

"You're not my Guardian, there's no Renewal."

Before Torny could make up some other excuse, and the bandit's loyalty would've been touching if it weren't so stupid, Livier and his cohorts arrived. They pulled up before Eujo, looking healthy—save a mark on Livier's hand where Wax's fork had found justice—and ready to deliver their Queen's verdict. Clean robes, clear eyes, and Livier's steady voice as he spoke.

"Good to see you again, my Queen, after our unfortunate encounter on Noctia," Livier began, offering Eujo the slightest of bows. The killer's look moved beyond her to Wax, the man's smile twitching. "And the Vis Renewal, still alive. How lucky you all must be to have made it so far."

"Not luck," Torny said, sidling up next to Eujo. "Skill. Lots of skill. The kind you wouldn't want to test."

"Oh, believe me, testing your skill isn't why we're here." Livier stepped back, gestured towards their former table, big enough for another two or three to join. "Please, we have room, and the ale is quite good."

For a brief, terrifying moment Eujo wanted to give into Wax's suggestion. Her own skars, too, were ready, the whispers picking up her discomfort. Unleash the stones, run back into the snow, try their luck at the next town. Hope, then, that word of their destruction hadn't spread. They'd be flying, then, wanted and without any Renewal protection.

Just common villains with uncommon power.

Livier couldn't do that to her.

"My friends are tired," Eujo said, reaching out with her

right to press on Torny's coat, keep the bandit from doing something dumb. "But I'll join you. It's been a long walk."

"I can only imagine," Livier replied. "We were so disappointed to arrive at the Animas only to learn you'd taken flight."

"Stage fright," Eujo said, following the Vientas trio back to their table. Wax, Bliss, and Torny must've picked up her vibe, because they didn't follow, instead heading towards the bar and the innkeeper. "Acting on a stage is different than sitting on a throne."

"I imagine neither is your favorite thing." Livier pulled out the chair for Eujo, let her sit in it. "Ale? The stew is quite delectable as well. Our kitchens could learn a thing or two from this isle."

Eujo nodded to both—if they were going to kill her, might as well enjoy a meal first. Livier dispatched one of his comrades to fulfill the order. Turned the same placid smile he'd worn this whole time back to Eujo.

"I'll admit, it's been difficult to find you," Livier said, flowing into a slow journey recounting the Vientas trio and their travels across Whent, to Tamas, and this little town. He told it slow, giving himself time to drink his own ale and for the promised food and drink to be delivered. "We picked up your trail off the road south of the roots and paced you for a day. After that, a look at the Tamas map said your options were limited, so why suffer amid the cold wilds when cozy inns like this abound?"

"Because you never know who you might run into."

A little laugh. One Eujo hated.

"But run into us you did, and good thing too," Livier said, the smile falling away. "Because the world has changed, my Queen, and I'm afraid it's left you behind."

CHAPTER 34

DEATH'S DESIRES

Veritrus rose, hands planted flat on the table, with determined grace. A man of certain action, and Annalyse figured she knew what that action would be. So she mimicked him, save one part: grabbing the crude knife—the Najahn outpost lacked Noctia's luxuries—and waving it towards the Najahn commander.

Intimidating, it wasn't, and Veritrus's mild eyebrow let her know.

"Come now, Annalyse. This hardly need be a fight. You don't even need to die." A warm smile. "Not here, anyway. Fassle, I'm sure, would prefer you tied and presented before him."

"You do know how to strike a deal."

Veritrus moved around the table's end towards her. Annalyse slipped behind her chair. The simple building housing their dinner remained empty, the other partakers scattering to witness or partake in what seemed certain conflict between Mottilan and Kitaye. The Najahn wouldn't, Annalyse figured, take a side. See who won out, whether they were worth fearing. Until then, enjoy the chaos and secure the skars.

"A better one than you would have received at the assassin's hands," Veritrus continued. The man wore Najahn robes, not the black armor. Had no voulge, no chakram. Maybe a knife somewhere in those folds, but Annalyse hadn't sighted it yet. "The Third Hand would've poisoned you, and if that didn't work, slice your throat clean. Fassle might offer you a chance."

"I've already been a working slave to your Ringed City. Not again."

Annalyse meant it too, and not just to Noctia. Deshiva also demanded obedience at spear-point, and even the Whent university pushed her onward with vague, dire threats about outside interference if Annalyse couldn't move fast enough. Always pressure, always demands, always accompanied by danger.

Maybe it was time she tried something different.

Veritrus hesitated, right hand trailing along the table's edge. "I thought Deshiva forced you to use the skars to burn our gate. Was I wrong?"

"She's not much different than you."

"No, I suppose not, except in one crucial way. She is trying to do what she thinks is best for her city, her isle. I am trying to save them all."

Annalyse retreated another step. Figured she had another ten or fifteen backward strides to bring her to the exit. Outside, shouts rose, a mixture of questions and alarm dulled enough by distance and focus on the Najahn leader to blur their specifics.

"Gladdring kept saying the same, but Fassle killed him anyway," Annalyse said. "Noble goals aren't worth anything."

"Not without the means to succeed." Veritrus tilted his head outside. "Deshiva and those Mottilan fools will get nowhere. Already, a Noctia force is heading towards Vis. They will crush these hunters, and with the skars in our hands, no fiend will—"

"Great. Keep your dreams and leave me out of them."

Veritrus opened his mouth for some threatening, insipid reply and Annalyse let the Foti skar talk over him. The fire stone's mauling rush flowed through the dinner knife, breaking free in a blossoming rose. The air snapped, light crackled, and Annalyse felt the heat through her own blinking lids. Veritrus cursed, stumbled back and tripped over a chair.

Annalyse took the opening.

A simple pivot had her running from the ramshackle dining hall, inn, or whatever the building's purpose was and into a scarlet night. Without the buffer, frenzied fighting's noise dominated. Hunters and Najahn mingled in a melee, and Annalyse would've lost her head to a rogue spear if she hadn't slipped on blood-soaked grass. The weapon thunked into the wood behind her, quivering as Annalyse crawled, ignoring the warm wet on her hands. The blood's owner lay to her left, glassy-eyed and unmoving.

Around her, an outpost undergoing meager repairs was again destroyed. Fire didn't play a part so much as wild blows against light walls: a makeshift shed before her crumpled as a Najahn swung his voulge wide of its mark, a dancing hunter who closed, tripped, and took care of her assailant with a well-placed knife.

Sichi illuminated it all, bolstered by torches, their merry glows at hard odds with the skirmish.

Still, escape wasn't hard to find. The jungle waited,

dark and inviting near the horizon. Annalyse started that way before a thought pushed her to the side, crouching behind stacked rubble meant, perhaps, for some future rebuild.

By her count, and the whispers in her head, Annalyse had a skar from every isle save Kance slotted into the necklace at her neck. Not one of those skars would feed her. Rana might be able to conjure water with some effort, but Annalyse had no skin to store it in. Her shoes were a frayed mess, damaged by fire and fighting. Her Vis weaves weren't much better.

A flight into the jungle now guaranteed starvation, dehydration, and likely death from some predator she neither knew nor understood.

Panic threatened.

Logic, as it always did, proved her bulwark.

Annalyse had wanted to get to Svarde's isolated cabin and disappear. A rosy view mismatched with her reality, her experience. Veritrus suggested Kitaye was about to be invaded, along with Vis as a whole. Which meant leaving the isle, which meant going to a place more hospitable to someone like her, that might protect her, value what she offered.

Whent would be ideal, but lacking a way to get northward, the next best option lay to the east.

As Annalyse scrunched up into a ball, wounded cries now outpacing calls of challenge in the air, geography danced in the blushed dark. What she knew of Mottilan and how to get there lay in the dinner conversation just curdled: a pass, some mountains, and a coast. Eastward.

Orders, crisp, clear, and mottled with curses slashed the general melee around her. Veritrus, giving commands to some obedient Najahn. Find the scientist, let the Vis hunters kill each other. Simple enough, though everyone seemed to look the same in these shadows. Which . . .

She leaned out, just a head's breadth, from the stacked satchels. To her right, the outpost sloped towards the jungle, burned out wreckage from this battle or the last rising crumbling here and there like flimsy toys. To her left, and east, the slope continued up, tight jungle closing in around the path to the Great Sana. A one way trip and a trap, there.

South? South would mean more jungle, then, if Annalyse remembered her maps, the ocean. Not an option.

Parading through potential plans kept the fighting, the horror, the blood staining her hands, knees, and robes at a remove. If she could keep in her head, let the skars whisper while strategies played out, panic, too, would remain distant.

North, then. Annalyse fell back into the satchels as Najahn armor, clicks and clanks as metal hit metal, gave its approach away. The soldier, voulge and eyes out and about, stalked near her, before her even, but not once did the shadow's gaze find her. Too preoccupied with some bashing fight back west. Staff on spear or blade.

The soldier stopped. Not a stride away from Annalyse. Turned to watch, the voulge laying across his hands, knees at a slight bend. Ready to run, charge, depending on whether the soldier was a coward.

The Foti skar whispered a solution. Roast the Najahn in his armor like dinner in a Noctia stone oven. Annalyse pushed the thought away. Tried holding her breath, scrunching up. Her hands pressed worn leather, her shoes scooted on grass up beneath her, and slipped. The damn blood kicked her left leg out, landing Annalyse on her butt. One satchel tipped, fell with a soft splat on the ground.

Soft, but not silent.

The Najahn whirled, already jutting with the voulge, and a new whisper surged. A different skar, the quietest one taking charge with a curved point diving towards her face.

Annalyse didn't fight it, didn't stop as a hungry cold ran through her and crossed in lines invisible and all too real from Annalyse to the Najahn. The man's skewer stopped, shivered, and a face hidden beneath a helmet twitched only once. The voulge dropped first. The Najahn came second, not to his knees, not to a collapse, but a crumble, a nothing, just a pile of metal.

She would've passed out right then, the whisper's satisfaction stealing Annalyse's breath, her fortitude, her muscles and bone all at once demanding rest. The only thing keeping her awake, forcing her to a crouch, was the confused shock at what'd just happened, and the likely cause.

A question to be studied later. Annalyse stumbled away from the satchels, the pile that'd been a living, breathing person moments ago, and found the carnage continuing without her input. The fight's range narrowed as outer conflicts resolved themselves and drew inward, though Annalyse saw Najahn armor glinting at the boundaries. A net waiting to snare what Vis made it out alive.

Deshiva would be in there somewhere, if she wasn't already dead.

Some loyal tinge threatened, one Annalyse thwarted with a stumbling, sneaking run to the east, around the mess hall. No battles here, and despite Veritrus's orders, the Najahn seemed more preoccupied with the hunter quarrels. A matter of luck, and one Annalyse wouldn't, couldn't waste.

She ducked away from torches, kept low to the ground,

and darted from shed to tent to storehouse. No alarms cried out, and Annalyse might've found success save for one dire reality: her stumbles grew more frequent, her eyes heavy-lidded, and her arms moaned every time Annalyse asked them to keep her up against another wood beam.

"What did you take from me?" Annalyse muttered, her voice not even a whisper.

The skar answered. They always did.

But the scientist didn't understand. She could, though, crawl. Through grass, and fern, and beneath the jungle trees. Far enough that when the sounds of fighting faded, when her feet wouldn't move any further, she believed she might stay hidden.

From some hunters, anyway.

CHAPTER 35
TO SEE FIRE

Ami pulled the cart by herself, well-made Whent wheels crunching over stone without pause. Three flame-proof tunics—Jochi promised a better name for the gear eventually—sat atop one another in the simple space. As heavy as an iron breastplate, Ami would've been buried trying to carry them through the tunnel, but the cart performed its task ably enough. Good thing, too, because this time Ami was alone.

And having a hand free to reach for the blade at her waist brought comfort, though the firewalkers waiting at the tunnel's end probably wouldn't find the sword frightening.

A diplomat. Ami didn't think back to her childhood all that often, but the circumstances, their utter clashing with her head-butting, biting, wrestling youth prompted a soft laugh. One that nudged the gold faceplate against her scarred skin. She hadn't had that as a kid either.

Time and violence tended to change things.

Svarde and Jochi would be watching the exchange from the leftward nook, a notch Ami couldn't even see as she tugged the cart from the tunnel and into the vast chamber. As ever, the firewalkers continued their steady march towards colonization, repairing damage from the latest fiend attack while bulking up dwellings along the pebbled gray slopes. The homes looked as sloppy as makeshift human huts, rock and sand melted together into sloping cups, tops wide open. An oddity until Ami remembered who used them, and what might happen if all that heat stayed compressed in a small space.

Could a firewalker burn? Immolate itself?

Theories could wait. Ahead stood someone more immediate, silent, and large. Its skin billowing in silent, flowing oranges and blues, the firewalker Ami had talked—if you wanted to call it that—with before strode up the slope. Tall enough for its obsidian skull, a triangle shape with edges that seemed to be unique to each firewalker, and the only way Ami knew to identify the fiends from one another, to rise over the plateau's jutting end. Sparks juddered along the black, dancing in patterns Ami couldn't decipher.

Instead, she stepped aside, pointed at the wide cart.

"They're for you," Ami said. "Don't know if you can understand me, but these, they'll keep your fire back. So you don't torch us."

The firewalker flashed motes back at her, gold and icy blue. Whatever that meant.

"You wear it." Ami forged ahead. "Like this."

She bent over the cart, pulled the first tunic out. Lifted it only for its bottom to drag along the rock, its top to press against her head. Awkward and ugly, and absolutely not how the damn thing was supposed to be worn. Ami worked her head into the tunic's armpit to see the firewalker's reaction: a single quiet gold mote, none of those four arms moving.

Sweat broke out, for once not caused by the fiend's heat. Ami considered shoving an arm through one of the tunic's slots, but the idea, how dumb she'd look attempting that, had her abandon it. Had Ami, instead, toss the outfit on the plateau before her.

"Put it on." Ami pointed.

The firewalker stared.

"Dammit, this isn't that hard." Ami nodded at the tunic, pantomimed scooping the thing up with her arms and sliding it over her head. "See?"

If the firewalker saw, it didn't say. Instead, the single mote fizzled, cracked in two, a redder glow marching to the skull's top while a quiet white bobbed to the bottom. The firewalker turned aside, putting its left arms towards Ami while its right pair waved towards the pool.

"Don't know what you're trying to tell me," Ami said, only to get her words answered by the firewalker's fellows.

The burning group, young ones playing, old ones working, others in spark-flashing conversation, stopped and shuffled aside. They all cleared away, leaving a path marred by melted rock and simmering coals right to the water's edge. As the separation concluded, with the firewalkers turning as one like some ceremonial guard, to watch their new row, Ami's leading fiend took off at a slow lope down the lane.

That she should follow was both obvious and insane.

Ami judged the tunic, its failed mission lying in the dust. She could shout, try to get the firewalker to turn around and, again, attempt some dance to persuade the monster to don the crafted raiment. Or . .

The Whent boots she wore went with her thick clothes, fashioned by those same engineers to keep her skin as heatproof as possible. An idea that held more promise in a forge than traipsing down a rocky slope, as the weight had Ami lurching from foothold to foothold, making her feel like she'd had too much Whent wine. That she'd definitely indulged last night wasn't important: the Vis skars made sure no hangover stung.

Nevertheless, her lumbering impression prompted no reaction from the watching firewalker ranks. Their constructs sat behind them, nozzles all, now, pointed back towards the water rather than the tunnel. Either they trusted Ami's friends wouldn't attack again, or the threat from new fiends was simply too great.

What that said about Jochi's arms, Svarde's undead cadres and their abilities, well, Ami didn't care to speculate. The isles had been losing, slowly, the fight against the fiends. The whole reason she found herself at the water's edge was to end the war before it consumed everything.

Her guide, her counterpart, stood well away from Ami, and not quite as close to the water's edge. The reason why wasn't hard to parse: water and fire tended not to mix. The firewalker wasn't standing still, though. Instead, it crouched, those four arms wrapping around itself as if in some sort of hug. The flames on its skin coalesced into a single candle, rising, only to get snuffed out as several other firewalkers broke their line to place a curling, black-iron shell around it. One plate ran over the firewalker's top, while four others came sliding in piece by piece, slotting against one another with deep, chunky clicks. As they placed each section, the firewalkers ran their hands along the joints, the metal growing hot and fusing together.

Mobile forges, these things.

In too short a time, Ami's firewalker disappeared inside the metal ball. With a final, hissing run along the last front piece, the firewalkers who'd trapped their friend stepped to one side and, together, gave the ball a shove. With no preamble, no ceremony, no shouting, the big orb rolled into the water and disappeared.

"What?" Ami asked, turning to the watching firewalkers. "What was that?"

The fiends seemed to understand, almost as one raising their arms and pointing to the dark waters.

Another swim in all this? After the first one had gone so well?

Ami started to shake her head, then laughed instead. Why not? She'd already gone beyond the goals of the mission—get the firewalkers to wear the special clothes—and bashing aside boundaries had brought her this far.

A different reality struck as she turned back to the deeps. Her outfit, heavy and fireproof, would just drown the Guardian if she waded in with it. Yet, if she shrugged it off to the light cloth beneath, any close firewalker encounters would be . . .

The skars. The Vis skars would keep her alive, and she'd left beauty behind long ago. A few more burns to understand what these fiends wanted seemed worth the sacrifice. Svarde had doomed himself to an un-death with that blade always by his side. Ami could risk a little more.

For Catya, for Foti, for herself.

The cool waters didn't steal Ami's breath this time. Their silky feel whispered of unknown things dead and decomposing at the chamber's bottom, mysterious fluids joining in the cavern's sea after leaking from creatures not of this world. Disgusting to some, ignored by Ami, who focused instead on the metal ball.

Against the water's dark cold, the ball glowed a soft gray. Bubbles rose around it, the pool reacting to the heat Ami felt now as she swam. The ball rotated, moved, and

Ami wasn't quite sure how until she noticed small nozzles dotting the shape. Boiling water dashed from those nozzles only to get cut off, a fresh gout appearing elsewhere to shoot the ball beneath the sea towards its goal: the red orange swirl.

Ami swam along at the surface, taking breaths as she watched the orb's progress towards that swirl. They passed by an emerald maelstrom, then an icy silver storm, both of which the firewalker dodged around with steam bursts.

Such fine-tuned control, moving underwater . . . what the Rana wouldn't give for something like this.

If Ami hadn't taken her own trip into the blue swirl earlier, she might've been surprised when the ball disappeared among the red motes. Vanished without sound, without bubbles. Instead, Ami gulped down as much air as her lungs could hold, and dove. Kicks, strokes, brought the Guardian closer, until those crimson lights danced about her head and body. They felt like nothing, yet they avoided her touch, even as Ami closed to the shapeless center.

Until, like exiting a bath, Ami wasn't in the pool anymore. Until air, sulphuric and acid, struck her gasping lungs like scalding smoke. Her eyes moved from murky dark to blasted reds and oranges, a dry landscape stretching before her, dotted with burning geysers. Clouds, scarred with purples and reds, coated the sky. Glassed obsidian ran underfoot as far as Ami could see, rising here and there in jagged spikes, like spears thrusting up from deep beneath the surface. That, though, was only the backdrop.

She stood on a cliff, near its very edge, the burning world sweeping away from her in all directions save at her back.

At her heels waited the pool Ami had emerged from, and as she turned around, Ami saw an obsidian hood wrapped over its small form. The black and clear shards glittered, as if grown off of one another, and blocked her view behind it. A cowl over anything emerging, or entering, the pool. To Ami's right, the black iron ball hissed as the welded joints split apart, the shell collapsing to reveal the firewalker within.

"This is your home?" Ami said, coughing as the air swiped at her throat.

The firewalker flashed dancing gold in return, before pointing with its two left arms back behind Ami, behind the obsidian cowl. What fear might've risen at being so far beyond anything known was calmed by the familiar Vis whispers, those skars mending her shocked lungs, her bare feet as they gathered cuts on the obsidian shards with every step.

That fear came back as Ami, walking opposite the firewalker, turned away from the cliff and went around the obsidian shell's side, giving her a view of what lay behind, beneath more blackened clouds and spitting flame.

Arrayed to the horizon stood a shifting swarm, metal and firewalker mingling. Massive constructs, far too large to fit in the pool, lumbered in the distance. The firewalkers themselves, each one a candle, merged in their brilliance with one another, so that it seemed like Ami looked across a single, pure flame.

The thousands, the tens of thousands, and all their terrible creations, spoiled the singular, strange beauty in the sight.

There was no other option against such a force, such a gathering. Ami would strike a peace with these creatures, or the isles would burn.

CHAPTER 36
CAST ASIDE

The salty sea spray and bitter ocean wind bore kisses Gladdring would endure for as long as he could, so long as the Kance Queen brought him to freedom. They were a day out from Noctia now, in the open ocean with the Ringed City and its isle beyond the horizon to the north. The loop, so the ship's captain declared, would take the Queen's ship almost to Vis before swooping further east and north to come into Kance from the south.

Too many ice floes to do it another way, was the excuse.

Whether the delay would be fatal depended on Fassle, on Yarvick, and how soon their chaos quelled.

But for the first day, at least, no purple and black ships chased after them. For the first day, Gladdring dined on fresh-caught fish and good Vis fruits bought from the Noctia ports before they became enmeshed in the . . . Gladdring grinned as he held the railing, looked over the waves.

The revolution, wasn't that what Yarvick wanted to call it?

Gladdring hoped the bandit lord succeeded. Yarvick, at least, could be bargained with, would be too busy getting control without Gladdring's token alliances and figurehead potential. What a mess that would be. And if Fassle won out, the old Circle's vengeance would consume too much time to attack their ship.

He'd reach Kance, and then—Gladdring turned, a not inconsiderable maneuver on the boat's rolling deck, with heavy coats on, to look across the sailor-covered and otherwise barren top deck—Gladdring would need to begin building loyalties anew. The Kance Queen made no secret that her tolerance for Gladdring's presence began and ended with his usefulness to her, a trait dwindling as their distance from Noctia grew.

Still, the Queen didn't know the skars like Gladdring did, and that alone would give the former Tenet some staying power. A chance, maybe, to carve out hope for himself.

"You spend a lot of time out here alone," came the Queen's muffled voice, protected by a thick indigo scarf. She'd appeared, as she often did, as if by magic. An open deck door with stairs leading down gave the sudden rise away, but Gladdring found himself frowning nonetheless.

Surprises were for fools who didn't pay enough attention.

"What do you think about, Gladdring, while you stare at the waves? Are you happy we survived, plundered the Najahn of their skars?"

"Why wouldn't I be?"

"Because a man like you is never content where he is."

"Wise words, my Queen." Gladdring, keeping one hand on the railing, gave the Queen a short bow. Like him, her royal highness wore bulky coats, though hers carried a finery, puffed furs and fitted sleeves that put her station clear of his own. A Queensguard, in their glass-like plate, stood behind her. "I've found contentment is often one day short of disaster."

"So then, where are you running to this time?"

"Sailing to Kance, I hope, and a reprieve from imminent doom."

"A reprieve?" the Queen joined him at the railing. The Tamas skar, slotted into a bracelet in Kance fashion around Gladdring's wrist, picked over her mood, declared the Queen wary, exhausted, and, yet, curious. "We've started the greatest war the isles will have seen in generations, all while fiends rampage. What sort of reprieve is that?"

"For a man about to see the gallows or the cold ocean, a good one."

The Queen laughed, then set about to stricter questions, beginning what Gladdring assumed would be a pattern. Breakfast, coffee, then a dialog on the deck about the skars, what Gladdring and his associates had learned, and their possibilities for turning the war quick. At the moment, the Queen held her objective as the defense of Kance, holding its cities and pushing the Najahn to stop the fighting.

From there, they could look to more worldly matters, like Gladdring's own professed desire to see the fiends wiped away with the skar's power.

"You'll give me that?" Gladdring asked. "A chance to find the fiend's source and use the skars against them?"

"If we survive that long."

Gladdring scoffed, "The Najahn, even if Fassle survives, won't press us hard. Once we train your soldiers, they'll be able to burn a frigate from afar, blow an adversary to the ground, or . . ." Gladdring found another path, veered away from where he'd been heading. "Change their minds and turn them to your side."

"The Najahn are only one enemy, Gladdring," the Queen said. "There will be others."

"None so powerful."

The Queen didn't reply, a long enough silence to make Gladdring doubt his own words. What adversary did she mean? Yet, before he could ask for more, she nodded and left, heading across the deck towards the raised bridge. An audience with the captain, more details and plans Gladdring wouldn't be privy to. The Queen was writing him out, and Gladdring had no other allies on the ship, save that Vis hunter, though Quik had kept to himself since the getaway.

Gladdring was alone. A situation he would have to rectify.

The Wind's Rose. A name as ridiculous as any other given a ship, but one Gladdring committed to uttering with the same reverence as all the other Kance on board. The vessel had a polished exterior that gave way to a mishmash inside, with different woods, patched over doors and new ones opened as the ship engaged in a continual resurrection. To hear the sailors tell it—and Gladdring talked more with them than anyone as the journey's second day wore on—Kance depended on the ship's legend enough to keep retrofitting it.

Every queen had to make their stamp on *The Wind's Rose,* and the one currently having an early dinner had done so with the ship's defenses. Notched along the railing at several stride intervals sat narrow ballista cannons and the taut strings to fire them. Tied ammo clusters lay next to every one, an impressive stock, and one Gladdring learned had been ordered on before the journey to Noctia.

Another mark in the Queen's favor.

Gladdring's random interrogations led him to *The Wind's Rose*'s forward cabins, stocked with critical cargo, and to the Queensguard pair standing outside the sealed room where the skars had been stashed. Glittering, as ever, they eyed Gladdring as he approached, the man donning as friendly a smile as he could.

"Good afternoon," Gladdring opened, giving each a nod in their turn. Both stared at him, offered nothing.

Typical. Even the Tamas skar gave no hints, just a muted caution.

"Do you know what's inside?"

Again no reaction. Gladdring tilted his head at the door. "Can I go inside?"

That, at least, earned a response. One put their arm—Gladdring found it hard to declare man or woman beneath their helms—across the door while the other put their hand on the rapier bound to the waist.

"So you are alive," Gladdring said, stepping back. "I had to make sure the Queen hadn't shielded her door with statues."

"What do you want, Najahn?" asked the one with her hand on her sword arm.

"Only to ask if you know what you're guarding, that's all. To ensure you're taking proper care."

Eyes narrowed.

"Skars can be very dangerous," Gladdring continued. "They hold the god's own power. One misstep, and this whole ship might be destroyed."

"Then you should tell the Queen."

"I have, she knows. In fact, that's why I'm here."

The Tamas skar kept him talking, a door edged open by possibility and forced the rest of the way by Gladdring's silver tongue. The Queensguard pair thawed as Gladdring described the skars, what they could do, how they could be wielded. Annalyse's notes, their progress sessions gave Gladdring the words to throw, the lures to cast out, and by the time he ran to the end, he knew their names, their shifts, and had the promises his guidance would be passed along.

Now, he had one more alliance to form, and Gladdring found his target near the prow. Quik, with little sailing knowledge but as much restlessness as the sailors, had his gauntlets at hand as he ran through one exercise after another. Jumps, curls, flexes, it all seemed like so much work, but Gladdring let the hunter wind his way through.

Quik must've noticed Gladdring standing there, buffeted by the endless breeze beneath the platinum sky, but the Vis took his time. Gladdring waited without a word, spoke only when the Vis hunter began putting on his own coats.

"I haven't thanked you properly," Gladdring said, drawing little more than a curious eye from Quik. It was, to be fair, a difficult place to hold a good conversation, what with the lapping waves, the sailors calling, and the wind's endless whistles. Gladdring, though, would make the effort. "Your actions back on Noctia saved all our lives."

"Thank me by saving my brother."

"To hear the Queen tell it, that is already being done. What you should be worrying about, now, is your own skin."

Those mighty brows furrowed. The Tamas skar spoke up. Good.

"The Queen is like any other ruler," Gladdring said, nodding past Quik to the ship's prow and walking that way. The hunter joined him, so they stood backs to the bridge, easily visible to anyone looking their way. "She seeks to preserve her country, and will use anyone to achieve that purpose. While ridding herself of the same when their usefulness is over."

"As I understand it, a war's coming to Kance." The Vis tapped the gauntlets, now hanging off his thighs. "I'm useful in a fight."

"But after?"

Quik laughed. "I barely know you, Gladdring, but you always seem to be scheming. Why so restless? We won."

"We made a good move, but the game continues. Preserving our place in it means working together, Quik."

"Does it?" Another chuffed laugh. "What now, Gladdring? Who am I supposed to gut for you? Or is the Queen again planning on murdering someone who doesn't deserve it?"

"Kill not a soul for me, Quik. Not right now, and maybe not ever. As for the Queen, that I cannot say." Gladdring let the Tamas skar free as he put a hand on Quik's shoulder. "What I'm asking is to watch my back, and I will watch yours. We're not Kance, we are expendable."

The skar found its footing and Quik's mocking look faded to straight concern. He didn't shrug off Gladdring's hand, returned the nod. When they went to dinner at the Queen's invitation an hour later, Quik sat by Gladdring's side, a shift noticed by the ruler.

And when the alarm came just past dawn that a Noctia ship approached, Quik was the first to Gladdring's cabin, waiting for a plan.

CHAPTER 37

BAR BRAWL

As stabs in the back went, Livier's came smooth and with little warning. Eujo, sitting in the one spare chair at their table, the inn's boarding room bubbling around her, reached for the offered flagon, felt a searing pain spread in her gut. Her eyes blurred, all coherent thoughts jumbling, and the Vis skar shouted nonsense in her mind. Burbling something from a dry mouth, Eujo fell off the chair and to the hard floor.

Sticking from her side, like some bloody victory flag, was a Kance dagger, silver and glittering.

Eujo saw her three friends, all standing near the inn's prodigious dark-wood bar, shout and curse as one. Bliss drew the thick root stick she'd been using as a makeshift staff and charged, dragging the weapon over her shoulder only to have it strike a lantern in the move, shattering glass and spraying burning oil across the floor. From her angle, Eujo found the blazing splashes mesmerizing, their sparks threatening to take her back—

The skars wouldn't have it.

Not just the Vis, but all of them, the Foti, Rana, Whent, and Kance stones slotted around her wrist snatched at Eujo's attention, her energy, both giving and taking what they could in desperate attempts to do . . . something. Eujo wanted to let go, sink into the dull death veil the dagger, probably poisoned, was drawing over her, but her friends engaged the assassins. They fought for her.

Letting the skars cut loose might well kill them all, and Wax, Torny, Bliss didn't deserve to die for Eujo.

The bandit and her Vis friend, her more than friend, found fighting first against Livier and the woman who hadn't stabbed Eujo. Bliss's staff gave her reach, the initial downward slam breaking into a straight on push at Livier, who used his Kance robes to misdirect, let the push sweep right on by to let him get within a rapier's strike.

Only for the man to fly aside, as if shoved by some invisible god's hand.

Which was, Eujo realized, exactly what happened. The Kance skar's residue crackled in Eujo's arm, her long day's muscles already exhausted and aching. Livier would be aching too, as his flight sent him crashing into another table, empty aside from chairs as the inn's more civilized occupants fled.

Torny danced with her opponent, daggers out and flashing as their boots stamped on, slipped over the burning oil. Behind them, Wax had his sword drawn, but seemed lost as to where to turn, who to fight.

The man wasn't a warrior, was barely a Vis hunter. This wasn't his place.

Eujo tried to speak up, tell her friends to run, an attempt cut off by new, biting agony: the dagger in her side lifted free, pulled out by the third assassin. Eujo curled her head, saw her own blood dripping off the knife's edge, saw the cold eyes behind the one who wielded it as she studied Eujo, looking for those signs life would soon be gone.

The skars surged again. Whent winning out this time, demanding a chance, and Eujo let it go.

Wood cracked, the floor beneath her, beneath Eujo's killer, roiling as though the ground had become a wave. Splinters flew, the assassin fell, and Eujo herself slid away, tumbling to a rest halfway across the inn. Flat on her back, the fighting in easy view, Eujo instead focused on the purple-red line following her trip across the inn.

Too much blood. Too much for any Vis skar.

Bliss, to the blood streak's right, swung her staff at the assassin pressing Torny—the spunky bandit's knife work wasn't up to Kance killer's standards, and her arms bore a desperate defense's telltale scratches. The root slammed the assassin's left shoulder, sent the killer into a sprawl through the burning oil, which finally found its purchase, illuminating the silver and blue Kance robes in a blaze.

The third assassin took no notice of her colleague's disaster, instead throwing the drawn dagger she'd pulled free from Eujo. The knife, in the unerring awfulness earned by long practice, jammed into Bliss's side, spinning the Vis into a half-crouch. As Torny cursed, dashed at the third killer, Bliss dropped the staff and pulled the knife free, now wet with new blood.

Sorry, Bliss. Eujo wanted to speak the words, would've, if her throat wasn't so damn dry. If her body wasn't so tired.

Still, the Vis skar worked. Attacked her wounds with as much skill as the assassins brought against her friends. Eujo found the next breath easier than the last, and if death might be inevitable, it wasn't right then, right now.

Livier must've thought the same, as the man rose up behind Bliss, rapier drawn and hunting for a fatal stab. Wax flew in, the brother at last rising to his sister's aid, like some diving bird, an almost shadow in the smoke. Wax's sword flashed, forced Livier into a counter, the Vis doing something smart and letting his momentum overpower the lithe Kance, pushing Livier into the same table he'd struck a second ago.

Wait. The smoke?

The burning oil had found more than the assassin's robe. The billowing black flew up into the inn's ceiling, roiling back down among them as wood beams became the second course to the floor's appetizer. If the assassins didn't kill them all soon, the inn itself might do the job.

Eujo pressed her right hand down, tried to rise and settled for a crawl. One along her own blood, towards the enraged Torny, dueling with the rapier-wielding, dagger-throwing assassin. Torny at least had the right idea of it: using her daggers to bat aside the rapier's stabs and step in close. The bandit scored a hit as Eujo made her second lunge, a quick jab along the assassin's leg, sudden red marring the dirty white robes.

A hit that cost her.

The assassin clamped her right, rapier-wielding arm against the leg, trapping Torny's wrist and its dagger against the torn robes. With her left hand, the assassin grabbed Torny's other wrist, one left too close with the leaning stab, and snapped it. A howled curse, the clatter of a dropped knife, and the assassin moved her hand in a fingertip stab at Torny's throat.

The skars spoke again, and Eujo let them.

Rana swept up the burning oil, the few droplets left, and flung them at the assassin, the tiny molten missiles lancing into the killer's face, burning through her robes, and breaking off the attack. The assassin stumbled away, batting at the oil, her back turning long enough for Torny to use the opening, the bandit's remaining dagger at last finding a home.

"Stop!" Livier, his voice no longer so pointed, so polite, shouted above the chaos. "The madness ends here, while your lives are still yours."

Eujo followed the looks, saw Wax, disarmed and bleeding, standing with a small knife to his throat. Livier, equally bloodied, held the Vis hostage, not a smidge of craze, of desperation in the man's stance. His two friends, associates, lay dead or dying on the inn's floor—the one who'd caught fire lay motionless as those flames feasted—but Livier gave them not one glance. Instead, he caught Torny, Eujo, and the stumbling Bliss in his look.

"We leave, now, and you have a chance at life," Livier continued. "Leave your weapons and go."

Torny aimed a wavering dagger at the man, the bandit's body disappearing amid the smoke. "Too late for that. Going to kill you instead."

"No," Eujo said, her voice a meek thing, but loud enough over the crackle. "He's right. Run."

The Kance skar whispered possibilities. Eujo listened.

A breeze rose, whipping the flames to new heights, but sweeping the smoke out through the inn's open doors, left ajar by frantic flight. Torny didn't seem moved by Eujo's command, but Bliss, easy to see in her halting, bleeding steps, drew a stronger response. The bandit ran for the Vis, caught Bliss as she fell, and pulled her towards the inn's exit.

"Sorry Eujo," Torny said as she moved Bliss, Livier and Wax walking after. "Wasn't how this was supposed to go."

Eujo tried to smile, failed. The Vis skar's early advances against her wound faltered as Eujo's own strength went to the other stones. The pain spread, a poison's classic burn sending aches along her nerves. The spreading fire's heat, too, added its own sear.

As a way to die, this had to be among the worst, but at least her friends, at least . . .

Livier coughed, the knife faltering. Wax drove an elbow into the assassin's gut, and dove. Landed at Eujo's side, sliding a battered shoulder beneath the Kance Queen's left arm. Before she could ask Wax why he was doing something so stupid, the Vis Renewal planted his left hand on the inn's floor, and the whole building lurched. Wood cracked and the ground itself surged beneath them, tossing Eujo and Wax towards, and through, the inn's front door. They smacked into Torny and Bliss, scattering the foursome onto the frozen street beyond.

Eujo flopped onto her back, looked up at the inn's pyre rising high into the dark, clouded sky. For the moment, the cold salved her burned and bloody body, the Vis skar muttering its approval at the change in scenery, in the removal of so many death-dealing elements. To her right, Wax, coughing up more smoke, struggled to stand. On Eujo's left, Bliss lay still, with Torny, cursing, trying to turn the Vis upright.

And around them, a whole town chattering, calling for water, wondering what was going on.

"No way," Wax muttered, kneeling over Eujo. She followed his look to the inn's door, wreathed in flame, and the silhouette lurching out between its beams. "He can't."

Livier, his robes cast off and standing in little more than a torched shift, stumbled free, two long steps before he landed, face first, on the hard ground.

"Look at that, Wax," Eujo whispered, townspeople clustering, the first offers of help, of wrapped bandages and warm resting places, pouring in. "We won."

Wax's ash-smeared face, bleeding gashes, and tired eyes seemed only to wonder at the cost.

CHAPTER 38

WHAT CHANCE REMAINS

The cold wet woke her, the way it pressed against Annalyse's cheek and left a slime trail at its touch. The scientists's eyes saw only dirt when they opened, mottled soil with scattered leaves mixed in. A worm wending its way in the early morning. No birdsong.

But a sniff. Deeper, louder than a human's, than a Whent dog's.

Annalyse turned her head towards the sound. Her body ached, demanded water. Her nose, crusted over, blocked any smells. Her ears and eyes, though, told her what she needed to know: a giant, gray-purple cat with six legs eyed her. The cat's mouth lingered open, revealing fangs that'd do exactly what they promised to Annalyse given the chance.

A pink tongue drooped. The cat leaned closer.

Terror found its hold, kicking away sleep's stranglehold, and Annalyse sat up in a sudden jerk. The cat—the hanoko, Annalyse found the word—edged back. Cautious, a trait that might've saved Annalyse's own life.

For now.

She had no weapons, no knowledge about how the hanoko fought, hunted, feared. Annalyse did, though, have the skars, and she felt them waking up with her. Whispers, curious and, in Foti's case, demanding.

The hanoko approached again, lead paw rising for what looked like a severe swat.

"Stay back," Annalyse said, a rasp the hanoko ignored.

The cat couldn't brush off the Foti skar and its fire so easily. Annalyse didn't let the skar go wild, tamping down the rush as the skar flooded heat through her fingers, fire sprouting up from the earth in small geysers. The heat, light, gave the hanoko enough evidence that this wasn't a meal worth fighting for, and the cat, hissing, turned tail and ran.

"Told you," Annalyse muttered, pulling herself up to a stand and brushing the dirt off her, well, dirty dinner clothes.

The sunny morning broke through with more warmth than the scientist had felt in weeks, perhaps a sign winter might be tilting towards its inevitable, wonderful end. The silent birds returned to chirping as the hanoko fled, their little forms dashing between the trees above. Those tweets added to the gurgling from her own stomach, a reality Annalyse couldn't dismiss despite the beauty around her.

The Najahn were her confirmed enemies now, planning to either kill her or send her back to Gladdring's—no, Gladdring had to be dead, Fassle then—towers to labor with the stones. Deshiva, an ally of chance, was probably dead too given the Mottilan attack, Veritrus's planned ambush. If the hunters from both cities had been wiped out or sent fleeing, and if Veritrus was right about a Najahn force heading this way, then Vis wasn't a safe isle anymore.

Annalyse almost laughed right there at the thought of

crossing the jungle on foot, making for Svarde's old cabin. What a dumb idea that'd been.

So where? And with what?

Annalyse still had her necklace, the skars within it. Nothing more than that, anymore. Her remaining stones had been back at the Najahn outpost, set in a small lockbox near her cot. That'd been smashed open by now, most likely, meaning any return would be both suicidal and pointless.

Which left the way she'd been going, a stumbling trek north and east. To the coast, to Mottilan, and there to a ship. One that would either bring Annalyse home to Whent or, if ice still blocked the sea lanes, to Kance. There, at least, was an isle that wouldn't accept Najahn control lightly. Annalyse could barter her knowledge for protection, for food and water.

With a direction decided, the scientist started off, picking through ferns and around mushrooms as she walked. Every plant offered a potential meal, but Annalyse hadn't studied Vis enough to know which were safe and which would make her more miserable than she already was. At least the sun shone bright enough to follow, its place along the sky giving Annalyse a good idea which way was north.

Long walks in the woods seemed to be the same as long walks in the Whent mountains or the Noctia streets: a chance to reset herself, to ask what Annalyse was doing and why. Her initial goal—save the world at Gladdring's behest—was so distant now as to be a delusion. Her Whent lab, its inventions, some that would've used the skars to great effect, felt equally impossible.

Survival, maybe with a side of stiff ale, ranked at the top and shoved all other dreams aside.

That sole focus held her through the day, till, sometime in the early afternoon, she stumbled through a fern bank onto a wide, eastward path. Wide enough for carts to pass and deserted, but the packed earth suggested recent travel. Only one thing that might be.

Her eastward turn and an hour's walk along it brought new sounds, ones Annalyse was closing in on. Groans, shuffling steps, and muted conversation. The scientist slowed as the path scaled further, curling around dense tree pockets in a wind uphill. Right now, Annalyse figured she hadn't yet been seen.

But her stomach still gurgled, her throat burned, and the Vis skar keeping her minor wounds at bay whispered for more. Banded together, her energy flagged, her legs took heavy steps. If Annalyse fell asleep, alone, near the path, she might never wake up.

Better a chance than none at all.

She broke into a stumbling run, setting her battered shoes one step before the other, dodging marred ground. Around another curve waited her salvation, stopping their own journey at the approaching steps.

A salvation that was, seemingly, fifteen or so Vis in various ruin. Annalyse slowed her approach as she took in disaster: three lay on stretchers made with bamboo and thatched branches, carried by others, while still more limped, wounds bleeding through makeshift bandages. A few scant pouches and water skins throughout the group gave little hope of refreshment.

This was a lost force, the casualties making a desperate retreat towards home.

"Who're you?" called one, his left arm limp but otherwise healthier than the others. He drew a hardwood club from his waist, brandished it towards her. "You don't look like a Vis."

"I'm not," Annalyse replied, running variables in her head. Making a decision. "But I'm not your enemy."

"Seems like everyone's our enemy these days." The man didn't lower the club. "What're you doing here, then?"

"Running from the same place you are, I think. The Najahn tried to hurt me too."

A calculated drop, there. Annalyse wasn't sure the Najahn had inflicted these wounds, but the man's slow nod confirmed her suspicions.

"Why?" the man asked. "You have no weapons, what would—"

"Knowledge. The Najahn fear anyone who wants to help the isles stay free."

"And you would travel with us, knowledge-giver? Even after seeing we are hunted?"

"Better than alone."

The man glanced up the path, "There's an inn not an hour's walk away from here, though we'll take three at least. You can go on ahead. We'll not stop you."

The hanoko dashed through Annalyse's head.

"Better with you than alone. If you'll have me."

"They're cowards," Reth snarled as they walked, he and Annalyse taking up the group's rear. "The Najahn waited until we were tired and bloody, struck while we were tying up the Kitaye captives. Most of us died quick. The rest of us ran."

"They didn't chase?"

Reth's grip tightened on the club, one that had yet to

find its way back to the cloth loop serving as its home. "They did. There were more of us. Brave souls who stood back to buy us time. That they've not caught up says they never will."

"You think the isle's lost, then."

Reth huffed, nodded at the wounded before him. "Vis is strong, but we're not an isle of armies. The Najahn will place a yoke upon us, and as long as it's not too tight, we'll accept it. Our mothers want to raise our sons and daughters, not bury them."

"And the fiends, at least, will have new enemies."

Reth said nothing to that, and Annalyse let the conversation die. Her throat could use the break anyway.

Minutes passed, the sun slipping near westward canopies. Green became orange and purple. The jungle symphony softened, and a new sound rose to replace it. A metal one. Reth cursed, gave a whistle, and the group picked up its pace, groans only growing.

"We're close enough now. With a push," Reth said, "we can make it."

Annalyse didn't need to ask what jangling metal meant: Najahn, approaching quick. How those soldiers could run this long after a day's fighting, in such heavy armor, seemed a mystery, but they were coming.

And with their arrival, Annalyse saw an opportunity. One she greeted with a fatalist's gleam.

"Reth, stay near me," Annalyse said, turning around. Behind them, the path carried on down twenty strides or so to the next curve. By the sounds, the Najahn would be rounding that turn in moments. "I'll need you to catch me when I fall."

"When you fall?"

The Mottilan hunter might not have understood, but he did as Annalyse asked. Why he'd trust a non-Vis only a couple hours after meeting her, Annalyse didn't have to wonder. The Tamas skar in her necklace had done its job, nudging Reth with every word she spoke to bring him around to her side.

She saw, now, why Gladdring put so much stock in the small topaz.

While the wounded Mottilan continued their slow flight, the Najahn pursuit arrived bathed in purple shadows. Their armor didn't gleam anymore, covered with dust and blood. Annalyse counted eight, and among them only three chakrams. The rest carried voulges and stolen Vis spears. Ramshackle as they might've been, though, their murderous intent was clear: they approached without words, with weapons drawn.

"Ready?" Annalyse asked.

"I don't know what you're planning, but I swear I am ready for it."

So, too, was the Whent skar. Annalyse bent down, the Najahn only a few strides away, those first chakram sliding off the backs. When her fingers touched ground, Annalyse let the skar loose. Like a thunderstorm bursting within her heart, the Whent skar took Annalyse's anger, fear, and hope, and sent it crashing forward. The path buckled, fissures spreading from Annalyse's fingers like earth-bound lightning. The Najahn faltered, fell as the cracks reached their metal boots. Upon contact, as if the Najahn themselves acted as a catalyst, the cracks widened, flinging rocks high into the sky and swallowing up the soldiers. Pits appeared where none stood before, and as the soldiers fell in, cursing, screaming, calling for help, the earth shut back over them, burying the Najahn in mounds.

Annalyse saw all this, directed none of it, the Whent skar shouting in her head a wordless victory. But she held herself steady, kept her hand touching the path till the last Najahn disappeared.

When the purple and black armor vanished, Annalyse slumped, but she never touched the broken earth.

CHAPTER 39

TO THE SILVER SEA

The gods weren't all that creative.

Ami came to the conclusion just like Fassle and his Adepts might bring about a Renewal: evidence, gathered piece by piece. The Guardian descended off the plateau, flanked by the firewalker who'd brought her here, and noted, beyond her sweat, cracked earth similar to Foti's lava wastes. A scorched sky nonetheless holding slight clouds. A hot breeze like the dry summers Ami had known.

Molten metal's familiar smell, biting at her nose as the firewalkers shifted to give Ami space.

All those obsidian crowns sparkled, seeming to float among the burning bodies. The firewalkers wore no clothes here, rising instead as burning shapes. A glance back towards the pool and the portal confirmed more constructs under assembly, more approaching. Safe passage through the water waiting beyond.

"Must've been a rough surprise, the first time through," Ami said, her escort's black head flickering blue sparks in reply.

Whatever that meant.

Still, Ami collected answers around her with every step. As she left the plateau, two carved stones rose on either side, taller even than the firewalkers themselves. Sigils she didn't know ran around the obsidian, the carved edges smoothed over, the rock melting as the artist signed the words. Warnings to any hoping to explore the portal, or mementos to the ones who'd already tried?

The firewalker mass revealed more of itself, the creatures not just waiting around the portal but crafting some society. The games Ami had seen back in the pool's chamber played here too: round rocks kicked in steaming circles, others throwing objects into the air to get struck by well-timed flail blows, and others stood in patterned lines with their obsidian crowns flashing at one another in repeating bursts.

Ami slowed at the sights, the heat building as she moved deeper into the crowd. A wondrous look at first, a marvel at the second, faded now to concern for herself.

"Why am I here?" Ami asked the firewalker by her side.

In that moment, she resolved to give the thing a name. Spark seemed suitable, obvious enough.

Thus dubbed, Spark reached its right mid-arm forward, pointing over the crowd to the distinct dark shapes rumbling across the land. Their heavy stomps made the ground tremble, a soft shake Ami hadn't noticed till she connected their motion with the vibrations in her thick boots.

"What, you want me to see those?" Ami laughed, one that turned into a cough as the dry heat snatched at her throat. "They look a little far away, Spark. Not sure I can make it that far and back."

Spark seemed to have anticipated the reply, as its arm

swung lower and leftward, towards a spot free of firewalk-ers, though not of their ash metal constructs. These contained the flame-spouting monsters Ami had seen on the other side, but those were tiny compared to the other machinations resting here. Among towering cylinders, squat iron balls, and sledge-like platforms, Spark led Ami near two silent, looming things that had looping lines running along what seemed like a band of knifes across their bases.

Ami stared up at the closer one, at the odd nodules springing off its sides. Vents perforated metal slabs, several cylinders shot towards the sky. Spikes jutted at odd angles, as if the vehicle needed to fend off some giant hand making for a grab.

Which, for all Ami knew, it did.

Spark rested its own hand on a charred ring halfway along the metal beast, a burning outline tracing its fingers before flowing along carved channels to a circular door. Once the heat completed the circle, some latch inside popped with an audible hiss. The entry swung in, and Spark stepped well back, waving for Ami to go inside.

The idea that she was about to walk into an oven with a giant burning flame crossed Ami's mind, and she made a silent prayer to Foti that those vents would keep the Guardian alive. Still, turning back now was the sort of thing she just didn't do.

You couldn't come this far and only now get scared. Svarde had stumbled deep into the Dark Below and hadn't turned back. Ami could do this.

For Catya. For the Isles.

Walking on metal brought unfamiliar sounds, ones, like the skar whispers in her mind, Ami ignored as she clomped into the construct. A lever litany ran around her, the machine's shape translating into basic box interior, uninteresting save for one thing: the lever heads, all of them, glittered with raw ruby stones.

With Foti skars.

Heat behind her made Ami advance further into the construct, Spark doing the kind thing and waiting for Ami to retreat to the back corner. Vents surrounded her, each offering a sliced view of the outside world, of the firewalkers moving again to make a path away. Spark's entry did just what Ami had feared: the air went from hot to sweltering, to suffocating. Her vision blurred, her Whent clothes finding nowhere to shove the heat to, and Ami sank to her knees.

Until, with a gentle sigh, the heat drained away. Fast enough to feel like a wind, and so thorough Ami shivered as she refocused her eyes. Spark stood at the construct's front, a hands on four levers and starting to work them in tandem. How those levers—

The skars.

The firewalkers used those skars to suck the heat away. Ami shook her head, cursing once again her home's utter lack of ingenuity. That these firewalkers were so far ahead of the Seven Isles seemed again obvious, and what it spelled for Ami's home wasn't good.

Then again, at least Fassle would get what's coming to him.

Spark's efforts cranked the construct to life. A rumble, a squeal, then both repeated time and again. Those knife treads found homes in the stone, every dig carving into the rock and sending the construct spinning around, then shooting forward. A lurching, uneven ride at first, a smoother one minutes later as the machine found its groove. Spark kept working the levers, a fast push and pull dance.

Like swinging a sword through a routine, or sailing a ship.

The view beyond the firewalkers became placid red and brown rock, dusted and cracked. Obsidian flakes dotted the landscape along with random stones, as if something large had chucked boulders here and there without regard for pattern or purpose. No plant dared contest the heat, no stream, water or otherwise, offered a break in the scenery. Canyons and mountains didn't exist, and what hills there were rose and fell like bumps, less a natural creation than some mistake in a monstrous process.

"How can you live in a place like this?" Ami asked.

Spark's obsidian slate rotated on the firewalker's body, a feat Ami hadn't seen before, but that shouldn't have surprised her. The firewalkers didn't seem to have bones like she did, nor blood. Whatever force powered their life didn't need muscles, so why not have a free-floating head?

The flashes didn't answer that question or any other, and after the gold cadence ended, Spark turned itself back to the front and the narrow slit offering a view of their path.

Time proved hard to measure. The sky never dipped towards darkness or grew to a brighter day. Ami herself tracked hours by the growing growls in her stomach, the thirst in her throat. She hadn't packed for a long trip, for anything more than carting the uniforms to the firewalker's camp, and now her comfort depended on one thing: the Vis skars embedded in her faceplate. The magical god stones salved her itches, smoothed her burns, and quieted Ami's desire to eat.

That those efforts wouldn't let Ami live forever was a fact she tried to ignore.

Spark, perhaps, realized Ami's existence wasn't eternal. The knife treads descended from a constant churn to individual slaps as the machine came to a halt, shuddering to a stop smooth enough Ami didn't even fall over. She'd been on Najahn carts with worse drivers.

One more mark in the firewalker's favor.

The exit opened with Spark's hand, and this time Ami followed the firewalker out onto another dusty plain. She'd spent the ride looking behind them and hadn't seen any trace of coming changes, so when Ami matched Spark's look beyond the construct's front, her whistle broke the grinding air.

The endless stone . . . ended. Not more than a dozen strides away, the rock vanished into a roiling silver sea. Familiar waves crested and slammed against the earth, at once defying that familiarity in the way their shimmering swirls coated everything the liquid touched. The sea itself stretched to the horizon, bending in against the rock in the distance.

An attack against the land.

"What is it?" Ami said, venturing past the firewalker towards the roil.

Spark made no move to stop her, and Ami closed, found a splatter leaking near her and bent down for a closer look. The globs separated and reformed, running into cracks amid the ground. As more waves struck, the silver built up, running into and overflowing the rocks. Never evaporating, never soaking into the surface. Beautiful, strange. Ami reached for one, quivering near her booted toe.

The yank sent her flying back, the sudden heat flaring against her. Ami hit hard, winced, and saw Spark stomping away. Red embers flared across the firewalker's obsidian, their meaning clear enough.

"Don't touch, got it," Ami said, pushing up to her feet, and stopping halfway.

A new sound approached, a familiar hissing grind like the other firewalker constructs. Her feet shook, the ground trembling. Ami and Spark both followed the sound to the right, to the giant spindly thing marching up the coastline. Several long legs, each driven by a piston, slammed into the stone with every step, the piston's head sliding down the metal leg to strike the ground. When it did, a loud hiss erupted and the silver building up amid the cracks launched sky- and sea-ward, splashing back into the shimmering miasma.

As the construct moved, raising the first piston leg, a second followed, striking the same point and spraying a thick mud down amid the ground. Ami and Spark waited another several steps, the construct continuing its march along the coast, before she could see what the machine had left behind: a thick sludge, forced into the same cracks the shining silver had been conquering before.

This time, Spark didn't stop Ami from touching the hardening leftover.

This time, Ami didn't need to ask what was going on.

She'd seen a windswept world getting blown apart. She'd seen all the firewalkers waiting by the pool, by the portal. The lands behind these shimmering gates were dying, and even the firewalkers, with all their miracles, couldn't save their own.

"But if you're all collapsing now, then . . . " Ami muttered, turning back to Spark, to the construct, and, far off, the way home.

Every fiend would be coming, because they had no choice. Nowhere else to go.

The Seven Isles would be getting very crowded.

CHAPTER 40

NOCTIA'S KNIGHT

Nobody caught a Kance vessel on the run.

That truth, as immutable as Gladdring's desire for something sweet with his morning coffee, had stood all his decades until today. Until he followed Quik and the curious Kance soldiers, sailers, and Queen's assistants to the deck and saw their pursuit slicing across heavy waves in the dawn sky.

The cutter's purple and black flag, Noctia's jagged golden ring centered on the waving fabric, caught the sun's early light. A damning beacon.

"Less than half our size," Quik said as they jostled, found their position against the railing. "We have to have more soldiers here."

"Which worries me."

"Our having more soldiers worries you?"

The hunter spoke sharp, alert, and curious. He'd either slept well the night before or beat Gladdring to that needed bitter tonic.

Good. The Tenet would need the Vis today.

"The Najahn wouldn't pursue or attack unless they saw

victory," Gladdring said. "Otherwise they would be desperate, and relying on that is a fool's tactic."

Quik leaned further over the railing, gripping the wood and staring as if answers could be found amid the approaching black ship. And maybe they could, but not to Gladdring's eyes. The Tenet backed off, stumbled as a wave sent the deck slipping, and caught himself on the door inside. Lanterns swayed in the halls, commands joined their creaks, and Gladdring heard what he wanted.

"Where are you going?" Quik asked as Gladdring shoved off, towards the ship's aft.

"To the only person here that matters."

The order calling the Queensguard aft proved the right one to follow, and Gladdring found the Queen surrounded by her protectors, looking at the Kance cutter now racing in behind them. Ballista and crossbows abounded, a ranged arsenal setting up for a first volley. Some aide slid sculpted Kance armor over the Queen's shoulders, clipped plates onto her legs and feet. No such protection waited for Gladdring, not that he'd wear it.

Anything heavy on the sea tended to take its wearer to the bottom.

While Quik watched with a look shifting between confusion and stoic amusement, Gladdring shoved his substantial self through the Queensguard until he neighbored his target, an achievement made clear when he noticed the Queen's flickering right hand delivering a don't-kill-this-man signal.

"I come to offer counsel," Gladdring began, eyes on the Najahn ship, trying to gauge the distance by the spraying water off its prow.

"Then offer it."

Iron as ever. At least the Queen was consistent.

"They think they will win," Gladdring said. "This—"

"I know. The question is how, Gladdring. Could they possibly pack so many soldiers in that tiny ship to take us?"

"Unlikely. Less than two squads could fit in one of those with any comfort."

As Gladdring spoke, the Queen raised her left hand high. Around them, crossbows raised. Ballistae slotted on the rear railing, soldiers sighting their shots.

"Then what is Fassle sending after me?"

"No Najahn ship could catch *The Wind's Rose*, not with our lead," Gladdring spoke, unraveling the truth as the Tamas skar found the Queen's icy demeanor only skin deep. The woman shared Gladdring's own fear. "They—"

A whistle from the Queen's left side and the royal dropped her hand. A hard stroke, one committing to a war perhaps inevitable but not quite real until this moment. Gladdring found his words dying as bolts small and large streaked into the cool wind. The missiles were too tiny to sink the Najahn ship, but would massacre anyone on her decks, steering her rudder, shaping her sails.

Or they would have, if the dark darts didn't swerve, sink straight into the tumbling waves. Down to the last one, the missiles flew off course. Gasps, curses, and clanking cranks followed.

"It seems we should have taken all the skars, Gladdring," the Queen said.

"And Noctia found someone, or someone's, who know how to use them," the Tenet replied. "I think it's time we bring our own to bear."

"Who would wield them? You?"

Before Gladdring could suggest that, yes, he would take that honor upon himself, the Queen sharpened her stare. He followed the look, noticed the Najahn bow wasn't empty any longer. A single form stood there, clad in purple and black, silver-blonde hair streaking out like the sea spray behind her.

"Of course," the Queen said. "Gladdring, the skars siphon your will, yes?"

"For heavier duties."

"Aim for the lady! Send every shot at her, and don't quit until she's down!"

Another round went forth, the shots less scattered but no more effective. The bolts neared the woman before flying askew, a couple lodging into the cutter's heavy hull with thunks loud enough to confirm how quick the Najahn ship was closing the distance.

"How many rounds, Gladdring, before she falls?" the Queen asked.

"Hard to say, but we know now how they're catching us. If they're using her Kance skar to speed their journey and deflect your shots, she can't have much left."

"Worth risking my ship and soldiers for?"

Gladdring frowned. "My Queen, you've already risked them. The Najahn will take their skars, and the rest of us will be left to die in these waters."

Another round, more bolts, and the same effect, save one thing: the woman slouched, her hands catching the Najahn cutter's prow. The downcast turn, the determined set, gave Gladdring the clue he needed to know her: the Noctia Renewal. Cast away from her mission by Fassle's declaration, held up in his esteem nonetheless. Gladdring tried to recall how many isles she'd conquered before being recalled, how many skars she might have.

"Who's that behind her?" The Queen asked, after calls to ready blades, prepare for a boarding.

"A prisoner," Gladdring muttered, seeing the familiar shift he'd worn not all that long ago.

Behind the shriveled man came another Najahn soldier, prodding the prisoner towards their ship's prow with the end of a voulge. As they neared, with Kance fire coming at will now, the bolts continuing to fly wide of their approaching target, the Noctia Renewal cast her left hand back. Reaching, it seemed, for the prisoner.

Reaching, soon, for nothing but dust. Gladdring gaped as the man, his shift, dissipated like a morning fog. No sudden fall, no struggling collapse, only a wide-eyed, open-mouth look before the prisoner ceased to be. Behind the vanished man, the Najahn guard put up his voulge, turned, and descended into the lower deck's relative safety.

The Renewal, the Renewal stood tall once more, a vibrant flush coloring her face.

"What was that?" The Queen asked. "Gladdring, what did she—"

"I don't know, but I suggest we leave." Gladdring began his back-step, sidling behind a Queensguard. "My Queen, please!"

"And go where, Gladdring? One of the fishing boats?" The Queen turned, glared his way as Gladdring retreated through the ranks, looking every bit the fierce leader she was supposed to be.

Until flame wiped the world away.

GLADDRING CAME to when his arm caught on a dead man's blade, the rapier free from its sheathe and shattered, the broken point cutting a new red line near the Tenet's elbow. The cut only happened because Gladdring was moving, his body sliding along slick wood.

No, not sliding.

"It would help if you moved," Quik said, the hunter grunting as he yank Gladdring further along the foundering vessel.

That Gladdring heard Quik's voice at all over the screams, the orders, the first sounds of steel meeting steel came because the hunter crouched low as he pulled. The reason why whistled overhead, Najahn fire making standing a sure way to die. Gladdring tried wriggling his fingers, toes, found his limbs all there and offered a quick thanks to Noctia that he hadn't yet joined her realm.

The Tenet didn't need to ask Quik what'd happened, why he'd survived. The Kance vessel's broken aft, much of it burning, offered all the answers. Bodies lay scattered about, some few sailors trying to pull wounded away while Kance soldiers struggled to meet Najahn scaling ropes tossed onto the few ends not too burned to hold grapples. The black-clad death dealers climbed with crossbow fire at their backs, voulges ready to spear at the front, a lethal combo claiming too many lives as Gladdring and Quik continued their retreat.

"You fled right on time," Quik said as they left the rear deck behind. The hunter scampered further ahead than Gladdring, stood while pressing himself to the rising cabins and top-deck structure. "The guards in front of you took the blast. Only ash remained."

Luck, or had he suspected what was coming?

Gladdring shook off the question, joined Quik on his feet. Pains sprinkled in, his body realizing Gladdring wasn't quite dead, but could be quite a lot better if he salved some new burns, that cut, and more than a few splinters.

"The Najahn's using her skars against us," Gladdring

said, looking for the Queen amid the wreckage and not seeing any sign.

"Figured that part out myself," Quik replied. "Think we ought to get some of our own?"

The Tamas skar in Gladdring's robes—a relief to find the stone still there—confirmed Quik's question came from confidence, not from fear. The hunter thought there was still a fight to be had here. A victory to be claimed.

"We take what we can, and run."

Gladdring pushed the Vis on. They passed by panicked, raging Kance heading the other way. They stumbled, slid as the damaged ship struggled with waves. Overhead, once-mighty sails burned like the world's greatest candle, flaming canvas falling around the pair. Not a soul questioned their path, threw them a look, or issued a challenge.

"Their queen is dead or missing," Quik said when they reached the skar's room and found it unguarded. "What else is there but vengeance?"

"Don't talk like some dire sage," Gladdring sniped back, trying the door's handle and finding it locked. "They're letting emotion lose them the war before it even starts." He stepped back, waved at the door. "Break this down, please."

"You think I'm just muscle?"

"I think if we expect me to get this open, we'll both be very dead."

Quik huffed, but did as Gladdring asked, throwing his shoulder into the door once. The wood buckled, but held. Another strike cracked through, and a third, this time delivered with the gauntlets, left a shattered mess clinging to warped hinges. Quik winced, favored his charging shoulder.

"Grab some Vis skars and you'll be fine," Gladdring said, stepping through.

The satchels, each with its separated plunder, sat in sealed crates amid the room. Quik didn't need to be ordered a second time, instead working his gauntlets to break each one open. The splintering wood added its sounds to growing groans and quieting screams, battle-cries. One battle ending and another, the ship's fight with the sea, getting into full swing.

"Take those four. I'll handle these." Gladdring directed Quik to the satchels holding Foti, Rana, Whent, and Vis. The Tenet would get Kance, Noctia, and Tamas. "Then we hope the Queen wasn't lying about those lifeboats."

Gladdring hoisted the first satchel, the Noctia skars within no light burden, but one desperation would let him carry. The second required a squat and a grunt, but before Gladdring lifted the third, Quik's curse called his attention.

The young woman who'd forced a war stood in the broken door, looking untouched and far from tired, for all the efforts the Kance had made.

"So many have tried to kill you, Gladdring," the woman said, her voice venom. "Now it's my turn."

CHAPTER 41

INTERMISSION'S END

By the third day, there'd been five attempts and zero murders. Livier, despite his wounds, had been on either side of them all, which was why he now laid on the flimsy straw mat with hands and feet tied. Eujo sat across the spare room, more of a closet by Kance royal standards, and relished the man's glare.

"If you weren't such a monster, maybe I'd let you try the skar," Eujo said as Livier roused himself in the late afternoon. "Can't argue they don't work."

"You'd be dead by now if they didn't."

The man's voice sounded like a snake's dying hiss, one soothed a minute later as he bent over and slurped some snowmelt from a pallid dish. Like a dog, though Livier deserved worse. Torny sided with Eujo on that, but Wax insisted Livier might have some use.

Eujo would bet more on Wax's reluctance to add another body to his list.

Nevertheless, this was a big day, a big moment, because Eujo herself was well enough—thanks to those skars and more judicious dressing changes, food, and drink—to interrogate the assassin. And Livier himself seemed ready to withstand it.

"Aren't I lucky," Eujo said, starting to stand up from the rickety chair in her corner only to drop back at an aching protest, her body not quite ready for the intimidating walk. "For now, I'm going to have to trust you'll tell me the truth. None of that Kance tongue twisting, no bending words, or I'll let Torny back in here so she can gut you."

"Is Torny the brat with the dagger?"

"The one she'd dearly love to shove into your stomach, yes."

"I like her."

Livier's grin had a sickly cast. Eujo let it slide off her. The man had no power here, not unless she gave some away.

"How much she likes you depends on what you tell me now," Eujo said.

"Let me guess, you want to know everything?"

"To start."

Livier laid back on the mat, eyes venturing towards the wood ceiling, boards that could use a refresher. The whole house met the barely-there standards for survival in a remote Tamas town, a refuge bought and paid for by blood money, by the rapiers, knives, and tools of Livier and the dead assassins. The weapons gave Eujo, Wax, and the others shelter and food for a week. At the end of that time . . . well, Eujo planned to go after the Tamas skar, and Livier would likely be burned in another pyre.

The assassin, though, seemed to think he had a way out. The confessional began with a short nod at nothing, then words flowed, slowing here and there for Eujo to get in a question, a jab, or just a sigh.

Because the whole damn thing was so stupid.

The Queen, the elder Queen, wanted the skars to shore up Kance in the face of what, she was sure, would be coming war between the isles. Whent and Rana had been heating up their fighting, and the Najahn were getting more aggressive in their territory claims. While the Queen suspected there was something more to the stones—the Najahn certainly seemed possessive of the things—the skars were more a tool to be bartered with.

"Fassle, she thought, would leave Kance alone if she had more skars to trade," Livier said.

"I had four, Livier. Four skars when my own guards turned on me. How much time was that supposed to buy?"

"A convenient bonus, that's all. Your life was the real prize, and sole control of the isle."

"Until they picked another Queen."

Livier shook his head, the straw rustling beneath his frayed, burned hair. "Kance wouldn't during a Renewal. The Queen would push it off, ensure she had full control as long as she needed it. You out of the way would hand her sole power."

"She never even asked me. Maybe I'd like her plan?"

"Cooperation's never been her style, Eujo. She won't share with you, or anyone, unless forced to."

Livier didn't know anything more about the Queen's plans, save that capturing Eujo became a higher priority after the Najahn ended the Renewal. The last missive that'd found Livier, waiting when they landed on Tamas, suggested the skars were even more valuable than suspected, that Eujo couldn't be allowed to fall into Najahn hands.

"As if I'd let them take me," Eujo muttered.

"A risk the Queen can't accept, which is why I'm here,

and why more will come after I disappear. Accept it or not, Eujo, your life is forfeit."

"I don't accept it, and anyone following you is going to wind up just the same."

"You're defiant now, but as the hours, days, maybe weeks wind on, every minute spent wondering if it'll be your last?" Livier wheezed a pathetic laugh. "Many break for less. So will you."

WAX DROWNED his sigh with the ale. He, Torny, and Eujo sat around the lone table in the squat house's center, a combination kitchen, living, and dining space dotted with scrappy wood furniture. The walls, though, were vintage Tamas, with dyed paintings running across the cherrywood boards. The inks didn't stop, just ran from one to the next in a dizzying array covering springtime dances, night skies, crashing waves, and solitary animals in snowy fields. If everything else in the place seemed cheap or barely hanging on, those walls were magnificent.

"So we're not done with this then," Torny said, her words sharing noise with the crackling fire built into the stone chimney behind them. "Guess we'll have to leave this paradise, stay ahead of their tracking?"

The paradise had two bedrooms lofted above, accessible by ladder and marginally more comfortable than Livier's mat. Bliss, barely upright herself, stayed with the assassin now, part of an all-day, all-night rotation wearing on the foursome but without any other obvious solution. Leaving Livier alone meant accepting a blade to the throat or worse.

"There's no staying ahead," Eujo replied. "Like Livier

did, they'll catch us soon. They know what we want, where we're going, and we can't change paths."

"Can't we?" Wax asked. "We could give up the Tamas skar. Go straight back to Noctia, then circle around. Throw them off."

"We'll just get caught by someone else. Better to play it straight. At least if we get the Tamas skar, Noctia will give me seven."

"And who cares about Wax, right?" Torny said. "You've got a few. That's enough to . . . what was it we're trying to do again? Destroy all the fiends, save the isles, give everyone all the food and love they'll need forever?"

"The bandit's got it," Wax laughed. "Simple, right?"

"Then—"

Wax cut Torny off with a mug wave, the laugh dying into something more serious. "It sounds like a joke, Torny, but I promised Pan I'd try for the Renewal. If that's been taken away, then I'm going to do something that'd make him proud. That'd make his sacrifice worth it."

"Not sure attempting the impossible is the way to honor a man's memory."

"I'm going to try anyway."

Eujo reached out a hand, put it on Wax's arm. "Not alone, either."

"A Kance queen and a Vis hunter." Torny whistled. "About the best pair these isles have ever seen. Those fiends better be running home scared."

"They will be, soon enough," Wax said, "once we figure out where we're going next."

The Kance Queen threw a look at Torny, one the bandit understood well enough to announce that she needed to go check on Bliss. "As your Guardian, I hereby say I don't give a damn what you decide, just that you pay me proper before this whole thing ends."

Eujo chuckled as Torny, refilling her mug, stomped off towards the closet. Wax only sighed—the Vis sighed a lot these days—and stared at the fire. "It's not impossible, you know that, right?"

"I can't believe that. I'm going to do it. Just like Svarde, I owe people."

"So do I. A whole isle of them."

"The same isle that tried to kill you? That's still trying to kill you?"

"They haven't yet." Eujo felt a touch, saw Wax shift his arm so her hand rested on his. "Don't mean to let them, either."

"Then we go on tomorrow?"

They were well enough to travel, and they'd already discussed getting provisions, a ride or a cart and pony for the trip: Wax and Eujo would give up their swords, their fancier Kance and Whent clothes for thinner, cheaper versions. Not a trade that Eujo looked forward to, but the Tamas skars were days away to the south yet, not a journey they could make by foot. Not without inviting more hostile pursuit.

"I'm ready," Eujo said, her look holding on the hands.

Did she need to say something? What, then? Words seemed as likely to shatter the fragile moment as anything else, so she fell silent, took in the fire while Wax finished his ale. He set the flagon aside, looked at her, the hangdog grin Wax wore so well finding his face. The cocky line, so full of himself, so confident, so . . . confused?

Wax's eyes drifted with his expression behind Eujo's shoulder, to the small home's front window, its fogged glass, and the door nearby. A door that shook with a hard knock, that opened with a harder kick a moment later.

"Some security," Wax said, standing up, casting about for his sword. Eujo matched him, though her rapier leaned against the wall near the door, near their coats.

No help dealing with the man who stood, grinning like some haughty devil, as the chill night wind raced in around him.

"What a trick," Daklin announced, several more hooded faces lurking behind. "At first, I thought our favorite Renewals had run off, but then we found some souls missing." He stepped inside, rubbed his hands together as if about to eat some tasty morsel. "The Tamas skar requires a show, and you'll be putting one on for us."

"Not likely," Wax said, finding his blade, raising it. "We're not your toys."

"No, no you are not." Daklin snapped his fingers. Those lurking shadows came into the room, wild costumes leaking beneath their cloaks and coats. Eujo would've laughed if Daklin hadn't soured into a scowl. "You're thieves. Criminals. If you were on Whent, we'd cast you into the Pits. Since you're on Tamas, you're going on the stage. You'll do your scene, or you'll die here and now."

"What do you care?" Eujo asked, standing by Wax's side, counting the steps to her blade and figuring it too far. "We're two—"

"The play, the theater, is sacred. You want our skar, you respect our rites. Now, set that sword aside." Daklin's furious grin returned. "It doesn't match your character, and you have some rehearsing to do."

CHAPTER 42

ERASED

Time flies when you're fighting for your life.

The constant stress subsumed the minutes, the hours into a stream Annalyse ignored. Day and night were background noise. Coffee and exhausted sleep took turns in unequal measure as the scientist, at first carried, then striding, arrived at Mottilan and grabbed hold of the cliffside city.

Annalyse didn't do it consciously, but when the hunters brought her into the broad, circular building just off Mottilan's empty port, the confusion among the elders, the other hunters, and even the few insects buzzing around was so apparent that to sit back would, once again, put Annalyse in the hands of people who knew less than herself.

"You have to prepare for war," Annalyse said first, loud and clear over the arguing gaggle.

Her audience held fisherman, weaving women, hunters aged beyond their prime, and sailors who thought they were going to spend the winter as they often did: drinking themselves silly until spring. Only Reth, taking his own new role as Mottilan's chief hunter in the wake of Najahn murders, accepted the verdict in the proper manner: by slapping a Najahn knife on a central stone table and declaring these were the city's new enemies.

"But how?" asked one of the elders, who indeed looked so frail and salted any armed conflict must've seemed impossible.

Annalyse knew that feeling, had shared it all too recently.

"With what we know, and what I can teach," Annalyse replied.

"And who are you?"

Annalyse didn't smile, didn't give a knowing nod like Gladdring might have. This wasn't a confidence game. Facts would win out, and facts she gave.

"Your last chance."

Mottilan would've cast Annalyse into the sea at those words if Reth hadn't backed her, explained how Annalyse had destroyed the Najahn squad. That earned Annalyse enough tepid support to lend the scientist leadership of a new war council, with her and Reth at the helm. Annalyse wasted little time, asking for and receiving details on the land around the city, resources in both goods and people, and talents.

Old lessons—Whent was a warring isle, between its squabbling warlords and constant conflicts with Rana—on how to counter raids and launch her own dredged free as Annalyse took in the details, plotted next steps. Dried fruit became chits marking possible Najahn positions, land-marks, and . . .

"Fiends?" Annalyse asked when Reth pointed to several melon rinds.

"Exactly," Reth replied. "We don't have the numbers to go after them all, and some of 'em don't move. The worst ones, maybe the hanoko, or some disease will kill them for us."

"But Deshiva—"

Reth spat to the side, a move echoed by the others in the room. "Kitaye's bigger, if they want to throw lives away chasing every creature on the isle, they can do that. Not our way."

The sniped attitude summed up Mottilan's approach: smaller, savvier, and with an eye always to being clever over being strong. Annalyse, with Reth giving her gentle nudges as necessary, fell in fast enough.

First, gather information. Mottilan's swiftest hunters scampered out from the city, looking for Najahn moves while confirming hidden paths through the mountains separating Mottilan from the Great Sana. Fishermen received orders to keep eyes out while on the sea, to scurry back if anything purple and black crossed the horizon.

Second, fortify. All those sleepy sailors kicked their hangovers with Reth's spear at their backs, their days filled now with shifting stone, digging spike pits, and building ambush platforms amid the trees on the main road coming into town. The fancier homes up on the cliffside became forts, stocked with supplies, darts, arrows, and spears. Any land invasion would be a bloody descent, any seaward assault would find themselves barraged by boulders and burning pitch from the high cliff point overhead.

And third?

Allies.

"When a new warlord comes in," Annalyse said at another of the constant circles around the stone table, "the first thing they do is change minds. Get all the knives pointed at their backs put in their sheathes. When's the last time the Najahn have had to do this?"

Blank stares greeted her.

"Exactly. They don't know how to change minds or win hearts. Even if Kitaye falls, the people living there won't work for Fassle. They'll give us information, or, with our help, disrupt anything the Najahn try to do." Annalyse tapped, then, the northeast part of the crude map overlaying the rough gray rock. "When I left Noctia, Whent and Kance were the only other two isles that cared about their independence. Whent's too far away, especially while ice clogs the lanes, but Kance could be a friend."

"A friend for what?" one hunter asked.

"Food, weapons, anything we can trade for. You're not going to get anything from Noctia anymore, so you'll have to replace it all with what Kance can provide. Or go without."

"That," Reth said, "is something we understand."

ONCE AGAIN ANNALYSE ran with Vis hunters through a clouded night, beneath not so much jungle leaves as mountain rock. Weaves thicker than the ones Deshiva gave her kept Annalyse warm, while Mottilan boots, sharp stones planted in their soles, dug into every step to keep her from slipping. She ducked beneath branches, followed Reth as he jumped over gaps formed by melting snow rivers.

Winter was still here, but on Vis, its grasp could be inconsistent.

Reth stopped atop a cutting ledge along the hill's westward face, a gap in the trees too clean to be natural. The forest swept away beneath them, giving way soon to the Great Sana's gray rise. Behind it sprawled orange and yellow flickers. The Najahn outpost.

"See that?" Reth said, pointing to swarming torches cutting to the north. "That's our doing, right there."

For a second, Annalyse wondered if Reth had sent Mottilan's few fighters on a crazed assault at the Najahn core. Then she heard the roar, loud and eerie, a gurgling, terrible thing. Awful at distance, and no doubt worse up close, where those Najahn soldiers would be facing something beyond their nightmares.

"That's the signal," Reth said, leveling a stare not at the several other hunters around them, but at Annalyse alone. "You're sure you want to come?"

"My idea," Annalyse said, damn proud of herself keeping her voice steady. "If something goes wrong, the skars are the best chance we have."

Reth only nodded. They'd had the argument in the days before, as the back-and-forth with the Najahn played out. The purple and black busied themselves more with Kitaye, whispers floating back through jungle meetings that the bigger city had been besieged, invaded from the north and south. Distractions meant openings, ones Mottilan had to maximize.

And that meant the skars.

They ran again, Reth picking the path down and around the Great Sana's base. Four Najahn guards stood around the entry, voulges ready. A dangerous target and not theirs, not tonight. Instead Reth kept them slinking through fern and tree to the south, around the Najahn outpost's base. As they went, the other hunters plotted out routes away, down to the southern coast where a fisherman's boat would be waiting.

Plots within plots. Gladdring would be proud.

They reached the outpost's southern edge as dawn approached, a too long run, those hideous roars continuing, though growing more distant, more distraught. Rather than diving right into the Najahn chaos, Reth held them back. Nuts and fruit passed from pouches to mouths, coffee beans among them. Little bitter bites delivering jolts, kicking away exhaustion.

Hiding, under the rush, the sick surge as Annalyse looked again on that awful outpost. Returning to the site of her near death, or worse.

To excise the trauma, confront it, destroy it.

Ami had said that more than once on Noctia, often while waving a blade around or three ales deep. That the Guardian hadn't followed her own advice was obvious. Maybe she had now, if Ami still lived.

Annalyse hoped she did, hoped the flame-haired fighter continued to slay fiends wherever she was.

Would've been nice to have Ami here, now, as Reth flashed the signal and their group broke cover. They stayed low, making for the first building, a low-slung stable. Once home to livestock, now a ramshackle prison, or so Mottilan's scouts suggested. A single Najahn soldier stood by the entry, helmeted head nodding up and down as he tried to dodge sleep's grasp.

Reth put the guard's worries to an end with a dart, blown when the man's head dipped and piercing his throat. The guard squirmed, tried to speak, and fell. A clanking disaster averted by Reth's own hands, catching the guard's collapse and redirecting it to the left, to where two other hunters completed the let down.

The grass would make a good bed for the man, soft and chilled with frost's latent kiss.

Annalyse kept herself pressed to the stable's outside wall. So far, better than expected. The fight with Kitaye, the fiend's attack, had pulled off so many soldiers as to leave the outpost all but deserted. What that meant for their goal, Annalyse didn't want to speculate.

She didn't, though, have to speculate on the light, and how their cover was dissipating every second. What'd been dark shadows now held grays, and color filtered in here and there. Reth caught it too, as did the other hunters, their looks going back to the jungle's edge and refuge.

But that would sacrifice the fiend's distraction, would clue the Najahn into their presence.

"No," Annalyse whispered, joining the hunters, the collapsed Najahn at their feet. The armor jostled. She smiled. Whent would provide. "Reth, I have an idea."

THE OTHER HUNTERS disappeared as the first rays broke the disappearing clouds, the Najahn guard, sleeping soundly without his armor, carried between them. Hands clasped behind her, Annalyse walked before Reth, hidden behind ill-fitting, but passable, armor plate. They wouldn't need to get far, wouldn't need to do more than find the prisoners, and ditch Annalyse among them.

Then, when night came again, she could break herself free.

Around the corner, through a loose gate—not barred, not locked, lax security for the Najahn—Annalyse walked into the long, narrow building. Beams and slats split the stable, and Annalyse listened, as she stepped on old straw and dirt, for the first questions, the calls for food, water, aid that populated every prison. None came.

"Where are they?" Reth whispered at her back. "The guards? The prisoners? Anyone?"

"Maybe our scouts got it wrong."

A hoped-for answer cast aside as they neared the first

cell row. Annalyse found her breath catch, her heart thunder with the skar whispers in her mind. The Kitaye and Mottilan prisoners were here, yes, and they lived, yes. They stared, sitting, at Annalyse and Reth, their mouths quiet, their eyes blank. In this cell, in the next and the next.

"What is this?"

Reth stepped past Annalyse up to a pair. He reached out, gave a slight slap to one hunter, pallid and bare save for a shift. The man swayed, but otherwise didn't react. He tried again, with the same result, and cursed. Annalyse kept going, found what she wanted, what she feared, in the last stall. Deshiva, battered but alive.

But Deshiva sat the same as the others, the fire gone. Soundless, vacant, waiting. Behind her, Reth, between curses, warned the day was getting on, a concern backed up by calls for breakfast, coffee, and shift rotation. They would be found out soon, and there would be no flight from here, no mass escape.

"Let's go," Annalyse said. "We can't help them."

"There's no hiding us now, Whent."

"Then we run, Reth. We run until we can't run anymore."

CHAPTER 43
THE LONG CLIMB

After getting cooked in what felt like a forge for way too long, Ami emerged, dripping, from the chamber's pool back into the world she knew. The firewalkers gracing the gray slopes watched her with flashing obsidian crowns, but none moved to bar her drenched walk up the slope, past the lumped vests she'd been sent to deliver, and down the tunnel towards Jochi, Svarde, and the other souls still suffering in blissful ignorance.

"They're all going to collapse?" Jochi said after Ami had changed her soaked, charred, clothes for new ones. They all stood in Svarde's favorite place, the stone cathedral, and the Dead King himself loomed nearby, a passive guardian over their discussion.

Ami found herself looking at the still giant, settled in his thick armor, while Maena, Svarde, and Jochi hammered opinion's on Ami's story back and forth. The Dead King had been down here for centuries, but offered no insight on Ami's words? Had he really been stuck with his risen bodies and never tried to understand what doomed him to this spot? What prompted the fiends to fly?

Or maybe he had, and assumed no isle would rise to help the fiends anyway, much less accept the ragged, monstrous refugees on their scant land.

"That's the problem, isn't it?" Ami asked in a lull, the conversation spinning around ways to contain all the fiends inside the Dark Below's caves. "We can't hold them down here. Can't."

"Haven't tried yet," Jochi replied. The warlord went without his bodyguards now, though the hefty ax at the man's waist suggested he wasn't undefended. Still, without the sycophant protectors, Jochi looked less a menacing tyrant and more an over-stuffed bear. "My engineers can knock down the right tunnels, keep these monsters running in circles until we decide what pit we want to put'em in."

"What if we don't put them in a pit?" Maena asked. "What if we send them up?"

"Lunacy," Svarde muttered.

"You've never been in a cage. You don't know what it means to try and get out."

Svarde wiggled the giant, jagged blade. "Not every cage has bars, Rana."

"You want out of yours? Just let go, Svarde."

"Okay," Jochi said, patting the air with his hands, as if putting out some invisible fire. "Let's calm down."

Ami snorted, "Jochi, you ought to know by now that insults and threats are just how we talk."

"Guardian's right," Maena said, crossing her arms and lighting up with a slaying grin. "There's no fun in just chatting, Jochi."

"There's fun in finding answers so I can get back to my ale," Jochi said. "By Ami's words, we don't have much time anyway till any fiend that can move's going to come crawling from those gates. Our firewalker friends might smash a good many of'em, but others are going to get out the far tunnels."

"And we don't want the firewalkers to die," Ami added.

"Right, which brings me back to the tunnels. We seal a few routes, keep the fiends moving in circles till we come up with something better."

Maena flicked her eyes up, "Already have something better: take'em to the surface."

"Noctia's not got the space for seven worlds worth of fiends," Svarde said. "No isle does."

"They all won't make it through." Jochi pulled out a pipe from his giant coat, stuck the small thing in his mouth. "Maybe it'll be few enough we can stick'em in a couple isles and nobody'll notice."

Ami sank back as the banter went on, solutions and problems whacking each other like soldiers in sad swordplay. The day's trip found the conversation a good chance to remind Ami that she was exhausted, the Vis skars eager for sleep's renewal. Maybe she could slink off, find a straw mat somewhere, and by the time she'd kicked a few dreams these three would have a solution.

Kivi, her rolling pebble snores rumbling in the corner, had the right idea.

"I'll go," Svarde announced, drawing Ami back to the interplay. "I'll march right up there and tell Noctia and the Najahn to get themselves ready. Get Catya off that throne." Svarde nodded at Ami. "And you're coming with me."

Damn.

. . .

They stood at the bottom of a god's strike. At least, what remained of it. The Dead King had built the cathedral near the Wound's bottom point, right where Vis's dagger had found Noctia's heart. Tunnels linked the stab here and there up above, letting more than a few fiends find its quick route to the surface, and a quicker end when they arrived. Now Ami and Svarde were set on taking the same route, a swift scaling to avoid a longer walk to Whent and frozen travel back to Noctia.

That they were heading to the Ringed City remained a doubtful choice to the former Guardian, but what was Ami supposed to do? Say no? Declare herself a coward before Svarde, Jochi, and Maena?

Not happening.

The plan, as Svarde described it, was simple enough: scale the Wound, get Catya to call off any Najahn attack, then use his and Ami's celebrity to get Fassle and his Circle to buy in. Stopping all future fiend assaults ought to make a tempting offer for Fassle, and with Najahn support, they might find a way to parcel any fiends able to function across the matching isles.

Jochi, Maena, and the firewalkers would handle any monsters too violent to be worth saving.

"And when Fassle decides he's going to have me executed anyway?" Ami asked.

"I'd like to see him try," Svarde replied, the big sword strapped to his back, hilt tied and touching the man's gray neck. A touch, apparently, could come from anything, not just his hands. "Every soldier he sends at us will be fighting on our side after a cut or two. The man won't have a choice."

"Because the best bargains are always struck under duress."

Svarde laughed, studied the rock wall before him. The Dead King and some Whent engineers had stacked enough stones and raised a ladder to get them to the cathedral's top, where the Wound proper began. Smooth pale stone awaited them, untouched for so many years. Not far above, though, the pristine climb would be interrupted by fiend claws, missed crossbow quarrels, and, if the Dead King could be believed, the very notches he and Demion carved on their first descent.

The climb would be a long one, every spot without a good handhold needing to be hacked out with chisels. Ami lugged pouches filled with mushrooms, bread, and water. Svarde carried the same, though the man didn't eat anymore. Said ale didn't affect him either, just pooled up and drained out of his cuts that never healed.

Ami didn't say it aloud, but Svarde's living death sounded worse than just, well, death.

"Fassle doesn't have a choice anyway," Svarde said, reaching and testing the first chisel. "What's he going to do when the fiends swarm the surface, our bones in their teeth? Noctia doesn't have enough voulges to save the isles."

"If he believes us."

The Foti man made the first lurch, leaping free from the stone platform to the Wound's lowest wall. Above him, working to speed carving those handholds, latched Kivi. She snorted, venting steam to Svarde's right to showcase the next leg.

"Ami," Svarde said, gauging the distance while Ami did the same to where Svarde hung now. "If you're going to be this sour, I'll swap you out for Maena."

"She's crazy."

"Not her fault, but she's still more fun than you."

"I bet Catya would disagree."

Svarde lumbered himself to the next handhold, clearing the way for Ami's jump. She bent her legs, judged the pouch's swaying weight, and took off. Her hands, gloved with a Whent scout's gripping cloth, caught the stone. Ami pulled herself up, slotting her feet into the first niche. The Vis skars whispered, tending to muscles well before they'd be sore.

"She would," Svarde said, and Ami glanced up to see him already several holds ahead. "She'd call me a grump and you the most fun she'd ever had." The Foti grinned Ami's way. "But we both know who she'd choose in a brawl!"

Oh, those were fighting words.

Days and nights burned on the climb up the Wound. Ami caught rest on larger cliffs, Svarde putting himself on the edge to keep her from rolling off. Kivi snoozed with her claws extended, secure on the walls even in slumber. They ate, drank, and shared memories good and bad, a journey at once a callback to the best time in Ami's life, and a hollow reminder of how far gone that time was.

That Svarde never slept, never seemed tired had eluded Ami back below. He'd sit there, silent, on the rock ledges and make not a sound for hours, glowing blue and purple moss their only light.

"How do you stand it?" Ami asked on the second night, curled into a narrow nook. The Dead King estimated four day's climb to take them straight up, if they kept a brisk pace. Ami's skars and Svarde's endless energy meant they were already feeling cooler surface air. "How can you sit there for hours in silence?"

"Not much different than my cabin," Svarde replied. "Nobody to talk to there either, for most of ten years."

"How'd you manage it then?"

"Live in the past. Try to think of ways I would've done it different."

"For ten years, you did that?"

"Some nights I got drunk too."

Ami's turn to laugh, "You know, I did the same thing."

"I know you did. You started on Vis, before we caught the boat to Noctia." Svarde didn't turn to look at her, just kept facing out towards the chasm, his blade in his lap, grip assured. "Part of why I left. Didn't want to watch you drown yourself either."

"Thanks."

"I know, I'm an ass. Never argued anything different."

"A stupid ass, too."

"But guess what, Ami? This stupid ass gets to save the world. Twice."

"Oh no, Svarde. I'm taking credit for this one. You're just the Guardian."

"Again?"

"Always."

Just after noon on the fourth day, Kivi snorted their impending approach. Conversation and unnatural noise had been drifting down for minutes already, and Ami wondered when the Najahn were going to make their first contact. The reason why they hadn't, why they didn't until Svarde hefted himself over the Wound's lip with a bold declaration that Catya's Guardian had returned, wasn't at all what Ami expected.

And Jochi, all the way down the Wound, likely heard the curse that left Ami's lips.

CHAPTER 44
AFLOAT

For most of the isle's history, a man caught without a weapon by those intending his murder wound up dead. In the current moment, with Noctia's Renewal delivering threats and two voulge-wielding Najahn behind her, Gladdring defied those grim odds.

His luck lay in a bag sitting to his left, where Gladdring's hand plunged even as the Renewal delivered her icy verdict. The black stones inside, like every skar, commenced their indecipherable barrage as Gladdring scooped them up. He ignored the torrent—as if Gladdring had fallen into a chattering crowd—and held his fist towards the Renewal and her guards.

"Approach, and you risk all our lives," Gladdring said.

The Renewal reached a hand towards her own neck, the necklace on it. "Don't threaten me with what you can't control. Drop the stones."

"Or what? You'll kill me?" Gladdring edged back a single step. Every stride gave him a split second longer to act when the Renewal or her guards charged. "You have no leverage, Renewal. You gave that away in your opening words."

To Gladdring's right, across the room, Quik watched them both. The Vis hunter stood before two satchels, his hands hidden behind his back. A chance, then, the man had a trap to spring. A confirmation, too, that like so many Vis, he'd been ignored.

The Kance ship, though, would not let its struggle be forgotten. The vessel continued to moan, the cracks and clangs now not those of metal blades but splitting boards, rushing water meeting little resistance. The Renewal's assault must've done more than damage the aft.

"It's sinking," the Renewal said as the deck shuddered beneath them. "Time's up, Gladdring. Use those skars, or—"

She cut off her own words, lunging forward. The hand that'd been near her necklace dropped in the motion to sweep free the long knife sheathed at her waist. Gladdring started, but there was still time, still time to feed the Noctia skars.

Feed?

The former Tenet didn't freeze, not quite. He collapsed, body going watery as the opals in his hand ravaged Gladdring with demands. Their wants, their needs didn't present themselves as words but as feeling, as raw, gnashing hunger wanting to snatch out at everyone within the room, at the two guards beyond it, at anyone left alive on the ship.

At himself.

And Gladdring would not, could not allow that, even as the Renewal's knife plunged towards his throat. At least, it did, until the Renewal flew aside, knocking over the Noctia satchel and smashing into the wall to Gladdring's left. The

Najahn guards outside started at the shift, only to find themselves bucked away, tumbling as their floorboards shot up, launched them along the tilting top deck. Their heavy splashes joined the continued chaos, another meal for fish feeding well today.

"Get up," Quik said, dashing to Gladdring's side. The hunter left several Whent skars in his wake, the stones glittering against the wood. "We're leaving before the ship breaks up."

"The skars," Gladdring whispered, taking Quik's hand with his empty right, lurching towards the Noctia satchel and dropping the opals back inside. Their hungry urges disappeared as they fell, Gladdring welcoming back control of his own body like recovering from too much ale. "We can't leave them."

"Damn the skars, Gladdring, we're going to die if we stay!"

"They're our only chance, Quik," Gladdring said, tying off the Noctia satchel and looping it over his shoulder. "When the Najahn come for Kance, we'll lose without their power."

He didn't mention the Kance soldiers might just kill Gladdring and Quik anyway, if the pair didn't have the stones to convince them otherwise. That was a problem for another day, another moment.

Quik seemed to gather Gladdring's stubborn goal and, steadying himself with every step as the ship continued its crumble, the Vis lurched back towards his satchels, scooping up the Whent skars along the way.

The Noctia Renewal groaned, lying on the floor. Eyes closed and hurting. Gladdring watched her as he tied the Tamas satchel, joining it with its opal brethren. Only the Kance stones left, and then . . . leave her to die?

The Kance ship tried to answer that question for him. As Gladdring made it to the last satchel, with Quik calling his own completion—the hunter could move fast when he wanted to—the vessel announced an awful crack. The room swung, the hallway outside its door falling away. Gladdring fell, grabbing the Kance satchel as the shifting doorway showcased a gray morning sky, one bright and clear and directly overhead.

Not a view desired when inside a ship's room.

"Too late," Quik snarled as Gladdring picked himself up. The Noctia Renewal lay crumpled, quiet now, in the room's corner. "You've killed us both, Tenet."

"Not yet. Turn around."

Quik cursed, did as Gladdring asked, letting the Tenet look at the four satchels Quik held, two around each shoulder. Gladdring's hand swept in one bag, snagged two stones, and pulled them free.

Unlike the Noctia skars, Rana's stones were more curious than killer, though their excitement picked up plenty when seawater leaked through the boards at Gladdring's feet.

"Grab the Renewal," Gladdring said, nudging the stones where he wanted them to go.

Quik shouldered by Gladdring as the seawater seeped away, seeming to disappear. Gladdring knelt on the wall, the small room now a prison turned on its side. The Rana skars listened, reached, and found what he needed.

"Have her," Quik said, and Gladdring's glance confirmed the hunter had the Renewal scooped under one arm, steady on the same back wall-turned-floor as Gladdring. "Now we can all drown together."

"Not quite."

The Rana skars answered Gladdring's question with a

surge, propelling the room up and forward. Clouds and sky disappeared as what once aimed above fell again to land flat against the sea. Gladdring hit the floor hard on his left shoulder. Quik, with enough dexterity to make Gladdring jealous, stepped with the transition, keeping his feet and dragging the Noctia Renewal with him.

The forced righting had its consequences: the nails keeping the room's walls together failed, boards breaking away. The walls sagged, the roof, again over their heads, moaned.

And Gladdring realized he'd grabbed the wrong skars. Despite their watery thrill, the Rana stones couldn't save them from getting crushed. He moved towards Quik, calling to the hunter to snag a Kance skar from Gladdring's satchels.

The Renewal answered his request instead, her eyes fluttering open. Held against Quik's side, Noctia's Renewal had the good fortune to be looking right up as consciousness found her, had the better fortune to hold a Kance skar within her necklace, and the best fortune to be too bleary to resist the skar's demands.

As the walls cracked, the roof didn't descend. Instead, like Gladdring peeling an orange, the wood above snapped away, flopping over the side and landing, the sea washing over their makeshift raft.

Gladdring started laughing amid the wreckage, the waves, the floating bodies. They were alive, they'd survived, all thanks to the damn stones. The skars that for so long had been ignored, relegated to the cursed Aegis.

"What're you laughing at?" Quik snapped, dropping the Renewal in the raft's center. "We're still doomed, Gladdring."

The hunter's assessment wasn't far off: the Kance vessel

had almost disappeared, its existence only marked by what lucky luggage, barrels, and bodies managed to stay afloat amid the waves. Some few people splashed around, but even as Gladdring took in their frantic attempts, wet clothes, armor, or the flurrying sea predators dragged them into the depths. Najahn and Kance both consumed without regard.

"My ship," the Noctia Renewal whispered from the raft's center, where Gladdring and Quik joined her. "It still floats."

She wasn't wrong. The Noctia cutter drifted among the waves, a distant target for any normal raft subjected to the sea's heavy battering. But Gladdring's wreck was hardly a normal raft. The Rana skars played about his mind, siphoning Gladdring's energy to keep their mangled boards atop the sea. As long as Gladdring could stay awake, stay alive, their little patch wouldn't sink.

Which gave them a chance.

"Quik, give me more," Gladdring said.

"More what?"

Despite his words, Quik seemed to understand what Gladdring wanted. Balancing on the wood, Quik again slid his back towards Gladdring, who scooped up several more Rana skars.

"What're you doing?" the Noctia Renewal asked, so flagged as to just lay in the raft's middle.

Without her soldiers, her skar-soaked bravado, the Renewal sounded just like so many hapless and helpless people. Gladdring almost felt sympathy for the young woman. Almost.

She was, after all, the reason they were in this situation.

With the extra Rana skars joining their brother and sister, Gladdring gave them direction, a wordless command to bring the raft to the Najahn cutter. He gasped as the skars took their orders, shoving the raft along the waves first slow, and then faster than any sail could muster. The battered wood shoved aside wreckage as it sped on, losing more of itself with every impact.

"You could try to steer," Quik noted.

"Not sure how," Gladdring replied, his voice stretched enough to draw a frowning look from the hunter. "Don't worry, I won't die till we reach the ship."

A bad joke, and one that only deepened Quik's worry. The Noctia Renewal, at least, seemed to have succumbed to her earlier trouncing, vanishing again into unconsciousness.

The best way, perhaps, to drown, should that fate still await her.

"Hold!" Quik shouted after another several minutes passed, the Najahn cutter and its empty decks drawing closer. "It's the Queen!"

Quik pointed to the left, to a charred wreckage patch not too unlike the jumble on which Gladdring floated now. The burned boards held several bodies, none moving, but the Kance Queen's glittering robes stood out, even if their feathers had melted together and their fabric was no longer blue but an ashen black.

A choice presented, and Gladdring made it.

"You're not turning?" Quik asked as their raft continued towards the cutter.

"I'm choosing us," Gladdring said. "She's either dead, which means we're risking ourselves to rescue nothing, or she's barely alive, and we lose our control."

"Control?" Quik's look mixed shock and anger so well, Gladdring wondered if the man's place wasn't, truly, on a Tamas stage. "You're talking control now?"

"I'm talking sense, Quik! Once she had the skars, she didn't care about you and I. We were fodder, expendable." Mustering up much vigor with the Rana skars sucking at him made Gladdring's vision blur, but he held his look straight at the hunter. "We'd be tossed aside at the first chance, just like your friend, the other queen."

Quik flinched. A reminder of something the man might've chosen to forget brought into harsh light. The hunter shook his head, spat a curse, but said nothing else as the raft continued on. He'd wrestle with his soul now, and that fight might continue forever.

Or Quik would do as Gladdring had, and choose survival over all else.

CHAPTER 45
SCENES ON THE MOVE

Daklin directed, dictated, and drove them forward. Eujo and the others, still in slow recovery from their inn-battle injuries, had few options other than to obey the mad actor. The man had loyal guards: leering jesters plucked from the Animas, handed a sword, an axe, or a whip, and tasked with watching the crew, spewing hideous, rhyming threats should Eujo and Wax veer off the assigned scene.

The rehearsals didn't take place on a stage, but on a rolling cart. A fat one meant for hay bales or other large crops, pulled by a four pony team, and decorated with a single table and chair for prop purposes. Two smaller carts hauled provisions, their own ponies leading the train towards the next town in a westward line. Every night they would pull into a new home, every night Eujo, Wax, Bliss, and Torny would collapse into a guarded room only to wake and do it all again.

Livier, as the assassin deserved, remained shackled. Daklin didn't care about the Kance killer except to order his limp movement from cart to cramped closet when they stopped. Whether Livier received water, food, anything necessary to survive at first lingered as a curiosity for Eujo, one she forgot as memorizing lines and hitting marks came to dominate her days and nights.

Back at the Animas, the rehearsals had been equally exhausting, but Eujo had nursed an escape's dream to keep herself afloat. Now, with cuts, burns, and a spreading bruise along her side where the dagger struck home, pains parlayed with exhaustion for the right to screw up her next scene. Wax, who'd left the inn fight with the fewest scars, would bandy about the cart spouting the next line in their insipid farce only for Eujo to miss her cue, fumble words, or repeat what she'd already said.

Daklin would demand another take, and another, until the man dipped into a silent, simmering fury for the day's duration.

By the fifth sunrise, Eujo pulled herself onto the rolling stage with little more than bleak acceptance. Coffee mingled with bread and broth—last night's town had been crowded, with only spare stables and dirty straw for sleeping—to give her precisely zero energy. The skars didn't help, the Vis mutterings ever-present as the stones sapped her strength to heal her wounds.

"Daklin says it's the last day," Wax said, jumping up beside her, then offering Eujo a hand to complete the lift. At the cart's front, the drive cracked the reins and the ponies started off. "Just one more, Eujo."

"Till it really matters."

Daklin tried to motivate his actors with threats, too, with one sitting supreme amongst the scattered, callous words: a final performance in Tamas's capitol city, Videgaud, a name Daklin pronounced with a different inflection every time he spoke it. When Wax had asked him why,

Daklin replied that as his isle changed with every passing day, so should the flavor of its name.

That ridiculousness aside, Daklin emphasized the pair—Torny and Bliss, as Guardians, didn't get the joy of delivering their scenes before an audience—would have to give their grandest performance in Videgaud.

"Do well," Daklin repeated often, "and your dreams will come true. Falter, and you'll never forget your failure."

What that meant, Daklin wouldn't reveal, though he didn't seem happy at the idea, given how hard he pushed his actors. Eujo figured their performance might weigh on Daklin's own reputation, which almost made her want to throw the scene. Serve the tyrant right.

"C'mon, Eujo," Wax said, the cart making its exodus as the town woke up. "One more day to get it right."

She blinked. Took a chill breath. Snow glittered in the plains and groves around them, Tamas turning from root-covered wilderness to pleasant farmland. Posts marked springtime hop fields, the harbingers of Tamas's much-loved ales.

Eujo would've loved more of that, but Daklin had withheld the alcohol.

"For celebrations," Daklin said, "and you've earned none of those."

Torny and Bliss sat back with Livier in one of the trailing carts, held not with shackles but with quiet threat. The bandit's fire had dwindled with Daklin's arrival, with Bliss still recovering, and the two often matched Wax and Eujo in sullen moods.

"Ready?" Wax said, positioning himself at the table's side. Eujo leaned against the cart's left wall, rubbing her forehead. "If we get a round in before Daklin gets back here, maybe he won't push us so hard."

"Believe that when I see it."

But when Wax gave the cue, Eujo spoke the line.

Videgaud emerged like a parade to the senses. At first a smudge on the forward horizon, heralded by more roads and cart-driven traffic. Walking travelers, too, suggested possible trips without needing carts. Stands appeared, farmers and merchants attempting to parlay cheaper, poorer goods into better barters without the city's crowds. Their calls interrupted Eujo and Wax as they continued their rehearsals—Daklin did not give them credit for their early start—and Eujo demanded a break, an end.

Daklin, who stood at the cart's head, surveying them from the driver's bench like some trumped up lord, scoffed.

"As much as any actors I've ever known, you both need the time and trials," Daklin said. "There's a place to set aside the readings and accept what comes, but it is not now, not with your journey at stake."

"Then my journey's going to have to risk it," Eujo replied, noting Wax flick looks between them both. That the Vis leaped into this with so much vigor had been impressive, now it was just annoying. "I'm done, Daklin. Done with these lines, with this cart."

She expected another cutting reply. Instead, Daklin hopped back into the cart with them, stomped to Eujo without once losing his balance on the rumbling boards, and put his hand to her chin. Eujo repressed a wild urge to bite him.

"Maybe I'm wrong," Daklin said, an admission Eujo had never heard the man make before. "We're so close, a little rest and recovery might do you good. For some, being brought to the brink of death brings out the best. For one like you, so coddled, perhaps some cushions, a goblet of wine, and a nap are more appropriate."

"Coddled?" Eujo snarled, rethinking her non-biting choice, but Daklin scooted back, waving her off the whole way.

"Truth needs no shroud. You're a queen, and you demand a queen's comforts. So take them, then. Enjoy one last day in the isles's greatest city."

"Only if you shut up."

Daklin, at least, did just that. He returned to his driver's side and let the two Renewals greet Videgaud on its own terms.

Architecture across the isles, in Eujo's experience, tended to be driven by need. In Whent, with its blasted tundra, thick stone and heavy roofs meant warmth and respite. Vis's treehouses gave shelter from prowling predators. Foti and Rana matched their isles's traits, as did Kance. But Tamas?

Tamas gave into its desires.

Videgaud continued its arrival, unrolling like a wondrous carpet before them. Like the Animas, buildings sprang from the ground in dream-like shapes. Wood, stone, mud, and stranger things jutted forth in all directions. Bridges, roped and otherwise, lashed between buildings. Windows fit the curving sides, catching light along gilded edges and splashing reflected rainbows around. Flags, some bearing sigils Eujo recognized—acting companies, merchant guilds, and so forth—mingled with patterned or solid-color cotton snapping in the wind. Music clashed with bubbling conversation, random instruments and their mismatched players bashing against one another as Daklin's train moseyed into the city.

Eujo expected some guard post, maybe a stiff superior

collecting a tax from any incoming travel, but Videgaud had no wall, had no order of any kind. Tamas, apparently, operated free and in a frenzy.

Even in Winter's heart, the trading buzzed, declared deals erupting as the ponies guided the cart through a growing throng. Eujo heard Daklin catch a price for the manure his creatures left behind, fertilizer scooped up by urchins bearing shovels and buckets. More appealing were the fruits, meats, and fish yanked off southern boats and delivered to restaurants and grocers.

"Kance star fruit," Eujo said as she and Wax sat on the cart's side, legs swinging free. Their thick, warm outfits kept things clunky, but if they weren't uttering those lines again, Eujo wouldn't complain. "It's been so long."

Harvested from sticky clusters high up in Kance's spiked mountains, the star fruit looked much like its namesake: speckled blue and white, with a breath-cleansing zest in every bite. That these were here and not yet rotten meant the merchants must've moved them quick. Something about getting off those high cliffs made the delights shrivel and brown in only a few days.

Wax moved without warning, pushing off the cart's side into the hard stone street. As Eujo called his name, the Vis scampered to the fruit-selling stand, yanked a star fruit from its basket, and whipped it Eujo's way. She caught it by reflex, snagged the second one when Wax sent it along. The fruit seller started asking for payment, delivered when Daklin, after stopping the train, handed over Wax's own sword.

"Are all Renewals this much trouble?" Daklin said, shoveling several more star fruits into a satchel to even out the trade. "Or is it just the Vis?"

"Definitely just me," Wax replied, not bothering to look

twice at his pawned blade. He hopped back up to Eujo's side, held out a hand. "Share?"

The Queen complied, dropped the second fruit in Wax's palm, "Thanks, Wax." The soft fruit felt perfect in her palm, like a thousand precious memories. She smiled, put her fingers up to one of the fruit's pointed ends. "Now, let me show you how to eat this."

"You don't just bite in?"

"Not if you're trying to be proper."

"That's me, always proper."

Eujo laughed, "Remember, Wax, you're in the presence of a Queen."

Wax snorted, though any quip died as the train rounded a corner and put Videgaud's center into view. There, like a molten bubble rising up from the earth, sat Tamas's Great Stage. Rather than wonder at the designs painted onto its arcing walls, Eujo found her lines running back through her mind.

The show was at hand, and, to hear Daklin tell it, the cost of failure was something worse than death.

CHAPTER 46

BURNING CHAINS

Reth made it two strides from the stable before a chakram struck him in the plated shoulder, threw the hunter to the ground. From her sight. Annalyse stood in the stable's center, plotting what would come next, her mind and body entranced by the still, kneeling forms all around her. Those faces so placid, those eyes so lost, yet still alive.

Her focus changed quick when that chakram hit, the metal clang snapping her back to the run, the flight, and its impossibility. The stable's door held a familiar figured flanked by two in the same purple black armor that Veritrus wore. He had a voulge in one hand, the curved spear catching daylight in a squinting glint. He wore no chakram, unlike his two guards.

Had he been the one to strike Reth?

Did it matter?

"A few days later than expected, but still you're here," Veritrus said, staying in the doorway.

He knew as well as she did that there was only one way out.

"Did you kill him?" Annalyse asked, because what else was there to say?

Ask him about the faded prisoners? Ask him about the Najahn betrayal? Ask about what all his purple and black killers would do to the people of Vis?

No. Reth first. The only ally she had left, first.

"If he's unlucky," Veritrus replied, casting off the question with casual indifference. "I'm not the chakram thrower I once was, and he did seem to have a suit of our armor on. Nasty bruise, maybe a bad cut." Veritrus smiled, thin and assured. "Perhaps I'll lend him a Vis skar."

"You don't want him dead?"

"Look around you, Annalyse. I would have thought a scientist more observant. Do these people seem dead to you?"

Annalyse gulped. Shook her head. Let her hand drift up her weave to the necklace. Not that she needed to touch the skars to hear their whispers, draw upon their god-given powers, but something about holding the black iron, those warm stones . . .

"Noctia and the Najahn are not about indiscriminate killing. It's much better to use resources than lose them." Veritrus took a single stride into the stable. "See, every one of your friends here is a valuable member of our outpost. We're still learning, but soon I expect they'll be finding fulfillment tending our fields, cleaning our plates, and repairing the palisade you so rudely destroyed."

"How?"

"Ah, see? There you are. Asking the proper questions." Veritrus reached into a small pouch at his waist, withdrew something Annalyse couldn't see but could easily speculate. "These skars really are wonderful, aren't they?"

"Which one, Veritrus?"

"How about I show you?"

Before Annalyse could protest, the Noctia leader shoved his closed hand towards her. Like a swinging punch, only one many arm-lengths away from connecting. Even so, Annalyse reeled. Not from physical force but a blunt attack upon her mind, like a seething headache attempting to barge through. Her vision swam, her ears pulsed, and Annalyse went to her knees, retching.

Veritrus approached.

"If you think this is bad, you should have been here on the first day," Veritrus said. "We lost more than a few. Only the wounded, you know. The ones with little use left. Their minds were too ravaged to retain." Veritrus went down to one knee before Annalyse, his head cocked, a close inspection. "Simply broke. Tragic. But the next batch was better. They merely spasmed until their bones snapped. Better than nothing. By the third, we could keep them alive."

Skars shouted in her mind, Vis and Tamas loudest while all the others scurried their curious emotions about. As if Annalyse had drank too much ale in a crowded room with a hundred conversations. That loudest pair, though, seemed a bulwark against the encroaching waves, drifting every attack into a shivering spike down her legs, arms, eyes.

"Some lasted longer than the others. Took multiple rounds." Veritrus reached out, gave Annalyse's shoulder a slight shove. The scientist fell back onto the dirt. "We had to chain them down, when all they had left was rage. Until the next session, when we could calm them the rest of the way and leave them how we wanted. How we want you."

The hit did it. The knock against the ground drove Annalyse's teeth into her tongue. Raw pain, physical, served to blunt the lacerating mental waves. She had to act, had to stop this, had to stop everything.

Right. Now.

The Foti skar, her faithful stone, answered Annalyse's desperate call. Heat sprayed from the necklace, lancing everywhere save her own body. Veritrus stumbled back, shielding his eyes, turning his armor to block the rays. The dried straw had no such defense. The Foti skar howled in wordless triumph as the stable caught fire, above and around Annalyse in an instant.

As those flames erupted, the mental assault vanished. Veritrus fled with nothing more than a curse, embers and the first ash landing around Annalyse as she tried to get her breath back, put herself into motion. Her body rose to the challenge slowly, as if waking from a deep sleep.

Her eyes traced the hungry fires as they raced along the roof beams, as they leapt from one straw pile to the next. Her nose burned at the first hot smoke.

Her ears heard the screams begin.

Raw, panicked, and confused. Annalyse lurched to her feet, followed the sound to the stall to her right, where a hunter pair backed against the stable's wall, fire blowing up as it found straw aplenty to devour.

What could be created, could be turned.

Annalyse called her skars again, found Whent waiting. Like a mad digging beast, the ground surged across the burning straw, burying the flames in a sudden dirt froth. The hunters, spared, stared back at her in wild confusion.

"Run," Annalyse said, heard more shouts demanding more action, shrieking more consequences.

The stable burned. No dirt tossing would save the engulfed roof, would keep the scientist and the captives alive. Annalyse needed something bigger. Broader. Desperate.

She needed Kance.

The wind stone answered Annalyse's summons with rasping delight. Annalyse pushed her ask, thrusting her arms out and praying for the wind stone to do what had to be done. The stone began, the air inside the stable whipping up, pressing the fire against the wood, crackling the walls.

And with its force, Kance demanded succor.

Annalyse hit the ground without knowing it, her legs at once little more than air themselves. Her arms flopped to the sides, muscles too drained to keep them aloft. Even Annalyse's tongue, bleeding, lay still in her mouth, her eyes drooped, and the smallest, smoke-filled breath was a labor.

The stable shook. The wind howled. But the walls did not collapse, and the fire began to fight back, began to take the air for its own.

"My turn," said a familiar voice, a hard one, and Deshiva's hand grabbed Annalyse's necklace, tore it from the scientist's neck.

The whispers vanished, a singular void Annalyse hadn't felt in . . . weeks? She stared up at the Vis hunter, in little more than charred rags, with more anger than Annalyse had ever seen in Deshiva's filthy features. The hunter held the necklace out as burning wood fell around them, the wind dying, their death approaching.

Until it didn't. Until the flames stopped their approach and went back the other way, until Annalyse rolled across the ground under something's power beyond her own, until the stable itself, what remained of it, split like a Whent boulder hurled from a high cliff and scattered in all directions.

Amid the straw, the burning splinters, the flying and flailing captives, Annalyse saw Deshiva continuing to stand there in the disaster's center, owning its focus and driving its force. The Kance-created explosion must've drained so much of Deshiva, should've brought her down just as it had Annalyse, but the Kitaye hunter didn't waver, didn't fold.

How?

Clanks and calls canceled that question just as they had too many others. Annalyse pushed her face from the dirt, found Veritrus standing with his bodyguards. One held Reth's wounded form hunched over, a Najahn sword near his throat. In the grass around, naked and nearly that hunters arose in the grass, heads shaking and mouths spouting curses and queries in equal measure.

They found their answers in Deshiva's call. A guttural whoop, like the kind Annalyse had heard in Kitaye, save this one bore a savage snarl at the start and end, a hanoko's howl before it pounced on some unlucky prey.

However sapped of their souls, of what made them human, Deshiva's howl spoke to something deeper. Something Veritrus had, evidently, failed to cleanse.

The Najahn, more soldiers coming at the stable's explosion, numbered between ten and twenty. Most of the outpost was still gone, pulled away by the diverting fiend. Those that remained found themselves outnumbered two to one, found themselves better equipped, but not so driven, not so brutal.

Annalyse sat, watched, a numb fascination holding her still as Deshiva's hunters, aligned in this visceral moment with their Mottilan counterparts, threw themselves upon the Najahn. Those purple and black held their poise for one moment, two, until fingernails found throats to tear and burning boards punched through gaps in their armor. Bodies, blood, and fresh screams lit a ruined morning.

The carnage ended quick. Veritrus, his pouch lost, his helmet torn away, and half his face with it, was dragged to

Deshiva. Annalyse, had she the energy to speak then, might've protested for the man's life, for the knowledge in his mind. Deshiva, with the Najahn's own voulge, put an end to that possibility.

The leader's death prompted a different awakening, as if the Vis realized that they weren't just vengeful ghosts but still alive, cracked free from their mind-prisons. Deshiva issued a different whistle, and the Mottilan who didn't understand had their directions clarified by Reth's companions, returning from the southern jungle with a ready escape.

"Get up," Deshiva said, her viscera-marred form gripping Annalyse's shoulder and pulling her to a stand.

"How can you move, after that?" Annalyse said, her own knees weak. The hunters around them shambled, some carrying wounded, others carrying stolen weapons. Grasses continued to burn. "The skars—"

"I can barely walk," Deshiva muttered, and Annalyse realized the hunter's arm on her shoulders was more for Deshiva than herself. "But together, we can run."

CHAPTER 47
CITY LIFELESS

Of all the people in the isles, few caused more angry nausea than Fassle and Yarvick. That they stood next to the person who inspired the exact opposite and quite a bit more besides had Ami reaching for a blade that wasn't there. Neither Flamebreak, her long lost bastard sword, nor the Whent-crafted weapon had come with her up the Wound. All part of Jochi and Svarde's quest for peace, to present a front crafted for diplomacy instead of death.

Ami would've dealt the latter in a second. Instead she settled for a curse and a spit down the Wound's long depths. With any luck, the splatter would land on Jochi's awful head for making her see this.

"Ami," Svarde said. "Remember why we're here."

She didn't have to work hard for that. Beneath the canvas roof around the Wound, at the foot of the Aegis's throne, stood the weapons and wielders of them that could bring the firewalkers home. Not just the burning fiends either, but the unknown others behind those swirling gates. Fassle, in his adorned purple and gold Noctia robes, and Yarvick, silky black and silver, with a broad hat shading the man's ghost-white face, crowned the entourage. The unlikely pair took up spots on either side of a too-frail Catya, each one greeting Ami's coarse welcome with thin frowns.

"An idealist and a traitor," Fassle said. "I see exile hasn't improved your demeanor. Would that you had died instead of Masayo."

"If she'd lived, maybe I wouldn't be here," Yarvick added, then swept his hat off in a swift bow. "So I have you to thank, Ami, for slaying my most persistent nemesis."

"You're not welcome."

Yarvick just laughed, a windy cackle. At least that made Fassle look even more annoyed, something that would forever brighten Ami's soured spirits.

"You're not dead," Fassle said, scowling at Ami, "because of your fellow Guardian." He raised his look to Svarde. "Your reappearance is, frankly, unexpected. Last I saw your unpleasant visage, you proclaimed a foolish quest and left here on a journey that seemed sure to end in your death. Yet here you stand, looking worse for wear. Explain."

"You don't give us orders," Ami said, crossing her arms as Svarde sighed.

The sound made her twitch, something she would've fought past and continued in a much-deserved insult barrage if Catya hadn't matched the sigh with one of her own. Coming from the Aegis, not a year older than Ami yet looking more than twice the Guardian's age, the whistling resignation caught Ami's fire in her throat.

Remember why she was here. Remember what this could mean for Catya.

"We come as equals," Ami finished. "Not to fight, but to, somehow, ask a favor. As friends."

Fassle and Yarvick glanced at one another, adding more questions on their relationship. That the bandit lord and the Circle's leader weren't friends had been as constant as Noctia's seasons. The Nimble Fingers picked pockets small and large, always keeping just shy of provoking devastating Najahn action, but any thieves who stumbled in their dirty tasks found the gallows quick.

Yet here they were, seemingly aligned.

"A favor . . . " Yarvick mused, then cast a look around the Wound, at the stationed guards and their listening ears, would-be whispering lips. "If you're not bringing an army with you, then I suggest we take this discussion to somewhere private. Wars can be started with rumors, and lives ended with one wrong word."

Despite Ami calling them equals, she and Svarde knew their lives on Noctia continued at Yarvick and Fassle's permission. While the Foti barbarian, with his immortal sword, might survive a crossbow assault, a chakram's edge, Ami would not. And she suspected Svarde's endless life might be strained if, say, an executioner's axe detached head from neck.

So they followed Yarvick and Fassle up from the Wound, climbing past snow-covered lelune flowers to a familiar tunnel. At Fassle's order, following guards stationed themselves at the openings, leaving the foursome distant enough to ensure difficulty eavesdropping, close enough that any surprised shout would bring certain death.

All the same, Ami wondered at the trust. Svarde refused to give up his sword, explaining nothing, and both lords accepted it. No argument, just a nodded agreement.

Why?

"We're giving you this moment because the isles have

fallen apart," Fassle said. "Because the *Najahn* nearly fell apart."

Nobody missed the glare Fassle dished to Yarvick, least of all the bandit lord.

"It's a time of crisis," Yarvick said, jumping into the gap. "The secret of the skars has been revealed, and their power is causing chaos across the isles. Our soldiers are—"

"Excuse me," Ami said. "Our? As in, you and Fassle? Together?"

"Noctia stands united," Fassle said, though his low tone suggested that unity came under some duress. "Rana, Whent, Foti, and Tamas are behind us as well, though their loyalties are not so concrete as we would like. Vis and Kance, however, have rejected our guidance for open war. Between those disasters and the continuing fiend threat, we are pressed to do what must be done."

"Which is?"

"Gather all the skars," Yarvick answered. "The god stones are the key, as you must know by now. Their power gives us a chance to eradicate the fiends forever. Yet, by the same, it might bring about our absolute destruction in the wrong hands."

The bandit lord seemed to fight against his own accent, his own mode of speech with every formal sentence. An awkwardness Yarvick didn't notice. Then again, why should he? The bandit lord defied countless orders for his arrest and execution by standing here. What was left, when you defeated death?

"You're hoping we can help you," Svarde said. "You let us climb because you think we will fight for you?"

"Fight, inspire, or bring some unexpected aid," Yarvick said. "There's little harm in learning why you're here. If it's not to our liking, we'll cut your throats and throw your bodies back down the Wound."

No doubt in those words. Yarvick's certainty snared Ami's response before it even began.

"Unexpected aid," Svarde murmured. "That's one way you could look at it."

The barbarian gave it all away then, detailed the swirling gates in the pool far below, the Dead King, Jochi's colonizing band, and, last, the firewalkers. He put the burning fiend's need for a home out as necessary, not a question or a demand.

"They will take it, if we don't give it to them," Svarde finished. "They will burn our cities and leave all the isles in ruins."

Fassle scoffed, "The skars would lay them low. I've seen—"

"How many of you know how to use them?" Ami asked. "The skars? Four? Five? A dozen? The firewalkers will ruin you." She found, deployed a sneer. "They won't be alone either. Jochi will stand with them. As will we."

"Against your homes?"

"Against you." Ami pointed at them both in turn. "Foti and the other isles might not care to fight you now, but they'll be happy to leave you behind when the firewalkers turn Noctia to ash."

"Threats, then?" Fassle asked. "You've come all this way to declare war upon us?"

"Back the firewalkers, and any other fiends that want more than blood," Svarde said, shifting to the right enough to impose his bulk between Ami and the other pair. "Prove you want peace for the isles, Fassle. Do that, and maybe we'll leave your head on your shoulders."

Fassle, red-faced, looked ready to bluster, but Yarvick cut the man off.

"Will these fiends fight with us?" Yarvick asked. "If they'll help us wipe away those resisters on Kance, on Vis, then they can have those isles for themselves. Except the skars, of course. A home for a few stones?"

THE *RAT'S FANG* hadn't changed much, though Ami's drinking partners tonight numbered among her strangest. She was the only one with ale before her. Svarde, to her left, stared at the flagon with such a look of despair on his face that she offered him a drink, only for Svarde to, again, decline.

"It tastes like nothing," Svarde said. "Don't waste it on me."

"Memories aren't as good as the real thing, are they?" said the third body at the table, in a voice so quiet as to escape the *Rat's Fang*'s conversation only because of the hour, the season. An icy port made for a dull dockside tavern. "But sometimes they're all we have."

Catya, wearing thick Najahn robes, sat in a high-backed chair. The *Rat's Fang* didn't have many of those, but Svarde secured one for the Aegis. The stools he and Ami sat on were too shaky, too prone to falling, a risk Ami would've called ludicrous not long ago, but that now . . .

She was here. The Aegis was here. Off her throne, away from the Wound, and without the skar necklace. Better still, Catya would never have to put it on again. The first provision struck and agreed to with Fassle and Yarvick, persuaded by the firewalkers and Jochi's own forces patrolling the caves far below.

Svarde should've looked happier, considering he'd

achieved his goal. No more souls would wither above that awful gash. That Catya would remain faded, unnaturally aged, wasn't his fault. That she had a chance to live another year, or ten, was.

Nevertheless, whenever Ami let her eyes settle on Catya for more than a second, she found herself reaching for the ale, waving for another round.

"Then here's what I say," Ami announced into the sodden silence around the table. "Let's relive a few of those tonight, at least until I can't sit on this stool anymore." Ami tapped the Vis skars embedded in her faceplate. "Takes a lot more with these little guys on my side."

Catya giggled. Her own mug, warm, with likely not-at-all fresh tea inside, rose to knock against Ami's, and Svarde launched into the first of many adventures, life seeming to return bit by bit as he spoke.

Yet Ami only felt the barest buzz by the time Catya slumped, almost asleep against the table. Svarde caught the Aegis with a tender arm, and together they left the tavern, hiked back to the Noctia quarter. After they dropped Catya in her assigned bed—Fassle thought he was being clever, giving Ami and Svarde their old rooms back—the Guardian pair settled up outside on the streets amid the thin remaining snow.

"We're welcoming these firewalkers with a war, you know?" Ami said, leaning back against the stone tower.

"If what you told me is true, they've been fighting a losing battle for a long time." Svarde fished out a pipe, a moldering pouch of foul Kance tobacco.

"Where'd you get that?"

"Left it here after my last visit," Svarde said, shaking the stuff into the pipe, used a small flint rock to spark it. "Maena didn't give me much time to pack."

"Grand adventures rarely do."

"Think we're about done with those."

Ami chuckled, "What makes you think that?"

"Crushing two isles with a horde of firewalkers doesn't strike me as grand, Ami. They'll fold in a few weeks or burn in a few months. Then it's done."

Svarde puffed on the pipe once, twice. Sighed and tossed the thing away.

CHAPTER 48
TO FIX A FLAW

A hostage's value should never be underestimated. Gladdring and Quik couldn't steer their battered, makeshift room raft with much accuracy, but the cutter came to them once the Vis hunter lifted the exhausted, unconscious Renewal into view.

Soaked with sea spray, Gladdring and Quik scaled the ladder let down from the ship, the Vis carrying the Renewal with him. They found a simple deck done up in the manner of Najahn method: tucked away ropes, emergency equipment, and chakram racks near the aft cabins. An open stair to the lower deck would lead to hammocks and cells for the crew and their prisoners. A few sailors greeted their arrival with suspicious eyes and worried questions.

Those questions, about whether the cutter's captain had been seen alive, whether any other soldiers were coming back, and what, just what was in all those sacks on the raft, told Gladdring more than enough: this was a threadbare crew thrown together for a fast pursuit, one now lacking in leadership and all that flowed from it.

"The Renewal first," Gladdring said, rebuffing their inquiries and directing Quik to carry the woman to the former captain's cabin. "Quik, see her settled. Trust no one else to go near her."

The hunter gave Gladdring the quizzical stare that remark deserved, but Gladdring didn't expound, only nodded towards Quik's ordered destination. He'd understand eventually. Or not. It didn't matter.

"We go on," Gladdring said next to the first mate, a swarthy woman who's stocky, tattooed self stood at odds with Najahn's preference for clean branding. "Kance is close now."

"Excuse me on that score, sir," the first mate replied, her thick speech suggesting a Rana or Foti origin, "But who are you and what're you doing giving orders on our ship?"

Muttered agreements hinted the four or five other crew standing nearby while the cutter rocked amid the waves were of like mind, but minds were malleable. Gladdring plunged his hands into his wet robes, felt not one but several topaz skars waiting for him. What with one amounted to a suggestion, might become a force with something more.

Time to put that theory to the test.

"I'm the one who knows best what's really going on," Gladdring announced. "The Kance Queen held me as a hostage, took me against my will to deliver the Noctia skars to Kance for her own ends. Your Renewal rescued me, and suffered much harm in the doing. When I say we sail on to Kance, I say we must deliver the Circle's edict: the Queen is dead, and Kance must reject her foolish defiance to join with the purple and black in destroying the fiends."

As he spoke, the Tamas skars transformed his words into plain emotion, a thick, invisible miasma coating the sailors in compliance. The stones squashed questioning thoughts in the same way a rapt story dispelled daydreams, or desire overrode rationality. The sailors may have started believing Gladdring suspect, maybe an enemy. They ended nodding with his every word as Gladdring assigned their new duties, gathered information on their food stores, the prisoners below, and learned what their mission had been.

"Stop the Queen and get the skars," the first mate said, her thick talk evening out as the Tamas stones dealt death blows to emotion, to slanted speech. "We're to help the Renewal in anything she asks."

Ah yes, the Renewal. Gladdring waved the crew off to do their tasks, to get the cutter back on the current heading towards the wind isle. A few calls came from the sea, some more shipwreck survivors demanding aid, but the Najahn crew paid them no heed. The desperate might be, as Gladdring suggested, enemies. Mortal threats. The ever-more panicked cries accompanied Gladdring to the Renewal's cabin, the former ship captain's residence rising up off the deck.

On either side of the cabin, stepladders led to the tiller. Black wood lined with purple and gold touches erased any natural brown on the ship, soaking in the sunlight and radiating its heat. An awful touch in the summer melting away any winter ice. Sails unfurled above, catching the day's wind and leaping the cutter forward, the ocean's steady slap a comfort. Too many years ago, Gladdring himself had stood atop one of these, measuring the stars and the sea for the purple and black.

A memory for another time.

They were underway, and Gladdring, once again, stood atop the others.

Entering the cabin threatened to knock the former

Tenet down. As Gladdring shut the slim door behind him, the price paid those Tamas skars took its bite. His head ached, his knees almost buckled, and Gladdring had to steady himself against cabin's wall.

"All right?" Quik asked, the hunter rising from the Renewal's bed.

A glance confirmed the Vis had played the good doctor, stripping off the soaked armor and wrapping the shivering, still-unconscious Renewal in blankets. Quik himself had tossed aside his own ruined outfit, and when the hunter confirmed Gladdring wasn't about to fall over, he resumed tugging on some spare breeches, a shirt left behind by the presumably deceased captain.

"Preserving our lives required effort, more than I wanted," Gladdring said. "But the crew is ours now, at least for the moment. We sail for Kance."

"So you suggested on the raft. What's there?"

"An isle for the taking, Quik."

The hunter frowned, "We're not their queen. I'm a Vis, Gladdring. At best they'll throw us on another ship home."

"No, because we have news, and an offer," Gladdring said, finally trusting himself to move off the wall.

The captain's cabin held the usual assortment given a Najahn sea leader: a bed against the far wall, a desk strewn with maps, and several chests filled with clothes and gear for bartering if the captain needed it. Gladdring went to that desk now, sat in the chair and rubbed his forehead. Quik finished dressing himself and waited.

The Vis would make a good servant. Pliable and loyal.

"Kance is at war," Gladdring said, "though they may not know it yet. We have the most powerful weapons the isles have ever seen on this ship. Ones they won't know how to use even if they pluck the stones from our dead hands. With that offer alone, we'll have protection, we'll have allies."

"Until they decide we're not important anymore. Just like the Queen."

"We'll be the ones deciding, Quik." Gladdring pulled his hands free, set the Tamas skars on the desk. "These skars can crush their minds, make anyone our ally, at least for a time. Long enough to learn who else needs ridding of."

Quik shook his head, "More murders, then. For what, Gladdring? You told me back on Noctia that our actions would save the isles. All we've done is start a war."

"The first step, and I'll admit, it's not been as clean as I would like, but i'm asking you to trust me, Quik. Together, we can see this through. Deliver the Najahn a defeat like they've never seen and watch Fassle's power crumble. Then we offer salvation, a united front against the fiends and an end to division, to chaos."

"With you at the top."

"With us, Quik. Together, we can lead armies, we can save your brother, and stop any more suffering atop the Wound's throne."

"You're talking big, Gladdring. I just wish I could trust you."

"Where would you be without me? Sitting in some school listening to a Najahn history lesson?" Gladdring's eyes glittered. "Or maybe you'd be on a ship like this, on your way to Vis to suppress your own people. Is that what you want?"

Quik only glowered.

"With me," Gladdring continued, because he never could let an opening go un-used, "you'll have a say. You'll pull the levers, lead the men and women of these isles against the endless threat and defeat it. It's not a curse, Quik, it's an honor."

When Quik continued his muted glare, Gladdring nodded to the door. Best give the man direction before Quik found a more dangerous course. "Check on the crew, would you? I fear I might not be able to leave this cabin for a while yet. No matter how you feel about me, neither of our ends are served by drowning in the depths at their hands."

Quik stood, headed to the door, scowling Gladdring's way all the while. "We're not done with this conversation, Gladdring. I'm not your pet. My brother's still the one that matters. I want him safe, skars be damned."

"Fassle's the one that wants him dead, not me."

Quik snorted, but opened the door and vanished onto the deck. As soon as the latch swung closed again, Gladdring stood and stumbled over to the Renewal's bedside. She lay there, indeed still breathing, eyes closed. She'd used so many skars already, Gladdring figured she'd sleep for hours yet if left alone.

His eyes traveled to the necklace still around her neck, black iron and holding all seven skars. Which one had given the Renewal all that extra energy, had sapped the sacrificial prisoners of their lives?

The answer wasn't hard to guess. Gladdring had felt the Noctia skar's snatching hunger. He reached, lifted the Renewal's head and her stringy, salted hair with one hand. Unclipped the necklace and drew it off. Too small for Gladdring's own neck, he shifted it in his left hand until his palm rested on the Noctia skar's warmth.

The stone bubbled up, curious and hungry.

The Tamas skars could change minds for a time, could push desires in the direction Gladdring wanted. People, however, would correct themselves, would return to what they knew to be true. The Najahn crew would be dealt with once they guided the cutter into port. The Renewal?

The Noctia skar read Gladdring's intentions, leapt to meet his request.

Yarvick had called Gladdring weak. Too weak.

No more.

CHAPTER 49

LAST LINES

Daklin gave them the tour guide treatment as the foursome left the cart —Livier, shackled again to a smaller cart's sides, waited with a guard. Muddy streets surrounded the lava-orange dome, broad avenues left free from haranguing stands if not wandering crowds. Actors stood immortalized as dark stone statues, blocks etched with their great plays, though Eujo recognized no names, no faces. Billowing, prismatic overhangs stretched out from the Great Stage: the theater itself seemed to be open at all sides, as if crowds coming to view a performance would swarm.

Eujo didn't listen to Daklin's explanation, whether such stampedes would happen. Instead, she ran over her lines again and again, matching Wax's steps as they headed inside the structure, trading wet paving stones for smoothed marble floors. Where that marble came from—Foti, Whent?—Eujo didn't know, but the sheer expense emphasized, again, how much weight Tamas put on their entertainment.

If the floor gave a sturdy spot to step, the walls provided

great places to look. Most held paintings, some slapped right on the beige stone while others hung on canvas or cloth. All depicted fantastical scenes, stages present beneath the action.

"You could be immortalized here as well," Daklin said, breaking Eujo's concentration by slowing up, talking right next to her. "As a Renewal, a good performance would be a legendary feat. Worth striving for."

"We're here to stop the fiends, not win your acting contest."

"Not a contest, a way of life."

If Eujo had offended Daklin with her comeback, the man showed none of it, instead continuing on his circuit. For every two outside portals, each an arch accompanied by thick double doors, a further funnel deeper inside waited. In between stretched spaces for dropping thick coats or ordering famed Tamas ales. At the moment, few others scampered inside the theater, and those that did greeted the group with confused stares.

Confused until Daklin identified their reason for being here. That inevitably drew wishes of good luck for Wax and Eujo.

"Sort of nice," Wax murmured as they approached Daklin's goal: backstage. "Not everyone wants us to fail."

"I don't think anyone does. It's more that we have to do this at all."

"Every skar has a task, right? At least we're not fighting a fiend or trying to outrun an avalanche."

"I'd prefer those."

Wax tilted his head, narrowed a single eye. "Don't kid with me, Queen. I'm good at spotting a liar, and I know you're looking forward to this."

"Why would you think that?"

Wax puckered his lips, threw a wink, and laughed when Eujo recoiled.

"Okay," Eujo said, falling into a smiling headshake. "Settle down. Focus on the lines, the steps. Not that you're kissing a Queen."

"Easy enough. Already kissed you a few times."

Another wink. Eujo went for a playful punch at Wax's gut, but the Vis danced back, laughing.

"Seems like our actors are in good spirits," Daklin announced, turning Bliss and Torny towards their Renewal pair. They'd reached a thicker door, one adorned, in gilded orange lettering, that what lay beyond was for actors and stage staff only. "I'm glad. Despite what you may think, I did not drag you all this way to witness failure. I hope you make us proud. The Animas, despite your escape, was your first teacher, and our efforts are on display today."

"Again, not doing this for you," Eujo said as Torny, facing away from Daklin, rolled her eyes. "Don't care about your Animas."

Daklin just grinned wider, yanked open the door to darker hallways beyond. "Good. Today, care only about your scene, and your spirits."

"Your spirits?" Torny asked as they sat in cozy chairs, munching on a late lunch waiting for them in the scalloped dressing room's center. "What's that even mean? Caring about my spirit?"

'You're a bandit,' Bliss signed. 'You've already lost yours. These two, though . . . '

"Guess I'll have to steal yours then."

Bliss smiled. She'd probably be okay with that, given what the two had become. Eujo watched the interplay as she dug into her own meal. Real, fresh fish and cooked carrots. Several oysters apiece too, plucked from the sea that morning and prepared with Tamas ice peppers. Briny bites perfect when washed down with malty ale.

Of all people, Daklin had recommended the drink and returned with flagons for them all. Calming for the nerves, settling for the stage, the man said, and while performing a whole play drunk wasn't advised, doing a scene with the audience a bit blurry might be helpful to fresh performers. After he'd dropped off the drinks, the man left, saying he'd be back in an hour.

Any ideas of escape disappeared when Torny, curious, tried the door and found a guard outside. The man, armed with a striped iron club, asked what the bandit wanted, and when she replied freedom, laughed and pushed the door shut again.

So they were left, the four of them, amid costume racks and walls decorated with old fliers like the ones that'd proclaimed Eujo and Wax's original turn back at the Animas. Hazy music floated in from somewhere, a player practicing. A single mirror, too, hung at one end.

"Want to run our lines again?" Wax asked, having devoured his meal faster than anyone else.

Eujo shook her head, swallowed her bite. "I have it as good as I'm going to, Wax. I vote we find some bad costumes and tell some stories."

'Stories?' Bliss signed.

"Memories, maybe. Something to take me away from here. We've been across a bunch of isles, faced all sorts of awful things, and maybe had a bandit fall in love." Eujo grinned at Torny, who blushed and stared at her ale. "Whatever happens on that stage, if Wax and I don't make it, or if we do, it'll be because we've done this together. So that's what I want. Your best, your worst, your funniest memories. If I'm going on that stage, I want to do it knowing just who I'm acting for."

"Well, Eujo," Wax said, "can't say I expected you to be heartwarming, but I'll say this: you want to go back? My vote's for those few fires in the Rana swamp. With Quik. Bantering, bickering, adventuring."

"With our soaked shoes?" Torny scoffed. "Give me those warm nights in Harrow's Edge any day."

As Bliss jumped in, signing away her love of Noctia city lights, Eujo sipped her ale, held back a smile. She'd not expected to find her three best friends during the Renewal's trials, but now that she had, the Kance Queen couldn't imagine being anywhere else.

Eujo could, though, imagine being anywhere other than the Great Stage. She stood, dressed in some flimsy maroon tunic, a tufted hat pressing on her ears. She waited off stage left, lurking behind a curtain as Daklin introduced the scene to what seemed to be a dark wall. Overhead lanterns focused their hot light onto the stage, rendering any view beyond its wood world pointless. To her right, a backdrop meant for the evening's main event showcased spindly trees and falling leaves, at odds with the summer fling scene she and Wax were about to enact.

Perform. Live. Embrace.

Eujo repeated the silent mantra as her heart thudded, Daklin reaching his conclusion. Wax stood across the way, done up in thin whites and equally ridiculous. He gave her a nod, a confident smile. Always believing in his friends, that one, even if he didn't believe enough in himself.

Daklin fell into a deep bow, backing up as he did so,

before turning Eujo's way and striding past. He put a hand, ever so light, on her shoulder.

"Just like breathing," Daklin whispered. "Be you."

Beyond, a trumpet picked up a merry tune—possibly the same musician that'd serenaded their dressing room memories with haphazard play—and Wax strode into the stage, arms broad and smile wide as he faced the audience, delivering the scene-setting lines. At their conclusion, Eujo would make her own way forth, would reveal her surprise to find him here, so far away from his coddling family.

And at the end?

No. Not yet. The next line, and only that.

Wax wrapped, sighed at the summer day's apparent beauty. Torny, stuffed somewhere in that hidden audience, whistled. Bliss, maybe, clapped.

Eujo made her entrance.

CHAPTER 50

THE COMING WAR

The small boat proved ample size for the few fleeing the Najahn outpost. Not every mind-wiped prisoner survived the stable fire, and some that did collapsed a few steps beyond, Veritrus's tortures proving too much to handle. Deshiva made the call to leave them, to carry Reth and a few others whose wounds let them stumble along with arms over shoulders.

To wait any longer, to build stretchers or heal what ailed those addled minds would've cost the group everything they'd gained. All the same, Annalyse, teetering on her own exhausted edge, was happy to let Deshiva make the call.

The shamble southward traded cultivated grass for jungle ferns and clinging vines, an hours-long hike continuing till dusk, till a hasty camp made on Vis's southern beach. The sloop found them when the fires lit, carting over food, bandages, and hope. Annalyse collapsed on the sand and slept until Deshiva shoved her awake, the morning sun well into the sky.

If the Najahn wanted to counter, to catch their escapees, they'd missed their chance.

"Like a fever," Deshiva said, later, as she spoke with Annalyse on the sea. "A sudden one. Defiant, angry, I was all of those things and then it was as if nothing mattered. I had no needs, no desires, no concerns about myself or what sat around me."

"So you remember it?"

They sat on the top deck, leaning on the starboard rail staring into open, shimmering ocean. Mottilan sailors danced around them, keeping the ship gliding amid the waves.

"Of course." Deshiva sniffed. "I wasn't dead. Wasn't unconscious. I saw everything, heard everything, I just *didn't care*. The skar Veritrus used . . . do you know which one?"

"Tamas, if I had to guess. The others are more blunt in their actions."

"The Tamas one, then. It obliterated who I was."

"Hid it, more like."

Deshiva frowned, "Because I came back?"

"The fire must've jarred you loose. Like it did most of the others. Tore away whatever veil the skar put over your eyes."

"Then thank you for nearly killing me."

"It wasn't planned."

Deshiva chuckled. Not a happy sound. "I'm aware. No military mind would've done what you did."

"It wasn't all my idea," Annalyse protested. "Mottilan's elders, and—"

"As I said, no military mind would've gone with your plan."

Annalyse let the argument die with a sigh. Deshiva was back.

Mottilan continued to transform, swapping a fishing village awash in grievance for a desperate chance at survival. Despite winter still keeping things cool and the seas turbulent, frames for new boats lay on the beach. Crossbows and quarrels, spears and stone blades lay newly wrapped in rows or hanging from beachfront racks. Those houses up on the cliffs had their conversions completed, spikes planted on the main road, shooting platforms nestled amid treetops. Baskets and barrels stuffed with salted fish and dried fruit found their way to stashes in caves along the coast, emergency reserves in case of relentless assault.

Because that, according to the hunters slipping in from Kitaye, who called themselves Lira, would be coming. Despite the disruption at the Najahn outpost, the purple and black continued to assert themselves. Kitaye remained under martial occupation, with more forces from the north landing every day. As the seas began to thaw, still more, with Rana and Foti mercenaries among them, would arrive. The Najahn would sweep south across Vis, fortify the Great Sana, and tell Mottilan to submit.

"Which we will not do," Deshiva said, much recovered —Annalyse's Vis skar could be thanked for that—and leading Mottilan's dreary war council. They sat around the same stone table, beneath the same thatched roof, and descended into details Annalyse no longer cared to listen to. "We have emissaries off to Kance. They'll be our best allies in this fight."

"Our only allies," one elder muttered.

"Until we turn the other isles against the Najahn," Deshiva said. "As winter lets up, we'll send for help, describe what the Najahn are doing. Foti, Rana, and Whent may change their minds."

"For us? What do they care about the Vis?"

Deshiva started up again and Annalyse backed away, slipped out into the afternoon sun. They would go at it for hours, flipping between in-your-face bickering and military minutiae. Annalyse hadn't spent much time around Whent warlords and their conquest conferences, but it seemed like so much talking, waiting for something horrible to happen.

Far more interesting, far more what she preferred, waited for Annalyse near the port. Two Mottilan hunters stood ready, spears pointed to the sky, outside the door. One even opened it as she approached, giving Annalyse easy access to the pitiful skar stores inside. Materials, from weaves to leathers to what armor and weapons Mottilan could spare, lumped around the place. Ideas and options, as if Annalyse could use the ten skars they still had—including the Tamas one taken from Veritrus's corpse—to even the odds.

And maybe she could. Those little stones could do amazing things in the right hands, and a strike delivered at the right time, in the right moment could swing a battle, change a war. The scientist set the stones in a line, counting them, listening as their whispers sparked up in her mind at the smallest touch. Which would be the key?

Her eyes found the single Noctia skar, its opal beauty sucking in the firelight from the cabin's lone globe lantern.

The door swung open. Annalyse grabbed the black skar and whirled, nerves flying, a hungry desire demanding to be set free.

It was: dropped, to bounce along the stone floor.

Before Annalyse stood someone that ought to be dead and that, to a degree, looked it. Sawi didn't have her Najahn robes, her Vis weave, but instead stood, with a set face, wearing battered Whent furs and leathers. Her outfit bore scratches, as did Sawi herself, and the Whent blade at her side bore stains of long-spilled blood.

Nevertheless, there she stood. Alive.

The hug was tight, hard, and long. Before that moment, Annalyse wouldn't have called them close, would've called them partners, at best. But war, death, and desperation strengthens frail bonds.

"How?" Annalyse asked, through happy tears. "How are you here?"

Sawi, smiling through her own, stepped back. "It's a long story, and I've walked a long way through some very dark caves to get here. There's a good inn nearby, with ale and a warm fire. Care to join me and my friends?"

"Friends?"

Sawi stepped aside, nodded at a Whent group standing outside, equally appearing as though they'd been battling the wilds for days on end.

"There's an invasion coming, Annalyse," Sawi said, "and if we're not ready, there'll be nothing left."

CHAPTER 51

TRAITOR NO MORE

Ami shooed away the handlers, let herself stare into the mirror for the first time since she'd vanished from Noctia a branded traitor. In the warm lantern light, the purple and black mail disappeared against her gold faceplate, her red hair, only catching here and there where the ringlets beneath revealed gaps to tighten. The armor's weight alone almost buckled Ami's knees, a reminder that life scrabbling for food in the Dark Below did little for her health. Yet, along with the hand-and-a-half sword at her hip, the pressure felt like home, like what she'd worn when Catya's quest took them into conflict, when Ami needed to stand on ceremony for her Aegis.

The faceplate, though, stole her focus. Hard to ignore the shine, the twin Vis skars embedded near her left cheek. Smooth, itching, omnipresent. Before the flight into the caves, Ami used to take it off at night. After, removal became too risky, the constant wounds requiring the skars presence. She'd learned to push the sensation away.

At least until someone's wide eyes centered on it.

"A few adjustments, but it will be ready by the morning," said a smith's assistant, one of the handlers, breaching her silent seconds. "If you'll stand still . . . "

Ami said nothing, and that served as a flag for the others, hands darting in from all sides to undue clasps, take further notes and markings to tighten, loosen, adjust to make the Guardian as protected a killing machine as possible. That metal armor like this would melt her in battle with the firewalkers went unremarked: Ami would lead the burning fiends from a distance.

Her real foes would be fellow humans, and against Kance rapiers, Noctia plate would make her nigh invincible. The set would be waiting for her upon arrival to Kance, the Najahn's coming sea assault aiming to claim the beach near caves known to lead to the Dark Below. Jochi would have his scouts marking the routes, keeping them clear of any creeping fiends.

Yarvick had asked what they'd do if the firewalkers couldn't fit through the narrow tunnels. To that question, Ami had laughed.

The firewalkers had punched their way out of a dying world. No simple rock would get in their way.

Catya sat on her balcony, thwarting the cold with a thick coat and hot tea. Ami joined her there, bearing two plates. One, overlaid with bread, eggs, and pillaged Vis fruit, and another with a simple Whent goat cheese spread over two thin wafers. Ami set the second before Catya and took her own spot on a hard wood chair.

"Svarde tells me you're both leaving today," Catya said as Ami rubbed her forehead. "Just after you arrived."

The Vis skars would clear the hangover, but they took time.

"There's people that need me," Ami muttered, digging

into the breakfast between words. "Well, not people exactly, but you get what I'm saying."

"That's what I told myself all these years. People need me. Now I'm not sure."

"What's that mean? You were the Aegis. You kept these isles safe."

"From the same fiends you're trying to save now, if I'm understanding it right."

Ami launched into a practiced defense, the same argument she and Svarde had pitched to the Circle, with Fassle's blessing, two days earlier. While many fiends were wild monsters, some appeared to be intelligent, worth working with and even saving. There wasn't blame to pass around here: with no ventures deep into the Dark Below, nobody could have known the Aegis's net was so dangerous to otherwise needy creatures.

"You say there's a portal down there, one for each of the gods," Catya said. Below them, scholars and vendors called out the morning's news, offerings, or reminders of classes that needed attending. "And that you think they're collapsing. Why now, after so long?"

The silver liquid lapping the firewalker's world came all too easily to mind.

"Because it takes time for something so huge to die," Ami answered.

"So I'm unlucky, then. Another ten years and I wouldn't have had to suffer like this."

"You bought us ten years of peace. That's not nothing."

Catya whispered a laugh before settling back into the far-gone stare to the horizon. "Do you think there's fiends like these firewalkers through all these gates?"

"You mean smart ones?"

"I mean ones worth protecting."

"Haven't seen'em yet," Ami said, her plate's contents running out and leaving her stomach still grumbling. Najahn chefs were always stingy with their portions. "Not going in after them, either. Too dangerous."

"Shouldn't we, though?" Catya asked. "If these gates are truly as small as you suggest, then it seems a random chance any fiend might survive."

"Catya, if you're trying to get me to go into every one of these things and go hunting for some monster that understands I'm not gonna kill it, or that it shouldn't kill me, you're—"

"Do you know how I made the net?"

"What?"

"With the seven skars," Catya said. "The old Aegis taught me. Said the one before that taught him, going all the way back to Demion."

"Okay?"

"I'm saying those stones can do incredible things, but I didn't get a chance to see what else they could do, working together. From the first hour, I made the net, and for ten years, I did nothing except keep it up." Catya flicked her wrinkled, faded look at Ami. "If you get those seven stones together . . . "

"I've seen what the skars can do, Catya. You do the wrong thing with that many, you screw it up, and we're not talking about lighting a house on fire, blowing over a chair. You could tear these isles apart." Ami tapped her faceplate, the twin Vis skars. "These two are enough for me. Those fiends want help, they've got to earn it."

SVARDE REFUSED his own armor set, preferring to keep his Foti leathers.

"What good's being immortal if I have to wear those hulking things?" Svarde said when Ami, her own armor packed away and ready for a roped descent. "I'm going to move fast, kill things. And laugh when they stab me back."

The blade-wielder waited for Ami at the Wound the following morning, several days after they'd arrived in Noctia. The short trip had its agenda sped along by necessity, the resistance in Kance and Vis pushing Fassle and Yarvick to expedited action. They'd approved the firewalker's entry into the isles, declared a victory as conditions to a permanent home, and passed along responsibility for both to Ami and Svarde.

Not that the two Guardians would be returning to Jochi's camp alone. Various Noctia scholars, guards, and diplomats were readying about the Wound. Engineers, too, swarmed the gap, pulled from other civil projects to construct, as fast as feasible, an elevator down the massive shaft. Pulleys, ropes, and wood slats ready to serve as platforms piled up around the entry.

Those would be for the followers, the Najahn. Ami, Svarde, and Kivi would return the same way they'd come up: with handholds and grit.

"The goal's not to kill them all, Svarde," Ami said, stretching, letting the Vis skars murder her would-be hangover. It'd been another long night at an ale house, with Svarde watching, envious, from start to finish. "We scare them enough, they give up."

"And what, Ami? Decide to give their isle to the firewalkers?"

"So you'd slaughter them all instead?"

"Kance has always been stuck up, in need of a smacking." Svarde grinned. "Why d'ya think I went to Vis? Those jungle lovers never bothered me at all."

"Where do you think we'll be going next?"

Svarde chose not to meet that question with his eyes, turning instead to the Wound, the first ropes waiting for their climb down.

"They'll have lost by then," Svarde allowed. "Vis never fought an organized anything."

"They're more stubborn than you think."

Svarde nodded, "But not as stubborn as you."

Ami was about to answer in the affirmative, only for Sawi's face to flit by behind her eyes. She'd be home by now, if Jochi's scouts had their routes right. What would the gatherer choose? Would she take up a spear against the Najahn?

What would Ami do, if Foti was invaded by another isle?

"Maybe we'll get lucky, as you say," Ami replied, finally.

Neither one, though, spoke for a long time as they began their climb down, following Kivi's snorts, and listening to the occasional wrapped message or package dropped behind them, to bounce and land in Jochi's hands. Replies would come back by Svarde's ferrite, who could scale the whole distance in less than a day when untethered from her slovenly human counterparts.

A war to save fiends, to crush resistance, was beginning, and Ami would be in the thick of it.

Behind her, withering in her bed, was Catya. Freed, at last, from her torment, and still alone.

CHAPTER 52
POWER AT LAST

Duty provided ample distraction, and Gladdring kept Quik occupied. The Vis hunter took the offered Kance skar, the command to send more wind into the cutter's sails, as sound advice, and soon the hunter spent his time up near the first mate, sending the Najahn ship screaming into Kance within a day.

Gladdring enlisted a couple Tamas-warped sailers to dump the Renewal's body over the edge, dismissing any questions of her demise as a tragic consequence of over-using the skars. Gladdring himself provided evidence of the danger, as relying on the Tamas stones kept him sitting in a deck chair, headaches pounding, and eyes half-lidded.

Yet, they lived. The cutter sailed.

The crew, however, grumbled whenever Gladdring relaxed his skar influence, as if waking from a collective nap. Quik would throw Gladdring a warning look when a sailor or the first-mate would ask what Noctia wanted, why they were listening to a Vis and a traitor. Gladdring would stride over, muster up some meandering story about their dwindling provisions, about a secret mission whispered to him by the Renewal before she succumbed, or whatever he could scramble up in the moment.

Never had seeing an isle brought so much relief.

Kance made a stunning first impression, gray spikes rising with the dawn on the horizon. Seagulls swarmed, followed by larger Daibens, or the sky falcons, as Kance called them. Those raptors looked like mistakes as their flew, seeming gaps in their wings really filament feathers that glared upon a diving strike, blinding the poor fish or rodent until it breathed its last amid killing claws. Kance fishing vessels provided easy food, their sails sending the darters blazing across the waves as their thin nets found meal upon meal, the Daiben striking any fish flopping free. Overheads, gliders added to the aerial clutter, darting through long, spidery cast-off seedlings from plants nestled high above in those peaks. Catch a seedling at the right time, Gladdring knew, and you could scrape off the protective fibers and turn them into the shimmering lace woven into so much Kance clothing, their sails.

The sparkles, the vibrant white, the wind-sculpting smoothness.

Gladdring let his view sink down, past the ship's prow towards the approaching docks. The Kance navy, always impressive as it so often stayed close to home, took notice of Gladdring's colors, and two clippers were racing to intercept.

"They might fire on sight," the first mate said. "Don't think we have much to persuade them not to."

"No," Gladdring replied, putting a steadying hand near the tiller's post, as if his palm could still the whole ship's anxiety at a touch. "What fool would think an invasion commences with a single, small ship? They'll ask what we're here for, then escort us in."

"What are we here for, Gladdring?"

"To bring news of disaster, and salvation."

The Kance docks howled. Shrouds like broken glass circled every pier, taking the swirling wind and sending it out at perfect angles to keep ship traffic from blowing over, and people from getting blustered into the sea. Flags declaring this and that merchant company crackled, and Gladdring found his robes coming to life, dragging him towards the ship's starboard side, as if his own wardrobe had decided the man deserved to rot beneath the waves. Still, Gladdring held his focus, kept his serious frown as he disembarked to meet the waiting Kance soldiers.

One Kance clipper had dashed ahead of the cutter, racing in to share the impending docker's desires, and the Kance were ready. Armored and glistening, seeming not the slightest bothered by the endless gales, at least fifteen soldiers and supporting staff stood ready to greet the Najahn vessel.

"They murdered your Queen," came Gladdring's first words, Quik on his heels, while the Najahn sailors secured their ship. "We were with her at the end. They used stolen skars, the same you'll find inside this ship, to kill her and all who came with her."

The soldier hearing the accusations, a man of slight bearing who seemed swallowed by his armor, yet nonetheless held Gladdring in a vice-like stare, gave no expression at the words. Were he left to his own impressions, Gladdring would've been lost.

The Tamas skar told him otherwise, said simmering rage and alarm lay beneath the man's narrow visage.

"The full story," Gladdring started, winced as his own

hair blew into his eyes with a sudden gust, "is not one to tell here. You'll find all the evidence onboard. Prisoners to power their god-spawned scheme, sailors all too willing to break under questioning, and sacks of skars, brought to devastate first the Queen, and then your isle."

"But not you," the soldier replied. "Or this one? This . . . " the man squinted at Quik, catching ink peeking beyond the man's robed neck. "Vis?"

Quik, for his part, played the silent bodyguard with marvelous perfection. Gladdring had to admire the hunter: for all Quik's gruff protests, the man understood how to put the goal before his personal feelings. A rare trait.

"We would be prisoners ourselves, if not for luck and desperation," Gladdring replied. "The Queen didn't go quietly, but destroyed their captain and soldiers. We persuaded them to come here, that their lives would be spared."

"If what you say is true, their lives are more than forfeit."

"As they ought to be." Gladdring nodded. "But, my friend, time presses. Where is Kance's second Queen? War is coming to your isle, and while we bring weapons, your people will need a leader to command them, and our knowledge to wield them. You need to send out fliers and find her, immediately."

At that ask, at last, Gladdring saw an eyebrow twitch, the soldier's gaze shift beyond the cutter and to places unknown. The future, the past, and a thousand worries in between. When the man settled himself, he flicked a hand to his left, down the dock.

"Follow me," he said, and as Gladdring, with Quik by his side, fell into steps, the remaining Kance soldiers swept up onto the cutter.

The isles needed to be saved, and Gladdring, now, at last had the real power to do so. Such developments had a way of keeping Gladdring's attention, so he didn't hear, didn't see the order given, and the howling wind ensured he didn't hear the screams.

CHAPTER 53

ASSASSIN'S TWIST

The lines came smooth and easy, the banter natural on a stage lit so bright everything else fell away. Just her and Wax, in faux fancy clothes, dancing around a dangerous romance. Sure, Eujo might've missed a cadence here and these as she focused on her footwork, and yes, she dropped one last line about some relative that'd be oh so mad to see the two of them together, but what did that matter?

The scene's core continued, and within some few minutes, both her and Wax stood in the stage's center. The climax, a much demurred, much denied inevitability, one they'd rehearsed time and time again—Eujo didn't even blush anymore—but at this moment, here, with nothing more than their voices echoing into the massive theater, time slowed. Wax dripped out his last line, fading the syllables as he slipped into Eujo's eyes, as his arms found her back, pulled her in close.

A bandit knows no love save the next score, the next meal. The romances stolen by kids in their quiet hours were never hers, used instead used to learn a new trick, or trick a new mark. Time lost forever when Eujo joined in the wrong, the right race and scampered across the floating gardens with too much speed. Earned herself a new life, and gave up a chance at things like this, at a kiss like this.

Wax stepped back, released her, the scene demanding a sudden recrimination, one Eujo stammered through. The lines broke. Words disappeared for three long seconds as she watched Wax, his ever-cocky grin receding into worry. Where had he come from, this Vis Renewal, to threaten her life in a way so different from her traitorous guards, from the deadly falls a misstep could deliver in the sky isles?

This should have been easier.

"Too much?" Wax said, an ad lib, and one serving to jolt Eujo back to the present, to her soft soles on the wood boards, the shining lanterns, the . . .

"Never enough," Eujo muttered, remembering her line, "yet impossible to continue. This was a mistake."

"Do you really think that?"

"It doesn't matter what I think, it matters what our world will allow."

She turned, Wax speaking her name, declaring some mad love, some deception that would give them their desired lives. In the play, that ruse would fail. Outside? Without the Renewal's chains?

Eujo hit her steps in measured time, leaving the scene even as she left the theater in her mind. A return to Kance, a declaration that the Queen had found a consort. Wax would leap among the cliffs with her, soar on the gliders with her, watch the shimmering dawns and dusks at the highest peaks at her side. There would be no Aegis, only a journey, bright and beautiful together. Why, Torny and Bliss could get roles in the palace, the bandit leading Eujo's security, and—

Claps. The curtain sweeping past Eujo's left to close off the stage and the audience beyond.

Eujo turned, found Wax coming across towards her, not the smile she'd hoped to see on his face.

"What happened?" Wax asked, reaching Eujo, but not touching her, not offering more than worry.

A thief knows what it's like to be crossed, knows how to raise walls to protect herself.

"What do you mean?" Eujo replied, folding arms.

"The lines? Your exit? You never looked back?"

"Who cares? We did fine. What could they expect?"

Before she could tell Wax off further, the curtains swept open again. This time, though, the lantern spotlights had been doused. The only lights left circled the stage floor, creating less a brilliant highlight and more a soft ring. Behind them, a stagehand blocked the exit towards the dressing room. The woman, sporting the theater's clean tunic and trousers, waved the Renewal pair back into center stage. Wax, still frowning, led. Eujo walked too, replaying the scene, discounting the flubs in turn.

Tamas skar or no, you couldn't turn a random person into an actor. Eujo stared that defiance into the dark, the shadows revealing more as her eyes adjusted.

And that defiance broke.

High seats ringed the stage, five rows out and another trio on an upper balcony. The seats themselves were each throne-like in their broad backs and wide armrests. Cushioned red and purple velvet ran along their boards, far nicer than than theater Eujo had ever seen before. Certainly, the Animas was put to shame by the comforts here, though those same amenities constricted any crowd.

Then again, those gathered to watch the Renewal pair seemed numerous enough. They'd abandoned their seats, clogging the isles and the gap between the stage and the first row. Every one wore deep crimson robes, every one wore a golden faceplate, a mask covering their forehead down across their chin, with dark holes across their eyes and mouth. The masks wore different expressions too, from smiles to frowns, gasps to wild grins. Disturbing enough, but what had Wax and Eujo making a lurch to the left came from the struggle on that side.

Torny, Bliss, both grappled by several masked Tamas apiece. The two struggled, but strong arms held theirs, while others pressed the Guardians back into their seats and covered their mouths.

"The performance is not done," announced a booming voice behind one of the masks, not one Eujo recognized, though the clear oratory gave hints to a theater career. "There remains the finale, the judgement. Stay in your places, please, and no harm will come to your friends."

"Wax," Eujo said as the Vis looked about to leap off after his sister, "do what he's saying. We have no weapons, and every Renewal has to do this, remember? They're not going to kill us."

"The other skars could've," Wax snapped back, his fists clenched by his sides. "Every single isle wants to kill its heroes."

"We don't wish to kill either of you," the voice replied, and Eujo traced its sound to center stage, just ahead beyond those lanterns. A straight mask, no real expression. "In fact, we wish to congratulate you."

As he spoke, the masked and robed figures swept up the small stairs on the stage's sides, their steps so smooth they appeared to float as they wrapped Wax and Eujo in a loose circle.

"To you, Vis," the deep voice spoke again, "we offer a

pass, and one of our isle's treasured skars. You put heart into your performance, you hit your marks, you spoke your lines with feeling. For that, you have earned our respect, and our wish for your success, Renewal or no."

One of the robed figures near Wax pulled free a gold tablet, just like the ones Eujo and Torny had stolen, and handed it to Wax, who held it as though the pass were some strange creature.

"See?" Eujo whispered. "Nothing bad."

"Sadly," boomed the voice, overriding Wax's reply, "the same cannot be said of your counterpart. Mistakes were made, owing less to the scene's complexity and more to a lack of preparation, a lack of pride, a lack of focus. We deny you, Renewal, a pass and a skar. Instead, to remind you of your lack of commitment, you shall wear your errors for as long as you live."

The crimson robes flowed, black-gloved hands drawing out finger-length golden needles. The points caught lantern light, flickering like stars as they advanced towards Eujo.

"What?" Eujo said, turning around, reaching for her bracelet with the skars, only to find it missing. They'd removed the things—Wax his necklace, her the bracelet— for the scene, and both waited in a lockbox back in the dressing room. "I don't—"

A first free hand, in utter silence, grabbed at Eujo's arm. The Queen jerked it back, delivered a kick to the robed figure's shins, and dropped the man or woman to a crouch. Another hand snared her left wrist, and, cursing, Eujo moved to slap it away only for Wax do it for her, the Vis yanking the hand off and pushing the offender back. Eujo took advantage, following the stumble to attack the same robed one, grabbing the needle-holding hand and tearing the tool free. The little scratch she earned in the process was worth it, as she brandished the needle like a sword, angling it towards the hesitant crowd surrounding them.

These were all actors, right? Not fighters? How brave could they be?

"Stop," the booming voice spoke again, not quite so calm as before. "You want the skar, you pay the price. You honor our traditions, or you learn for your disrespect. This is not a choice. Attack again, and we will take your Guardians from you."

That the last seemed an improvised threat was obvious, and Eujo pounced on it, backing up next to Wax.

"You don't seem like the murdering type," Eujo snarled back. "How about we call it even? I promise to think about my bad performance, and you let us all go free, keeping your eyes in the bargain."

"Oh," said the voice, amused. "We won't kill them. Tamas has other uses for its prisoners. So many costumes to weave, so much ale to brew. Their lives will belong to the isle, yes, but they will live them still."

"And I thought Tamas was going to be the easy one," Wax muttered.

"None of'em are easy," Eujo replied, then, raising her voice, addressed the robes. "Keep your damn hands off me and my Guardians."

Defying her words, the robes surged forward. Wax cursed, Eujo angled the needle towards an incoming mask and stabbed, only for the tilting faceplate to knock the blow aside. Arms grabbed Eujo's shoulders, her wrists, her ankles, her neck. A hand clapped over her mouth. She tried to kick as her sleeves, her pant legs were pulled up, her body pressed down onto the stage boards. Those gold faceplates loomed, needles descending to make the first marks.

She wanted to scream, but the shout echoing through the theater didn't come from Eujo.

"Leave off her," called Livier, the man's formal diction underscored by dead certainty, "or I will dismember you all, limb from limb."

The assault hesitated, though grips still held Eujo down.

"News comes from Kance," Livier continued, his closing voice making clear the assassin's walk down the theater's central aisle. "The sky isle has lost one of her queens. The remaining one lays before you, and any harm to her will bring our vengeance."

Now the hands released her. Stood back and away, clearing to the stage's side. Eujo said up, saw the haggard Kance assassin make his limping way near the stage, Daklin at the man's side, supporting him in grim-faced silence. Livier dropped to a single knee, nodded at Eujo.

"Kance is yours alone, my Queen, and war is at her shores."

THE SEVEN ISLES **are at war.**

Wax and Eujo, pursued by assassins and soldiers alike, head to the spire isle of Kance to prepare for invasion. They expect an onslaught of metal and magic, but the truth is something far, far worse. Beneath the earth, an army the isles have never seen marches towards Kance, with their own survival at stake. Win, and the fiends can save themselves from their collapsing home.

They can not, will not, lose.

Continue The Seven Isles series with *The War of Winds* by clicking here or scanning the code below:

. . .

After a disaster on the Moon, Mox's search for strength brings him to a dangerous scientist and a choice between the life Mox knows and the vengeance he desires.

Jump into a new science fiction adventure with *The Metal Man*, available free when you sign up for my author newsletter by clicking the link or scanning the code below:

ACKNOWLEDGMENTS

There's this idea that writing is a solitary act, but that couldn't be further from the truth. Every writer depends on friends, family, and, yes, the readers to keep spinning their stories.

Specifically, I'd like to thank my wife, Nicole, who's endless love and encouragement make every day brighter. My brothers, Jonathan, Justin, and Matthew, and parents, Bob and Mary, who help keep a smile on my face.

And, of course, all of you readers that make this life possible.

Thank you.

About the Author

A.R. Knight writes sci-fi and fantasy in the frozen north of Wisconsin. With a pair of cats keeping him company, he enjoys delving into adventures that are as much about the villain as the hero.

After getting a degree in journalism and touring the country installing healthcare software, A.R. Knight thought it would be good to get back to what he loved. So now he's got a small office and early mornings to spin whatever tales come into his imagination.

When he's not writing, A.R. Knight tends to travel anywhere he can, whether that's islands off the coast of Ecuador, the rainforest, snowboarding in the Rocky Mountains, or sipping scotch in Edinburgh. That's the nice thing about the writing life, you can take it anywhere.

To contact or see what he's up to, visit www.blackkeybooks.com

arknight@blackkeybooks.com

For Holly and Ryan